THE DEAN, DILLINGER, AND DAYTON, OHIO

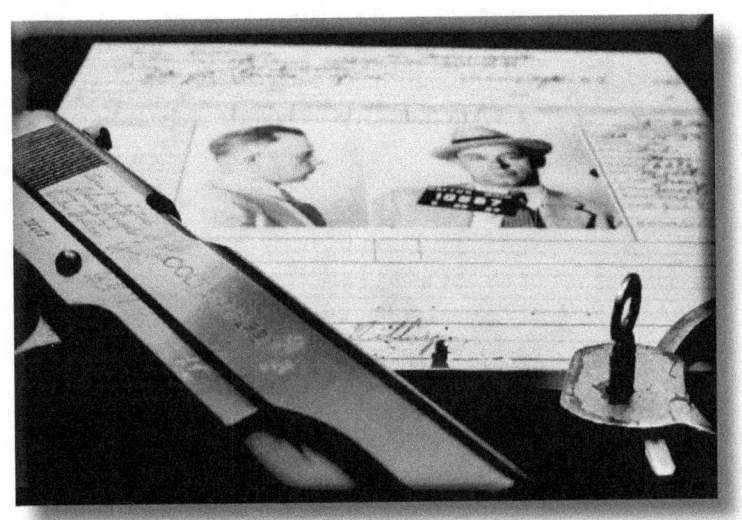

LEGEND – LORE – LEGACY

STEPHEN C. GRISMER

PUBLISHED BY
DAYTON POLICE HISTORY FOUNDATION, INC.

STEPHEN C. GRISMER

This book was enhanced with
the attentive assistance of
SUSAN D. JANSEN, ESQ.
DOLL, JANSEN & FORD

The contents of this book are the author's own research
and interpretation of this aspect of history.

Contributing editor,
MICHAEL J. SAMMONS

Title page photograph by
AMY M. SIMPSON
and
Cover design by
AUSTIN KIRKPATRICK

Library of Congress Control Number: 2020914418

ISBN-10: 0-9895302-4-8
ISBN-13: 978-0-9895302-4-8

Produced in the United States of America
10 9 8 7 6 5 4 3 2 1

Published by
DPH FOUNDATION, INC.
P.O. Box 293157
DAYTON, OH 45429-9157
www.DaytonPoliceHistory.org

DEDICATION

To all the unwavering men and women of law enforcement;
notably those in service with the Dayton Police and
"Twin Cities" Minnesota Police Departments.

May all law officers stay safe in their duties as they
serve and protect American communities
during this most unsettling of times.

A special thank you to THE FAMILY of
DAYTON POLICE CHIEF RUDOLPH F. WURSTNER

In Memory of Two Special Friends...

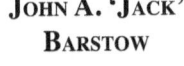

JOHN A. 'JACK' BARSTOW

Grandson of Dayton Police
Chief Rudolph F. Wurstner.
Jack was the Chairman of
Dayton Police History
Foundation, Inc. at the
time of his passing on
on January 11, 2018.

Jack Barstow in the role of Chief Wurstner
in 2012 for a filmed reenactment.

JOHN R. THOMAS

Dayton Public Safety Director
and retired career policeman.
John, a lead supporter of the
Dayton Police History Foundation,
unexpectedly passed away
on May 23, 2020.

ACKNOWLEDGMENTS

Had it not been for the creation of a very special police exhibit at Carillon Historical Park, this book may not have been written (see Introduction). I sincerely appreciate the contributions of countless supporters and local history buffs in completing that particular project (see Afterword). Pure imagination produced a storyboard framework, expressed in topics conceived by **Steve Lucht**, the exhibit coordinator, and **Gwenyth Haney**, the collections manager. I am truly grateful for their spirit of cooperation leading to the writing of the book, *THE DEAN, DILLINGER, AND DAYTON, OHIO*.

As far as the book itself, *my heartfelt gratitude* is extended to the following individuals without whom this story would not have been as far-reaching as it became.

First, the individuals listed on the copyright page:

Michael Sammons painstakingly proofread the entire final draft manuscript for grammar, punctuation and word usage; suggestions for rephrasing passages were offered as well. **Susan Jansen** often made herself available whenever I needed another viewpoint in shaping some important passages. **Austin Kirkpatrick** of *Austin and Shilo Creative* took a rough concept and turned it into an attention-grabbing book cover design. I also reached into a well of incredible photographic images by **Amy Simpson**, depicted on the cover and title page.

Secondly, the individuals who aided by conducting research used for this story:

Walter 'Butch' Smith, a retired inspector for the State of Indiana jail system, is a mentor and an enthusiast for this topic with a superb network. Besides material support, thanks to Butch I was able to electronically link with established "Dillinger" authors Ellen Poulsen and William Helmer.

Butch also introduced me to **Larry Wack**, a retired FBI special agent out of Washington D.C., now deceased, who was instrumental in providing records from the FBI archives.

Good friends **Dennis Murphy**, **Curt Dalton**, and **Gary Siler** individually provided research material used in this book, particularly on the life of Mary Longnaker. Dennis is an old hand at this. He and I teamed with Dr. Judith Monseur in authoring a 2017 book. Curt, a prolific author of local history, introduced me to **Virginia 'Ginny' Stewart**, who provided fresh and little-known background on Longnaker.

Gary Siler deserves *special mention*. He is a "pen pal," true friend, and an incredible researcher whose skills I have drawn upon often; an invaluable asset. He always graciously assists and goes far beyond expectations as he did with background facts on Mary Longnaker, Ptl. William 'Tom' Wilson, and Al Fouts. His exceptional research on Fouts took the mobster from having a single storyline to being a key recurrent character.

Another unexpected key character is that of Detective James Crumley, developed thanks to the direct assistance of his great-granddaughter **Bridget Sperl**. The result is a fascinating sub narrative of police and gangland connections between Dayton and St. Paul, Minnesota.

Robert 'Bob' Makley, a St. Marys resident and the grandnephew of bank robber Charley Makley, is another friend who contributed considerably. Bob provided background material which allowed me to expand on the book's account of this gangster. Other essential research contributions came from **Jack Barstow** in the years before he passed away; local historian **Margaret Peters** in a 2010 interview; and Wright State University Special Collections archivists **Dawne Dewey**, now retired archive manager, and **William 'Bill' Stolz**.

I am indebted to other resource contributors too numerous to name. They are identified in the **Bibliography**.

Particular recognition goes to retired Dayton Police **Chief James Newby**. In 1988, he authorized the official transfer of many historically significant Dayton Bureau of Identification records to the archive managers at Wright State University (WSU). Aware that the documents were destined to fade and disintegrate with time, he ensured the arrest records related to John Dillinger, George 'Bugs' Moran, Al Fouts, et al., were preserved by the professional archivists at WSU's Paul Laurence Dunbar Library.

Every one of the many archived documents related to Dillinger's arrest was thoroughly researched for this book *and placed in context* with other source materials. The availability of the original records opened the door to a more complete understanding of the relationship between Dillinger and Mary Longnaker as well as the 1933-1934 investigative time line in Dayton. Individually, the preserved documents are of perfunctory interest. Comprehensively, those original records were the key to the story.

THE DEAN, DILLINGER, AND DAYTON, OHIO is the grand narrative of those archived records so safely tucked away. This is another reason to be grateful.

Lastly, the individual who should be listed at the top but prefers not to be listed at all, my wife, **Teri**. The love of my life supports my undertakings like no other person should or would.

I always like to mention that the private non-profit organization, **Dayton Police History Foundation, Inc.**, motivates all research that is conducted on local law enforcement and garners warm support.

Thank you to all.

— Stephen Grismer

FRONT BOOK COVER IMAGE

Dayton, Ohio Police: The Colt Super .38 auto pistol taken from John Dillinger when arrested; the Dayton B of I arrest card and mug shot of Dillinger; and the handcuffs placed on Dillinger when arrested in a Dayton boarding house.

Photography by Amy M. Simpson - Cover Design by Austin Kirkpatrick

OTHER FRONT BOOK COVER IMAGES:
CHIEF RUDOLPH F. WURSTNER, CIRCA 1940
Courtesy of Julie Utley, great-granddaughter

JOHN H. DILLINGER, 1933
Miami Valley Regional Crime Lab
(nitrate negative donation to DPHF)

ALL BACK BOOK COVER IMAGES:
"ALBERT" G. FOUTS, CIRCA 1930;
GEORGE 'BUGS' MORAN, 1946;
AND ALFRED J. BRADY, 1936
Wright State University (WSU)
Special Collections and Archives

TABLE OF CONTENTS

INTRODUCTION

Bootleggers, Bandits, and Badges:

From Dry Times to Hard Times in Dayton, Ohio

The full-size *"Title Graphic"* on display entering the **Carillon Historical Park** exhibit.
Taken **January 1921**: Patrolmen Chester Mapes and Charles McElhaney (axe)
readying to bust a bootlegger's still at South Jefferson and Market Streets.
Today, this is the location of the Regional Transit Authority Central Hub.

INTRODUCTION

PROHIBITION – One of the most romanticized periods in United States history began in earnest 100 years ago on **January 17, 1920**. That was the date the National Prohibition Act (unofficially, the Volstead Act) went into effect allowing for the federal enforcement by lawmen of a newly authorized amendment to the U.S. Constitution. Ironically, the ban on the manufacture, transportation, and sale of alcoholic beverages came at a time when society chose to burst forth in cultural liberation, expressed by the period dubbed the "Roaring '20s."

Enveloping 1920 through 1933, Prohibition was ushered in a year earlier when Congress ratified the 18th Amendment on January 16, 1919 then followed with the passage into law of the Volstead Act on October 28. The latter provided a centennial date for the 2019 opening of a new, temporary exhibit at Carillon Historical Park, sponsored by Dayton Police History Foundation, Inc. (DPH Foundation), titled: *Bootleggers, Bandits, and Badges: From Dry Times to Hard Times in Dayton, Ohio.*

This exhibit also gave rise to this commemorative book.

The Prohibition Era was bookended by two other significant, closely tied periods in our nation's past: **The Temperance Movement** of the 19th and early 20th centuries – which led to the legal ban on distilled and brewed beverages – and **The Great Depression** – a period that brought the Roaring '20s to an abrupt end with the stock market crash. Prohibition was the gateway to the recognized age of "big-name" gangsters.

The *Bootleggers, Bandits, and Badges* exhibit visually guides visitors through all three eras with photo imagery, artifacts, and storyboards post-Civil War through 1941 when the collapsed economy found restoration with wartime production.

Dayton, Ohio, the setting for this story, was profoundly affected by all three eras as were most other locales throughout the country. But the city of Dayton's story is unique and as compelling as those of other, more celebrated metropolises. The development of local law enforcement in the "Gem City" is the major component of this book and with it comes the other main title subjects, two larger-than-life figures:

Dayton Police Chief Rudolph F. Wurstner who would become the nation's "Dean of Police Chiefs."

John H. Dillinger who would later be named the nation's first "Public Enemy No. 1."

All three – **The Dean**, **Dillinger**, and **Dayton** – come into their own in different ways in the year **1903**, making it the starting point for this story. The first two chapters chronicle events that shaped early **Dayton** – a major U.S. city – with law enforcement as its backdrop. Although it receives third billing, it is central to this account but has within its tale the two principal figures as characters in contrast.

Chief Wurstner served Dayton citizens over the course of five decades while **Dillinger**, a victimizer, was in and out of Dayton over a mere five months in **1933**. Yet is it Dillinger who is best remembered locally, and of course, nationally.

When it comes to The Dean and Dillinger, this book's goal is twofold: 1) To capture the career of, and deliver a genuine appreciation for a historic local lawman who earned national standing; and 2) To give the notorious bandit's interaction with the Gem City the fuller narrative it deserves. Often publications –

when addressing Dillinger's time in Dayton and with his local girlfriend, Mary Jenkins Longnaker – gloss over the episode; Mary was not a gangster moll and his coming to Dayton happened before the famed Allen County jail escape. The general misimpression is that Dillinger passed through Dayton once or twice, was arrested, and then conveyed elsewhere.

The local story is more involved, and not surprisingly a mix of facts and folklore. Omitted from this book are baseless urban myths (i.e. Dillinger robbing an A&P grocery store in 1929 or committing a Vandalia, Ohio bank heist). However, weight is given to convincing tales; moreover, gaps in recorded accounts are developed with common police practices of the day (e.g. chain of command notifications or conveyance by paddy wagon to the county jail).

Another objective is to also draw together the many storyboards related to Dayton law enforcement that are currently displayed at the *Bootleggers, Bandits, and Badges* exhibit. Consequently, this book is not meant to impart a comprehensive account of policing in Dayton, Ohio for the years 1867 through 1941. Rather it offers a compilation of exhibit vignettes (some expanded) for that time frame, often focusing on the darker elements of our past.

Readers will also be introduced to the gangsters and mobsters with Greater Dayton connections – such as local crime figure Al Fouts, the more infamous Chicago mobster George 'Bugs' Moran, and many others. The accounts promise to be surprising as is the backstory of the long but dubious career of exalted local lawman James Crumley.

More importantly, this book, as well as the exhibit, highlight heroic actions by Dayton law enforcement officers and their bloody sacrifices in protecting our local community ... the individuals who truly deserve acclaim – such as Ptl. William Jenkins and Det. Russell Pfauhl. Readers will appreciate their dedication to duty.

In the end, this saga will tie Dayton, Ohio to legends from arguably the most notorious period in American history. This will also be the definitive tale of Dillinger in Dayton and bring to light a forlorn love affair. The many other figures and events from the Gem City's past provide an astonishing untold legacy.

A Closing Note:

Bootleggers, Bandits, and Badges was scheduled for exhibit at Carillon Historical Park until December 2021 but its popularity has prompted two extensions through 2023. *Come to Dayton and tour it!* The exhibit is designed to be the catalyst for a far larger vision of a Dayton Metropolitan Police museum facility at Carillon Historical Park. The exhibit, as well as this commemorative book, are but glimpses into the Gem City's remarkable law enforcement past.

Major support is needed for the museum initiative; in particular, businesses and individual benefactors willing to embrace and financially anchor the project. Interested parties that recognize the intrinsic value that a police history museum offers the community are asked to please contact <u>DaytonPoliceHistory.org</u>.

In the running narrative of the book, take note that individuals highlighted with **bold text** <u>*when first named*</u> are generally those who have <u>*recurring*</u> appearances as the history unfolds - retain their names while reading.

1888 – UNIFORMED DAYTON PATROLMEN 50 YEARS APART – *1938*

1888: Front Row Left - **Ptl. John Boes**, who would one day be the Montgomery County Sheriff. Front Row Right - **Ptl. John Allaback**, who would one day be the Dayton Police Chief. Front Row Center - Ptl. Edwin Fair, who would serve 41 years. His hooked cane is on display at the exhibit at Carillon Historical Park.

Circa 1938: Below is Ptl. Paul Geralds. Hired in 1929, he would become Dayton's Chief of Detectives in 1949.

Courtesy of Tina Young, granddaughter of Ptl. Geralds

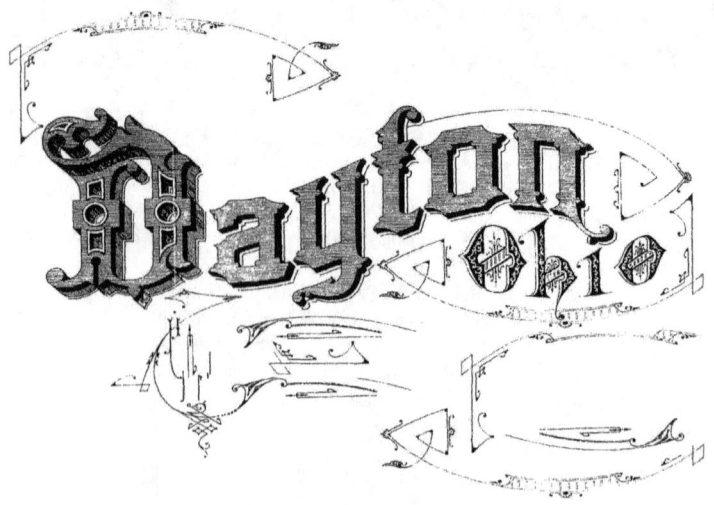

PROLOGUE

LAWMEN, TEMPERANCE, AND VICE

CINCINNATI DAILY STAR, SAT

OFFICER LEE LYNAM

Shot and Killed by a Dayton Desperado.

miles, thereby
ing all through
city, as it were,
hich our people
being taxed as
ar thing. Clay

January 17, 1880
Cincinnati Daily Star
newspaper story on
a Dayton police
officer's murder.

MACE CABLES SALOON

Dayton, Ohio in 1880 - East Third Street looking toward Jefferson Street.
Mace Crable's Saloon was located at 109 East Third Street as indicated.
The three-story structure; fifth row building from the corner.

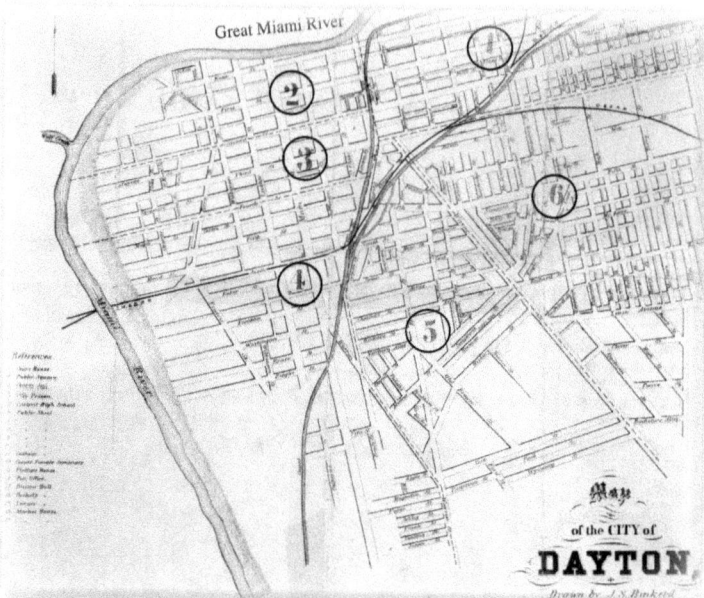

1862-1863: City of Dayton map showing the town divided into six wards *(above)*.
1873: The *earliest-known* photograph of uniformed <u>Dayton police officers</u> (below).

Ptl. John Madden *(right)*. Patrolman *(left)* and civilian are unidentified.
Courtesy of Sally Crowe, great-granddaughter of Ptl. Madden

DAYTON, OHIO – In 1795 Dayton was a river wilderness on the edge of the new frontier, then the Northwest Territory. Five families made a hard travel upstream from Cincinnati, and in 1796 settled on land at the confluence of the Great Miami and Mad Rivers. At the time, George Washington was our United States President. Local Shawnee Indian Chief Tecumseh and indigenous tribes were feared threats for Dayton pioneers.

When Ohio was admitted to the union as its 17th state in 1803, Montgomery County was carved from Hamilton County where Cincinnati was the center. Dayton was designated the seat for Montgomery County. The settlement became a town in 1805 and then an incorporated city of the second class in 1841. By the start of the Civil War, Cincinnati was the sixth most populated U.S. city while its northern offspring had become the nation's 45th largest city and was growing. By the time of U.S. entry into World War II, the city of Dayton was the nation's 40th largest metropolis and a mere two decades away from having over one quarter-million residents.

Law Enforcement is Established in Dayton

The foundation of local police service began early in 1797 with the appointment of Dayton's first constable. Then in 1805, and each year thereafter, a single town marshal was elected to serve. In 1833, the first watchman, "under the pay of individuals," was assigned to walk a downtown beat… the trades square contiguous to the Court House.

In 1858, City Council authorized six city-paid uniformed watchmen to assist the marshal – one per each of six political wards – while a resolution was passed to form a police department.

The traditional underpinnings in the ward-watch system were those men appointed as watchmen were residents of the ward and obligated as sentries for only their ward. They were recommended by and thus duty-bound to the elected ward official. It was a vocation vulnerable to venality from the start.

1861: The *first-known* photo of a uniformed <u>Dayton lawman</u>, a **ward watchman** *(left)* standing next to a Union Army soldier.

Even though Dayton was Ohio's third largest city in 1860 – behind Cincinnati and Cleveland – state law did not permit it to have a police department. Delayed by the Civil War and state-level political wrangling, the General Assembly of Ohio finally authorized the formation of the Dayton Metropolitan Police Force well over 150 years ago.

Dayton established its police department in April 1867 consisting of 22 men – two men per each of the then 11 wards – including veteran Union Army Colonel Patrick O'Connell, the new "police captain and acting superintendent" (the official title for the police chief).

The Dayton Metropolitan Police Commission, a board comprised of four political appointees and the mayor, oversaw the activities of the police force. The police superintendent was elected to two-year terms and acted at the directive of the commission. Many of the early heads of the police force were Union Army veterans of the Civil War. General William Martin, appointed in 1873, is recognized as Dayton's first police chief because, unlike the three others who preceded him, he "retired" from his term in office. [1]

By 1873 the size of the police force increased to 33 men (three per ward). Patrolmen were paid today's equivalent of $3.78 per hour and worked 12 to 14 or more hours a day, seven days a week, 365 days per year. There were no days off. Then on June 3, 1874, Dayton patrolmen were granted a new benefit... six (6) days off every year but only on the condition that they took no more than one day in any one month. They also received a commensurate cut in pay. Policemen were not highly regarded and the job was not considered a "profession."

The Women's Temperance Crusade in Dayton

The first major crisis that the new police force confronted was the Women's Temperance Crusade in 1874 when the consumption of alcoholic beverages was five times what it is today. The temperance movement was in its 50th year, and as a national organizing effort it promoted the moderate consumption of intoxicating beverages or preferably complete abstinence.

The crusade was born 60 miles south of Dayton in Hillsboro, Ohio. The women were victorious in closing all the town's saloons (a triumph that later led to the official formation of the Women's Christian Temperance Union, the WCTU, in Cleveland in November 1874). The crusading efforts found similar success 25 miles to Dayton's northeast in Springfield, Ohio where many saloons were closed. The crusaders were ready to take on a far larger target.

The reforming ladies decided that the Gem City was ripe for their words and acts. Thus, Dayton became the first major city in the country to be challenged by the temperance crusade.

The New York Times followed the women's cause with interest. It reported that Dayton had "520 drinking places," ... an exaggerated number although there were certainly over 300 saloons in town.

In February 1874, 200 crusaders in bands of 22 ladies began to visit the bars and pray for the imbibing men's souls. At first a novelty, it became an annoyance and then caused near rebellion. Saloon keepers offered free beer and whiskey whenever they were visited by the praying women.

Men hurled insults at the ladies as well as bologna and crackers. Knives and pistols were brandished. The developments were reported monthly to the readers of *The New York Times*. After 43 days touching three months of entrenched battles of passions, on election day, April 6, the local whiskey candidate running for mayor, Lawrence Butz, soundly beat the temperance candidate, David Houk.

The following day, Mayor Butz had the Board of Police Commissioners issue an order for all local taverns. Strict rules on the tavern keepers were established for the sale and on-premise consumption of alcohol. The saloons found in violation of the order would be declared a nuisance, shut down and abated by Dayton patrolmen. At the same time, the women were also prohibited from blocking the entranceways to the saloons.

The door-to-door saloon crusading came to an end locally. Unlike Hillsboro and Springfield, the movement did not find success in closing saloons in Dayton, Ohio, a city comprised largely of German and Irish immigrants and early descendants. *The Times* later reported four of 302 taverns had closed.

The crusaders continued their protests in New York, Chicago and other major cities throughout the nation. Along with the Anti-Saloon League (founded in Oberlin, Ohio in 1893) and other groups, it was a movement that would eventually find success 45 years later with Prohibition.

First Dayton Officer Killed is in a Saloon

In the last quarter of the 19th century, taverns could be found on nearly every square and corner. Patrolmen would canvas these drinking establishments looking for drunks, troublemakers and violators of liquor laws. Lee Lynam was one such patrolmen.

On January 17, 1880, at 12:15 in the dark, frigid morning, Ptl. Lynam entered Mace Crable's saloon located at 109 E. Third Street. [2] He was followed inside by 22-year-old John Francis, a known troublemaker, seeking warmth and revenge for his arrest the day before.

Near the bar, Francis fired a revolver, mortally wounding Ptl. Lynam. The officer pulled his club while attempting to chase his assailant fleeing to the back room, but staggered and fell heavily to the floor, bleeding profusely.

Having heard the gun fire from nearby, a private watchman and two other patrolmen rushed to the tavern. Officer Lyman died on the filthy saloon floor as Francis was taken into custody.

The murder case was tried in Butler County, Ohio (city of Hamilton). Francis was sentenced to 10 years in the state penitentiary for killing the lawman. Ptl. Lee Lynam was the first local police officer killed in the line of duty. Others would follow in coming years.

System of Corruptive Influences

An appointment to the police force in the early days often had less to do with qualifications and more to do with patronage known as "the spoils system." An early low point for the Dayton police force, still in its infancy, was in 1885 when the appointed male secretary for the Board of Police Commissioners embezzled $2,500 ($70,500 in today's money). He "absconded" and was never captured.

Decent, upstanding men were also appointed to the police department. The most decorated Dayton combat veteran of the Civil War, Major William Shoemaker, was an original member of the 1867 police force. In 1887, he was appointed "superintendent of police," becoming the first officer to rise through the ranks to become police chief; however, after a little more than two years, he resigned his commission for reasons unknown. Although he would remain on the police force until 1911 as the police court bailiff, he was replaced as police superintendent by a city councilman.

Dayton Police Supt. William Shoemaker

The appointment of a city councilman to head the police force was characteristic of practices during the formative years of both public safety departments – police and fire. Politics played a significant role in appointments to the safety services. At least one historical account indeed suggested that "it existed according to the caprice and schemes of the politicians, who either became councilmen, or who governed those who did. The consequence was progress and desired improvement [in the public safety services] was retarded…." [3]

Political appointments by the Board of Police Directors to head the police force this century included four more Civil War veterans, two former county sheriffs, and two city councilmen. As a system that was susceptible to graft and vice, many of the appointed leaders completed no more than one full term or even less. This situation of failure at the helm would leach into the rank and file of the force.

Good Men, Bad Men, and Tarnished Cities

In January 1881, **John Allaback**, an Indian scout and sergeant serving in the U.S. 2nd Calvary, escorted Civil War combat veteran, Union Army General Philip Sheridan, to the site of the Battle of Little Big Horn. Their mission was to erect a monument in remembrance of General George Custer and his massacred troops.

That same year, on August 5, **Rudolph Wurstner** was born in Fort Jennings, Ohio, a small village 20 miles northwest of Lima. Both men would someday become Dayton chiefs of police and both would bless their community with honorable careers, particularly during the century to come.

A decade later, in October 1890, **Albert Fouts** [4] was born in Dayton. A local hoodlum turned roaming gangster, he would come into his own early in the 20th century, finding common interest in bootlegging and robbery alongside an associate with the birth name Adelard L. Cunin. Better known as **George 'Bugs' Moran**, he was born in 1893 in **St. Paul**, Minnesota, a hometown that attracted gangsters because of Police Chief John O'Connor's welcoming policy. Moran's hometown was sullied as was his playground of **Chicago**. Years later, Bugs Moran himself tarnished the Gem City.

In the coming century, Dayton law enforcement would strive to rise above failings found in far larger cities, but according to the local newspaper, the Dayton police force was subject to influences of the day which could be described as "rotten politics at that." In 1892, "...the Department was up to its eyebrows in... sensations in the shape of shakeups, usually attended by... unsavory rumors..." [5]

A Distressing End to the 19th Century

The Dayton police superintendent in 1892, a former Montgomery County sheriff, was accused of being in cahoots with jewelry thieves. Although never charged with a crime, he resigned under pressure.

He was replaced by a native of New Orleans, **Thomas Farrell**, who had achieved notoriety as a Chicago detective with the private Pinkerton's National Detective Agency, the most sophisticated investigative agency in the United States at the time.

Pinkerton's Detective
Thomas J. Farrell

In 1893, Chief Farrell appointed a fellow Irishman, **James Crumley**, to the police force. Soon Ptl. Crumley was "detailed to detective duty," a prized assignment. This Dayton sleuth's law enforcement career would take to the rails and eventually end as the chief of detectives in the employ of the St. Paul, Minnesota Police Department.

During the eight years Chief Farrell was in charge, he decentralized the police force by opening three police precinct stations, moved the patrol house downtown, and instituted the "Gamewell System of Police Telegraph" among other notable achievements.

Dayton Police Superintendents 1867-1900
(clockwise from top center):

William Patton (1883–1887); **Albert Steinmetz** (1889–1890);
Thomas Steward (1873); **Charles Freeman** (1890–1892);
William Martin (1873–1875); **George Butterworth** (1881–1883);
Thomas Farrell (1892–1900); **William Shoemaker** (1887–1889);
Amos Clark (1870–1873 & 1875–1881); **Edmund Zwiesler** (1890);
and **Patrick O'Connell** (1867–1869) *[center image].*

Tragically, the end of the 19th century was fatal for two Dayton police officers and tumultuous for the head of the force.

In 1897, Sergeant Amer Keller was killed at a fire scene when a fireman fell from high on a ladder onto him.

Sgt. Amer Keller

Then, in 1899, Dayton Patrolman William Dalton, a former Miamisburg, Ohio constable, was thrown from his galloping horse and killed when its front hoof entangled in a crossing wagon's wheel. Both officers' skulls were fractured.

Ptl. William Dalton

And then, in 1900, Chief Thomas Farrell resigned after years of public indiscretion at the local houses of ill fame. It was a nasty separation with accusations and public counter accusations.

Farrell's second in command, **Captain John Allaback**, was placed in charge of the police force on an interim basis until a permanent replacement was found.

Capt. John Allaback

The Dawning of a New Century

In 1901, after a 15-month outside search, John Whitaker of Butler County, Ohio was appointed to head the Dayton Department of Police. His command was distinguished by the introduction of the civil service system (which ended the spoils system), new police identification methods (the Bertillon system), mug shots, physical fitness standards, and discipline.

Whitaker would be elected the vice president of the International Association of Chiefs of Police, a prestigious and influential position.

The arrival of Whitaker in 1901 and his actions thereafter inaugurated the *Modern Era of Policing* in Dayton, Ohio.

The following year in October, Dayton Police Superintendent John Whitaker became the City's first police commander to be conferred with the official title of "Police Chief" by municipal code.

Dayton Police Chief
John Whitaker

While a new label does not necessarily assure altered patterns, there now was police optimism ... and fresh prospects.

On December 6, 1902, a young man named **Rudolph F. Wurstner** joined the Dayton police force. He was assigned to jail cell duty inside the 2nd Precinct Station, located on the corner of East Third Street and Linden Avenue.

He was a turnkey ... the bottom rung.

Dayton City Jail entrance from East Sixth Street near Tecumseh Street.

1902: The only known image of **Jail Matron Loanda Bowman** *(below).*

1911: Police ambulance driver **Ptl. Frank Johnson** *(above left and in cab).*
Courtesy of Carolyn J. Burns, granddaughter of Ptl. Johnson.

Sidebar: Dayton Police Matrons and a Dayton Police 'Motorman'

Mrs. Loanda H. Bowman: The role of women with the City of Dayton police force had its roots in **1888** when the needs of women prisoners were recognized. The first woman was appointed to the police force on a temporary basis and *"with reluctance"* as a jail matron until 1894 when the permanent position of police matron was established. Loanda (also Louanda) Bowman was that matron. It was not a city-paid position. The Woman's Christian Association paid the matron's salary at the start. Under pressure by women's groups, in **1897** Mrs. Bowman became a permanent full-time, city-paid jail matron, making her Dayton's first female police employee.

Loanda Bowman lived at the Central Police Station 24-hours a day, seven days a week, 365 days a year. She was reportedly beloved by the patrolmen as a mother figure. After Ms. Bowman's death in **1906**, the City hired two women for police matron duties that she alone had managed: **Kate Allen** to handle the 12-hour night shift and **Ida Van Skaik** to handle the day shift. They shared the duties together for well over 16 years. When the Bureau of Policewomen was formed in **1914**, policing forever changed.

Patrolman Frank W. Johnson: Appointed in **1902**, 'Big Frank' Johnson worked in the days when bounties for fugitives were offered ... but not to police officers. However, Ptl. Johnson became the first Dayton officer to receive a monetary reward, $25 ($720 today), for his valor when he tracked a highway robber to a downtown saloon and then successfully fought off the fugitive's accomplices to bring him to jail. Ptl. Johnson began his career as a horse-drawn patrol wagon-ambulance driver. When horse-and-wagon was transitioning to motorized travel, most police officers had to be trained to drive; most supervisors used a "police chauffeur" well into the 1920s.

Ptl. Frank Johnson was a **link from past to present**. He was one of the few who knew how to drive an automobile and became the first officer to operate a motorized Dayton police vehicle, a paddy wagon, in **1911**. Because of his skill with firearms, Ptl. Frank Johnson was appointed as a member of the "Emergency Squad" in **1920** and made crime runs in Dayton's large Buick. Later he became the official motorman of the "Flying Squadron" and cared for the "Bank Flyer" Cadillac beginning in **1930**.

Circa 1915: A newsboy quizzed by **Policewoman Lulu Sollers** *(note her badge)* outside the Western Union Telegraph Company at 28 S. Jefferson Street in Dayton. *National Cash Register (NCR) Lantern Slide Collection at Dayton History*

PART ONE

THE GEM CITY 1903 – 1919

1910-1922 - Chief John Allaback's Gem-studded Badge *(above)*.
Presented by his troops during the Policemen's Ball in 1910.
Courtesy of Tom Petkewitz, badge owner

CHAPTER 1

1903 AND THE IMMINENT RISE IN CRIME

Circa 1903: Downtown Dayton - South Main Street looking north from Sixth Street.

WRIGHT BROTHERS RETURN HOME

ARRIVED IN THE GEM CITY, LAST NIGHT, FROM KITTY HAWK, N. C.

THE PROBLEM SOLVED

AERIAL NAVIGATION MADE POS-SIBLE BY THE NEW INVEN-TION.

December 24, 1903: Small local headline in *The Dayton Herald* about the success of the Wright Brothers' ground-breaking first flight.

September 29, 1909

Dayton native
Wilbur Wright
(flyer pilot left)

New York City, NY
An early demonstration
of powered flight circling
the Statue of Liberty

Wilbur and Orville
Wright

1903: Dayton police inspection on St. Clair Street.
Ptl. Rudy Wurstner *(4th from right looking left)*.

THE YEAR – The **City of Dayton** was growing at an incredible pace in 1903. Industry was prospering and Dayton became known as "The City of 1000 Factories." The population, which stretched east and west, was spreading north of the Great Miami River. Dayton was a major municipality, the nation's 45th most populated, and would become far larger. It was 30 years before the man regarded by many as the most notorious criminal in U.S. history stepped foot in the city.

In 1903, the least senior patrolman served his first full year on the police force having been appointed in late 1902. Released from turnkey duties handling jail prisoners, **Ptl. Rudolph F. 'Rudy' Wurstner** was initially assigned a beat in the Huffman Hill neighborhood, south of East Third Street and east of Torrence Street. It was a modest start for a police officer who would have a police career like no other in the annals of the Dayton Police Department.

Patrolman
Rudy Wurstner

Soon, Ptl. Wurstner was reassigned across town where he pounded the West Third Street pavement on foot, stopping to visit the owners of businesses on his beat ... and that included the proprietors of a uniquely active bicycle shop.

In 1903, Dayton's Wilbur and Orville Wright conquered the skies with first powered manned flight; a magnificent advent to the 20th Century's age of modern transportation. *This is the event that defines Dayton to this day.*

And yet, Dayton police officers were operating with only two horse-drawn wagons and a horse-drawn ambulance out of a patrol house at St. Clair and East Third Streets.

The year 1903 marked 70 years of traditional police foot patrol in Dayton, Ohio. Patrolmen walking an assigned beat would be augmented in the next decade with some bicycles and motorcycles, but for the most part law enforcement work was left to the men derisively labeled "flat foots." Dayton patrolmen wore rounded constable hats, wool coats, and with leather straps around their wrists, swung hickory night sticks with vigor.

What else happened in 1903?

On June 22, directly due west in the closest major U.S. Midwestern city, an infant was born by the name

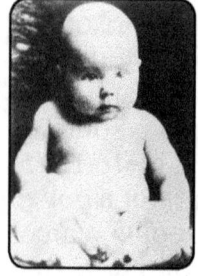

of **John Herbert Dillinger**. This child would be raised in a middle-class section of Indianapolis this decade and the next. In his late teens, he moved to a farm in a small town on the outskirts of the center city. Then he would find home in a cell block in upstate Indiana during most of the cultural clash of the Roaring '20s with the legal ban on spirits.

The infant,
John Dillinger

But as Prohibition faded in 1933, Dillinger would emerge from prison. Almost immediately upon release, he was drawn east to Dayton, Ohio. His name renowned today, Dillinger's infamy is forever linked with the Gem City.

On the flip side, Ptl. Rudy Wurstner's exceptionally long career bore witness to the greatest overall growth in Dayton's history. That growth would include the modern evolution of police transportation and that growth covered world-changing transportation history rooted in Dayton.

As a foot patrolman, the officer was expected to get to know every resident and shop owner. Ptl.

Wurstner would stroll into the Wright's bicycle shop in 1903 only to find them out back tinkering on a contraption of theirs that he little understood. The young patrolman got to know the **Wright Brothers**; their respective callings in life episodically brought them together. Over the course of his career, he would mingle with **Orville Wright** at social affairs, such as formal or public dinners and ceremonies.

Rudolph Wurstner would come to know the brothers' fame. And, he would later earn a place of honor alongside Orville and Wilbur.

The 30 years between 1903 and 1933 is the story of bootleggers, bandits, and those who wear badges … dedicated centurions as well as opportunists.

In July 1903, **Detective James Crumley** found himself out of the employ of the Dayton Police Department. One account has that he resigned; another that he was dismissed. In either case, he had made a name for himself as "one of the best that had ever been established by any member of the local force. He was courageous, fearless and diligent in pursuit of his duty. He was likewise conversant with the conditions attending police activity and was always regarded a veritable terror to criminals of all types." [6]

Chief Thomas Farrell

Patrolman Crumley was certainly the latter and was believed at times to be a crony to a few law breakers. Appointed by **Chief Thomas Farrell** in 1893, Crumley was a large, athletic man who once made a living as a professional pugilist. He

illustration *(undated)*

was not hesitant to take out a combative foe with a "single uppercut on the point of the chin [or] let go his right" to knock out teeth. [7] There was one time when glove-covered fists hampered the quick use of his hands as reported on Christmas Eve 1894.

Officer Crumley stopped a "prowler" at three o'clock in the morning near the train station when he was suddenly and repeatedly slashed savagely with a knife. He could not pull his pistol. Spewing blood from five deep lacerations to his face and neck, the officer tried to subdue his attacker who fled. The assailant was soon thereafter arrested. One deep wound barely missed Crumley's jugular vein, and in all, the gashes required 48 stitches. It was an encounter so brutal that it made the newspapers across the nation including, in a foreshadowing, Minnesota's *St. Paul Globe*.

The detective, having survived the wicked attack, returned to duty to be the subject of hundreds of local news

Circa 1900

Detective James Crumley
(center)

Standing with two large detectives:

Sergeant Frank McBride *(far left)*

and Detective Frank Bassett.

Courtesy of Bridget Sperl, Crumley's great-granddaughter

accounts over the next five years, many glowing. However, shortly after Chief Farrell was forced to resign in 1900 – at a time when loyalties were often paramount for those in valued positions in police service – Det. Crumley was also dismissed from the police force. The alleged offenses were unspecified conduct unbecoming an officer, and for the temperance lobby admonishment of drinking alcohol. In his case, it was while on duty.

James Crumley was quickly hired by the Pennsylvania Railroad out of the Pittsburgh office. His role, in his words, was to "protect the public from pick pockets and con-men." [8] Still, his local popularity was such that he was congratulated in the press on his new job and lauded for his work as a Dayton investigator. Within a half year, and two months before the appointment of Chief John Whitaker, Crumley was rehired by the Dayton police force and immediately reassigned as a plainclothes officer. It was not long before he was the focus of a stirring newspaper account of an arrest during which "bare knuckles were used with effect by the detective who felled his man...."

An "exciting capture ... of a daring Negro sneak" [9] by Det. Crumley was fodder for the newspapers. The detective had enthusiasts in the press but he once again faced scrutiny when a gang of six or seven pickpockets working a crowd downtown victimized a citizen in the near presence of the detective. A complaint was lodged with the Chief that not one of the "dips" was arrested, implying that something sinister was afoot. Det. Crumley told the Chief there were too many suspects for him "to tackle" but the press was perplexed that this tall man of action could not apprehend at least one thief. Chief Whitaker felt the same way and dismissed the detective from the force (although Crumley contended that he resigned).

In the absence of employment in law enforcement, James Crumley opened a saloon on South Ludlow Street in July 1903 where two thieves were spotted and arrested by Dayton detectives. A stolen trunk containing silk goods was suspiciously recovered outside the back of the bar. Crumley was not implicated but it left a stain not forgotten by one newspaperman.

By April 1904, Crumley was back in the service

of the Pennsylvania Railroad as a railroad detective. In September, he briefly appeared in Dayton to capture "the most celebrated pickpocket in America, 'Hockey' Cavanaugh." [10] Over the course of the next 30 years, whenever Crumley returned to Dayton, or made national headlines, he was championed by the local newspapers for his exploits. One newsman found exception.

James Crumley

Circa 1902: Police File Card
Detective James Crumley

On December 15, 1916, a *Dayton Journal* writer was asked by an outside source if Crumley had been prosecuted for a crime when he worked as a policeman in the Gem City. The reporter replied in a letter with negative anecdotes as well as an assessment: "Unable to dig up indictment on J.P. Crumley. Officials say know nothing.... Known as a good detective but prone to fall for easy money." [11]

The lawman, James Crumley, was destined for controversy in a larger venue.

The opening of the 20th century did not change the landscape when it came to alcohol. Intoxicating beverages were viewed as the greatest evil by many in society. And, so, it was with excitement when on October 24, 1904 the nation's "most spectacular old temperance warrior," Carrie Nation, brought her crusade against saloons to Dayton the second of two times. The first had been in 1901. Advocates greeted "the hatchet-waving, bar smashing, booze destroying crusader" at the Union train station. [12]

It was 30 years earlier that Dayton police had been confronted for well over six weeks by the women's temperance crusaders. Their praying tactics in Dayton to close local taverns made national news. Now the WCTU woman, who was known for the lawless, ruthless destruction of saloons with an axe, was in town for a week of speaking engagements. She always drew huge crowds.

At one event, an attention-seeker decided to masquerade as Carrie Nation by clothing in a black sunbonnet and full-length dress. Wielding a wooden hatchet, the individual arrived at a Third Street saloon. A throng of people gathered expecting to see a Mrs. Nation bar-bashing episode. Instead, the crowd watched as Patrolmen George Hankins and Isaac Lightner latched onto the impostor and walked the man to the Central Police Station.

WCTU Leader, Carrie Nation

As it turned out, Carrie Nation spent the week in 1904 simply lecturing the local church circuit and criticizing the "cowardly" Christians that were not voting for candidates who favored the complete prohibition of alcohol. In one of her last local appearances, she drew "nearly 4000 people" to a lecture at the Armory on East Sixth Street.

Many Daytonians were disappointed not to see the violent outbursts for which Carrie Nation was popular. She left the Gem City and no saloon was subjected to her swinging axe.

Between 1904 and 1908, the rank and file of the

Dayton police force gradually increased in size to 122 sworn officers. Although patrolmen continued to work regular 12-hour days, their days off had expanded to 26 days per year.

Still, more police officers were needed because the crime rate in the city at the turn of the century was on the rise as the population rapidly increased. Generally, there had been two to four murders a year, [13] if not less, and an average of 10 to 15 armed robberies committed annually. But those numbers exploded in the new century.

At the start of the decade, Dayton police had to deal with the dangerous Frank Cook gang of thieves and ruffians. The Cook gang, also known as the Bungaloo gang, had as a member Earl 'Pete' Fouts, the older brother of Al Fouts.

In 1902, a notorious killing was committed by one of the gang leaders, Charles 'Dayton Slim' Stimmel. He and Frank Cook's sister fled to New Orleans but were tracked down by Dayton detectives and captured. Defended by a local criminal attorney who served many underworld clients, **John E. 'Jack' Egan**, Stimmel was found guilty and, seated on "Old Sparky," executed at the Ohio State Penitentiary in 1904. [14]

Defense Attorney
John 'Jack' Egan

At the end of the decade came the public's realization that a series of strangulations of five young local women, predominantly between 1904 and 1909, had been committed by a serial killer. Later, Dayton's "Jack the Strangler" was suspected of a number of similar murders in Cincinnati. The heinousness of the crimes shocked the community, puzzled police, and made for good press.

The 1907, '08 and '09 killings gained national attention and prompted *The New York Times* to liken these strangulation murders to London's "Jack the Ripper" serial mutilations only 20 years earlier (1888). Dayton's serial killings were never solved. [15]

Much less sensational but far more common in terms of criminality was **Albert Fouts**.

Al Fouts / Foutz

He first came to the attention of the Dayton police force in 1905 when he was arrested for "Suspicion" – a catch-all reason to be taken into custody without evidence to charge – for loosely matching the description of a crime suspect. Fouts was questioned and released. He was 15 years old at the time and diminutive in stature. A mere 5'1, he never grew taller in adulthood. He was a thief and his minuscule size made break-ins a perfect fit for him.

The first adult arrest of an 18-year old Al "Foutz" [16] was in June 1908 for "B&L" – burglary and larceny. Sent to the Ohio State Reformatory, he was twice paroled and twice returned to jail for violations of his parole until released five years later. Over the course of 40 years, he spent as much time in prisons as he would on the outside. But when he was outside, he committed crimes and drew the company of police.

Crime aside, Dayton police again faced a blow to its reputation in October 1908 when Chief John Whitaker was dismissed from the force. This occurred after his return by train from Cincinnati late at night in a highly-intoxicated state. Then, while venturing from saloons to hotel bars proclaiming his police authority, he acted confrontationally with patrons.

The flow of booze and Dayton's large number of bars added to local societal woes as was the case here. Widely regarded as an accomplished police leader, Chief Whitaker's fall from grace was steep and dismaying. But into the vacancy created by his forced resignation for unbefitting conduct stepped Whitaker's second in command, Captain John Allaback.

Chief Allaback had been the interim commander for 15 months prior to Whitaker's appointment after then Chief Farrell was forced to resign for engaging in inappropriate conduct. In 1908, the former Indian fighter conveniently lived just around the corner from the Central Police Station, ironically, in a house on Tecumseh Street. Taking the helm once more, this time permanently, Chief Allaback proved to be a reserved commander; however, there was never a doubt who was the leader of the Dayton Police Department over his long tenure. He took charge at the time of some noteworthy happenings for Greater Dayton as the decade closed out.

Although there were only villages and townships throughout the region, by the end of 1908, a community adjoining Dayton named Oakwood became the second incorporated city in Montgomery County. As the year closed, a former Dayton patrolman who had joined the force in 1886 with then Patrolman Allaback, John Boes, served his final days as the Montgomery County Sheriff. After his one term in office, Sheriff Boes was appointed the Montgomery County Prosecutor's "Secret Service Officer."

Patrolman John Boes; later elected Sheriff of Montgomery County.

Boes new duties included, under an amended Ohio 1909 act, "providing against the evils resulting from the traffic in intoxicating liquors." The temperance movement was gaining serious political traction. [17]

Arguably the greatest achievement in history, human flight in 1903, had received scant notice from the local newspaper reporters while national publications turned a blind eye to the feat. However, in 1909, after the Wrights flew exhibitions throughout Europe, and then New York City, it suddenly dawned on the press that the miracle of manned flight had been realized.

1909: Crowd forms at Union Station to greet hometown heroes, the Wright brothers.

Returning home from their worldwide tour that year, Wilbur and Orville Wright were honored with a huge parade and festivities, paying tribute to the hometown brothers, embarrassingly, six years after the fact.

1907: Third Precinct Police Station, located at 1828 West Third Street.

Ptl. Rudy Wurstner sitting, third from the right.

Ptl. William Jenkins standing, third from the left.

Circa 1910: The boy, Johnnie Dillinger.

Circa 1910: Patrolman Lucius Rice
Courtesy of Robert Rice, Jr., grandson

The year 1909 also saw an uncommon appointment of a black man to the Dayton Police Department. **Lucius Rice**, a sergeant in the Ohio National Guard, stepped over the color line to join the man recognized as Dayton's first black patrolman, **William Jenkins**, appointed 11 years earlier in 1898. Both police officers brought credit to the force throughout the course of their careers. Together these officers patrolled the familiar streets of West Dayton. They were soon joined the following year by a third man of color, **George Wheeler**.

Ptl. William Jenkins

It was 1910.

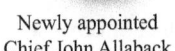

As that year began, Chief Allaback was honored by his loyal troops. It was during the Policemen's Concert and Ball, the first social event ever held at Memorial Hall which was dedicated just two days earlier on January 5.

He was surprised with the presentation to him of "one of the handsomest badges worn by any official in the United States." [18]

Newly appointed Chief John Allaback

Later that year, on August 14, 1910, a figure central to the local story of John Dillinger (now a boy of seven growing up in the Hoosier State) was born in Indiana as well.

Mary Jenkins, later **Mary Jenkins Longnaker**, would eventually call Dayton her home.

Sidebar: Police Methods of Communications and Identification

The Patrol Call Box: In an effort to keep the city sprawl
under watchful care, the City of Dayton purchased and placed into
operation the Gamewell system in **1896**. The $25,000 system
($777,400 today) consisted of 64 patrol call boxes strategically
located around the city. In years past, patrolmen could sound an
alarm by blowing a whistle or banging an ash can with a nightstick.
The call box was the new, high-tech way for local lawmen to contact
the police "central exchange" to request help. Officers also had to
check in on the hour to receive assignments.

Although patrolman could speak into a telephone, the telegraph
feature was the primary identifying function of the police patrol
call box. When the "hook" was triggered by inserting a key in the
"Wagon Call" keyhole, a telegraph signal would transmit the call
box number (i.e. box location) to the police "central exchange."
There it would imprint the box number on a paper ticker tape. The
"exchange" operator could then send a wagon or other officers
from the patrol house to that location.

The call box was the main police method of communicating
throughout the first 40 years of the **20th Century** until in-car radio
transmission came into practical use in **1940**.

The Bertillon System: In **1879**, the Dayton Police Directors
required the head of the police force *"to have photographs taken
of noted criminals and suspicious characters to be preserved...."*
The photographs as a collection was called the "rogues gallery."
The beginning of Dayton's Bureau of Identification is traced to this
directive. In **1902**, the Dayton "B of I" was fully established
with the local introduction of the "Bertillon System for Criminal
Identification" at a cost of $1,000 ($30,500 today).

The Bertillon system - founded on a science called anthro-
pometry - was "based upon measurements of certain bony parts
of the body that were thought never to change over the life of
an individual." Early police identification clerks that logged
anthropometric measurements on mug shot arrest cards were
known as "Bertillon operators." Front and, later, side facial
pictures of criminals – mug shots – were adhered on the reverse
side of Bertillon cards.

The Bertillon identification method was used during the
first 20 years of the **20th Century** until the Henry fingerprint
classification system became the standard in Dayton by **1920**.

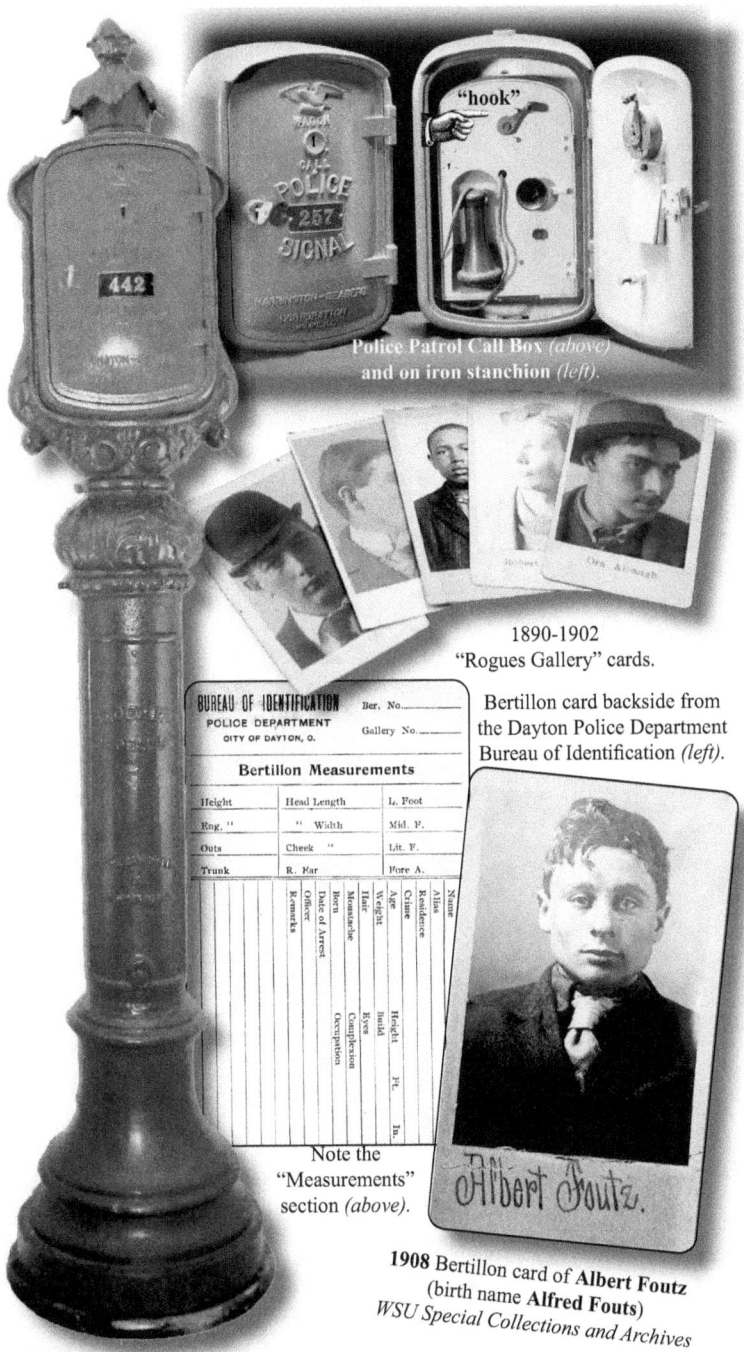

"hook"

Police Patrol Call Box *(above)*
and on iron stanchion *(left)*.

1890-1902
"Rogues Gallery" cards.

Bertillon card backside from
the Dayton Police Department
Bureau of Identification *(left)*.

Note the
"Measurements"
section *(above)*.

1908 Bertillon card of **Albert Foutz**
(birth name **Alfred Fouts**)
WSU Special Collections and Archives

CHAPTER 2

DECADE OF DEATH – THE NEXT 10 YEARS

March 27, 1913: The devastation of the Great Dayton Flood is national news.
Circa 1918: 15-year veteran Dayton Police **Sergeant Rudy Wurstner**.

1911: Ptl. John Reiter with his "DPD" Flying Merkel motorcycle. First known photo of a Dayton "motorman" and "machine." *Courtesy Ron Reiter, grandson.*

1913: The Great Dayton Flood devastated the city and region.

Martial Law was declared by Governor James Cox.

Circa 1916: Sgt. Thomas Grundish walking a police beat at a downtown railroad yard. *Courtesy of Tom Grundish, grandson.*

RESILIENCE – The second decade of the 20th century saw Chief Allaback and his troops on the front lines severely challenged and often repeatedly burdened with death. And, as the 1910s rolled in and on, the now street-experienced Patrolman Rudy Wurstner continued his many years conducting walking patrol. He was still assigned, along with Patrolmen William Jenkins, Lucius Rice, and George Wheeler, to the 3rd Precinct station house located at 1828 W. Third Street alongside the City Railway tracks. [19]

Ptl. Rudy Wurstner

In the demarcated third police precinct, the Wright Brothers rented space to build airplanes at the Speedwell Motor Car Company of Dayton on Wisconsin Avenue. Construction was underway on their new factory near Brooklyn Avenue, also in West Dayton. The Dayton Police Department, still using horse-drawn wagons, purchased its first motorized "machines" ... motorcycles. One had been placed on patrol on a trial basis in October 1910 and a second was purchased two months later.

In February 1911, the City of Dayton requisitioned four Flying Merkel motorcycles for its patrolmen – two for the 2nd Precinct and two for the 3rd Precinct – making Dayton police, arguably, the first in the nation to conduct police motorcycle patrol. Then in April 1911, two Speedwell automotive patrol wagons were placed in the "police fleet." That year ended with Ptl. Rudy Wurstner as a nine-year veteran. He and his fellow officers would face an unimaginable and harrowing natural disaster the following year.

In 1912, air and motor vehicle travel were in their formative years. Long-distance transportation was through steam locomotion for well over a half century. As a business operation on rails, it employed lawmen to protect passengers and the train industry alike. James Crumley had been a special agent since he left the Gem City in 1904, first with the Pennsylvania Railroad and then, beginning in 1909, with Great Northern Railroad for both the Willmar and Sioux City Divisions.

On July 11, 1912, Special Agent Crumley was hired by the Minnesota-St. Louis Railroad after being in charge of security for the St. Paul and Minneapolis terminals. His work brought him to the attention of St. Paul Police Chief John O'Connor. Twenty years after Dayton Police Chief Farrell appointed Crumley to the Dayton police force, another fellow Irishman, did the same in St. Paul. Crumley was proudly hired by a man he admired and was assigned to detective duties by Chief O'Connor in 1914. By this time, a thuggish local gang member, Bugs Moran, had left his birth city for new gangland territory on Chicago's North Side.

James Crumley

Chief John O'Connor had been appointed to head the St. Paul Police Department in 1900. He immediately instituted his "layover agreement" to reduce crime within the city limits. He had a contract with gangsters to "check in" with police upon arrival; make payments to the police and city officials; and agree not to commit major lawbreaking in St. Paul. What may have begun as a well-intended initiative did indeed work but it ultimately created a safe haven for many of the nation's most notorious criminals in decades to come. Detective Crumley would eventually fall victim to the "O'Connor Layover Agreement." [20]

While both St. Paul Det. James Crumley and Dayton patrolmen were destined for unforeseen troubles, Indianapolis in 1912 was the home to a troubled boy trying to navigate his youth in a family struck by death.

When nearly age four, John Dillinger had suffered the painful loss of his mother to a stroke. He became the only child at home when his 18-year-old sister married in 1907. Living with his stern father, he was both indulged and knocked about. After several years, "Johnnie" moved to his sister's house so that she could care for him. But his sister was soon a young mother with a number of small children.

Johnnie was sent back to his father who remarried in 1912. The elder Dillinger was a successful grocer by trade and a churchgoer. The youngster had the benefit of a moral upbringing in a family of affordable means. On the other hand, he was often at odds with a father, who was strict by nature and physical with the lad, and a stepmother he loathed (he would come to love both parents later in life). Johnnie was rebellious even before his teenage years.

Dillinger reportedly bullied other children but was also described as a normal, pleasant kid, contrasting traits that were later evidenced in adulthood.

The bully, Johnnie Dillinger

Out of boredom, he quit school when he was age 16. Interested in making money, he found employment at an Indianapolis machine shop. Despite efforts by the elder Dillinger to convince his son to return to school, the boy remained a dropout. As a teenager, it was not uncommon for Dillinger to be in trouble with the law for brawling, petty theft, and knocking back booze.

Ills at homes that bred delinquent teenagers, such as Dillinger, was a swelling problem for urban America. Having experienced the likes of Al Fouts and others, Dayton was no different than Indianapolis. Law enforcement had long been monolithic and exclusively a man's occupation. But in this decade, the world that belonged to men was confronted by women asserting themselves and their views as never before. They were determined to remedy disorders at homes, oftentimes bred by alcohol consumption.

In 1914, a policing bureau was formed in Dayton comprised of female social workers wearing badges. Their role was "handling home life cases" that were more familiar to "women folk." Society demanded the women do the kind of work that "should not be handled by men." [21]

Circa 1914: The Dayton Bureau of Policewomen is established by the Public Safety Director. Policewomen Annie McCully and Lulu Sollers. Aide Gertrude McClure. *Wright State University Special Collections and Archives.*

The sworn policewomen were expected to deal with some of the responsibilities that had previously been those of patrolmen, especially "the management, arrest and commitment of drunken women and wayward girls." [21 ibid]

The Dayton Bureau of Policewomen was a social reform born from various women's movements including the temperance lobby. Appointed in early 1914, the Dayton Bureau's first member was Policewoman Annie McCully who was joined later that same year by Plwn. Lulu Sollers. These two Irish women, seen authoritatively traversing the city streets in their post-Victorian dresses, formed an enthralling team. They captured photographers' lens and the public's curiosity for the next few years until McCully left, as the Great War was ending, to engage in surveillance of federally identified women.

In the interim, the Policewomen's Bureau had "prostitutes, child deserters, unwed mothers, drinking fathers and mothers, the cruel and the ignorant, the misguided and the criminal file through [its] office day in and day out." [21 ibid]

The impact of women inside and outside of law enforcement cannot be overstated. In the years during and on either side of her police career, Annie McCully also guided Dayton suffragists and was later identified by the press as the city's "suffrage pioneer."

Plwn. Annie McCully

The temperance and women's suffrage movements transformed society which also changed law enforcement practices. Both long-fought causes – respective 96- and 72-year campaigns – would find their ultimate goals met with success as 1920 approached.

While patrolmen yielded to the unfamiliar formation of the Bureau of Policewomen and, later, tolerated a reduction of force due to the Great War, uniformed officers on Dayton's front lines repeatedly withstood the misery of deaths this decade.

———————

On January 21, 1913, in assessing ways to manage funds, the City of Dayton reduced an already understaffed police force of 160 officers by a full 15%. The timing could not have been worse. On March 24, 1913, the Gem City was overrun by turbulent flood waters in what has been described as the greatest natural disaster ever to strike Ohio. It was one of the nation's greatest natural catastrophes of the 20th century.

By any measure, the Dayton police force was undermanned, under-equipped, and under water ... but its officers were undeterred. Patrolmen William Jenkins and Rudy Wurstner were two of those 136 officers who remained in the field for days on end until certain that the urgent nature of this crisis had abated.

At four o'clock in the morning, Ptl. Jenkins – by then a 15-year veteran – walked door-to-door waking sleeping citizens residing along the Wolf Creek levee. At this unreasonable hour he implored families to move to high ground. After saving 40 people on one street alone, he was suddenly swept away in a barrage of water. Frantically, he struggled to survive from being battered to death by the heavy debris churning in the cascading water or drowned. [22] He suffered a severe hip injury but he remained in the field.

The community suffered 92 "recorded" deaths with unofficial estimates up to 128 lives lost. In addition, 2,000 domestic animals and 1,400 horses perished in the city of Dayton alone. It was the worst struck Midwest city.

The small force of 136 policemen – doing what they could to maintain social order in a devastated city bent on immediately rebuilding – required the assistance of 2,400 National Guardsmen. When two men were caught by the military pillaging unsecured buildings, they were taken before Chief Allaback. Perturbed by the disruption, the Chief made his position quite clear to the soldiers when he said, "Don't bring looters to me. Kill them if you catch them looting." [23]

In the wake of the 1913 Great Dayton Flood, [24] members of the Dayton police force were initially assigned the repugnant duty of hauling away dead animals. Ptl. Wurstner headed a detail responsible for the removal of horse carcasses from the city. His detail carted the animals from West Third Street six miles south to the disposal site; grounds on the Great Miami River. [25]

Ptl. Rudy Wurstner

March 1913: 1,400 horse carcasses lined Dayton streets in the flood aftermath.

The clean-up work on the heels of the initial four-day human rescue and recovery efforts was so demanding that Ptl. Wurstner, as well as many of his other fellow officers, never made it home until a week after this destructive deluge.

Five years later, a dark wraith of nature visited post WWI. The horrific fervency of the 1918-1920 Spanish influenza pandemic found the police on the front lines, once more at great risk, especially those handling police ambulance duties such as Ptl. Frank Johnson. Beginning in October 1918, Chief Allaback gave patrolmen orders to close saloons that violated health orders. Extra officers were placed on duty to arrest those who did not heed the cancellation of holiday celebrations.

Chief John Allaback

This was not how the temperance activists expected tavern closings to come about.

Maintaining order on the streets of Dayton, six otherwise healthy policemen, ages 24 to 31 (three recently schooled appointees) – Patrolmen Clement Francis, Emerson Glotefelter, Lawrence Graham, Vinton Harsh, Edward Hennessey, and Troy Sine – were afflicted with this attributed World War I plague and died. [26] And other untold officers may have as well. In the first four months through January 1919, 701 Daytonians died from the Spanish flu, a distressing number far, far higher than from the Great Flood.

Between the Great Flood and the Great War, the year 1916 was personally tragic for Dayton police officers. Three fellow Dayton officers were killed in the line of duty, evenly spaced with one death every four months. The first of the three was in January.

Ptl. John Stapleton fractured his skull when his motorcycle slammed into the side of a moving motorized fire engine. Closely following the engine, he had not anticipated its quick right turn from North Main Street onto Burton Avenue. Ptl. Stapleton's death was a modern, blended reprise of the casualties of both Sgt. Amer Keller and Ptl. William Dalton at the close of the last century.

Ptl. John Stapleton

Not surprisingly, a saloon and a bootlegging venture were the backdrops for two police murders.

The last of the three, in September 1916, was inside George Kerns' saloon on South Euclid Avenue at Germantown Street. Ptl. George Purcell entered the bar on a report of a man with a gun causing a disturbance inside.

Ptl. George Purcell

The officer approached the notorious local gang leader, Robert 'Alabama Slim' McCullough, and asked him to step outside when, suddenly, the officer was shot and then stabbed by Alabama Slim.

McCullough fled and was later arrested during a manhunt. The officer died as he was being placed in a police ambulance. Ptl. Purcell's murder was reminiscent of the killing of Ptl. Lee Lynam in 1880.

Only a week earlier in September, Ptl. William Jenkins had arrested four of six of McCullough's "Alabama gang" members on Dunbar Avenue, but not without a fight. The officer suffered severe injuries and was nearly blinded in the brawl from blows to

the head. The examining doctor noted in the pension records that "Officer Jenkins is in a pitable condition.... so crippled up... that he will be unable to properly protect himself...." *[sic]*

The Gem City's groundbreaking lawman was driven into retirement due to the debilitating nature of his injuries.

Ptl. William Jenkins

In between the killings of Patrolmen John Stapleton and George Purcell was an attack in May 1916.

Patrolmen Charles Thomas and Chester Mapes, in a plainclothes assignment, were searching for bootleggers near the river's edge, an area commonly known as the "Edgewood Dump."

They came upon two men beneath the Washington Street bridge with suspected bootleg whiskey. After sampling it, Ptl. Thomas told the men they were under arrest.

One moonshiner suddenly pulled a revolver, shooting Ptl. Thomas in the chest. The bootlegger attempted to flee but was gunned down by Ptl. Mapes who then took the other bootlegger into custody. Ptl. Thomas was rushed to the hospital in a police ambulance but died from his wound a week later.

Ptl. Charles Thomas

It was not policemen alone who fell victim to murder. Mrs. Ethel Mullen was slain on November 28, 1916 while her husband, Edward 'Mike' Mullen, a "Bungaloo gang" member, sat in prison for a burglary in Troy, Ohio.

Her killer was familiar to police.

Three years earlier, after a "final parole," Al Fouts had been suspected of committing a number of hold-ups in nearby Xenia, Ohio. He was convicted in January 1914 of a reduced charge of carrying a concealed weapon. Sentenced to the Ohio Pen, he was again paroled in December 1915.

He had frequent run-ins with the law in Dayton but this time, on December 3, 1916, Al Fouts was arrested for driving a butcher knife into the chest of his purported "sweetheart" and charged with second-degree murder.

It had been a lovers' quarrel and Fouts was "in a fit of insane fury." The knife punctured Ethel Mullen's lung. She lingered for a little over three days inside her older brother's house on East Fifth Street as Fouts watched her slowly die from internal hemorrhaging.

The killer, Al Fouts

As soon as she drew her last breath, he deeply slashed his own throat with a razor blade. It was the suicide attempt that brought the police to the house.

Scarred for life, Fouts survived the terrible wound to stand trial. He was defended by local criminal lawyer Jack Egan, the attorney who could not save Charles Stimmel from the electric chair.

Luckily for Fouts, he was convicted of the lesser offense of manslaughter and would be sentenced once again; this time to three years.

A week before his 1917 conviction, Fouts filled out his draft registration card but was spared by prison from induction into the military at a time of war.

The suffering this decade by families from Dayton was made worse by the killings of warfare. Between April 6, 1917 and November 11, 1918, the U.S.A. engaged in the Great War of Europe and Greater Dayton was on the front line, literally and industrially.

On the home front, Dayton contributed mightily to support its troops overseas. Its police officers took into custody about 900 "Huns" – German-born Daytonians – so that they could be registered and photographed by the Bureau of Identification. And, there were local enlistments of patrolmen and civilians for overseas battles. In the end, the Montgomery County death toll was, conservatively, several hundred.

To support U.S. troops, the city was heavily involved in war manufacturing and was even the "tank [production] center of the nation." As the birthplace of flight, three aviation facilities, including McCook Field, were also involved in Army Air Service training and testing. [27]

Rudolph Wurstner was 36 years old at the war's start. He had risen to the rank of sergeant two years earlier on February 3, 1915, and reassigned to the 2nd Precinct in East Dayton.

While Sgt. Wurstner, a martial art "master," molded a Dayton Police "Crack Jiu-Jitsu Squad" to conduct

Sgt. Rudy Wurstner

exhibitions, he was called upon during WWI to train U.S. Army Air Service soldiers stationed at McCook Field. The press reported: "Men of McCook field are preparing themselves to do things to the Huns when they met [sic] them in hand-to-hand conflict.... Sergeant Wurstner declares the soldier class to be among the best he ever instructed." [28]

Only a month before America's entry into the war, the Dayton Police Department instituted a training school, under the command of Lt. Thomas Lanker, for new recruits who were required to go through a "course of instruction" to learn police work. (Lt. Lanker would eventually oversee private security for the Dayton Wright Airplane Co.)

Having demonstrated his leadership skills, Sgt. Wurstner was selected to be the city's first police instructor. He was sent to the New York City Police Department school for training. Not long thereafter, he was joined as a police recruit instructor by **Sgt. Thomas Grundish**.

Sgt. Thomas Grundish

These two sergeants taught the city ordinance book, and proper procedures for handling criminals, evidence preservation, public courtesy, calisthenics, as well as self-defense tactics based, of course, on the principles of Jiu-Jitsu. The first recruit class graduated as the United States entered the Great War. Two other recruit classes would follow before the war's end.

———————————

Leading to, during, and after the Great War, the Temperance Movement had increasingly gained American citizen support but not so with the German-American population. This ethnic group had offered the most opposition to Prohibition. However, anti-German sentiment silenced much of their argument and the U.S. Congress passed the Wartime Prohibition Act, banning the sale of most alcohol in order to preserve grain for the war effort. [29a]

An amendment to the U.S. Constitution prohibiting alcohol had been *proposed* during the war by the U.S. Senate on December 18, 1917.

Sidebar: *The Great War – Two Combat Soldiers, later Patrolmen*

In 1914 the drum beat of war was in the air, and in **1917**, U.S. entry into The Great War brought about national patriotic fervor.

A tale of two combat soldiers who became police officers:

U.S. Army Sgt. William T. 'Tom' Wilson voluntarily enlisted in the armed services in 1914. In September 1917, Pvt. Wilson was promoted to the rank of sergeant as part of the 372nd Infantry Regiment which deployed to France in March **1918**. The 372nd was a "colored" regiment.

Sgt. Wilson was on the front lines of combat during the fierce battles of the Meuse-Argonne offensive and the "Battle of the Argonne Forest," lasting until the war's end in November 1918. There were heavy casualties but victory was achieved.

Sgt. Wilson and his entire Division were awarded France's highest honor, the Croix de Guerre. The heroic black combat veteran was later appointed to the Dayton police force where tragedy struck him in **1928**.

Courtesy of Gary Siler, researcher

U.S. Army Pvt. Horace C. Moore voluntarily enlisted in **1917**, *at age 14*, to become one of the youngest soldiers in the American Expeditionary Force. Trained by the Wright Airplane Company at McCook Field, he was stationed in the air fields in France which were machine gunned and bombed by the enemy.

He survived WWI, joined the Dayton police force and partook in the **1933** arrest of John Dillinger.

When WWII erupted, Ptl. Moore took leave to accept a commission in the U. S. Army Air Corps for combat in Europe. After being discharged at the rank of captain in 1947 he was reinstated to the police force and involved in a police shooting.

He retired in 1951 at the rank of sergeant but, with the U.S. engaged in the Korean War, this experienced combatant of two wars reactivated in the Army, retiring at the rank of lieutenant colonel.

Courtesy of Steven Moore, grandson

WWI-era: Aerial view of McCook Field training facility in Old North Dayton. The biplane flyover is at Keowee Street where Webster Street intersects.

WWI: Dayton Police "Crack Jiu-Jitsu Team" at McCook Field for an exhibit and the training of U.S. Army Air Service Soldiers.

WWI-era: A wider version of the photographic image depicted on the chapter introductory page (45). Sgt. Wurstner seated at left. Taken in front of the 1st Precinct Station & City Jail on East Sixth Street.

The 18th Amendment was *ratified* by the requisite 36 of 48 states on January 16, 1919. In the end, only two states rejected it; however, passing the amendment did not immediately bring about its enforcement.

In Ohio, the struggle between wets and drys came to a climax when the Anti-Saloon League pushed for a state constitutional amendment prohibiting the sale and manufacture of intoxicating beverage. The issue came up for a vote in 1914, 1915 and 1917. Each time it failed. However, in 1918, the league put more resources into the campaign and the amendment passed. Ohio's rural counties, where prohibition sentiment was strongest, carried the amendment to victory. Montgomery County, with its larger German-American population, voted against it. Prohibition began in Ohio on May 27, 1919, seven months before national Prohibition began. [29b]

On October 28, 1919, Congress passed the National Prohibition Act (the Volstead Act) which authorized the enforcement of the ban on alcohol. It became effective on January 17, 1920.

PROHIBITION ... Temperance prevailed as constitutional law in the United States!

The enforcement of prohibition laws in the Gem City was not immediate ... it could not be described as an eager undertaking.

Circa 1922: Dayton Liquor Squad - **Ptl. Russell Pfauhl** (standing left) across from Sgt. Newton Haywood and two unidentified officers with a seizure of bootlegger stills inside a storage room at the Central Police Station on South Ford Street.
William Preston Mayfield Collection at Dayton History

PART TWO

THE TEMPTATIONS 1919 – 1933

1890-1927 - Chiefs Thomas Farrell, John Whitaker, John Allaback,
and **Rudolph F. 'Rudy' Wurstner's City-issued Badge** *(above)*
Courtesy of Chief Richard Biehl and Dayton Police Department

CHAPTER 3

PROHIBITION ENTERS THE ROARING '20S

1922 - 1925: An assortment of local newspaper articles regarding Prohibition. Dayton Liquor Squad showing a seizure from a raid of a bootlegging operation (location unknown) in cooperation with State of Ohio liquor agents.

Legal Dayton saloon on Williams Street destined to close with Prohibition *(above)*.

Illegal bootlegging operations in Dayton destined to open with Prohibition.

Bootleg liquor seized by the Dayton's Liquor Squads during Prohibition.

WSU Special Collections and Archives

Mayfield Collection at Dayton History
(below)

LIQUOR SQUADS – As with any initiative passed by legislators – whether local, state, or federal – law enforcement had to make adjustments to the new reality. Additional or redirected funds were necessary as were strategies and new assignments. Cooperative efforts between agencies had to be developed. Attitudes had to be ... massaged.

The U.S. government appointed over 1,500 federal agents to enforce the National Prohibition Act. The Ohio government appointed its share of state liquor officers. Montgomery County's battle with bootleggers was a singular assignment belonging to Deputy Sheriff Ford Long from 1923 to 1929. He would draw on other deputies, or state and federal agents, when conducting raids. The Dayton police force remained a few years away from designating two "Special Liquor Squads" which required reallocation of manpower.

Chief John Allaback had already restructured the police organization over a three-year period between 1918 and 1920. The Chief chose to elevate four men to the second line of command by creating a new position – "Police Inspector" – replacing a single assistant chief. Each inspector was assigned a "Bureau." After three years training police officers, on March 1, 1920, Sgt. Wurstner was one of four promoted to the new rank.

Police Inspector Rudy Wurstner was part of an upper command team that included **Inspector Seymour 'Cy' Yendes** as well as Inspectors Thomas Grundish and Otha Greger. Together, and beginning in 1920, these four commanders oversaw the Dayton Police Department for an incredible 15 consecutive years. They

Police Inspector
Seymour Yendes

comprised, arguably, the most influential command staff in Dayton police history.

Inspector Wurstner was placed in charge of the "Uniform Bureau" (patrol operations), the largest bureau. This was a good fit for him because he was popular with the troops. He also had within his bureau all motorcycle officers and a police fleet of a few "emergency" automobiles. It was clear early in Inspector Wurstner's command that he was not one to be removed from the rank and file uniformed officers. He patrolled the streets with his troops.

Police Inspector
Rudy Wurstner

Society would undergo dramatic changes as well in this coming decade. At the time, Ohio was a powerhouse in the nation and Dayton was prominent on the national stage. In 1920, the Democrat nominee for United States President was a Daytonian and Ohio's governor, **James Cox**, the founder and publisher of the *Dayton Daily News*. His vice-presidential running mate was **Franklin Roosevelt**.

1920: Governor Cox campaigning with Roosevelt in Downtown Dayton.

The cultural landscape was anew.

The vital role that women played during World War I pushed forward women's suffrage. In 1919, after several false starts, Congress passed the 19th Amendment with more than the two-thirds majority vote required in each house. Women triumphed in 1920. They attained voting rights when the states ratified the amendment. [30] The 1920 national election was the first under this amendment and women aligned with Republican Party principals far exceeded attendance at the polls than those with Cox's political party. The opposing candidate, Republican and Ohioan Warren Harding, was elected to the U.S. Presidency, but Franklin Roosevelt had elevated his national profile by being on Cox's ticket.

There was much "roaring" to be witnessed in Dayton when it came to transportation, aviation, philanthropy, local economy, city improvements, and sports. A hallmark year for Dayton was in 1920 when it came to professional sports.

The Dayton Marcos was one of the eight chartered members of the professional baseball Negro League in 1920, joining the famed Kansas City Monarchs and Chicago Giants, which the Marcos defeated in their first game. That same year the National Football League was founded in Canton, Ohio as the American Professional Football Association.

PRICE, 10 CENTS
N. Y. FOOTBALL GIANTS
vs.
DAYTON (Ohio) TRIANGLES

Sunday
November 29, 1925

Polo Grounds
New York

The Dayton Triangles was one of the original 10 chartered members. The Triangles played at home what is recognized by the NFL as the first NFL football game. Dayton's team scored the NFL's first touchdown and scored the first NFL victory.

The Dayton Triangles vs. the New York Giants (program). Game at the Polo Grounds.

During the decade, Dayton played the Green Bay Packers, Chicago Bears, and New York Giants. In 1929, the Dayton professional football team moved to a new sporting venue, Brooklyn, New York ... sold to a convicted bootlegger, 'Big Bill' Dwyer.

Police patrol was changing in the 1920s. The local police force had to find ways to address issues that could no longer be resolved by conducting basic foot patrol. There was the management of traffic. In Dayton, horse travel, on a broad practical level, ended after the Great Flood of 1913. Motorized travel had gained popularity. Rotating semaphores were used by police officers to regulate travel at main intersections.

The number of police investigators gradually rose from one detective in 1900 to 15 by 1920. Specialized police units, known as "details," were being formed to handle traffic, crimes, and public ruin related to vice activities.

Traffic Semaphore
Main and Third Streets

One of those details was the special liquor squad because the biggest change to the landscape entering the 1920s was from the triumph of the 90-year temperance movement. Even though the liquor squad's formation was a year away, enacted new laws effectively erased from the city surroundings Dayton's 230 saloons ... but not the desire to consume alcoholic beverages. Underground drinking establishments, "speakeasies," emerged intensifying bootlegging and making it – and associated crimes like armed robbery – even more dangerous for law enforcement officers.

In the rough-and-tumble world of policing in the early 20th century, Inspector Wurstner was as likely as his troops to engage in the dangers of the profession. The self-defense instructor and martial arts master was willing to take care of business when necessary. But his willingness to take action opened him to claims of brutality as well. The newspapers savored in reporting one incident in which a robbery suspect complained that the Inspector struck him three times in the face and knocked out one of his teeth by the blows. The accusation was later dropped. The press report was reminiscent of stories about former Dayton Detective James Crumley.

Placed on a special detail at the St. Paul Union Depot in 1920, Det. Crumley still recalled the sting of the complaint against him in Dayton. It was fresh years later because he wrote in a letter, "Can say that while there [at Union Station], I never had a complaint of a touch of either a pick pocket or a con-man while I was working." [31]

The police chief he so admired had been in command of the St. Paul Police Department, with one two-year interlude, since 1900. On June 1, 1920, **Chief John O'Connor** retired but his "layover agreement" remained to the benefit of bootleggers and gangsters. Crumley allied himself with fellow detective Thomas 'Big Tom' Brown during this decade while the police force saw a turnover of six police chiefs until Brown himself was appointed to the top post. This alliance would later prove to have a downside.

St. Paul Police Chief John O'Connor

June 1920 also found Al Fouts paroled from the

Ohio State Penitentiary. Maybe it was for a change in scenery or maybe to create distance between himself and Mike Mullen, the husband of Al's dead "sweetheart," Fouts decided to head for California. Another move took place in 1920. It was from Indianapolis and the distance was much shorter.

In 1920, John Dillinger's father retired from grocery store ownership. He sold his property and relocated the family to a farm about 20 miles southeast in the small town of Mooresville. This was not a move that the younger Dillinger wanted. The older man was seeking a way to provide a better environment for his increasingly unruly teenage son who refused to get a formal education.

Johnnie, now 17, had a job in an Indianapolis machine shop and a motorcycle. He commuted on his "machine" from the farm to the shop. "His wild and rebellious behavior continued with nightly escapades which included, drinking, fighting, and visiting prostitutes." [32]

The teenager,
John Dillinger

John Dillinger was on the cusp of adulthood and was not inclined to engage in responsible behavior.

In 1921 the Dayton Police Department finally formed its "Special Liquor Squad" to enforce Ohio's Crabbe Act, which provided for compensation directly to local officials based on the number of arrests and fines of prohibition violators. But it was not until the following year, two years into Prohibition, that the squad began taking recorded enforcement action.

On March 8, 1922, the city of Dayton passed a local ordinance. Under the ordinance, prohibition violators were charged and revenue from liquor enforcement was split with the state 50-50.

Prohibition – *If money could be made from unlawful practices, it was happening on both sides of the issue.*

The special liquor squad was comprised of two sergeants and eight patrolmen divided for two shifts. They were issued a "Police Raid Car," a motorized wagon with an enclosed bed to both look like and be a freight hauler.

Dayton "Police Raid Car" parked on Sears Street.
Collection at Dayton History.

The dry law was unpopular with the public and reflected negatively on the officers, considered "appointed shoals," who allegedly discarded due process.

They "battered their way into homes, clubs and ... businesses and carted away all the wet goods." [33] The press reported that Dayton had 250 bootleggers but little progress was made to eliminate their "750 speakeasies and 150 private stills." [34]

Dayton police did not make the laws, but they enforced them and they did make progress. They had to confront the bootlegging of alcohol made in illegal stills throughout the city. In 1922 alone, the special liquor squad conducted 1,156 raids, destroyed 192 stills, made 595 arrests and confiscated 47,400 gallons of mash, liquor and home brew. [35]

That same year, 1922, the three precinct stations closed when the Dayton police force permanently

The "Emergency Car" outside the new "Ford Street Station." Members of the team are *(left to right)*: Patrolmen George Feirstine, Frank Ganger, Frank Johnson, and Albert Oberer; Police Inspector Thomas Grundish; and Sgt. Harvey Siferd.

moved its jail and patrol officers into a new Central Police Station, commonly called the "Ford Street Station." Many bootleggers and gangsters would pass through this building, handcuffed by liquor squad officers. John Dillinger would rest there, too.

In May 1922, the officer who would one day arrest Dillinger, **Ptl. Russell Pfauhl**,[36] wrote a detailed report to Chief Allaback about a boot joint operator who tried to bribe him. He refused the money but was told, "It's alright, your sergeant takes money." Ptl. Pfauhl went on to report that his squad had raided a number of houses but the suspects arrested were never worried because, they said, the sergeant will "take care of it." It was a pattern.

Ptl. Pfauhl related in writing that he had conducted a number of these raids after getting the Anti-Saloon League to petition for warrants. He insinuated in his report that a judge and a local attorney had received favorable treatment from bootleggers as well.

The patrolman turned in his report to the Director

of the Dayton Public Safety Department (in charge of police and fire) listing a dozen witnesses to payoffs.

Soon thereafter, Ptl. Pfauhl was removed from the liquor squad by his sergeant. The public safety director examined the entire case and found there was insufficient evidence of "bribery and protecting bootleggers." And, with Pfauhl having no "personal knowledge" to substantiate his claim, instead found the patrolman "guilty of accusing a superior officer of graft...." [37] Ptl. Pfauhl was then issued departmental charges for disrespecting a superior officer and submitting a false report. The defiant patrolman pleaded "not guilty" to the charges ... *at first.*

Ptl. Pfauhl went to the newspaper with his allegations, which were published, but within a week the officer suddenly sent a report to the chief withdrawing his accusations and offering his regrets. He also changed his plea to the charges to "guilty" and offered to work for the best of the department. Ptl. Pfauhl was required to forfeit all vacation days for a half year and was ordered to publicly apologize to his sergeant and to do so in front of the first and second reliefs ... but he was allowed to keep his job.

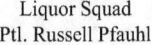

Liquor Squad
Ptl. Russell Pfauhl

This was Prohibition.

Chief Allaback was able to celebrate 36 years in law enforcement on June 16, 1922. He was approaching 14 consecutive years as the head of the Dayton police force, over 15 years when his time as interim chief from 1900 to 1901 is taken into account. His career as chief was not defined by high individual achievement but was lengthy, steady, and marked by significant events in Dayton history, particularly in the preceding decade.

The only taint to his office was the resignation of his second in command in 1918 for conduct unbecoming an officer for a sexual indiscretion. The Chief, as Dayton's longest-serving commander at the time, was a steadying presence for a department with a history of leadership scandals. Then, on October 29, 1922, Chief John N. Allaback took leave of his command when he died of natural causes while still running the Department.

Chief John Allaback

His time at the top, throughout the entire history of the Dayton Police Department, would be surpassed by only one man.

Although consideration was given to Inspector Thomas Grundish for the top spot, a former chief special agent for a railroad line was appointed the new Dayton police chief.

James Woodward was brought in to reinvigorate a police force of 198 officers viewed as having become stale. He was much like Det. Crumley in that he had been a long-serving railroad lawman who was experienced in dealing with transient thieves. Woodward was not unfamiliar with the Dayton Police Department or it with him going back 20 years.

Dayton Chief
James Woodward

In 1902, Woodward was appointed as a "special policeman" by Dayton Chief Whitaker. In 1903 he was engaged to train and care for a pack of bloodhounds the city purchased which were kept at the Patrol House on St. Clair Street. Using Dayton's first police canines, Woodward often tracked and captured criminals with the bloodhounds "which were of the finest stock" and regarded as "the best in the country". [38a]   He trailed a Dayton killer to Coshocton, Ohio. He tracked two highwaymen over four states to Parkersburg, West Virginia after they escaped the Ohio State Penitentiary.

In 1904, with his many exploits recorded, Woodward sold the bloodhounds and became the "chief special agent" in charge of 26 railroad policemen and

detectives for C.H. & D. Railroad. [38b] By then, Agent Woodward had established a reputation in Dayton for his detective work, just as a Pinkerton's detective, Thomas Farrell, had done in 1892. And just as

1923: Police inspection by Chief Woodward (in civilian attire). Inspectors Grundish and Wurstner on the right.

it had 30 year earlier, the achieved notoriety led to Dayton's top position on the police force.

The surprise appointment of Woodward – someone from outside the ranks – was not well-received by the troops in general. As happened with the other lawmen that came from outside Dayton's ranks – Farrell and Whitaker – history repeated itself with an unpleasant and even briefer ending to his command. Only two-and-a-half years from assuming the highest post, Chief Woodward resigned in 1925 after a Dayton city manager panel probe was conducted into bootleg liquor protection and pay offs.

Racketeering was an allegation brought against the Chief but it was determined by the investigation to be "unreliable," thus never proven. Although the criminal accusations appear to have been unfairly lodged, he was still found "unfit" for command. This finding may have had more to do with the internal politics of the police department at the time. Nonetheless, he was forced to resign his command. He would be the fifth of six Dayton police chiefs, going back to 1889, who was removed from office under charges of misconduct.

A new chief was needed and that man was certain to come from within the ranks.

––––––––––––

While Prohibition was the law of the land, familiar neighborhood taverns re-purposed or simply disappeared ... but not so for the taste for liquor. Speakeasies thrived. Illegal gambling operations prospered as well in this new environment. Even though the decade began with a declaration for self-discipline, the general public found ways to skirt the law with a constant flow of bootleg liquor. As early as 1922, a Dayton bootlegger complained that his kind was "losing trade because many people were learning to make their own 'hooch'." Competition was "getting awful." [39]

The infection of illegal brewing within homes was enough that by 1923, Dayton school teachers were reading the 18th Amendment to the U.S. Constitution to all students on "temperance day." That same year, home supplies of liquor for "medicinal purposes" were no longer overlooked by the Dayton liquor squad. The police claimed they had been so effective over the past few years that they were turning their attention to "illegal *private* stocks." [emphasis added]

Liquor could be found anywhere. On one occasion, "pedestrians stared in blank amazement as the occupant of an automobile careening madly northward on S. Main Street [near the Montgomery County Fairgrounds] tossed bottle after bottle of whiskey from his machine."*[sic]* [40] As each bottle hit the ground, people ran to retrieve those which were unbroken but then had to rush for cover as local township constables in a pursuing vehicle sped through to catch the "booze car" before the last bottle of "firewater evidence" had been "tossed overboard." The lawmen succeeded and placed the driver under arrest.

The constables tried to recover the rest of the liquor but "the mystery of the disappearance" remained unsolved. The arrested man was a whiskey runner for the "king of Dayton bootleggers," **John Friend**. Two years later, in a twist of "fate," one of the constables and three others from two area townships would be convicted for being in cahoots with Friend by providing protection.

The temptation for police patrolman to profit from liquor, or to consume the liquor itself, was certainly there but many more officers were quicker to take principled action.

Ptl. George Wheeler strolled his beat on West Fifth Street. He was known for making "teenagers toe the line, not go into those places they were not supposed to go [for instance, bootleg-joints], and speak respectfully to all of the women." [41] On one occasion in local lore oft told, Ptl. Wheeler was passed on the sidewalk by a man but the officer heard the sound of bottles clinking. He stopped the fellow wearing a bulging overcoat to ask what he was doing. The sheepish response was, "Oh, nothing, nothing."

Ptl. Wheeler took out his night stick, whacked the bulges breaking bottles, and then walked away leaving the man drenched in alcohol.

This was Prohibition.

PTL. GEORGE WHEELER
(right) circa 1916
alongside fellow bicycle
squad members:

Ptl. John Shimmoler
(center) and

Ptl. Walter Cussick.

Wolf Creek

Hell's Half Acre

MIAMI CITY

"MIAMI CITY" in West Dayton, south of Wolf Creek and West Third Street, in a neighborhood now called "Five Points."

"HELL'S HALF ACRE" was across the river, south of Eaker Street, and less than one mile from the Montgomery County Fairgrounds.

POLICEWOMAN DORA BURTON RICE *(right)* in the Roaring '20s with her daughter Lillian. *Courtesy of Robert B. Rice, Jr., grandson.*

Sidebar: Black Dayton Officers – Few in Number; Noteworthy Careers

Dayton's black population of 500 in the mid-19th century was a small number. While still relatively few by 1920 – roughly five percent of the city population – the number had risen to 10,000. Black citizens settled in "Hell's Half Acre" and then across the river in a section of West Dayton known as "Miami City." White police officers patrolled those neighborhoods but, by 1910, three black police officers, an unwritten quota, were in the workforce. Two were newly hired and joined **Ptl. William Jenkins** who was hired in 1898. The quota increased to five black officers after WWI and then rose to eight after WWII. In spite of limited numbers, those who served shone, including:

Patrolman George W. Wheeler: Born in 1884, he came from a prominent local African-American family that had settled in Dayton as early as 1824. After appointment to the police force in 1910, he became one of few early Dayton bicycle officers in a squad supervised by **Sgt. Rudy Wurstner**. He often worked in tandem with Sgt. Lucius Rice and was with him during two critical incidents during their careers. Ptl. Wheeler became the second black man on the Dayton police force to hold a supervisory rank. When he retired in **1943**, no other black officer would surpass his nearly 33 years of service until 1994 with the retirement of Major Dallas Hill.

Sergeant Lucius J. Rice: Born in 1876, he served as a Second Sergeant of Company C, Ohio National Guard for two years before joining the police force in 1909. His skill and character pushed aside barriers within local law enforcement. Ptl. Rice was Dayton's first African-American lawman to be appointed as a plainclothes detective (vice detail); to be teamed with a white officer, **Detective Seymour Yendes**; and to be promoted to the rank of sergeant in 1916. His career, which ended in **1939**, was dangerously eventful and consequential.

Policewoman Dora Burton Rice: Born in 1876, she was the first cousin of internationally celebrated poet Paul Laurence Dunbar. She married Lucius Rice in 1909. Mrs. Rice played a key role in her church as its treasurer and organist for over 20 years. After years as an outstanding community figure, she was appointed to the Dayton Bureau of Policewomen in 1929, becoming its first black policewoman. Plwm. Dora Rice devoted herself to protecting neglected and abused children. After 10 dedicated years, Plwn. Rice resigned in **1939**, a year in which a phone call to her from the police operator would prove personally tragic.

CHAPTER 4

The Klan, Kings, and Killings

September 14, 1927: *Dayton Daily News* article on the new police arsenal. Dayton Police Captain John C. Post (inset) demonstrates a Tommy gun.

September 21, 1923: KKK Rally at the
Montgomery County Fairgrounds

September 21, 1923:
Kluxer Parade Downtown Dayton

CROSSROAD – An anti-immigrant, anti-Catholic sentiment of a growing number of white evangelical Protestants, with strong temperance leanings, helped bring about a national resurgence of the Ku Klux Klan.

Prohibition fueled the ugly movement and Dayton was not immune. In fact, local episodes were quite visible.

The press and public officials could see the wave of sentiment and publicly condemned it. It began with a September 9, 1921 newspaper exposé on the KKK's attempt to enroll local county officials. This was followed by criticism on May 25, 1922 of Klan efforts to have a large rally inside Memorial Hall.

In January 1923 a grand jury was charged with probing into an election circular distributed throughout the county by the KKK although the court inquiry was halted due to a "fund shortage." Then on February 7, 1923, a Klan publication, *The Fiery Cross*, appeared on the streets of Dayton.

An open assembly for the initiation of 600 male Klansmen took place in Montgomery County on April 20, followed by the first open "KonKlave of Dayton women" on July 24 and then another gathering of women on September 11. In 1923, KKK rallies took place throughout the region in places like Miamisburg, – Montgomery County's third city to incorporate (and the last until 1955) – nearby Xenia in Greene County, and New Carlisle in neighboring Clark County.

In Dayton, the worst was to come.

Dayton Police Inspector Rudy Wurstner was faced with the task of ensuring that order be maintained on the streets of Dayton as one of the largest crowds assembled downtown on September 21, 1923.

The bystanders spanned nearly two miles from Monument Street to the Montgomery County Fairgrounds for a white hooded-robed "Kluxer" parade. It was huge with the route from the Fairgrounds to the river and then doubled back.

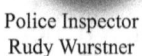

Inspector Wurstner, never one to assign unpleasant duties to others that he himself would not do, preceded the march with Sgt. Dan Wetzel and Ptl. Ben Hudson nearby. Order was kept.

Police Inspector
Rudy Wurstner

Finally, in the dark of that evening, a 100-foot cross was torched during a ceremony at which an estimated 32,000 people were in attendance.

Even though this rally was without incident, two months later, beginning in November, the Catholic University of Dayton (formerly St. Mary's College until 1920) was targeted three times by the KKK.

The last was the wickedest with the burning of a cross near Alberta Street and the "exploding of a dozen bombs." [42]

Inspector Wurstner alongside an unmarked
Dayton Police Buick Touring Sedan.

Fortunately, no one was hurt. The perpetrators of the violent attacks were never identified by police.

In May 1924, another citywide episode occurred when crosses were set aflame the same night on the grounds of the Art Institute in Riverdale and in four quadrants – Soldiers Home in West Dayton, McCook Field in North Dayton, Huffman Hill in East Dayton, and South Park.

Overt Klan activities began to fade from then on. Nevertheless, local KKK membership was estimated at 15,000 and that appalling reality endures as Dayton's shameful cross to bear. While Ohio may have had more Klan members than any other state, Dayton was one of six cities nationally recognized as a "hooded capital." [43]

One of the other six "mecca" cities was, coincidently, Indianapolis.

At age 20, and still a motorcycle transient between employment in Indianapolis and his father's farm in Mooresville, Dillinger acquired a four-wheeled vehicle one night to impress a young lady. John Dillinger was traveling the path of crime. Stopped by police, they soon discovered that the acquisition was not quite legally transacted. He was arrested for auto theft. The fissure in the relationship he had with his old man was beyond mending short of dramatic action. Believing salvation might rest with the armed services, Dillinger was pushed to enlist in the U.S. Navy in 1923. Conforming to discipline and shoveling coal was not in his wheelhouse. Within five months he deserted. Dillinger was fortunate to be granted a dishonorable discharge and not sentenced to time in the brig.

The deserting sailor, F3c J. H. Dillinger

Beryl Hovious Dillinger

In 1924, John Dillinger moved into his father's house once again, Now approaching 21 years of age, he married 16-year-old Beryl Hovious. After a brief time together in Mooresville, they moved to her parents' home 20 miles further south.

This was a union that was destined to not last past the year in being physically together. The marriage was certainly strained after Dillinger committed a bungled grocery store heist in Mooresville, Indiana.

Late on a Saturday night in the first week of September, Dillinger, along with an older accomplice named Edgar Singleton, hid in the shadows of a church next to a small grocery store. The owner, Frank Morgan, had cash from his shop's returns when he was attacked from behind by Dillinger. Swinging a machine bolt wrapped in a rag, he twice struck Morgan in the head and then pulled a .32 caliber revolver. Stunned, the grocer still managed to fight back and grabbed at the gun which fired. At the sound of the loud blast, Dillinger ran to the awaiting getaway car operated by Singleton. He had stolen nothing.

Upon learning of the incident, the elder Dillinger convinced his son to turn himself in to police. He did so, confessed, and then snitched on his partner in crime. Following the advice of his father to do the right thing, he entered a guilty plea with hope for a light sentence.

Instead, he received 10 to 20 years of hard time and crossed from freedom into the state prison in Michigan City,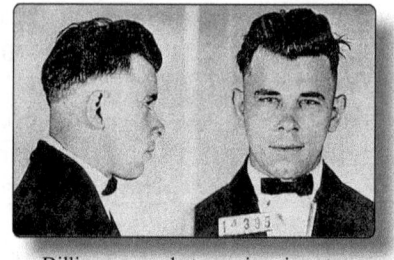

Dillinger mug shot - a prison inmate.

Indiana. Resentful, upon being booked into prison Dillinger reportedly swore: *"I will be the meanest bastard you ever saw when I get out of here."*

While the unknown Dillinger festered in confinement for the remainder of this decade into the next, Dayton's local killer, Al Fouts, alias W. E. Davis, did not find his change of surroundings on the West Coast rehabilitative. Years earlier, he had learned the fine skill of safecracking from his older brother, Pete Fouts. This, combined with his small size, gave Fouts all the talent needed to prowl, infiltrate, and commit sneak thievery.

And so, in 1922, Fouts committed a first-degree burglary in Los Angeles. He still had not learned how not to get caught.

Convicted and sentenced to one to 15 years, he began serving his hard time in upstate California on July 30, 1922. Unlike Dillinger, Fouts would be released from prison much earlier. He was paroled on September 15, 1925, and found this way back to Dayton by 1928. He would happen upon another criminal trade in the later 1920s – bootlegging. Fouts, who crisscrossed throughout the Midwest – Ohio, Kentucky, Indiana – drew

Fouts mug shot - a prison inmate.

a connection with the Chicago mob, and made the consequential acquaintance of one George 'Bugs' Moran.

Throughout the 1920s, Dayton's two police liquor squads successfully raided speakeasies, garages, homes, and other bootlegging havens in search for illegal stills and the product of those stills. At the same time, the greater Montgomery County was also beset by illegal liquor operations. Federal agents were aggressively pursuing violators inside and outside the incorporated boundaries of Dayton with the assistance of local lawmen.

Bootlegging operations were often so large that federal agents were inclined to declare their targets as the "king of Dayton bootleggers" when brought before federal grand jurors. Locally, there was a succession of "kings" after each conviction, such as Albert Robinson in 1923, followed by Steve Kender in 1924 – a legal "saloonist" before and after Prohibition – followed by John Friend.

But no one in Dayton was quite as renowned as the nation's "King of the Bootleggers," **George Remus**.

As a lawyer representing bootleggers in Cincinnati – the center of Midwest whiskey distilling – Remus saw that his clients were made wealthy by their acts. He decided to get his slice of the action. Purchasing distilleries to produce and sell bonded (legal) liquor for medicinal purposes, he had his employees hijack his own liquor to sell illegally throughout the Midwest, supplying Chicago mob boss Al Capone as well.

Dayton was in his distribution network which would lead to his local prosecution. In March 1924, Remus and his gang were sentenced to serve time in the Montgomery County jail as "guests of

George Remus, Rum King, Is In Jail Here

September 3, 1925
Dayton Daily New
"'bootleg king' now a prisoner in the Montgomery co. jail."

County Sheriff
Howard Webster

Sheriff Howard Webster for one-year."[44] A federal judge decided, instead, to first send Remus to serve time in Atlanta. Dayton, as well as the city of St. Louis, had to wait to impose its justice on the bootlegger.

After 21-months incarceration in the south, on September 3, 1925, the "bootleg king" was finally transferred to the Montgomery County jail to serve his overdue sentence. Remus' jail time was shorter than anticipated. The defense lawyer successfully argued that his Dayton sentence should run concurrent with his Atlanta sentence.

The infamous "Bootleg King" was released five days later.

The local bootleggers whose names most often surfaced in the press were **John** and **Mary Friend**. They were dubbed the "king and queen of Dayton bootleggers" and reigned from 1923 until 1931. The newspapers reported they made "thousands of dollars out of their alleged illegal transactions in liquor."[45]

On January 20, 1927, the couple was raided at their home in an exclusive Oakwood neighborhood after a secret federal indictment. Their indictment led to the arrests of "nearly 100 persons" including four township constables for taking protection payoffs.[46]

These were some of the same constables that had chased down the Friends' fleeing "booze car" on South Main Street several years earlier.

The "king and queen of Dayton bootleggers" were defended by Jack Egan, the attorney who a decade earlier represented Al Fouts.

Only the headlines of Charles Lindbergh's cross-Atlantic flight overshadowed the bold front-page caption of the May 20, 1927 trial.

Lindbergh Holds Furious Pace Near New Foundland Fog Bank

Woman Says Constable Told Her to Give Him $100 Sum [47]

Still, the testimony and courtroom drama was a full inside-page account. In the end, the couple was convicted and sentenced as were many other indicted co-conspirators.

John Friend served federal time in Atlanta's penitentiary as had George Remus. Upon release, he and his wife returned to the illegal local liquor trade. Their last prohibition-era police raid was in 1931 at their Xenia Pike home. The two were convicted for violating the National Prohibition Act and sentenced... a one-year prison term for Mary and a two-year, six-month term for John.

After again serving time, and with the collapse of Prohibition soon to follow, the "king and queen" continued in the legal liquor trade but added illegal gambling to their profit-making ventures. They remained troublesome tavern owners for state liquor authorities long after Prohibition ended.

On the outskirts of the city border, Deputy Sheriff Ford Long had served the residents of Montgomery County as its bootleg officer from 1923 to 1929 during local enforcement's most active years. He made his most accomplished raid on November 19, 1927. Deputy Long uncovered an illegal distillery operation in the north Salem Avenue area on Jefferson Road. [48]

November 1927: Deputy Ford Long (right), in the company of federal and state liquor agents, proudly displaying the County's largest bootleg liquor seizure.
William Preston Mayfield Collection at Dayton History

Deputy Long, in the company of two federal agents, three state officers, and three other deputies, conducted the "largest ever" seizure in the county's history to date. Two large 200-gallon-capacity stills, 400 gallons of liquor, 1,100 gallons of mash, and 500 fake bonding labels were confiscated in the raid. The estimated value of the liquor and equipment was $21,000 ($308,000 today).

A retired national-circuit race horse jockey by the name of Douglass Hoffman was arrested. The stills and whiskey were destroyed.

It was a good day for lawmen and a bad one for a bootlegger.

Two years beforehand, on June 18, 1925, Inspector Rudolph F. Wurstner was appointed Dayton's chief of police. The keynote speaker during the promotional ceremony was Chief Wurstner's close friend,

Inspector Thomas Grundish, who would often be called upon as his second-in-command for the next 10 years. The celebratory reception was adorned with 14 floral arrangements, the centerpiece gifted by the AAA Dayton Automobile Club.

June 1925: Chief Rudolph F. Wurstner poses alongside floral arrangements received on the day of his promotion to head the Dayton Police Department.

The perfect in-house selection, Chief Wurstner had the respect of his officers and was the one to bring unity to a police force that had experienced considerable discord over the previous two years. His first act was symbolic. His predecessor chose to never wear a uniform while in office and visually appeared detached from the police force, especially when conducting inspections. Chief Woodward's leadership found itself under the critical eye of his police officers.

Chief Wurstner, on the other hand, made it clear who he was. "I have worn a uniform for 23 years and I don't propose to discard it now." [49]

Chief Rudy Wurstner flanked by Ptl. Thomas Dunlavey *(right)* and Ptl. Henry Gray.

September 23, 1926 Dayton Police Inspection

Chief Wurstner, with his appointment, would embark on an incredible quarter century, bringing stability to area law enforcement previously soiled by repeated misconduct or incompetence at the top. He insisted on the professional integrity of his men and set the bar for his successors.

In uniform, he proudly held an impressive, panoramically photographed police inspection in September 1926. He was not one to sit in an office. It was no surprise to see him on the front lines with his troops. The Chief, though, was also an administrator and clearly a recognized leader.

Within two years of his ascendancy to the top, Chief Wurstner hosted a three-day conference in Dayton for what had been the "Ohio Police Association." It took place on June 28, 1927 and was a transitional convention; the following year, an official new organization was established as the "Ohio Association of Chiefs of Police" (OACP), which still exists today.

On the last day of the conference held at the downtown Gibbons Hotel – and as happened with Chief Allaback 15 years earlier – Chief Wurstner's dedicated troops surprised him by presenting the Chief a diamond-studded badge. He wore that badge for the next 22 years.

Conference Portrait

As one of the OACP founders, Chief Wurstner would later be named the association's president during one of the most noteworthy periods in Dayton police history – 1933 and 1934 – when a brazen Midwest bank robber was under the intense hunt of the nation's law enforcement.

One of the many topics discussed among the chiefs attending the 1927 convention was the surge in violence against police officers and the need for a better arsenal of weapons to better protect themselves.

The Dayton Police Department had seen the decade begin with **Detective Edward Poland** critically injured in a gun battle with two highwaymen. It was 1920 and on a street between the Fairgrounds and the "Edgewood dump" where Ptl. Thomas was killed.

Det. Edward Poland

The assailants were caught two days later in a manhunt, tried, convicted, and sentenced to prison. One bullet remained in Det. Poland's body but he recovered to return to duty.

In 1922, Miamisburg Ptl. Frank Weidner was fatally stabbed, the only police officer murdered in Montgomery County outside the city of Dayton during this first half century. In 1923, Dayton Ptl. George Clark was shot and killed during the daytime while questioning a man about a burglary. The police were on edge and reacting to dangers, both real and perceived. The killings of Patrolmen Weidner and Clark were emblematic of the experiences and violence in store for patrolmen in Dayton, as well as nationwide, throughout Prohibition and the impetuous Roaring '20s.

Ptl. George Clark

Continuing... on the afternoon of December 16, 1925, six months after Chief Wurstner was promoted, Ptl. Perry Heywood was shot and critically wounded in a gun battle at 324 Bruen near Ludlow Street.

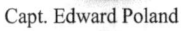

Chief Wurstner was one of the first, if not the first, to arrive on the scene moments after the shooting. He and **Captain Edward Poland** arrested the armed suspect, Pearl Shortill, who had also shot a second officer, Ptl. Todd Sloan, and killed another man at that scene.

Capt. Edward Poland

In 1926, Sgt. Lucius Rice attempted to arrest an assailant when a shootout ensued. Although seriously injured by a gunshot wound, Sgt. Rice was able to kill his attacker. These wounded officers were as fortunate as Capt. Poland had been six years earlier. They all survived to return to duty. But Dayton police officers would be far less fortunate from September 1927 to February 1928.

Local law enforcement was at a crossroad in its history. Still conducting day-to-day foot patrol with wooden nightsticks and hard-to-pull pistols concealed beneath uniform coats worn both winter and summer, new measures were needed to show that the police were capable of engaging in its battles against criminals and the onslaught of police attacks.

Two months after the topic was raised at the OACP Conference, the Dayton Police Chief and the Montgomery County Sheriff authorized the combined purchase of four Colt Thompson submachine guns.

The shipment was received in September 1927, a tragically fateful month. The police force also received a shipment of eight rifles, eight shotguns and two short-hand shotguns in slings for motorcycle officers, gas bombs, steel vests and more.

Inspector Thomas Grundish and Capt. John C. Post

The arsenal in full, and exhibited in action, was depicted in the Dayton newspapers. On September 14, **Captain John C. Post** and Inspector Thomas Grundish demonstrated the Tommy guns. They were sending a message to criminals.

The message was not received.

Police tragedies as never before began the following day with the shooting death of a Dayton railroad detective, Alfred Knight. In checking box cars at the rail yard north of town, he was shot by a drifter.

This was followed by the killing of Dayton Ptl. William Horn three days later on September 18 by a man with a concealed handgun stopped at the crossroads of Warren and Hollencamp Streets. And then...

Ptl. William Horn

THE ROARING '20s: LOCAL LAWMEN KILLED IN THE LINE OF DUTY.

1927
B&O Railroad
Det. Alfred Knight

1928
Dayton Police
Ptl. 'Tom' Wilson

1922
Miamisburg Police
Ptl. Frank Weidner

1927
Dayton Police
Ptl. Walter Rauch

... a third slaying with the wounding of Captain John C. Post and Patrolmen Edward Frick and Vernon Kuntz in a September 24 gun battle with a barricaded shooting suspect. Captain Post died the next morning, and only 11 days after his machine gun exhibition for the press.

While Daytonians mourned in disbelief the killings of three lawmen in a single month, they were shocked on Christmas day.

In the early holiday morning hours, Ptl. Walter Rauch was ambushed by robbers, shot and killed. Left lying on the cold sidewalk, he was discovered by a churchgoer walking home from Midnight Mass at St. Joseph Catholic Church

Two months later, Ptl. William 'Tom' Wilson, the decorated WWI combat veteran of the "Battle of the Argonne Forest," was shot by an intruder ambush. He died two days later, becoming the first black Dayton officer killed in the line of duty.

When these five Dayton lawmen were killed by gunfire in five separate incidents in little more than five months, it marked *the bloodiest period in Dayton police history.*

Sidebar: A Sergeant's Ill Omen and a Captain's Legacy in Death

Sergeant Lucius J. Rice: In **1926**, the 17-year veteran detective was conducting an investigation on Dunbar Avenue when he happened upon a man stabbing another man to death. In attempting to arrest the assailant, a gun battle ensued. Seriously injured from a gunshot wound to the abdomen, as he fell to the ground Sgt. Rice was able to shoot and kill his attacker. Rushed to the hospital by a responding black policeman, Sgt. Rice's wound was described as potentially "fatal." Yet, he survived to return to duty.

Then, in the summer of **1927**, Sgt. Rice was teamed with **Det. George Wheeler**. Traveling in a Dayton police touring auto, another car forced them into the path of an approaching street car on West Fifth Street. The force of the head-on collision fractured their skulls, broke bones, and caused internal injuries. Both men were listed in "critical" condition but survived to return to duty. They would be together again at the scene of a critical incident in **1939** that would prove fatal.

Captain John C. Post: The only killing in city history of a Dayton police commander was the mortal wounding of Captain John C. Post in **1927**. In search of a shooting suspect, he led two other officers in ascending the stairs of a boarding house on Franklin Street, a few doors west of Emmanuel Catholic Church. Suddenly, the suspect emerged from hiding and opened fire, wounding all three officers. Despite being injured, the officers returned fire and shot the suspect. All were removed to Miami Valley Hospital.

While this police shooting was taking place on September 24, **Chief Rudolph Wurstner** was attending the "Police & Fireman Field Day" sports competition at the Montgomery County Fairgrounds with his wife, Carrie, and Mrs. John Post, also named Carrie. An officer arrived and advised the Chief of the shooting. Chief Wurstner later said that the most difficult experience in his long career was telling his good friend's wife that her husband was in a gun battle and gravely wounded in a nearby hospital.

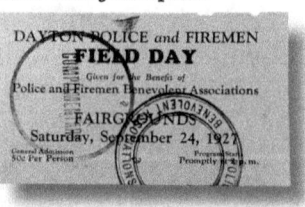

Carrie Post's Field Day ticket.

Two of the three officers recovered from their wounds. Capt. Post died the next day. His death was devastating to the community and, in particular, to his brother officers. In tribute to him, less than 11 years later on March 4, **1938**, the members of the newly chartered **Dayton Fraternal Order of Police** named its lodge after Capt. John C. Post. It is the 111th F.O.P. lodge in the nation to be chartered. Thousands of lodges have formed since.

PRINCIPALS AND SHOOTING SCENE

FARMER IS HELD
AS WITNESS IN
DEATH MYSTERY

Dayton
Police
Captain
John C. Post

CONSTITUTION
and BY-LAWS
John C. Post Lodge No. 44
Dayton, Ohio
FRATERNAL ORDER of POLICE
STATE OF OHIO

Organized at Dayton, Ohio,
Chartered by Fraternal Order of Police
of Ohio
March 4, 1938

Police-Fireman Field Day Ticket *(left page)*
and Captain Post in touring auto *(above)*
*Collection at Dayton History courtesy
of Marilou Routsong, grandniece*

1938 Dayton FOP Lodge
Constitution booklet.

The year 1927 was a mid-point in the long career of Chief Rudy Wurstner. It may have been the most eventful and tragic of all years for him. On either side of the OACP Conference, internationally renowned aviator Charles Lindbergh visited Dayton, specifically to meet Orville Wright. This was another time when the career road of Chief Wurstner crossed with a Wright brother. This crossing of paths would reoccur over time including long after both had died.

A few months before the September 1927 heartbreak of local police killings, Charles Lindbergh made international aviation history. He flew 33½ hours in a single-engine airplane, the 'Spirit of St. Louis,' the first solo, non-stop flight between the U.S. and Europe. Departing from New York, he landed in France on

1927: Orville Wright and Charles Lindbergh in Dayton.

May 21, 1927. A month later, on June 22, the celebrated worldwide hero, Lindbergh, came to Dayton as a guest of the first man to fly an airplane back in 1903.

Local political officials planned a procession through downtown Dayton but upon arrival, the aviator expressed no interest in participating in any fanfare. His motorcade bypassed the parade route to go directly to Orville Wright's Hawthorn Hill home.

The Lindbergh crowd, which waited hours, was disappointed but many assembled outside the Wright's house to see their hero. Chief Wurstner, who oversaw the security for the motor escort, was none too happy about the abandoned parade.

He sharply remarked to the press, "It was a contemptible trick ... a 'back alley' trick.... My heart goes out ... especially [to] the children and aged women, who stood on the streets for four or five hours ... only to be fooled...." [50] Chief Wurstner was invited by Orville Wright to stay at Hawthorn Hill and the Dayton Police Department was charged with Lindbergh's security while there. Less than two months later on August 5, 1927, Lindbergh returned to Dayton to be honored by a public deprived of a parade appearance in June.

Throughout the remainder of the decade, Dayton police had an annual average of 1,170 liquor arrests. Its effect could be measured in the number of alcohol stills bashed or confiscated. When the liquor squad began its campaign in 1922, 192 bootleg and home-brew stills were seized. In 1923, another 120 stills were seized. But with each passing year, the number of stills confiscated diminished in number: 37, 15, 7, to zero. Yet, the campaign moved forward with government reports of statistical triumphs.

The true measurement of success or failure was best gauged by public sentiment and backing. The unpopularity of Prohibition among the citizenry was reflected by the fading will of politicians to support the means necessary to enforce the laws. Funding was cut. At the close of 1927, the Dayton police liquor squad was reduced in size and then merged with the vice squad. These police units were pressed to take legal action despite the publicly unpopular social and political agendas of the day.

By 1928, Prohibition enforcement was no longer a subject of detailed police record keeping or receiving the kind of local press that it had the previous seven years. In fact, the number of newspaper articles written about the activities of the Dayton liquor squad in the last five years of Prohibition, 1929 through 1933, were a quarter the number than written the first five years of enforcement, 1922 through 1926.

Still, police were threatened by ever-present dangers from gangs, many protecting lucrative bootlegging and gambling operations. Gang violence was on the rise in the U.S. and the public was enthralled with press reports and movie reels recounting battles over bootlegging territory in the Windy City between the likes of Al Capone and George 'Bugs' Moran. At the same time, citizens were deeply fearful that underworld gun battles jeopardized their own safety. Prohibition was seen as the root of the problem.

The horrific massacre of seven men in Chicago on St. Valentine's Day in 1929 intensified the sentiment. Capone, the leader of the South Side gang, reputedly authorized a mob hit on his North Side rival, Bugs Moran, and others in his gang. The mobster escaped

his own gangland execution because he was late for the meeting at the garage that held his bootlegging trucks. But with a core seven of his gang brutally gunned down, Bugs Moran took to a lower public profile and gradually drifted from the Chicago scene only to later find himself in Dayton.

The year 1929 was crimson. The second month, saturated blood red in a bootlegging mob garage, had given the nation its starkest image of a decade of Prohibition; and, two months before the year closed out, the U.S. economy frighteningly dripped red ink.

1929: Al Capone's soup line for unemployed workers.

When 16 million shares traded on the New York Stock Exchange, Wall Street was aghast as billions in collective savings vanished in one session.

On October 29, 1929, unexpected and exactly 10 years and one day since the passing of the National Prohibition Act, the harshest financial free fall happened.

THE GREAT DEPRESSION ... The deepest and lengthiest economic ruin in U.S. history!

Nationwide, the rising crime rate brought on by Prohibition accelerated after the stock market collapsed on "Black Tuesday" in 1929.

CHAPTER 5

PROHIBITION SEGUES TO THE GREAT DEPRESSION

May 4, 1930: *The Dayton Herald* newspaper story on the Xenia Avenue Trust bank robbery and running gun battle. One of many articles with pictures.

North Main Street in Downtown Dayton at the close of the Roaring '20s.
This view is looking north from Second Street to the Great Miami River.

Typical of a press release image created by the Dayton Police Bureau of Identification
toutng the investigative expertise of the Dayton Detective Bureau. In this case, the
Wesley brothers had held up the Fifth Street branch of the City Trust & Savings Bank
but were tracked to Chicago by Inspector Seymour Yendes and Sgt. Oscar Kincaid.
The robbers were arrested by the two detectives and returned to stand trial in 1929.

REVENUE – The unabated killings over bootlegging territory in major cities factored into a general attitude among America's citizenry for a repeal of national, state, and local prohibition laws. The web of underworld connections, spun throughout the full 14 years of Prohibition, was manifested by a local crime described beneath *The Dayton Herald* newspaper headline:

Second Racketeer Dies – Officials believe battle climax to local liquor war

This was as much about emerging local gang warfare over rival revenue interests as it was about booze. In this case, gambling and racketeering shakedowns were in the mix.

This war may have begun when two henchmen for local gangster and major 35-race-horse "books" operator, **Floyd Shawhan**, bludgeoned a rival nearly to death. It ended the following year when one of

Local Gangster
Floyd Shawhan

Shawhan's local henchman, Glen 'Fat' McCrosson, and another gangster, Lonnie Carmer, were killed by Meyer Ostrov, described by police as a "'big shot' in the liquor racket." [51]

Protecting criminal interests was brutal and often fatal business, locally as well as nationwide.

Gang ruthlessness rooted in illegal alcohol, along with the despair brought on by the Great Depression, changed the public's principal and principled focus. Its interest in the notion of imposed temperance had hurriedly faded.

In 1930, the keeping of prohibition-related statistics by the Dayton Police Department officially ended, three years before the coming repeal of the amendment. Although there were clearly different and newer priorities, police department and city officials still assured the community there would be no relaxation in the enforcement of prohibition laws. The downsizing and renaming of the liquor squad, they said, was merely a customary "shifting of men."

In fact, revenue was at the heart of a surging crime wave, armed robbery, particularly holdups of financial institutions. Free-wheeling gangsters, coveting other sources of dough, found armed bank robbery profitable.

"Banks had been robbed before but not to this level.... It was the perfect storm of several circumstances." [52]

1921 Colt Tommy gun
Montgomery County
Sheriff's arsenal

A combat product of the Great War, the Colt Thompson submachine gun, affixed with drum magazines capable of discharging 50 to 100 rounds of .45 caliber ammunition with a single trigger pull, were sought by gangsters with murderous intent.

This gave them the upper hand over law enforcement officers, most carrying .38 caliber six-shot revolvers.

Chief Wurstner's 1920 Colt Police Positive Special revolver

Those lawmen in the Gem City mainly walked police beats covering two to four miles as had been done by downtown watchmen going back nearly 100 years.

Dayton Police "Emergency Car" leaving the Ford Street Station, with four officers inside, armed with shotguns, responding to a crime in progress.

Dayton's few "emergency cars" were brought out of the police building bay only after crimes occurred. Bandits with the incentive to flee crime scenes were also attracted to cutting-edge automobiles with large engines capable of traveling at remarkably high speeds.

"Bank robbery was a state crime and [bandits] could easily jump from one border to the other and it was very easy to escape justice." [53]

Even though there was a national Bureau of Investigation (BOI), it had little authority and its agents had no power to arrest unless deputized by the local police. Its director, J. Edgar Hoover, had been placed in charge of the BOI in 1924, but his agents were unarmed until 1934.

Crime fighting was a local police challenge which had little clout beyond its own jurisdictional boundaries, in and out of which gangsters traveled.

The fast pace of the Roaring '20s triggered two decades of unprecedented bootlegging, underworld crime, break-ins, highway robberies, and bank holdups.

Roaming gangsters assailed the Midwest and Dayton was not untouched. Greater Dayton financial institutions were thrashed and emptied by armed robbers: the East Fifth Street City National Bank, the South Park Savings, the East Fifth Street Union Trust Company, to name a few.

Inspector Seymour Yendes and his detective squad were called to investigate holdups in smaller towns as well. One such holdup attempt was by the notorious **Bob Zwick** gang at the Phillipsburg State Bank in a community 15 miles northwest of Dayton. A bank cashier was abducted before opening hours, a disturbing development. This was in January 1930, followed soon that year by a succession of other unrelated Dayton and regional bank holdups.

Three members of the notorious Bob Zwick Gang: Allen Sherrer, Oscar Wehner & Raymond Lee

"Activities of bank bandits ... aroused Dayton bankers" so they held a local April 15, 1930 conference to discuss the "frustration of future robberies...." [54]

Chief Rudy Wurstner and his chief of detectives, Inspector 'Cy' Yendes, recommended placing bullet-proof glass around cashier cages and installing silent alarm systems inside the bank facilities that would be directly linked to Dayton police headquarters.

Faster, modern automobiles for police use was also a topic of discussion. Some of these safeguards were instituted, but more were needed, and more would come.

In order to meet the challenges posed, Chief Wurstner undertook additional measures to enhance his department's equipment.

In January 1930, the police force purchased another Tommy gun for its arsenal which was stockpiled inside the Ford Street Station House. The Chief later displayed it to press photographers as a firm warning to outlaws.

Although not necessarily readily available, the weapons could be signed out by officers for stakeouts. One such occasion came just one month after the bankers conference.

1930: Chief Wurstner shows off a new police Tommy gun to a Boy Scouts troop and newspaper reporters.

The Union Trust Company on Xenia Avenue was targeted by outlaws repeatedly. The bank had been held up three times, the last time on April 4 by gangsters with ties to Al Capone traveling north from Hamilton, Ohio. But on the morning of May 6, 1930, Dayton police ensured there was not a fourth robbery at this bank.

Based on a "tip-off," Chief Rudy Wurstner authorized **Ptl. Walter Dempsey** and his less-experienced partner, Ptl. Bryan Hock, to stakeout the bank armed with a Colt Thompson submachine gun and shotgun from the police stations stocked arsenal.

As the two officers "stationed" outside the back of the building, entering the front were two heavily armed bandits, Indiana Reformatory parolees from Chicago. The robbers were spotted. As one attempted to strike the bank manager Phillip Kloos [55] with the rifle barrel, police gunfire blasted into the rear of the bank.

Ptl. Walter Dempsey

The four bank employees and a customer dropped to the wood floor. Ptl. Dempsey then ran with his Tommy gun to the front of the bank while Ptl. Hock remained on watch at the rear door to protect from being ambushed. Ptl. Dempsey later described to the press what next happened:

> "Before I could bring my machine gun into action, the bandit nearest me fired at me with a pistol. I started firing immediately through two windows that were between the robbers and myself. I must have fired 20 shots. I saw both of the raiders fall to the ground. One was bleeding about the face. Hock and I ran to the door, saw the ... two bandits...."

It looked like a fresh Chicago crime scene with the smolder of gunfire and machine gun-riddled building windows. Both hold-up men had been wounded by Ptl. Dempsey but through the haze the outlaws still managed to escape the building, running east on Xenia Avenue. The officers gave chase and a gun fight erupted at Dover Street. "Both of these men staggered from the effect of our gunfire," Dempsey later said. [56]

The "running gun battle" quieted with capture and soon the street was filled with gawking citizens. The press anxiously took photographs of the excited throng around the bank building and the gathering of bystanders, including awestruck kids, huddled around the get-away car. Again, it was like a crowd scene out of Chicago; ideal pictures for local front-page newspapers with bold headlines.

Dayton Policeman Kills Bank Bandit, Wounds Another in Running Gun Fight

May 6, 1930

In the end, one robber, Orral Farley, was killed. The other, James Brink, with a head wound, was c a p t u r e d, tried, and later sentenced to prison. The two fearless officers made names for themselves that would last throughout their long and outstanding police careers.

A visual of this nature further inspired bankers to support the police cause.

In August 1930, Greater Dayton financial institutions presented an automobile to Chief Wurstner specifically designed to deter bank robberies. It was maintained in the Police Headquarters' north-side garage bay at South Main and Market Streets.

Description found at the bottom of Page 119.

The Dayton Police "Bank Flyer" was an eight-cylinder Cadillac V-8 "refitted" by a company in Cincinnati with special racks built inside the vehicle to hold "an assortment of machine guns, rifles, shotguns, tear gas bombs, hand grenades, gas masks and bullet-proof vests." [57]

The car had a heavy steel bumper making it "possible ... to go through a brick wall." [57] It had a special three-quarter inch steel shield to protect the radiator, impenetrable tires and bullet-proof windshield. The Cincinnati company, oddly enough, was the one that similarly customized in bullet-proof fashion two of Chicago mobster Al Capone's Cadillacs.

The Dayton police weapons arsenal was now fully mobile. In the event of an armed robbery, a bank official could activate – "by hand, foot, elbow, or knee" – a silent hold-up alarm. It would sound in both the garage and upstairs at police headquarters.

The motorman in the bay, Ptl. Frank Johnson, would have the Bank Flyer engine running by the time the three-man "Flying Squadron" scrambled down the stairs from the offices of the Bureau of Identification (B of I). The squadron, with this customized, heavily armed special-purpose vehicle, would hasten to the crime scene. The armored Cadillac was often promoted by Chief Wurstner and the police department through local newspaper stories. It was a "land battleship."

Ptl. Frank Johnson,

The Bank Flyer made for good press and reassured a frightened public.

August 1930: Chief Wurstner, the Bank Flyer and the Flying Squadron *(left page)*. Captain Harvey Siferd, Detective John Blake, Detective Howard Reed, Patrolman Brenton Collins, and Detective Walter Geisler.

Dayton was not lacking local bootleggers, bandits, racketeers, and gangsters during the 1920s and '30s, some with ties to larger-than-life crime figures in Southwest Ohio such as George Remus. One of the era's most vicious gangsters, Bob Zwick – a Remus accomplice – had his local ring using the Gem City as its base of operation in 1929 and 1930. But Dayton was more a convenient big city stop-in and pass-through for gangsters crisscrossing the region.   Between Cincinnati and Toledo, **Hamilton** (population 52,000) and **Lima** (population 42,000) were the next largest cities. They were a quarter the size of Dayton but often frequented by gangsters as well.

When the Xenia Avenue Union Trust Company was robbed by five bandits in April 1930, local police authorities long believed two of the culprits to be Fred 'Killer' Burke and Ray 'Crane Neck' Nugent, two of the gunmen that Chicago police suspected of committing the St. Valentine's Day Massacre.

Dayton criminal defense attorney Jack Egan was also a common thread tied to underworld characters. He had a practice both in Dayton and Chicago. He had built an attention-grabbing client list and it was not uncommon as well for him to represent associates or gang rivals of the likes of George Remus, Bob Zwick, and Ray 'Crane Neck' Nugent.

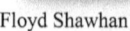

Surprisingly, Egan did not represent one particular city of Dayton "racketeer" and club owner who lived in the fast lane and had been on the scene since 1921.

Floyd Shawhan got his start as a 1920s' bootlegger, but expanded his domain over time with gambling interests. In 1930, he found himself dangerously

Floyd Shawhan

at odds over racketeering profits with Bob Zwick (an underworld rival of 'Crane Neck' Nugent who once tried to kill Zwick over a gang dispute in Hamilton).

Zwick decided to take retribution against Floyd Shawhan for not yielding the extortion payoffs Zwick expected to receive. He robbed a Shawhan gambling club.

ROBBERY IN DAYTON SAID TO BE WORK OF NOTORIOUS GANGSTER

PROPRIETOR MAKES IDENTIFICATION OF WIDELY-SOUGHT MAN

Alleged Murderer Made Threats Against Floyd Shawhan, It Is Reported.

STORY OF HOLDUP IS TOLD BY WITNESSES

Dayton Robbery Believed to Be Act of Reprisal Against Victims.

ROBERT ZWICK

The notorious gangster, Bob Zwick.
February 1, 1930: *The Dayton Herald*

Just as willing to engage in hard-nosed clashes when necessary, in an unrelated incident in 1931, Shawhan had a "pistol duel" at his Crystal Gardens night club on Brandt Pike. Using two automatics, he shot local racketeer 'Alex the Greek' Pitakos, killing the man with 10 bullet holes, but was himself badly wounded.

The court ruled Shawhan's actions were in "self-defense." His wound was serious, later resulting in his leg being amputated, and ultimately his death.

Identified in the local press as "Dayton No. 1 public enemy," Floyd Shawhan was a hoodlum who often made news with his shady persona. Although dangerous, he was not a local mob boss.

Leon Gleckman

There was no one of "mob boss" stature in Dayton. However, former Dayton Detective James Crumley was an employed lawman at a place that did have one. His adopted city's "bootlegging boss," Leon Gleckman, was also known as the "Al Capone of St. Paul."

What Dayton – a city of 200,000 and the nation's 41st largest – had instead was a police chief in Rudy Wurstner who was "often quoted as invoking the *Golden Rule*." On the other hand, St. Paul – a city of 270,000 and the nation's 31st largest – did not have a top commander sharing that philosophy. Its chief's prism view was shady.

Dayton Chief Wurstner
Dayton Daily News
illustration *(undated)*

Appointed to take charge of this Twin City police force on June 4, 1930, **Thomas 'Big Tom' Brown** was committed to preserving an *olden rule* – the "layover agreement" initiated by Chief John O'Connor in 1900. It worked for 30 years to keep the crime rate in St. Paul considerably lower than its "twin," Minneapolis. But it had corruptly mutated into a city-sanctioned criminal protection scheme.

Mobsters and gangsters were sheltered from local arrests and extraditions for crimes committed elsewhere. Consequently, Bugs Moran's hometown was a safe haven for its infamous visitors: Ma, Fred and 'Doc' Barker, Al Karpis, Al Capone, 'Baby Face' Nelson, 'Machine Gun' Kelly, and later, in 1934, John Dillinger and his gang of Harry Pierpont, Charles Makley, Russell Clark, John Hamilton, Homer Van Meter, and others.

It was in this environment in January 1931 that Chief Brown promoted his old gumshoe partner, James Crumley, to be his chief of detectives in command of all St. Paul criminal investigators.

In his later years, Inspector Crumley took pride and credit for solving, in 1931 alone, the   First State Bank robbery, two high profile murders, and a major kidnapping.

St. Paul Police
Chief Tom Brown

Inspector Crumley laid claim to directing the investigation that led to the capture of suspects in the Chicago kidnapping for ransom of St. Paul mob boss, Leon Gleckman. Gang associates had paid a portion of the $200,000 ransom to gain the mobster's release; however, within two days, Crumley's detectives apprehended five of Gleckman's six abductors... but the lifeless body of the leader of the kidnapping gang was found on a lake shore.

St. Paul Police Inspector Crumley

St. Paul and Dayton had more differences than the similarities it had in James Crumley, Bugs Moran, and John Dillinger.

Al Fouts, having been freed from a California prison for a number of years, returned to Dayton. He lived for awhile in a boarding house with five tenants owned by his brother, Pete. Having a base did not keep Al from roaming with criminal intent. Between 1931 and 1933, he was involved in a number of burglaries, safecrackings and other such acts.

Records are sketchy but some of his movements are known. In July 1931, using the alias George Lawson, Fouts was arrested in Richmond, Indiana for being in possession of burglar tools and two revolvers. He was charged for carrying a concealed weapon.

Convicted, Fouts was given a sentence of "one year on the state farm." [58] Then on February 14, 1933, he was arrested by Dayton police as a fugitive from Wapakoneta, Ohio and returned. The crime was burglary.

In June 1933, Fouts with two accomplices held up two Dayton stores. He was indicted for the crimes six months later after an investigation. In August 1933, still using the alias of George Lawson, Fouts was arrested by Dayton police detectives on an active federal warrant.

Circa 1930: Al Fouts; Dayton Police mug shot.
WSU Special Collections and Archives

A month earlier, he and his brother Pete had burglarized two Kentucky post offices, one in Johnson Junction and the other in Mayslick. Stolen was cash and stamps valued at $490 ($9,800 today). He was turned over by Dayton police to federal custody but later freed on bond.

Al Fouts was 43 years old in 1933. After the Kentucky escapade, he kept on lawbreaking at a distance from Greater Dayton. He largely evaporated from the local stage, although he continued to peddle tax-free bootleg whiskey to blue-collar saloons and for labor union hall events in Dayton. There is reason to believe that he turned to swindling as a shrewder way to profit from wrongdoing. But he would resurface locally in the next decade, and when he did, he returned to his tried and true methods of old. And the methods were typical of a series of crimes committed by Fouts at the start of this decade

———————————

Federal, state, and county investigators had discovered a "gigantic" illegal distillery in an old factory with "countless" underground tunnels in the city of Hamilton. The entire bootlegging operation was valued at $50,000 ($777,000 today). Several arrests were made.

Two months later, in February 1931, the state "dry officer" investigating this case drew a connection between Al Fouts and the bootlegging operation. The link was found inside a car parked nearby the distillery – explosives and burglary tools, "the most complete [set] ever discovered in Butler County." [59] Fouts was known to authorities as a member of a safecracking ring which operated throughout Butler and Hamilton Counties. In addition, he was observed during another liquor raid conducted in the area, implicating him with authorities. He was in circulation.

In the meantime, three auto businesses up north in Lima had been burglarized and their cannonball safes looted. Regional police knew Fouts' M.O. as an active "yegg" ... he had a reputation as a skilled safecracker. He was around Lima, too.

Lawmen working for the cities of Hamilton, Lima, and Dayton were able to connect the crimes to the local suspect by the distinctive burglary instruments. Four Dayton detectives arrested Al Fouts at 336 Xenia Avenue. Auto tires and tools were recovered along with two revolvers. Fouts was held for Lima authorities in the Dayton City Jail until taken into custody by the Allen County Sheriff.

This was not the last time that **Sheriff Jess Sarber** would travel from Lima to take into police custody a gangster arrested in Dayton...

JESS L. SARBER
Democratic Candidate for
SHERIFF
ALLEN COUNTY
Election, Tuesday, November 4, 1930

Allen County Museum and Historical Society

... but the next time would be his last.

The Great Depression strained the resources of the City of Dayton. This was exacerbated by a decision made by the city commission to annex seven square miles where the residing 36,000 new citizens could not afford to pay taxes. The annexation added to city operating expenses. And yet, there was a curious juxtaposition between two decades.

Funding had been withdrawn from the police efforts to enforce prohibition laws during the prosperous Roaring '20s. Conversely, financial resources were allocated as never before to law enforcement during the Great Depression era.

The Dayton Public Safety Department (police and fire) was able to invest in automobiles, communication and forensic technology, weaponry, uniforms, and police equipment as well as street engineering and electronic innovations. By 1931, 46 traffic lights were added to the signal system bringing the total number to 100 citywide.

On September 9, 1931, a conspicuous major patrol transformation occurred, as one local newspaper noted, for the "modern Dayton officer [because now] a Sam Browne belt supports a revolver on his hip, in plain view and readily accessible, [while] a black jack rests in his hip pocket." [60]

Chief Wurstner had authorized a complete change in the appearance of Dayton officers. Winter coats no longer extended full length; they dressed with shorter wool coats called "reefers." Patrolmen wore long-sleeve worsted shirts with neckties in the summer. Although they caused skin irritation on hot, humid days, they were more liberating than the practice of wearing military-style coats year-round.

Unidentified
Dayton
Police
Patrolman

Leather puttees covered calves while leather gear wrapped around the waist, and a lanyard extended over the shoulder to support an exposed cross-draw holster with flap. No longer did officers carry 'pocket pistols' and have to struggle beneath their coats to pull them out.

Chief Wurstner was preparing his officers for battles but there was more coming.

As personal police equipment improved in an effort to offset growing dangers posed by heavily armed gangsters and roaming bandits, police technology improved dramatically just as well.

In October 1931, the Chief and Inspector Seymour Yendes attended the International Police Chiefs Conference in Paris, and also traveled to seven other European countries. Upon his return, the Chief told the press that "throughout the world, law enforcing bodies are adopting radio… systems in their fight against the steady rise in crime." [61]

Three years earlier, in 1928, the City of Dayton had opened its new police and fire "Signal Building." The timing for this shared public safety communications center could not have been better. In 1928, Detroit was the first city in the nation to equip its fleet of police cars with radio-receiving sets. This huge advance in police technology came to Dayton on September 24, 1932.

Dayton installed radio receivers in its limited marked cars. One-way broadcasting to police "radio cars" allowed for immediate police responses to calls for service, especially crimes in progress, and for receiving "all-points bulletins" on wanted suspects.

On the first day, Chief Rudy Wurstner sat at the first modern Dayton police dispatch desk to demonstrate police radio broadcasting for press reporters.

No longer would officers assigned to its handful of marked cars have to go to call boxes to receive instructions from the police central exchange (although patrolmen still had to go to a call box or telephone to speak to a dispatcher).

Dayton's Signal Building

In 1932, the number of patrol cars were few. One-way radios forever changed the approach to police patrol and responses to crimes in progress. As time passed this decade, the number of police motorcycles was reduced because the success of "radio cars" hastened the expansion of the Dayton patrol car fleet.

One success would come almost exactly a year later. It was as if this technological innovation set the stage for September 22, 1933.

Sidebar: *The Dayton Signal Building and One-way Radios*

Signal Building: In **1932**, the Dayton Public Safety Department moved into a new direction from changes initiated four years earlier in Dayton and Detroit. In Dayton, the "Fire Alarm Telegraph and Police Signal System Building" at 15 E. Monument Avenue, more familiarly known as the "Signal Building," was dedicated in **1928**.

The Signal Building, located atop the river levee alongside Fire Station No. 4 (the Fire Headquarters) and across from Steele High School, was the new "central exchange" for both the police and fire departments. Initially, the building centralized telegraph signals that came from police call boxes, and fire alarm boxes, into its many tickertape machines. It was also the central site for all electrical components regulating the ever-expanding city traffic signal devices.

Circa 1932

Signal Building *(white)* dwarfed by the school's tower.
WSU Special Collections and Archives

WPDM: The first radio receivers were installed in Detroit in **1928**. They were installed in Dayton patrol cars and officially used on **September 24, 1932**. The press noted that, suddenly, Dayton police "advanced in quality and speed." The Dayton police call letters were WPDM for the one-way radio communication from dispatcher to patrolmen. A single dispatch desk with a radio signal transmitter and microphone was set up. Dispatching would greatly expand with time. The few police cars were termed "radio cars."

One-way radio broadcasts were broken into three (3) classes:

"**Runs**" - Dispatches to a police squad to proceed to a call location;

"**Station Calls**" - Orders to return to the police station house, or to call the dispatcher;

"**Teletypes**" - Broadcasts of holdups and "BOLO's" ("be on the lookout" for ...), et al.

When the **1932** radio system was first established, it was proudly demonstrated to the press by **Chief Rudy Wurstner** who spoke into this Western Electric microphone to a Dayton Police "radio car".

The "farmer": His forthcoming view of incarceration since his parole from the Indiana State Prison. The entranceway to the welcoming cell blocks of the Dayton City Jail.
John Dillinger (inset): *Wright State University Special Collections and Archives*

PART THREE

THE FARMER 1933

1927-1949 - Chief Rudolph F. 'Rudy' Wurstner's Replicated Badge *(above).*
Presented by his troops during the Ohio Police Chiefs Conference in 1927.
Courtesy of retired Dayton Detective John Ness (donated to DPHF)

CHAPTER 6

1933 and an Imminent Tie to Crime

July 21, 1933: The fugitive **John Dillinger** pictured with his girlfriend, **Mary Jenkins Longnaker**. He was accompanied by Mary (pictured) to the World's Fair along with her friend, Mary Ann Buchholz.

The new method of police patrol.

1933 Dayton Police marked "Radio Car," a Chevrolet Master. *(above)*

1932 Dispatch Center in the Dayton Signal Building. *(left)*

Motor and Walking Dayton patrolmen unidentified.

Circa 1930: Downtown Dayton. **Old-school patrol practice.** Officers on Walking Beats.

PRIORITY SHIFT – In September 1932, the Dayton Police Department installed "Sparton short-wave length radio receivers" in a fleet of 20 motorcycles and 11 newly marked police cars, now called "radio cars," at a cost of $11,000 ($217,000 today). The Bank Flyer was equipped as well and in its second year of service. It was always on call with weapons and all "means conducive to the restoration of order" [62] as were the men of the police force, outfitted in modern, action-ready uniforms.

In September 1932, John Dillinger had served eight years in prison, missing most of  the prosperity of the Roaring '20s. He also missed out on married life; Beryl Hovious was now his former wife having divorced him while he was in prison. She tied the knot with a new man in 1932, turning the page to a new chapter in her life.

John Dillinger

Dillinger was an ex-husband, freed from the bond of marriage. In the not-too-distant future, he would be an ex-con, freed from the confines of the Indiana State Prison. He would enter an economically depressed America. But, it was a nation that was shedding the restrictions of Prohibition in the not-too-distant future.

The seemingly endless killings over bootlegged liquor factored into greater public insistence for the repeal of Prohibition. It was a campaign issue for Franklin D. Roosevelt, the man who had been the unsuccessful vice-presidential running mate with Dayton native and Ohio Governor James Cox in 1920.

In late 1932, Roosevelt won the presidency himself and would take office the following March. By April, Congress amended the Volstead Act in an early first step. Beer, with a volume of no more than 3.2 percent alcohol, could be sold and served.

Full repeal of Prohibition would happen at the end of 1933.

LAUREL and HARDY at the Loew's Theater in "The Devil's Brother"—Say: "*I Tolde You So*"

It Is the Best | Ye Olde Lager Beer

PONY HOUSE
The OLDEST and BEST in DAYTON
125 SOUTH JEFFERSON ST.

Even with the passing of the 21st Amendment to the U.S. Constitution, Ohio's old legal counterpart – the Crabbe Act – was not repealed until December 23 of the following year. This allowed time for the establishment of state-controlled "hard liquor" stores.

Post Prohibition – *If money could be made from what was previously a crime, the government could do it....*

Although the repeal of Prohibition was still opposed by the Women's Christian Temperance Union and others throughout the nation, the enforcement of prohibition laws had waned long before 1933. And, while bootlegging tax-free alcohol was ongoing, limitless profits had also waned. The focus of law enforcement after the crash of the stock market had shifted at the start of the decade

Gangsters roamed the U.S., the Midwest, and regional cities seeking soft, lucrative targets. Banks and jewelry stores were vulnerable. This threat had become the priority with police officials.

As much to warn criminals as to reassure the public, Chief Rudy Wurstner was more than pleased to have his department's weaponry and skills spotlighted in Dayton's newspapers.

Captain Edward Poland, Officer Walter Dempsey and **Sgt. William Aldredge** were three of the best trained police marksman on the national level. They were members of pistol teams often at the top in firearms competitions. Dayton was in the national finals against the Boston Police Department team in 1931. In 1932, it ranked third to Washington D.C. and Los Angeles Police Departments in the national standings.

Sergeant William Aldredge *takes aim!*

POLICE PISTOL TEAM LEADING IN INTERSTATE

Sergt. W. J. Aldredge Has Marked Up Two Perfect Scores in Matches.

Dayton Daily News
March 28, 1932

Ptl. Aldredge was particularly adept. In 1929 at National Guard Camp Perry on Lake Erie in Ohio, he won the interstate meet, and would do it again in 1932 with two perfect targets as the Dayton Police pistol team scored 996 of a possible 1000 to win the title.

Sgt. Aldredge had a good year in 1932. He would have the kind of on-duty success the following year that his thorough practical preparation was meant to bring.

1932 was a bad year for a young Indiana woman, **Mary Jenkins**, now living in Pleasant Hill, Ohio, one hour north of Dayton in Miami County. At 22 years of age, she found herself in the fourth year of an unhappy marriage. Born in 1910, Mary had reached this stage after a childhood often burdened by the recurring despair of death.

In late 1913, when she was three years old, Mary's older brother, Paul, age 5, died of diphtheria.

Mary Jenkins

This was followed by her infant sister, Martha, dying in child birth in February 1915. Then, in February 1917, and just three weeks after the birth of her youngest brother, Daniel, her mother, Laverna, passed away from pneumonia. Mary was only six.

Little is known about how Mary's teenage years unfolded. Her father, George, had a girlfriend whose last name was Jessee. The two moved to Kansas City, Kansas after Mary and her brothers, Jim, age 10, and John, age 5, were placed in an orphanage. The infant, Daniel, was adopted.

But Mary Jenkins started life anew at age 18 when she wed Howard Longnaker on February 19, 1929, in Newport, Kentucky.

Though newly married, the specter of death continued to haunt her family. Just 17 weeks later, on June 18, 1929, Mary's younger brother John, now age 17, drowned while swimming in a creek in Bedford, Indiana.

This was exactly two months after their older brother, **James 'Jim' Jenkins**, was imprisoned for life for fatally shooting a Mitchell, Indiana grocer.

James 'Jim' Jenkins

On the other side of death, nine days after marriage, Mrs. Longnaker gave birth to daughter Alice Ann "Clara." Then, on August 17, 1930, another daughter, Betty Jean, was born.

Whether domestic abuse or because she was a vamp, Mary abandoned both girls in 1932 (although she moaned to those who listened that she was desperate to have her children). An institution of the bureaucracy later held that she separated from her husband "to run away with another man." [63]

It was winter when **Mary Jenkins Longnaker** moved to Dayton where dance halls were abundant and parties routine. Initially, she lived at 212 Clay Street sharing a room with a friend, Ruth Keeney. The Clarendon was a two-story, red brick row apartment building with basement units.

Not far away at East Fifth and Pine Streets was Recreation Hall, a place of "Music–Songs– Other Features" like the "Walkathon," the popular marathon dance contest of the day. Here she met a new friend, **Mary Ann Buchholz.** They would share a trip to Chicago not long after Longnaker moved to a downtown boarding house on West First Street.

Meanwhile, a court in Miami County, finding that her daughters' father was also unsuited to properly care for the two girls, saw to their institutional placement. Registered as Clara Ann and Betty Jean, they entered Knoop's Children's Home near Troy, Ohio on April 1 the following year.

Both girls would be adopted by separate families soon thereafter; their first names and last names forever changed. [64]

Circa 1930: Miami County Knoop's Children's Home near Troy. Montgomery County is adjacent and south of Miami County.

On New Year's Eve 1932, the Dayton Police assignment detail was typed for the Year 1933 and authorized by Chief Rudolph F. Wurstner.

There were 209 lawmen assigned to the police force with 23 vacancies to be filled in the coming year. The field operation was divided into three eight-hour "reliefs" with police officers assigned to traditional "foot" patrol. Triple the number of walking officers were now assigned to motor vehicle patrol – both motorcycles and two-man "radio car" crews.

The Dayton Police Department had officers in other specialized assignments, notably the Bureau of Identification (B of I) and Detective Bureau, both under the command of **Inspector Seymour Yendes**.

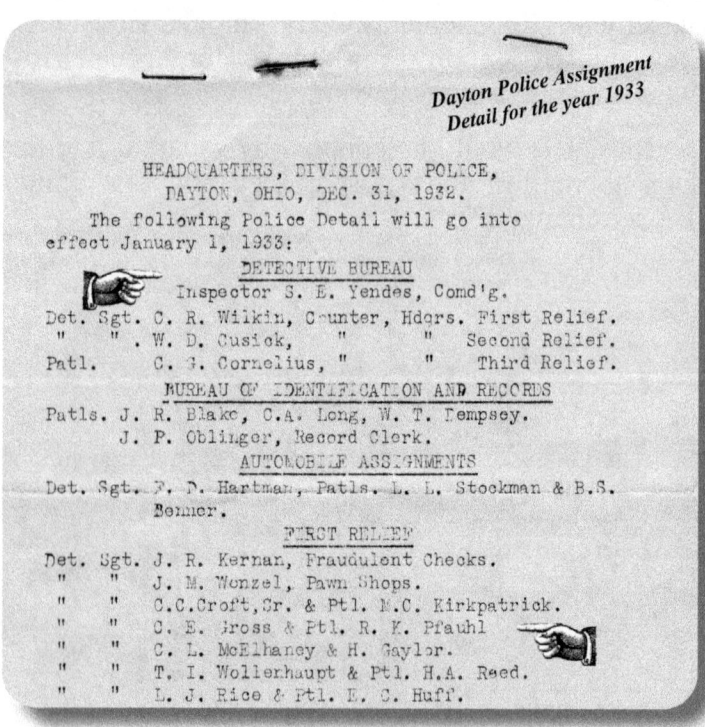

Dayton Police Assignment Detail for the year 1933

HEADQUARTERS, DIVISION OF POLICE,
DAYTON, OHIO, DEC. 31, 1932.
    The following Police Detail will go into effect January 1, 1933:

                      DETECTIVE BUREAU
             Inspector S. E. Yendes, Comd'g.
Det. Sgt. C. R. Wilkin, Counter, Hdqrs. First Relief.
  "   " . W. D. Cusick,   "   "   Second Relief.
Patl.   C. G. Cornelius, "   "   Third Relief.
                BUREAU OF IDENTIFICATION AND RECORDS
Patls. J. R. Blake, C.A. Long, W. T. Dempsey.
       J. P. Oblinger, Record Clerk.
                   AUTOMOBILE ASSIGNMENTS
Det. Sgt. F. D. Hartman, Patls. L. L. Stockman & B.S.
          Bemier.
                   FIRST RELIEF
Det. Sgt. J. R. Kernan, Fraudulent Checks.
  "   " J. M. Wenzel, Pawn Shops.
  "   " C.C.Croft,Sr. & Ptl. M.C. Kirkpatrick.
  "   " C. E. Gross & Ptl. R. K. Pfauhl
  "   " C. L. McElhaney & H. Gaylor.
  "   " T. I. Wollerhaupt & Ptl. H.A. Reed.
  "   " L. J. Rice & Ptl. E. C. Huff.

The latter unit had seven investigative teams, each consisting of a sergeant and detective. **Sgt. Charles Gross** with **Det. Russell Pfauhl** formed one of those teams. In the field, **Captain Earl Yates** was in charge of the overnight Uniform Bureau (patrol operations), a command position once held by Inspector Wurstner. **Sgt. William Aldredge** was in charge of Third District patrol and assigned to "Radio Car #17."

All five men would find their professional lives forever tied to an event that later unfolded. At the same time, Chief Wurstner would also find his profile further raised when he was elected president of the Ohio Association of Police Chiefs in the coming year. It was quite an honor for a man who had led his troops for eight years.

Now, 30 years after the Wright brothers first flight of 1903, John Dillinger's birth, and Chief Wurstner's appointment to police service, this was the state of local law enforcement and direction of the Dayton Police Department with the opening of a new year.

Most of the 1920s and first few years of this new decade passed by as John Dillinger served hard time in the state prison in Michigan City, Indiana, developing close ties with inmates convicted of robbery such as Harry Pierpont, Charles Makley, Russell Clark, and John 'Red' Hamilton, among others. While some in the lot had killed, others that had not had no compunction for committing assaults with murderous intent. Dillinger was exposed to a dangerous brew.

He also had a new cellmate, James 'Jim' Jenkins, who had himself robbed and murdered... and Jim had a sister about whom he often bragged.

It was 1933.

Troubles percolated for Mary Longnaker in Miami County, but the Gem City was her retreat from her troubled marriage in Pleasant Hill. Now living in a Dayton rooming house, free from the burdens of family, Mary traveled as she pleased. Occasionally, she visited her relatives in Indiana, including brother Jim serving a life sentence in the Michigan City, Indiana prison. When she appeared, she was dressed for the occasion ... attractively. The siblings were very close; he carried her picture.

It was not long before Jenkins' cellmate developed a growing interest in the tall, slender, young brunette and Jim let Mary know. Smitten, Dillinger sent her a telegram upon his coming release, pledging his plans to visit her. Four months short of nine years since he pleaded guilty to a slipshod Indiana grocery holdup in Mooresville, he was soon to keep his promise.

John Dillinger was paroled from prison on May 20, 1933. Although released to the outside world, the dangerous influences from within cell blocks had prepared him to resume his earlier life of crime, albeit less amateurish. He was now wiser and hardened.

John Dillinger

Traveling in a ragged Model A Ford, Dillinger came to Dayton in May to satisfy his prison obsession with Mary Longnaker. He drove around downtown looking for her. He shouted to pedestrians in his search as to her whereabouts. He found the place she roomed – in what has been described as a "respectable boarding house" – at 324 West First Street, owned by 48-year-old **Mrs. Lucille Stricker**. [65] The landlady accepted Dillinger's claim to be Mary's brother and rented a room to him for his visit. Thus began his local romance with Mary Longnaker.

After a few days in Mary's company (who at first did not much like him but soon grew on her), Dillinger left for Indiana... but he would rendezvous in Dayton with Longnaker in June, July, August and September. He was in town eight and likely more times through the course of the summer. In between, the two engaged in a letter-writing relationship that fueled infatuation.

In the meantime, he and members of a cobbled gang committed unspectacular department store and restaurant holdups around Indianapolis. But Dillinger wanted more and so, in mid-June 1933, he and three members of his gang traveled to New Carlisle, Ohio, a community just 18 miles northeast of Dayton. The four bandits staked out the National Bank at 100 E. Jefferson Street at South Main Street. [66]

In the darkness in the early morning of June 21, three of the hold-up men broke into the bank through a back window and waited. The get-away driver parked their Ford two blocks away on Jefferson Street. He was in front of a doctor's house so his sitting at that spot caused no particular alarm. The Ford had a license plate believed to have been issued in Dayton.

Sometime around eight o'clock in the morning, a clerk, Horace Grisso, unlocked and then entered through the front door where he was surprised by the waiting Dillinger and two of his gang.

Circa 1933: The National Bank in New Carlisle, Ohio.

They had white handkerchiefs covering the lower half of their faces. They operated in a calm manner.

Told to open the vault, the clerk stalled for time, saying he was a new employee who did not know the combination. Soon a woman bank assistant, Mata Taylor, entered and then a bit later the cashier, Carl Enoch, and a patron, Grant Widner. The last clerk to enter was forced to unlock the vault. All four people were tied up with cords and told they would be shot if any of them yelled out.

As one outlaw stood guard, Dillinger and the other bandit placed $10,600 cash in money bags ($212,364 today). The three robbers fled through the rear window to the get-away car which took off eastbound on State Route 71. [67]

The gang threw roofing tacks from a keg onto the road behind them for a distance of a mile. There was no pursuit and with the heist, Dillinger committed his first bank robbery of what would become many bank holdups.

In June, Dillinger stopped in Dayton to enjoy Longnaker's company once again. More visits to Dayton were to come so he paid for the on-going reservation of a room on the first floor of the boarding house. Either during this visit or during another in June, Dillinger and Mary decided to drive to Pleasant Hill. He had a compulsion to track down Mary's spouse. Johnnie wanted to give the man his due when it came to the divorce for the way this estranged husband of hers was mistreating his gal.

Howard Longnaker was found at his job site west of the town, the water pumping station. Words turned to heated confrontation and soon to physical jostling.

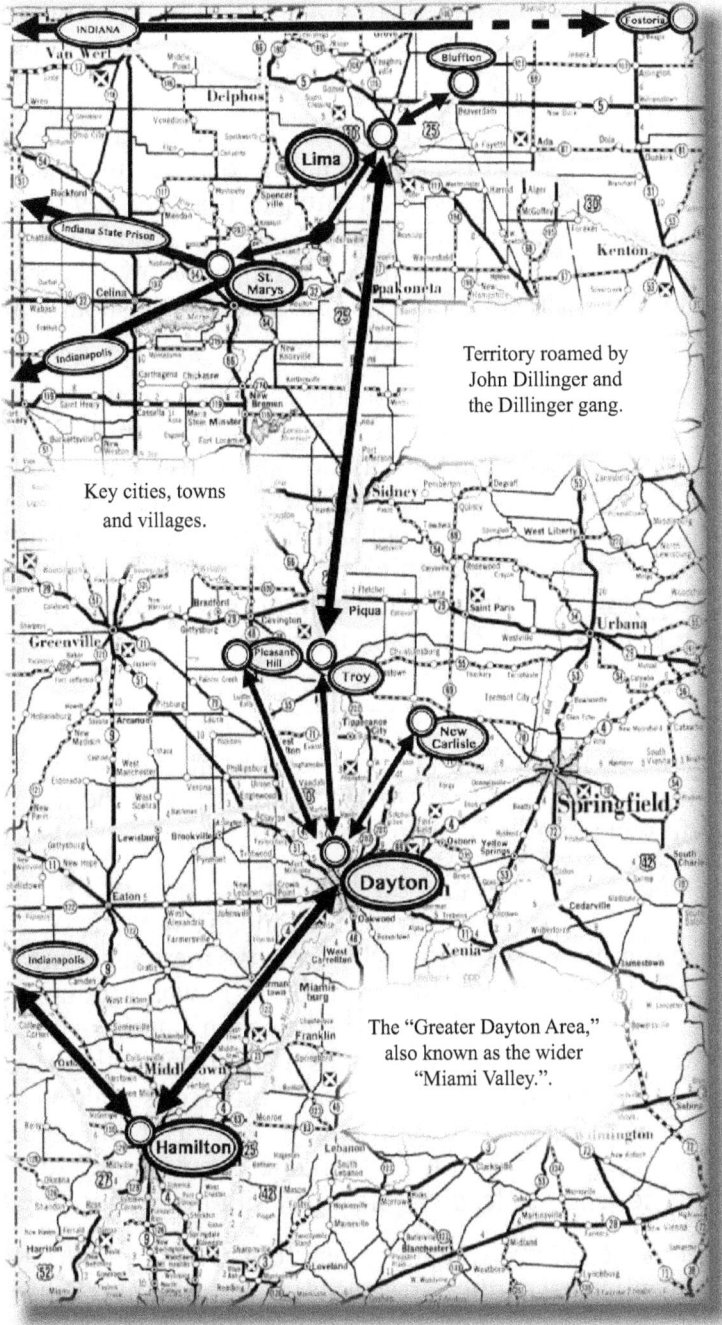

Territory roamed by
John Dillinger and
the Dillinger gang.

Key cities, towns
and villages.

The "Greater Dayton Area,"
also known as the wider
"Miami Valley.".

1930 Map: Southwest Ohio between Lima and Hamilton.

The threat of fisticuffs promptly ended with the quick arrival of the town marshal, Orth Stocker. The lawman escorted Dillinger back to the out-of-towner's car.

The lore is varied. The constable intended to either direct Dillinger to leave town or to drive himself into town. If the latter (not an unusual practice, perhaps, for small town law and order), it was to appear before the mayor or to be jailed. What is known is that Marshal Stocker stepped onto the running board of John Dillinger's motorcar.

As the lawman stood on the footplate, the scofflaw decided he wasn't about to be told what to do by a copper and, certainly, was not about to be arrested. Dillinger hit the gas and sped through the streets as the marshal held on with all his might. An abrupt stop, followed by a quick maneuver, threw Marshal Stocker free from the automobile, which then hightailed south out of town. [68]

Back in Dayton, Dillinger and Longnaker did not stay hidden from the world. They enjoyed the night life whenever he was in town.

Now that Prohibition was on the verge of full repeal, Dayton's Olt Brothers Company was one of 21 local breweries, mostly all German-American owned, back to near full-volume business. It was producing its Olts Superba Beer for the open market. Mrs. Stricker's boarding house was a short one-mile drive for Dillinger to take Mary to the Pony House saloon at 125 S. Jefferson Street. [69] There, Olts, Ye Olde lager, and Red Top beer where available "on draught" for a public ready to legally consume adult beverages.

Light conversations often dovetailed to Mary lamenting her awful marriage to Howard, his hold on their

PONY HOUSE SALOON

two children, and the expense of a divorce proceeding. To cheer her, Johnnie would treat his gal with dinners at places like Pete Lohana's Greek restaurant (a place police believed catered to patrons of Dillinger's ilk).

It was a mere two-block stroll from her West First Street boarding house south on North Wilkinson Street. Here, in the mood for a dream retreat away from the gloom, they marveled about the attractions to be seen at the World's Fair in Chicago and entertained going there. It was fantasy for Mary for the evening.

It was doable for Dillinger – a man who traveled about, never staying in one place more than a few days – although it would come later. At the moment, he was ready to leave Dayton but would return.

In late June, the outlaw was suspected of being involved in a bank robbery in Kentucky. When he was on the road, Dillinger often wrote to his girl.

In one letter to Longnaker he said, in a veiled way, that he hoped to profit handsomely from several bank robberies. In doing so, he could free her brother Jim from the prison in Indiana. He was more direct in saying he would shuttle all three of them to South America.

In July, the robberies continued at a tavern and three banks in the Hoosier State, one of which was a failed attempt in Rockville, Indiana.

On Thursday, July 20, the day after the Rockville crime, Dillinger drove his 1928 Chevrolet Coupe to Dayton to visit Mary once again. They traveled for drinks to a place by the tire factory, Vargo's restaurant on West Riverview Avenue. [70] Longnaker introduced her friend, 20-year-old Mary Ann Buchholz, to her suitor. Dillinger offered to take both women to the Chicago World's Fair that very day.

An excited Buchholz left Vargo's and headed home to pack. It was about a 10-minute fast walk for her across the Rosedale bridge. Not long thereafter, at around six o'clock that evening, the couple traveled along a dirt road. They arrived at Oakridge Drive [71]

where they picked up Buchholz, and then headed north to the Windy City.

There was a quick stop at a diner on Eaton Pike not far from Dayton,

Mary Ann Buchholz's residence on Oakridge Drive.

a 10-minute break for a drink of water. They dropped in on Dillinger's dad at the Mooresville family farm. Then they made a momentary stop at a filling station to give a ten-spot to John's teenage half-brother, Hubert.

The drive to Chicago was long, but by three o'clock early morning, the three checked in the Hotel Crillon on Michigan Avenue at East 13th Street. Dillinger paid for a three-night stay in adjoining rooms. The gentleman had one room for himself and another for the two ladies, although they were in and out of his room. At one point, Buchholz spotted a pistol on top of Dillinger's dresser as he was showering. Longnaker opened the wallet next to it and said, "How'd you like to have this amount of money?" [72] She spread the leather billfold to show several $50 bills.

The cash – equal to a couple thousand dollars today – paid for a spectacular weekend for three inside Chicago's *"A Century of Progress International Exposition."* The outlaw's time was fully devoted to the two women; there was never any contact with Dillinger acquaintances. They were able to enjoy an array of performances, like the burlesque fan dancing of Sally Rand, a "dream cars" exhibit, the food, the amusements, and some picture-taking experiences. When Mary snapped a picture of a policeman, Dillinger looked at her "with the queerest face," a look she later said she would never forget.

Three 1933 tickets

The 1933-1934 Chicago World's Fair

The weekend in Chicago was an escape ... unlike the one that Dillinger would not have from Chicago exactly one year later.

The weekend retreat over, the three left the Windy City in the morning bound for the Gem City. On the return trip, the trio traveled an eastward Great Lake hook beneath the base of Lake Michigan. They were headed to the Indiana State Prison... Longnaker had suggested that they go to Michigan City.

It was an hour's drive to visit her brother, Jim Jenkins. Before arriving, they stopped for a sandwich and coffee at a diner, and then at a stand where Dillinger purchased a variety of fresh fruit – bananas, plums, apples, oranges and grapes. Wrapping a $50 bill in black paper, he secreted it in a small hole he bore into a banana, sealing it with some pulp.

Indiana State Prison at Michigan City

Arriving at their destination about 10 a.m., John Dillinger waited in the coupe while the two Marys headed to the prison entrance. Unwittingly, Longnaker was abetting, in one small way, Dillinger's long-range plan for a massive inmate breakout from the slammer.

Following his instructions, the young ladies entered the jail facility and were admitted by a guard. Upon reaching an inner chamber, Longnaker passed a $50 bill to a prison official and told him the money was to have "a dentist get [Jim's] teeth fixed." [73] Once inside the visitors' ward, Buchholz sat idly by as Mary was seated across from her brother.

Keeping to her beau's directions, Mary suggested to Jim to "eat the banana first" and then, in quiet deliberative way, read from scratched notes to convey that the money was to be divided and distributed in $10 amounts to specific guards and inmates. She ended by telling Jim to "sit tight."

After a half hour, the two young women parted company with Jenkins and hopped back into the waiting Chevrolet, satisfied their mission was accomplished. Mary laughed at how dumb the guards were not to check the fruit.

The trio continued home making Indiana stops in Fort Wayne, where Dillinger met with someone briefly in "a cheap-looking shack," and then into Richmond to pick up a few candy bars before arriving in Dayton. It was the evening of Monday, July 24. Dillinger stayed the night with Mary but left the next day.

By this time, possibly as early as July 15, Dillinger had visited a local attorney to engage him to represent Mary.   J. Farrell Johnson was with the firm of Pickrel, Schaeffer, Harshman & Young at the Union Trust Building located at 25 N. Main Street, across the alley from the "new" and massive court building that rose above the "Old Court House."

The Union Trust Building and the "New" Court House to its left.

The brief meeting between the two men inside Office 620 did not go well, but in the end, Dillinger fronted money to hasten Longnaker's divorce from her husband, Howard. This effort to secure Mary's divorce, their weekend together, and letters of his desires spoke to the long-confined convict's intention ... marriage was clearly his state of mind.

The following morning, Dillinger headed west into Indiana. The very next day, July 26, Johnnie mailed a love letter to his gal which lovingly expressed, in part:

". . . Honey, I miss you like nobody's business and I don't mean maybe. You know I must be thinking of you for I just got up.... I hope I can get fixed so I can spend more time with you, for baby I fell for you in a big way and if you'll be on the

level I'll give everybody the go by (goodbye) for you and that isn't a lot of hooey either. I know you like me dear but that isn't enough for me when I'm as crazy as I am about you. You may never get to feel the same toward me as I do you in which case I would be better off not to see you very much for it would be hell for me.... *[sic]*

John expresses love for Mary

"Well, sweetheart I guess I'll ring off for this time, love me a little or do you love me a lot? Well, baby, ta ta for this time hope I hear from you soon. *[sic]*

"Lots of love from Johnnie"

He added that he hoped Mary had seen her girls and he wanted to see them as well. He wished she and he had "two or three sweet little kids." He also promised:

"If that lousy husband of your bothers you any more just let me know and he will never bother you again." *[sic]*

Around July 31, a special delivery letter was received from Mary, but Dillinger was disappointed that her words did not match his craving for her. By August 2, he received a second letter from Longnaker, but this one was relatively lukewarm as well. It was dispiriting for Johnnie. He wanted to feel her passion, and so he responded in early August, first mentioning her children before getting to the point.

> "Gee! I would sure like to see the little darlings.... how in the hell did I know I would fall for you....
>
> "Honey I wish you would get your hair fixed up and put on your black gown and have your picture taken especially for me how about it?" *[sic]*

He continued by asking her to write him, as one historian related, "a long, sweet letter telling how much she loved him and that she couldn't live without him." [74]

> "Ha! Ha! Kid you've sure got me tied up in a knot but dont leave me dangling for I want to know something when I see you again. *[sic]*
>
> "Lots of love from Johnnie"

The U.S. mail, and Longnaker's inability to keep secret her romance with the bandit, would be his undoing. Longnaker kept confiding in her landlady, Mrs. Lucille Stricker, about her relationship, and later she, in turn, would secretly tell Dayton police about the visits and mail.

In August, robberies continued at two more banks, including one in Bluffton, Ohio near Findlay in Allen County. By August 15, Dillinger was a suspect in at least six bank robberies in three states and a host of store holdups. During these first months after his release from prison Dillinger had remained unknown to the public.

By mid-August, however, Dillinger started to gather the widespread attention of financial institutions, police, and the press.

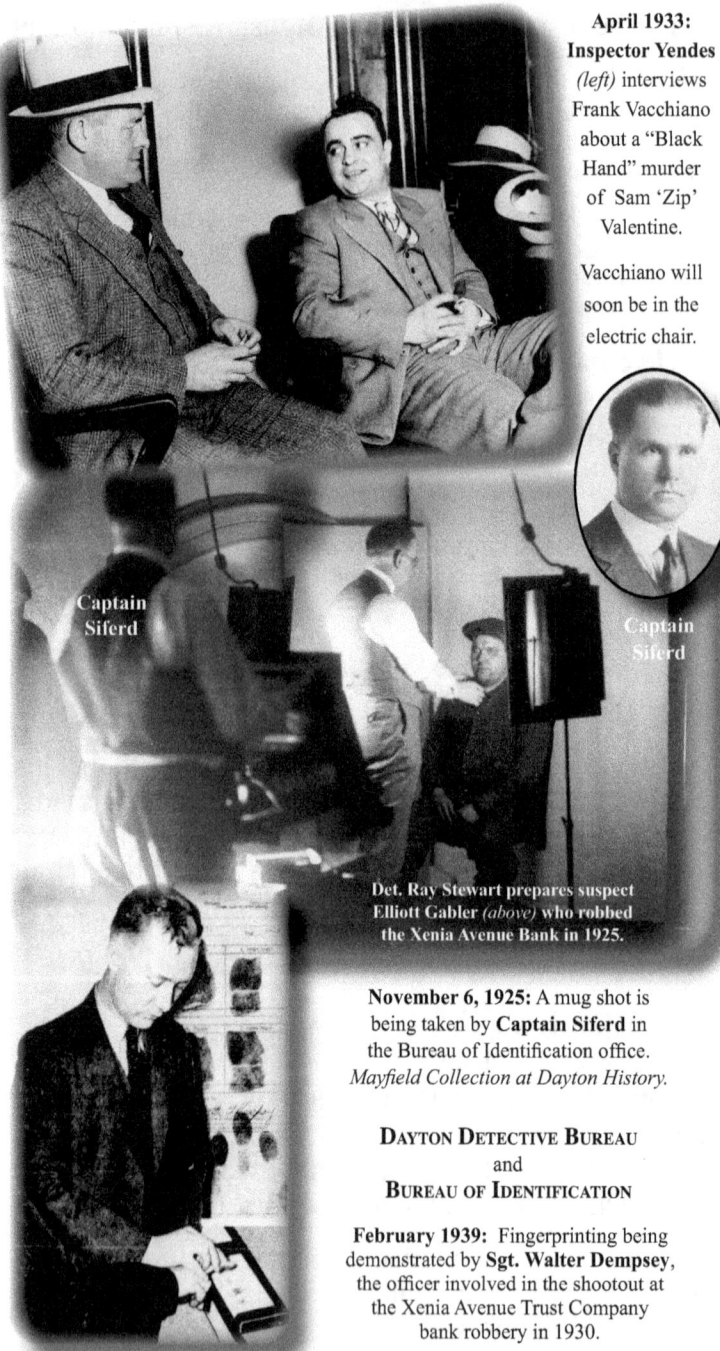

April 1933: Inspector Yendes *(left)* interviews Frank Vacchiano about a "Black Hand" murder of Sam 'Zip' Valentine.

Vacchiano will soon be in the electric chair.

Captain Siferd

Captain Siferd

Det. Ray Stewart prepares suspect Elliott Gabler *(above)* who robbed the Xenia Avenue Bank in 1925.

November 6, 1925: A mug shot is being taken by **Captain Siferd** in the Bureau of Identification office. *Mayfield Collection at Dayton History.*

DAYTON DETECTIVE BUREAU and **BUREAU OF IDENTIFICATION**

February 1939: Fingerprinting being demonstrated by **Sgt. Walter Dempsey**, the officer involved in the shootout at the Xenia Avenue Trust Company bank robbery in 1930.

Sidebar: Dayton Detective Bureau and Bureau of Identification

The Detective Bureau: Much had changed for Dayton police investigators since 1902. At the time, it was a squad of one sergeant and four detectives.

Sergeant Walter J. Hughes was appointed "Chief of Detectives" in October **1903**. The squad became a Bureau under his 17 years of supervision and tripled in size to 15 detectives. But the Detective Bureau suffered a great loss with Sgt. Hughes' unexpected death in **July 1920** after a brief illness.

Sgt. Walter Hughes

Inspector Seymour E. Yendes was quickly placed in command of the Detective Bureau. He had developed a reputation as an exceptional investigator during his eight years in the Bureau. Believing his investigating detectives and Dayton's identification experts shared a common lane, he brought the Bureau of Identification under his command as well. He would become a police official of national acclaim over the next 17 years with his greatest notoriety coming from the arrest of John Dillinger in **1933**.

Bureau of Identification: Known as the "B of I," much had changed since the Bureau was established in **1902**. Previously, it was an office for Dayton's "Bertillon officers" that were handling the old "rogues gallery" while changing over to a Bertillon recordkeeping system, the accepted national law enforcement standard at the time. But in 1910, the International Association of Chiefs of Police endorsed fingerprinting as the better practice. Dayton's B of I began transitioning to this new identification method in 1915 when Patrolman Siferd was assigned to B of I. He was promoted to sergeant and then, in 1923, promoted once again.

Captain Harvey W. Siferd assiduously studied fingerprinting – a categorizing method using the Henry classification system of ridges and loop, whorl, and arch patterns – to perfect criminal identification. He had become a nationally renowned fingerprint expert. But the Dayton Bureau of Identification also suffered a great loss with his death in **July 1932** after a year-long illness.

One of Capt. Siferd's detectives was a crime-fighting patrolman reassigned in 1930 to the Bureau of Identification and then later promoted to run it.

Sergeant Walter T. Dempsey succeeded Captain Siferd in charge of the B of I. He eventually, brought state-of-the-art ballistic investigations to Dayton and was credited with making the Dayton B of I "known throughout the United States." The B of I office in the Market House Police Headquarters maintained the police weapons arsenal in a South Market Street garage bay where the "Bank Flyer" was housed. Sgt. Dempsey – an expert competitive marksman who often teamed with Sgt. William Aldredge in shooting competitions – oversaw the "Flying Squadron," the SWAT Team of its day.

CHAPTER 7

FUGITIVE: UNDER THE COVER OF DARKNESS

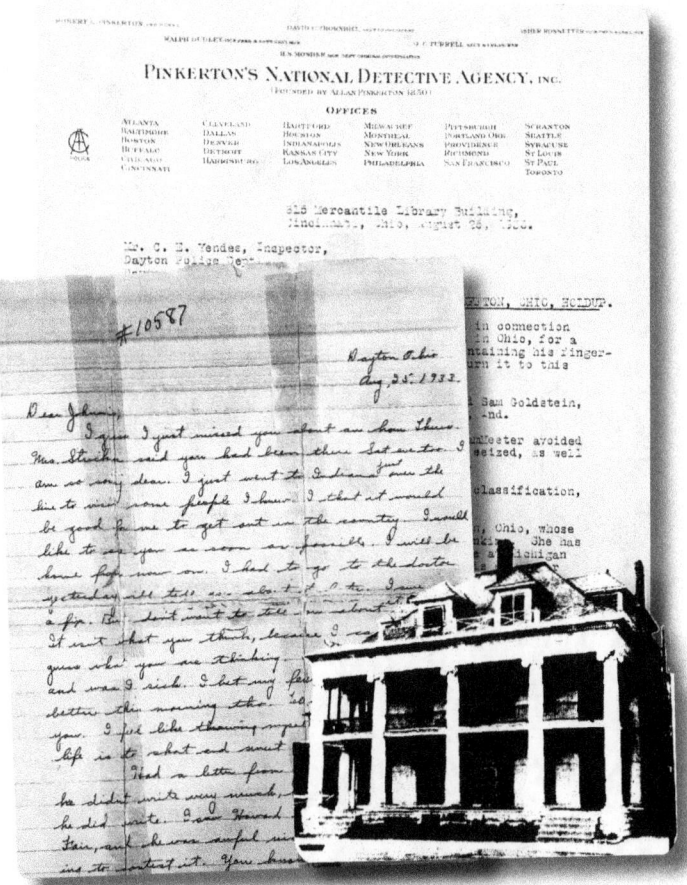

August 25, 1933: Two letters written and mailed on the same date. One is from Pinkerton's National Detective Agency to Dayton **Inspector Seymour Yendes** and the other is from **Mary Longnaker** to **Johnnie Dillinger**. Her residence, a boarding house at **324 W. First Street**, Dayton, Ohio, is in the foreground. Letters: *Wright State University Special Collections and Archives*

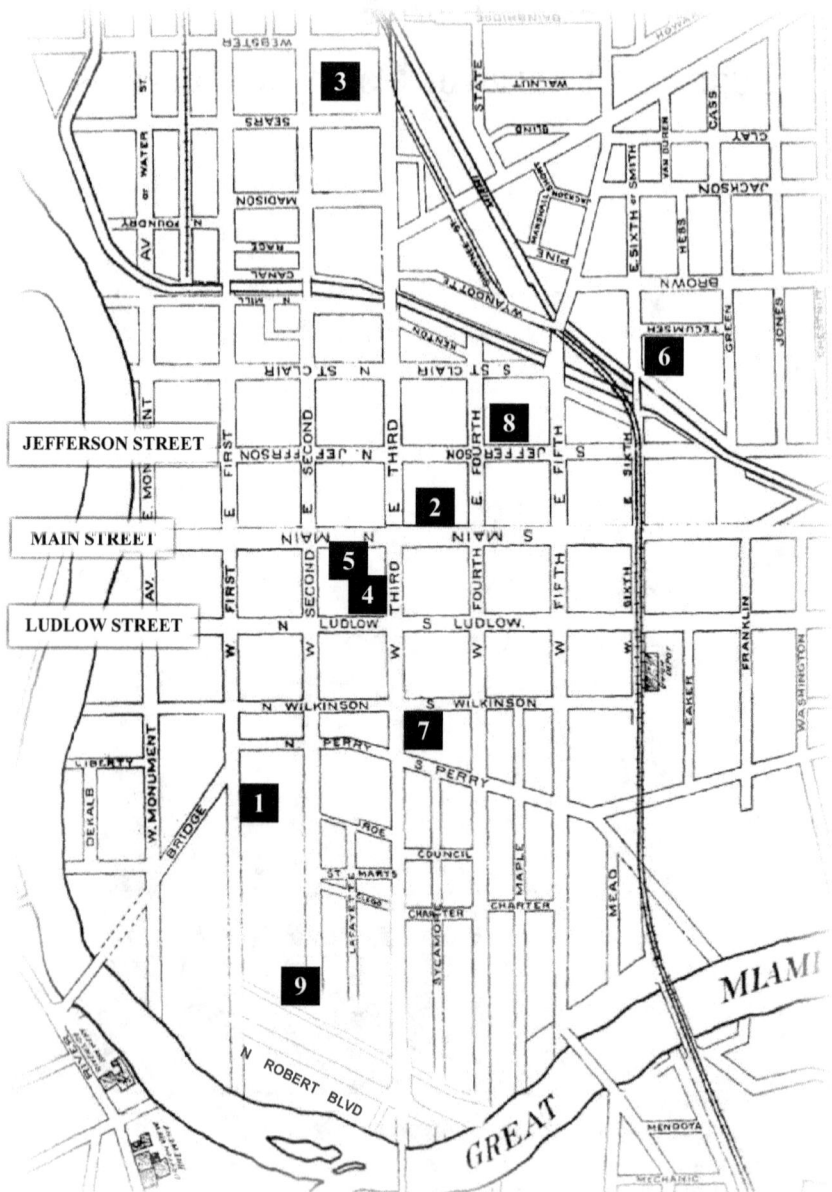

Legend: **1** Stricker's Boarding House - **2** Dayton Police HQ - **3** Ford Street Station/Jail - **4** Montgomery County Jail - **5** Old & New Courthouses - **6** Old Central Police Station (1867-1922) - **7** Pete's Restaurant - **8** Pony House Saloon - **9** N. Robert Blvd Hideaway

TAKEDOWN – John Dillinger was a hot topic of conversation in the Midwest. The Indiana State Police were issuing wanted posters in the state, and to agencies in other states, to aid robbery investigations spearheaded by Captain Matt Leach.

The Pinkerton's National Detective Agency – still the country's highest-profile private police agency – was contracted in Ohio to investigate the $2,100 Citizens National Bank holdup in Bluffton ($42,072 today).

Circa 1930: Downtown Dayton looking at three (3) city streets extending south from First Street to Fifth Street - **Jefferson** (far left), **Main** and **Ludlow** Streets.

In the last half of August 1933, Dillinger dumped his old coupe and obtained a speedy new 1933 Hudson Essex Terraplane.

Letters continued to be exchanged between he and Mary in the month of August.

The now notorious outlaw was in Dayton on Saturday, August 19 and again on Thursday, August 24 but the two lovers missed each seeing each other.

On August 25, a disappointed Longnaker wrote a letter closer in tone to what Dillinger had hoped to receive.

It said, in part:

> "Dear Johnnie;
>
> "I guess I just missed you about an hour Thurs. Mrs. Stricker said you had been there Sat eve too. I am so sorry dear. I just went to Indiana just over the line to visit some people.... I would like to see you as soon as possible. I will be home from now on.... I sure am in a fix.... Tell you more when I see you. I feel like throwing myself in the river. But life is to short and sweet anyway.... If you can come down over Sun. I want to see you so bad *[sic]*
>
> "Well honey I guess I will sign off. Hoping to see you soon.
>
> "Lots of Love. Mary."

Her letter also mentioned that she had seen Howard at the Greenville (Ohio) Fair "and he was awful nice." Her estranged husband had asked if she was really planning to go through with the divorce.

She wrote Johnnie that she told him, "Sure I was."

Around the same time, the Pinkerton's Detective Agency had learned that Dillinger was periodically visiting Dayton and was paying for a woman's divorce proceeding.

All they knew was her maiden name, "Jenkins."

Coincidently, on the day Mary mailed her impassioned letter to Dillinger – August 25 – Mr. Edward Clark, a division manager for the Pinkerton's

PINKERTON'S NATIONAL DETECTIVE AGENCY, INC.
(FOUNDED BY ALLAN PINKERTON 1850)

Agency, wrote to Dayton Police Inspector Seymour Yendes. The letter said, in part:

> "John Dillinger, alias John Hall, is wanted in connection with some of the bank holdups, in various towns in Ohio, for a period of the last year.... "Recently.... John Dillinger, Harry Copeland and Homer VamMeeter avoided arrest. [sic]

> "John Dillinger has a female friend at Dayton, Ohio, whose given name is unknown, but her maiden name is Jenkins.... Dillinger calls upon this woman regularly and, no doubt, can be apprehended at Dayton, Ohio. He is driving a new Essex Terraplane 8 Sedan, black color.... The thought is ... you could hav e the Police ... get some information concerning this woman and cause the arrest of Dillinger, and/in all probability, Copeland, as they spend considerable of their time together." [sic]

The Pinkerton's Agency sent a copy of Dillinger's fingerprints and his physical description to Inspector Yendes. Dillinger was about 5'8½ and 160-170 pounds. Physically, he was average: medium size, medium build. He had two small but noticeable facial moles but two features stood out: a "deep dimple" in his chin but also "grey" eyes ... cold grey eyes.

As she had hoped, Dillinger visited Longnaker, on Sunday, August 27, arriving in Dayton driving his new Terraplane. Feeling brash so soon after the Bluffton Bank holdup, Dillinger told Longnaker that "business was getting better." After his Sunday tryst with her, Dillinger again left Dayton as was his habit.

Mary Longnaker

John Dillinger

In the meantime, acting on the correspondence he received from the Pinkerton's Agency a few days earlier, Inspector Yendes dictated a letter on August 28 for Chief Wurstner's signature. Addressed to Indiana State Prison Warden Walter Daly, it was a simple request:

> "We would like to ascertain the marriage name of James Jenkins sister, and since we understand that James Jenkins is serving a life sentence in your Institution, would ask that you kindly obtain her name for us from him...."

Inspector 'Cy' Yendes was the right man at the right time to head the Dayton Detective Bureau. He had the confidence of Chief Wurstner. He was three years the Chief's junior, having been appointed in 1906, but had risen in rank quicker. He was promoted to sergeant in 1912, and was a detective sergeant in 1915. He and the Chief often worked in tandem throughout their careers.

While then Sergeant Wurstner was detailed to the red-light district in East Dayton to rid Pearl Street of its "painted" women, Sgt. Yendes was teamed with Ptl. Lucius Rice to do the same in West Dayton along "the crimson trail" of Home Avenue. Houses of ill fame on this street, such as "Hedgewood," were owned by the same infamous madam, Lib Hedges, [75] who oversaw the Pearl Street district and Warren Street brothels.

By 1933, the Chief and Inspector Yendes had been in positions of command together for 13 years. They often traveled to conferences and meetings with each other. They socialized together. Cy could and did issue directives on behalf of Chief Wurstner and wrote communiqués in the Chief's name.

When Inspector Yendes spoke with police officials from other jurisdictions, his was the voice of Chief Wurstner. Theirs was a tight-fitting relationship as Dillinger came under local investigation.

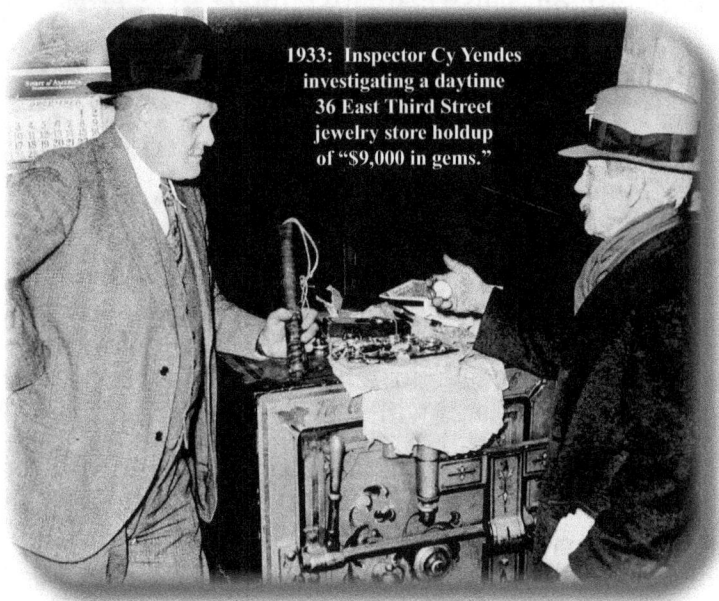

1933: Inspector Cy Yendes investigating a daytime 36 East Third Street jewelry store holdup of "$9,000 in gems."

As September opened Dayton police received a second, but more precise communiqué, again from Pinkerton's Manager Edward Clark. He advised that he had learned Mary Jenkins' married name and address.

Although this newest tip had been written on Saturday, the 2nd of the month, Dayton police had learned where Dillinger's local girlfriend lived by Wednesday, August 30. The Pinkerton's Acting Superintendent, Mr. J. A. McCarthy, had come to Dayton to personally meet with Chief Wurstner that day. Police Inspector Yendes immediately assigned a plainclothes squad to contact Mrs. Lucille Stricker.

His investigative team was Sgt. Charles Gross and Det. Russell Pfauhl.

The detectives had photos and circulars of John Dillinger to show her. She recognized the bandit as the male friend of her tenant. She promptly consented to a surreptitious search of her tenant's room. It was there and then that Dayton police found letters tying Dillinger to Longnaker. Under

Dayton Police
Sgt. Charles Gross

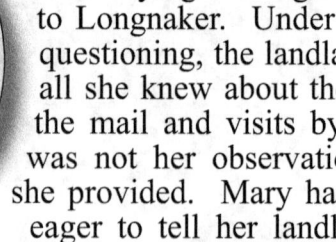

Dayton Police
Det. Russell Pfauhl

questioning, the landlady poured out all she knew about the frequency of the mail and visits by Dillinger. It was not her observations alone that she provided. Mary had always been eager to tell her landlady about her dates with Dillinger and their letters.

When speaking with the detectives, Mrs. Stricker – realizing the threat the fugitive posed – agreed to secretively assist the police. Whenever letters came to Longnaker, she offered to steam the envelopes open, read the contents, and reseal before turning them over to her tenant.

She would immediately alert the police to the letters and, most certainly, would telephone when the gangster himself next arrived. It did not take long.

Heeding her vow, Mrs. Stricker called police within a few days when a letter arrived. The letter had been opened without Longnaker's knowledge. In it was a promise made by her beau, Johnnie Dillinger: *"I'll be seeing you soon."*

That phrase caught the attention of Inspector Yendes, and with it, Chief Wurstner authorized Sgt. Gross and Det. Pfauhl to begin a stakeout. In early September, the two detectives moved into the boarding house.

Mrs. Stricker placed them in a room opposite the first-floor sleeping quarters reserved for Dillinger, and directly beneath Longnaker's room.

Dayton Police
Chief Rudy Wurstner

And then they waited and waited. But Dillinger was nowhere in the vicinity. [76]

In September, the robberies continued at two more banks, including an Indianapolis heist of $24,800, the second largest bank holdup in the state's history ($496,853 today).

Law enforcement throughout the nation was warned by Indiana State Police Captain Matt Leach, "The Dillinger gang are not men to be captured single-handed. It's going to take a well-organized army, ready to shoot and kill in a split second." [77]

The tracking and chase of the elusive fugitive was intensifying. At the same time, Dillinger had no intention of slowing down. He was delayed in a return to Dayton because he was in the midst of planning an elaborate scheme.

Now flush with the cash from the recent bank robbery, Dillinger amassed weapons which he was arranging to be smuggled to his inmate buddies in

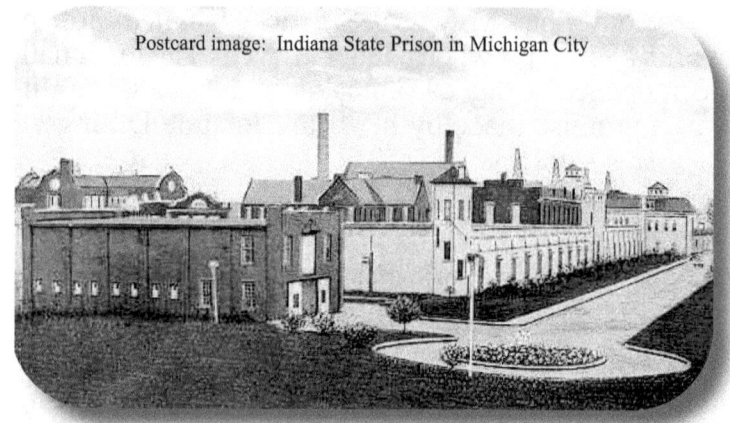

Postcard image: Indiana State Prison in Michigan City

prison with the aid of accomplices both inside and outside the walls. The time spent on this scheme kept Dillinger away from detectives staking out the Dayton boarding house and from Mary, much to her unhappiness.

But a visit was forthcoming, and an escape from the Indiana State Prison was imminent.

Distracted, Dillinger was not focused on Mary Longnaker in September. The first week of the month, he robbed a bank. Back in Chicago, on September 15, he was consumed with other affairs – as small as having his Terraplane fenders repainted and the car washed at Supreme Motor Sales (under the name of "Mr. Donovan") to planning a massive jail break.

Planning and committing bank holdups, networking with gang members, plotting conspiracies ... these all took time.

Yet, he would finally find time to think of his "honey" by the third week of the month. Although he had written to Mary often, and visited Dayton three times in the month of August, Dillinger had only one overnight stay with her since their July 24 return from Chicago, and that was on August 27. His "sweetheart" was not getting the attention she craved.

Mary Longnaker's divorce had not moved forward. She needed Johnnie's cash for legal expenses, and now rightly suspected he was a sought man. She was in a bleak mood and fretful that Dillinger might show at Mrs. Stricker's boarding house while she was away (knowing he had already done so twice before).

Frustrated when an earlier letter she had mailed to Dillinger came back *Dear Johnnie* from the postal service, she penned her discontent on the letter itself for no one to see: *"Why don't you stay at home?* [signed] *Mary."* Adding an annoyed, *"This was returned unclaimed."*

Mary was *not* a happy woman. But sometime in September she attended a dance and met a 28-year-old man by the name of Claude ... Sherman Claude Constable.

Ruddy complected, he was 5'11 and 170 pounds of muscle. He lived at 217 Reisinger Avenue, about six blocks from Mary Ann Buchholz's Oakridge house. He labored at a local GM DELCO plant. Unlike Dillinger, Claude had a job! He also had a father in Richmond, Indiana who was running in an election for the office of Wayne County Sheriff.

And, much like Dillinger, Claude had eyes for Mary. As was the practice of the day, he wrote a letter to her that said:

"Hello Honey.

"I am at Work as You see. Hope you Will please excuse This paper & pencil

But I decided That I must try and get in Touch With You. *[sic]*

"After You left The dance fast Mon Nite, I got With a bunch I knew & We Went To Russels point & Spent The day. I tried to locate you before leaving, But Was unable to. Hope You Will forgive me. Yes? No? *[sic]*

"I do not Know if I Will have to Work This Sat. Nite but Think not. If not I Will Be at The dance at Lakeside Hoping to be With You. *[sic]*

"Give me a ring on The phone.... Call me any time in The morning up until 2:00 P.M. & I will be sure and be here. *[sic]*

"Hoping to see & be With You Soon. You remember The One You danced so much With Well That's me. ly ly. Ans. Soon" *[sic]*

They met. Mary found comfort in Claude Constable while she longed for Johnnie Dillinger.

She mailed a letter to her brother, Jim, along with some pictures of she and Claude together. Mary spoke kindly of Claude in breaking the news of this new guy who had entered her life. She also bemoaned the loss of her two girls (to a children's institution).

Coincidently, Jim also received a letter from Claude in which he expressed his intentions to woo Mary. Jim replied to both.

First, Jim wrote to his "Sweetheart Darlin ... I'll bet a cooky you're peeved at your big bud for having neglected to write you." *[sic]* He missed her birthday on August 14 but flipped his guilt to her for not visiting him.

*Mrs. Mary Longnaker
3 2 4 W. First St.
Dayton Ohio   4   Sept. 11, '33
Hello "Sweetheart Darlin';"
I'll bet a cooky you're peeve; at your big
bud for having neglected to write you. But here I am*

When it came to Claude, Jim said she need not worry how he felt about her dating someone other than his former cellmate. "What you do is your business. No one else's." Then, in his separate reply to Claude, Jim reassured him by saying, in part:

> "I read your letter and was very
> pleased to hear from you.... Mary says
> you're a good fellow and I'll except
> her opinion. *[sic]* You have been plain
> spoken in regards to this. And let me
> say, admire your frankness. I like the
> tone of your letter and believe you will
> do well by Mary. She's a swell Sis....
> Sincerely yours – Jim."

James Jenkins' letters to Mary and Claude were written on September 17 and postmarked from Indiana State Prison on September 19.

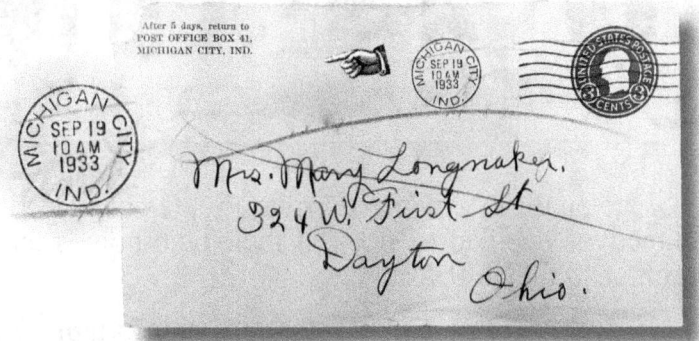

Seven days later, the inmate confined for life by iron bars, behind stone walls, under guard for murdering an innocent man, would breathe fresh air; a free man.

Imprisoned by assignment within the confines of a sleeping room – in stifling heat and miserably close quarters – Dayton Police Detective Sergeant Charles Gross and Detective Russell Pfauhl spent the better part of two to three weeks inside Lucille Stricker's boarding house without any luck.

It was a monotonous police stakeout post that continued day-after-day-after-day....

Mrs. Stricker's boarding house

Late on the afternoon of Friday, September 21, the detectives decided to sleep at their own homes that night... so they left.

It was overcast and a relatively comfortable 74 degrees outside. Det. Pfauhl would later recount his evening. He had flipped a newsboy a couple of pennies before arriving at his house on Salem Avenue near

Catalpa Drive. He was able to unwind from days of stakeouts by soaking in his bathtub. Later that evening he relaxed on his bed, reading the sports section.

Detective Russ Pfauhl called it a night ... but then his telephone rang.

Det. Russ Pfauhl

Sometime after midnight, in the tranquil early hours of September 22, 1933, the low engine rumble of an automobile echoed between houses at the rear of 324 W. First Street. A black Hudson Terraplane rolled in the alley and the engine cut off. Under cover of darkness, John Dillinger strolled up the porch steps from the quiet streets of Dayton.

The fugitive carried a Colt .38 Super auto pistol concealed on his waist beneath his coat. He held a satchel packed with more than $2,600 cash in "bills of small denomination" ($52,170 today).

Dillinger's Colt Super

The ever-observant Mrs. Stricker had seen the arrival of the gangster before he lightly rapped on the boarding house door. The landlady answered. When asked if Mary was there, she answered, "Yes, she's upstairs in her room, first door on the right." [78] The outlaw quietly ascended the steps.

Straight away, Mrs. Stricker's index finger spun the rotary dial six times to complete the telephone number – "ADams-1234" – connecting her to the police desk. Sgt. William Aldredge calmly answered, "Police."

By a quirk of fate, she had connected with the

officer on the police force who was most skilled in the use of firearms. She was very uneasy and highly anxious as she blurted, "He's here!"

Sgt. Aldredge: "Who's here?"

Mrs. Stricker: "John Dillinger, you God damn flatfoot!" [79]

Sgt. Aldredge immediately phoned Inspector Yendes, and then alerted patrol Captain Earl Yates. In turn, Sgt. Gross and Det. Pfauhl were telephoned by Capt. Yates who told them to "get down here right away, your man has showed up." [80]

Sgt. William Aldredge

Thanks to the installation of one-way radios almost a year to the day earlier, Capt. Yates was able to coordinate with the dispatch operator to broadcast instructions to police "radio cars" to position out of sight within proximity to the boarding house. Then the Captain held a relatively quick 45-minute briefing for some uniform officers at headquarters while an alerted Inspector Yendes notified Chief Rudy Wurstner.

Dayton Police
Captain Earl Yates

In short order, eight plainclothesmen and up to 32 uniformed officers had surrounded the area central to West First and North Perry Streets. The men waited for the arrival of Inspector Yendes.

Parking a block away, the Inspector did not see any officers in the darkness. He had thought about walking down an alley but realized, wearing a cap and sweater, he could startle a hidden officer who might yell out. Instead, Yendes strode the sidewalk across the street, actually passing the boarding house.

The local press later reported that "a shadow stepped from behind a tree. There was a gleam of metal and a click as a rifle came to an officer's shoulder and the hammer drew back." [81]

A patrolman's weapon, aimed at the figure in civilian attire, was pushed aside by another patrolman who firmly whispered, "Don't shoot! That's the Inspector."

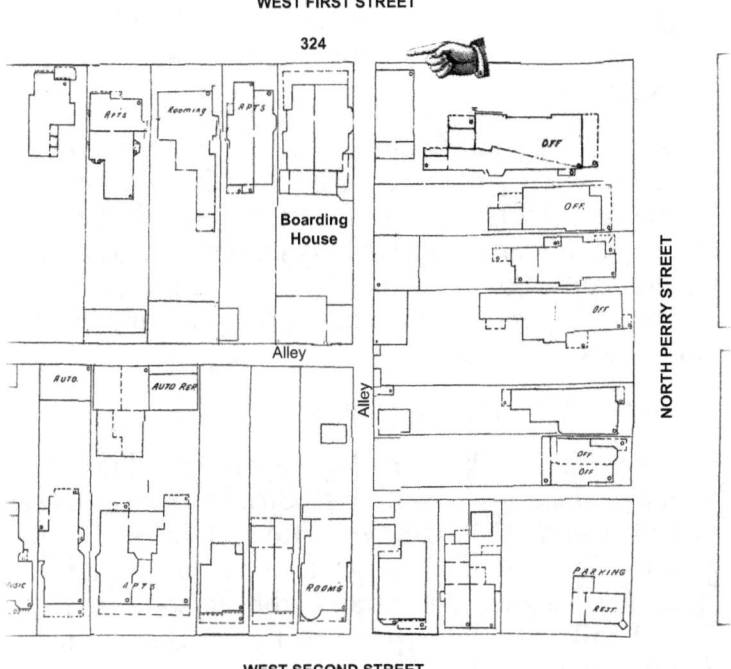

Now positioned, and with their commander's arrival to direct the team's movements, an offensive was about to occur. The Bank Flyer was certainly on the scene with its arsenal of weapons. A Tommy gun and a "short-hand" shotgun were used during this raid. The detectives wore bulletproof vests, secured in the armored Cadillac for such an occasion.

"Everyone wanted to get into the act," Det. Pfauhl recounted, "but Gross and I knew every nook and corner of the inside of that house, so we were the ones to go in." [82]

Directly outside, taking positions were Inspector Yendes, Capt. Yates, Sgt. Claude Cadot, Patrolmen Horace Moore and Ed McFadden as well as Patrolmen Albert Gaylor and Frank Hardesty. Inside and unaware, Dillinger was with Mary discussing their trip from two months earlier. As they looked at the photo snapshots taken at the World's Fair, the landlady met Det. Pfauhl, Sgt. Gross, and Sgt. Aldredge at the back door.

Mrs. Stricker softly mouthed, "He's up in the room now." [83] Sgt. Aldredge positioned himself inside on the first floor while Mrs. Stricker quietly led the other two officers up the thickly carpeted steps to her tenant's room on the second floor. Once there, and as planned, the landlady rapped on the door and called out, "Mary, can I talk to you?" [84]

Mary simply replied, "Sure."

When Longnaker cracked open the door, the police suddenly pushed past Stricker and barged into the room. Dillinger was sitting on the bed. The pictures flew out of his hands as the stunned fugitive stood up realizing that a trap had been sprung. Det. Pfauhl hollered, "John, police officers. Stick 'em up and face the wall." [85]

Dillinger at first brought his hands up toward his shoulders, but then lowered them in a feeble move toward a holster on his hip, stopping short when, as Det. Pfauhl later described, he jammed a short-hand shotgun into the fugitive's face insisting, "I'll kill you if you don't put them up." [86] Sgt. Gross did the same to the bandit's chest with his Colt Thompson submachine gun.

Dillinger froze, palms exposed, while Sgt. Charles Gross held aim at the fugitive. Det. Pfauhl frisked him for weapons as Sgt. Aldredge arrived upstairs and stood guard. Dillinger was found to have a sidearm in a hip holster and another auto pistol in a shoulder holster.

Det. Pfauhl, who had no interest in being gentle in his approach, contended, "I would have killed him. That shotgun would have blasted him right out of that room." [87] In an understatement, the outlaw observed, "You caught me off guard." He later said, "I would have been a damn fool to have pulled that gun." [88]

Mary Longnaker, who collapsed to the floor at Dillinger's feet, had pretended to faint from the tension. Det. Pfauhl yelled at her, "Mary, quit it. Stay right where you are," [89] until Sgt. Aldredge directed Mary to "crawl to the wall and put your hands up." [90]

The fugitive was told he was under arrest by Dayton police. Sgt. Gross ordered the bandit to place his hands behind his back. He was handcuffed.

Sgt. Gross' handcuffs placed on Dillinger

John Dillinger, alias John Hall, alias John Donavon, alias Frank Sullivan, was taken into police custody at 1:30 in the morning. It was his first arrest since paroled from the Indiana State Prison, and also the <u>first</u> <u>arrest</u> of Dillinger as a notorious gangster on the national scene.

Mary Longnaker cried as she, too, was taken from her rooming quarters into police custody. Claude Constable, who incredibly was elsewhere in the boarding house, was grabbed as well.

Through history, Dayton Police Detective Russ Pfauhl has often been singularly credited with the arrest even though it was clearly a team effort.

As Dillinger was walked out the building, he scanned the scene of heavily armed Dayton police officers and noted, "You fellows don't take any chances, do you?" to which an officer remarked, "Not with fellows like you, we don't." [91] Ptl. McFadden was instructed to drive a red unmarked police Chevrolet carrying the two detectives and Dillinger to headquarters.

Dayton police officers confiscated Dillinger's .38 Colt Super auto pistol, $2604 in cash, the 1933 Hudson Terraplane, three other .38 handguns, boxes of ammunition, papers, and a bag with eight pounds of roofing nails. One coded map the detectives knew were plans of some sort – possibly getaway routes from New Carlisle, they thought – but the meaning was not clear at that time. Five days later, its significance would become clearer.

Dillinger and the two boarders were transported to the Dayton Police Headquarters, located on the second floor of the old Market House on South Main Street. [92] There, prisoner No. 10587's mug shot and fingerprints were taken by the Dayton Bureau of Identification. Dillinger had committed no crime in Dayton, but he was a wanted fugitive in other cities. Longnaker was questioned and released. Her role was not deemed important to the matter at hand. Constable was questioned and released as well.

As Dillinger was seated under a harsh light in an interior room of the building, he noticed the detectives removing their bulletproof vests. He asked, "What are those things?" When told what they were and why they were worn, Dillinger smirked, "Hey, that sounds like a good idea. I'll have to get me some of those." [93]

Entrance to the Market House Police Headquarters *(left)* with the offices of the Detective Bureau & Bureau of Identification on the second floor.

Dillinger, interrogated primarily by Inspector Yendes in the company of Sgt. Gross and Det. Pfauhl, was uncooperative. More than that, he was a surly prisoner who ignored many questions posed by the detectives. The fugitive was mostly quiet but commented that he first thought the lawmen barging into the room were kidding. He then remarked, "I thought you were some of the boys [from a rival gang]. I can spot a cop and I didn't think you guys were cops." [94]

Under intense inquiry, the captured armed robber flippantly countered that he carried his life's savings in cash because he did not trust banks. And, he knew nothing about any bank holdups. Dillinger's reply to the detectives' many questions was:

"I want to call my lawyer." [95]

Sidebar: The Obscurity of the Dayton Police Takedown Team

There is no doubt that the life and crimes of John Dillinger have been recounted often in print and on film, but little is told about his arrest in Dayton, little is known about the items recovered, and virtually nothing is known about the takedown team.

In spite of being in the custody of law enforcement officials many times – the Indiana State Prison, Montgomery County Jail (OH), Allen County Jail (OH), Lake County Jail (IN) – often overlooked is the fact that the notorious bank robber Dillinger was tracked down and arrested by police only <u>twice</u> in his criminal career. The first time was by the **Dayton Police Department** in 1933, and the second time was by the Tucson Police Department (AZ) in 1934. He turned himself in at Mooresville. Chicago is a story to come....

This is an early and deserved, but brief postscript on the careers of the five lawmen who apprehended John Dillinger.

Inspector Seymour E. 'Cy' Yendes: Appointed to the police force in 1906, he became the City of Dayton Public Safety Director in 1937, and retired in 1941 after a 33-year career. Five years later he opened a private detective agency.

Captain Earl S. Yates: Appointed to the police force in 1907, he retired in 1944 after a 37½-year career, making him the 19th longest-serving law officer in Dayton history (spanning 1797 to present).

Sgt. William J. 'Joe' Aldredge: Appointed to the police force in 1922, he rose to the rank of Captain, and retired in 1947 after a 25-year career to become the Mound Laboratory Chief of Police.

Sgt. Charles E. 'Tony' Gross: Appointed to the police force in 1917, he retired in 1944 after a 25-year career. There are no known public statements from him about the arrest of Dillinger but his handcuffs, placed on the bandit, are in the Wright State University archive collection.

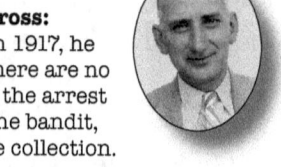

Det. Russell K. 'Russ' Pfauhl: Appointed to the police force in 1919, he retired in 1947 at the rank of sergeant after a 27-year career. He opened his own private detective agency which operated until 1976.

The bandit, taken into Dayton police custody while looking at snapshots, is ironically soon photographed by Dayton's Bureau of Identification, fingerprinted, and then interrogated by Dayton detectives.

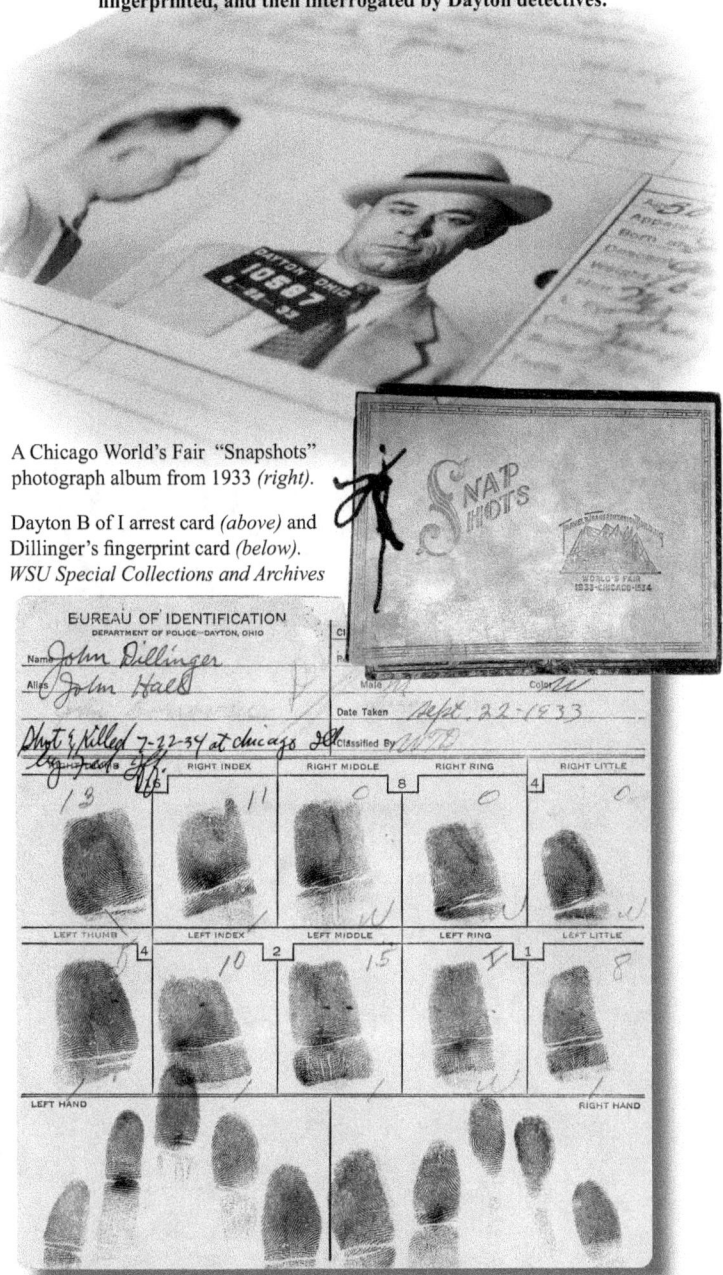

A Chicago World's Fair "Snapshots" photograph album from 1933 *(right).*

Dayton B of I arrest card *(above)* and Dillinger's fingerprint card *(below).*
WSU Special Collections and Archives

CHAPTER 8

CAGED – CAGED – CAGED – CONVEYED

September 22, 1933: The fugitive John Dillinger, alias John Hall, was
arrested by Dayton police detectives and booked in the city jail.
Wright State Universtiy Special Collections and Archives

Circa 1933: Downtown Dayton looking north from Fifth Street toward the Court Houses.

Ptl. Everett Plummer *(right)* ticketing an automobile near the Court Houses

JAIL CELLS – When John Dillinger was taken into custody by Dayton police detectives on Friday, September 22, 1933, he was in a jail cell and in a fix. He needed sage and shrewd legal counsel. The bandit's Chicago connections provided the local choice – **John E. 'Jack' Egan**. Born in Middletown, Ohio in 1873, Jack began his career as a newspaper reporter, first with *The Middletown Daily Signal* (near Hamilton) and then *The Lima News*. He switched his career choice by attending college up north. He graduated from the University of Michigan Law School where he was the senior president, and played guard on the Wolverine football team.

The now experienced lawyer had been in practice since 1899, representing local clients such as murderers Charles 'Dayton Slim' Stimmel and Al Fouts as well as the "king and queen of bootleggers," John and Mary Friend. Often aiding underworld characters, he had law practices in both the cities of Dayton and Chicago.

John E. 'Jack' Egan

He was the perfect attorney of record for this bank-robbing gangster.

Dillinger remained at the Market House Police Headquarters for the time being. When he was taken to his holding cell, Dillinger pronounced, "You can't keep me. My gang is around here and they will get me out," to which Sgt. Aldredge replied:

"We're putting an officer on these steps. If your gang come for you, his orders are to shoot you first." [96]

Inspector Yendes knew theirs was a rare and precarious catch. Gang members Homer Van Meter, and Harry Copeland were subjects of Ohio and Indiana manhunts and treacherous.

The Inspector emphasized to news reporters that he had *"officers armed with rifles and shotguns ... throughout headquarters ... to meet any possible attempt by confederates to free the prisoner."* [97] [emphasis added]

Late Friday morning, after unsuccessful questioning at the police headquarters, the fugitive was conveyed in the back of Ptl. Thomas Dunlavey's "Black Maria" police paddy wagon to a second jail cell located at the Dayton Central Police Station, also known as the "Ford Street Station." [98] Booked in the city jail, Dillinger was posed the standard questions and when asked his occupation, he said:

Dayton Police "Black Maria"

"I'm a farmer." [99]

It was not long for word to spread to police authorities throughout the Midwest of Dillinger's capture. That very first morning, Muncie Police Chief Frank Massie, along with Delaware County Deputy Lester Corn, arrived in Dayton to argue for Dillinger's return to Indiana to face charges. Morrow County Sheriff Fred Struble of Mount Gilead, Ohio escorted the Cardington Bank cashier, Edward Willits, to view Dillinger regarding a July 14 robbery.

Clark County Deputy Sheriff Arthur Shuman brought the New Carlisle Bank cashier, Carl Enoch, to look at Dillinger. He could only say Dillinger resembled a bandit he saw. Sgt. Gross and Det. Pfauhl were with all and filed reports on these meetings.

Entrance to the Dayton Central Police Station and City Jail, known as the "Ford Street Station."

Indiana State Police Captain Matt Leach, along with State Investigators Claude Dozier and Harvey Hire, also arrived on the first day.

In the spirit of cooperation, Inspector Yendes allowed the lawmen to conduct ballistic comparison with a bullet taken from the body of a murdered La Crosse, Indiana bank cashier (the tests were reported as negative a few days later). He also allowed the state investigators to interview Dillinger.

Det. Pfauhl showed the agents from Indiana the recovered letters and map. The Dayton detective speculated that the diagram may be plans for an escape from the Indiana State Prison. The Captain, known to have an arrogant tone, scoffed that Pfauhl "had been reading too many detective magazines" [100] insinuating that Dillinger was not of the caliber to pull off a plot that outlandish.

When Leach abruptly reconsidered and demanded the papers, Yendes had enough and ordered the Captain out of his office. Yendes then called Detective Hire back into the room and told him that he, and not Leach, was welcome to have any papers he needed for the Indiana investigations.

This episode initiated what later became a public rift between Yendes and Leach. Indiana, which had five banks assailed and wanted Dillinger extradited to the state, had not made a good impression with the appearance of its state police captain.

The word of Dillinger's arrest most definitely spread to the press and the local papers reported events daily. Chief Rudy Wurstner wanted the kind of news coverage that the arrest of a highly-sought, four-state bank robber would bring to the Dayton Police Department. Inspector Yendes was to become the face of the investigation. He provided a B of I photograph to the *Dayton Daily News* for publication.

As much as the suspect himself was wanted nationwide, so was his photograph. Over the course of the next few months, official letters and telegrams were received from police departments in Indiana, Michigan, Kentucky, California, Florida, and around Ohio requesting his fingerprints and his Dayton police mug shot (now and forever infamous).

On Friday evening, Inspector Yendes himself appeared in the *Dayton Daily News* proudly exhibiting on his desk all that was seized – "money, guns, shells" – as he held the Colt .38 Super taken from Dillinger. The caption:

Examines Guns Found in Suspect's Room

There were four guns depicted in total. He told reporters that the police also recovered "detailed notes explaining the speediest ways to escape from various cities."

Sidebar: Arrest Report – A Portrait of Ambiguities and Omissions

The Dayton Police "Report of Arrest" on the capture of **John Dillinger** is confounding. It is handwritten, not typed, and should have been completed on the day of arrest; however, it briefly relates the October 12, 1933 events in Allen County. Since the last two sentences of the report do not look to be added on, it leaves the impression that this was executed at least three weeks after the fact. Dillinger was taken into custody for being a fugitive and not for a Dayton crime. It could be that the report was initially deemed as unnecessary.

The Arrest Report is very brief. It mentions **Homer Van Meter** and **Harry Copeland** as wanted, but does not offer any details on how the arrest took place, or the disposition of the items seized, including the Essex Terraplane. It does not identify where the guns were recovered (in the room or in the car). It only describes the guns as .38 auto pistols without providing any serial numbers. And it mentions there being only three guns when photographic evidence depicts four guns.

Much of what can be gleaned about the actual arrest is from press reports, some of which quote first-hand witnesses. **The finding of facts is a challenge:** Accounts are limited in scope and there are discrepancies to sift through. The number of guns have been reported to be as few as three and as many as six. **Det. Russell Pfauhl** himself identified the guns as "revolvers" when they are all semi-automatic handguns. There has always been the supposition that a "Dillinger Tommy gun" was seized. There is no evidence that a submachine gun was confiscated.

There is one picture of a display, presumably, of all that was seized by police. It appeared in the *Dayton Daily News* the day of the arrest. It shows Inspector Yendes sitting at a desk that exhibits money, guns, nails, and shells. There are two semi-auto handguns on the desk and two in the Inspector's hands to total four. If there was a Colt Thompson, it would have been shown, or listed in a report, or described in a news article. This photo is the best record.

The "**Dillinger Tommy gun**" that police officers often contend was taken from the bandit is very likely lore. The Tommy gun held by **Sgt. Charles Gross** at the time of apprehension was used for police training over many decades thereafter. In all probability, it was called 'the Dillinger Tommy gun' and the characterization became misconstrued with the passing of time.

Inspector Seymour Yendes

Police were aware for seven weeks that Dillinger was in the area. "He was probably planning a bank robbery here," [101] said Yendes.

When later asked what was to happen with Dillinger, Yendes said that he "will be turned over to the city where the best case can be made." New Carlisle really wanted the bandit and planned to bring bank bookkeeper, Horace Grisso, on Sunday morning to identify Dillinger.

As the following week unfolded, Indianapolis, Bluffton, and Farrell, Pennsylvania also became front runners to win this prize catch.

John Dillinger was kept in the Dayton City Jail the remainder of Friday and then overnight. Chief Wurstner was determined to thwart any possible escape by the fugitive. He authorized a contingent of uniformed officers, including Patrolmen Bryan Hock, Everett Plummer, and Lee Eyer, to be on post around the clock, *"cradling submachine guns in their arms."* [102] [emphasis added]

Ptl. Eyer was detailed to special duty from 7:30 to 10:30 in the evening recording the license plate numbers of suspicious cars traveling near the station house. He submitted his report to the Chief.

As Det. Pfauhl later said, "We didn't want any of his boys trying to spring him." [103]

Attorney Jack Egan filed a petition with the County Common Pleas Court on Friday for a writ of habeas corpus contending, of course, that Dillinger was being unlawfully deprived of his liberty and should be released.

Habeas Corpus, Montgomery County Court: "John Dillinger vs. Rudolph Wurstner, Chief of Police…, Seymour E. Yendes, Chief of Detectives of the Police Department…, and all other Police Officers and Stationhouse Keepers of the city of Dayton."

"We command you that the body of John Dillinger and all effects taken from him and belonging to him, save and excepts certain guns, by [named parties]… imprisoned and restrained of his liberty as it is said… [have said parties] to appear in this court to show the cause of the taking and detention of said John Dillinger." Signed by Judge Patterson.

The hearing was set to be in front of Judge Robert Patterson for Saturday morning, September 23.

The Montgomery County Jail fronted by the Sheriff's Office.

That very day, heavily-armed officers accompanied Ptl. Thomas Dunlavey's "Black Maria" paddy wagon in transporting Dillinger to the third cell in which he would be held by police... this time inside the Montgomery County Jail. [104] He was turned over to the custody of Sheriff Eugene Frick from this point forward.

A weekend headline in *The Dayton Journal* set the tone of press coverage in the upcoming week:

DILLINGER LINKED WITH OHIO BANK HOLDUPS AND IDENTIFIED AS INDIANAPOLIS ROBBER

Dillinger stewed in the Montgomery County Jail as employees from banks in three states were brought in to look at the fugitive. The outlaw stared with the dirtiest scowl at every witness in an effort to intimidate them from identifying him as the ringleader of bandits who held-up their banks.

Dillinger was suspected as the gang leader who robbed banks in New Carlisle and Bluffton, Ohio; Farrell, Pennsylvania; Gravel Switch, Kentucky, and four Indiana cities: Muncie, Daleville, Indianapolis, and Montpelier as well as the Rockville attempt. The take from these eight banks totaled $69,800 ($1.4 million today).

Authorities from several of these cities, upon learning of Dillinger's arrest, began requesting the suspect be turned over to them for trial, including the Indianapolis Police Department. After the morning hearing next door in Common Pleas Court, Judge Patterson ordered Dillinger remain in custody, without setting any bail, until the resumption of the hearing the following Saturday. This gave police agencies time to get witnesses to identify the suspect and prepare warrants.

Old Court House alongside the "New" Court House

That same morning, Chief Wurstner sent a Western Union telegram to Indianapolis Police Chief Michael Morrissey: "Hearing of John Dillinger Set for September Thirtieth at Ten AM. Demands Extradition." The telegram was received.

On the very same day, Chief Morrissey wrote a letter to Inspector Yendes. He thanked him for the treatment given to Detectives Emmet Englebright and Ernest Whitsett the day before when they met with

Dayton detectives to interview Dillinger. He also referenced the long-distance telephone conversation Yendes had with Chief of Detectives Fred Simon. A capias was enclosed for Dillinger and an assurance that they would be in court on September 30.

The local newspapers reported the following day (Sunday) that arrest warrants were forthcoming from Indianapolis as well as New Carlisle. (Bookkeeper Horace Grisso said that he could tell that Dillinger recognized him; peculiarly, not the other way around.)

Mary Longnaker

Over the weekend, Mary Longnaker had tried to visit her Johnnie at the Montgomery County Jail but he was in isolation and was allowed no visitors.

Mary reflected on what had happened to her and her Johnnie early Friday morning. On Monday, September 25, Mary wrote him a letter saying, in part:

"Hello Honey:

"I thot if I couldn't see you I could write to you. I love you Johnnie. Don't forget I'll always be thinking of you.... You remember you asked me to marry you. *[sic]* I am still willing to marry you if I had my divorce. I didn't know how much you meant to me. Just when I can't have you. [...]

"I guess my divorce won't come up until next week. It is going to be contested. But I guess it all goes in life. His bringing up everything he can think of. Well Darling, I must close and go get something to eat. See you Sat.

"Loads of Love. Your sweetheart. Mary."

Was this genuine love or simply concern that Mary's regular source of funding was drying up? Or could it be that Mary was attempting to cover a sin? Inspector Cy Yendes would later say that during his interview of Dillinger, the bandit believed Mary had set him up to be nabbed by the police. Did Johnnie believe he had been betrayed, or was he simply venting on the night of his arrest?

Mary addressed the envelope containing her letter: "Mr. John Dillinger, % County Jail, Dayton, Ohio | % Sheriff Frick." The Sheriff received the letter; Dillinger did  not, at least not right away. It would go with his effects wherever he landed after the next court proceeding.

That same day local newspapers underscored conditions as stated by Inspector Yendes three days earlier ... that Dillinger was at the Montgomery County Jail *"under heavy guard following his removal from the city police station house."* [105] [emphasis added]

Sheriff Frick had Dillinger placed in a cell on the second floor and the gate at the jail entrance tightly secured.

Montgomery County Sheriff Eugene Frick

Yet, one evening, Deputy Sheriff Fred Parsons was approached by a strange man who came to that gate leading to the jail. Not identifying himself, the suspicious man asked to see Dillinger in his cell. When he was refused entry by the deputy, who held his hand on his pistol, the man hurried away toward a second man standing outside the screen door leading to the jail lobby. Moments later, the man returned with his hand covering his mouth claiming that he had been punched.

When this did not cause Deputy Parsons – who was described in the newspaper as a "Negro deputy" [106] – to open the barred door, the man dropped his hand from his mouth and reached though the bars saying, "Well, we can at least shake hands." At that point, Deputy Parsons ordered the man to leave… which he did.

Montgomery County Deputy Fred Parsons

This peculiar and troubling episode reinforced for local law enforcement to remain alert and on guard ... and with good reason.

As a number of jurisdictions filed court papers in an effort to gain custody of John Dillinger, on Tuesday, September 26, his gang was preparing to make its move in the Indiana State Prison in Michigan City. Using plans many believe were devised by Dillinger, as well as the weapons he had smuggled into the prison, there was a mass escape of convicts, including his former cell mate and Longnaker's brother, Jim Jenkins.

While Dillinger resided behind bars in Dayton, 10 of his gang broke out of the Michigan City penitentiary. They split into two groups. In only two weeks, five of those inmates would reunite with their now incarcerated liberator.

As the Indiana manhunt for the prison escapees took place, Chief Wurstner, knowing that Jim Jenkins was one of the inmates, immediately sent a letter to Mr. Walter Daly, the prison warden. He advised that when Dillinger was arrested, a letter was in his possession that named Jenkins' father, and his Kansas City address. That information was passed on. At the same time, Inspector Yendes promptly informed Sheriff Frick of the local connection of this one particular inmate.

Jim Jenkins,
the gang's link to
Dillinger in Dayton!

The fact that Mary Longnaker's brother was one of the escapees gave the local press several story lines on Wednesday, September 27; the headline in *The Dayton Journal*:

DILLINGER LINKED WITH DESPERADOES

Would Jim Jenkins direct the gang to Dayton "in a desperate attempt" to free Dillinger? Sheriff Frick assured the press that "every precaution" had been taken. *The Dayton Herald* reported the Sheriff stressing that his *"deputies were heavily armed and the night force was doubled, with all other deputies 'on call' for the night."* [107] [emphasis added]

Had Dillinger been informed of the prison break? The Sheriff said he had not, and he would not allow anyone to do so. There would be no visitors, and that included meddlesome newspapermen.

The more interesting storyline involved Indiana State Police Captain Matt Leach. Less than a week earlier, he had derided the notion by Detective Russ Pfauhl – that the papers seized from Dillinger might be escape plans – a suggestion witnessed by Inspector Yendes and Sgt. Charles Gross. And, this was an account that was backed by Forrest Huntington, an Indiana state investigator. [108]

The press, in learning that the papers seized from Dillinger had been offered to Capt. Leach, began asking about them. In a face-saving effort after the escape, the Captain professed that the jail break might have been prevented had the maps been provided sooner by the Dayton Police Department. Furious, Inspector Yendes refuted the charges lodged by Capt. Leach, insisting that the Indiana State Police had access to all of the documents.

Yendes was out-publicized. Although Dayton readers were interested in the escape, their level of attention was less than that of the Indiana public which was more vested in the matter.

Leach relentlessly assigned blame to Yendes, but in the end Leach's reputation held him less credible. Historical accounts have carried the truth pertaining to the root of the quarrel. What historians have never uncovered are: 1) when the papers actually ended up in Leach's hands and 2) what the papers ("maps") actually were.

They vanished over time.

Whether the maps were coded routes for the Indiana State Prison fugitives once outside the walls, or something other, the inmates were on the run and indebted to John Dillinger. They had split into two bands. One group, which included Jim Jenkins, was intent on reuniting with their now caged rescuer who happened to be in Dayton, Ohio. In addition to these escapees, others in Dillinger's gang prior to his arrest – Copeland, Van Meter, and get-away driver Hilton Crouch – were still dangerously on the loose.

All posed serious threats to local law enforcement. Thanks to daily newspapers, all of these gangsters were well aware of Dillinger's location and circumstances.

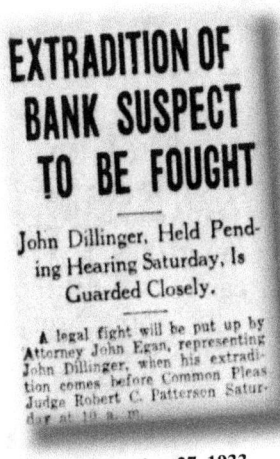

EXTRADITION OF BANK SUSPECT TO BE FOUGHT

John Dillinger, Held Pending Hearing Saturday, Is Guarded Closely.

A legal fight will be put up by Attorney John Egan, representing John Dillinger, when his extradition comes before Common Pleas Judge Robert C. Patterson Saturday at 10 a. m.

September 27, 1933
Dayton Daily News

In Dayton, news reports had begun to say that Dillinger was being held pending his return to Indianapolis to face bank robbery charges. Although Clark County filed charges, New Carlisle fell out of the picture because its case was weaker than the others. The drive for Dillinger's extradition had been reduced to three jurisdictions, each from an individual state – Bluffton and Indianapolis had a rival in Farrell, Pennsylvania.

This third reasonable possibility was announced under a headline in *The Dayton Journal*:

DILLINGER LINKED WITH BANK THEFT IN PENNSYLVANIA

Even though Pennsylvania bank robbery victims traveled to Dayton on Wednesday and readily identified Dillinger, the article below this Thursday morning headline still made Indiana the odds-on favorite. It related that Dillinger "is to be returned to Indianapolis for the robbery of the Massachusetts Avenue State bank September 6." Bluffton, Ohio was not even mentioned in the newspaper story.

While Indiana and Pennsylvania authorities prepared for the scheduled Saturday extradition hearing, Allen County officials made clear to their Dayton and Montgomery County counterparts during the early week that they wanted John Dillinger to stand for arraignment on the Bluffton, Ohio bank robbery ... and it had the necessary paperwork in order.

Local criminal attorney Jack Egan, the man with a Chicago law office, had his local office on the eighth floor of the downtown Schwind Building. The 11-story "tower" was located at 27 S. Ludlow Street (this same building once held the office of the Dayton Women's Suffrage headquarters before becoming the Dayton League of Women Voters). Egan easily walked the half block to meet with his client in the Montgomery County Jail.

Circa 1933: Ludlow at Fifth Street with view toward Third Street.

Schwind Building directly below

As much as Sheriff Frick did to suppress outside news from his prisoner, there is little doubt that Egan informed Dillinger of the Michigan City escape, and of the three cities vying for his custody.

After the shrewd attorney and his cunning client consulted, Egan managed to gain an audience with the presiding judge, Robert Patterson, on Thursday, September 28. In chambers, the attorney conferred with Judge Patterson. Egan saw the landscape for what it was. He would no longer argue that Dillinger was being held without just cause. Allen County had a valid warrant, and Bluffton was in Ohio. So, by God, Egan now believed the Common Pleas Court should send his accused client to a county within the state.

An agreement was hatched with the court to extradite Dillinger to Lima to face arraignment for a relatively meager $2,100 Citizens National Bank robbery. This over the not-yet-argued positions of out-of-state officials seeking transfer to Indianapolis for the $24,800 Massachusetts State Bank holdup, or to Farrell, Pennsylvania for the $14,000 S.J. Gully Bank robbery. The court decision was sudden and Allen County Sheriff Jess Sarber, who had picked up Al Fouts two years earlier, was again prompt when called in arriving in Dayton.

Indiana and Pennsylvania authorities had prepared for a Saturday morning hearing, so the Thursday morning ruling took both off guard ... although Pennsylvania State Police Captain Jasper Oftedahl, upon hearing that a decision was made, wrote a letter that very day to Chief Wurstner asking for the date of transfer to "the State of Indiana," assuming that it had to be there. Indiana, he knew, had at least four banks robbed including the huge Indianapolis heist.

Jack Egan believed the move of his client to Lima to be legally and personally advantageous. Even though Bluffton was a viable aspirant, and could be rationalized, Judge Patterson's ruling seemed perplexing to some and begged questions:

Was the real risk of attracting Dillinger's gang the incentive for Dayton authorities to hurriedly rid itself of this menace? Did the private investigators of the

Bluffton bank robbery from the Pinkerton's Detective Agency exert some influence over this matter? Did Indiana State Police Captain Leach so incense Inspector Cy Yendes that no Indiana city would get custody?

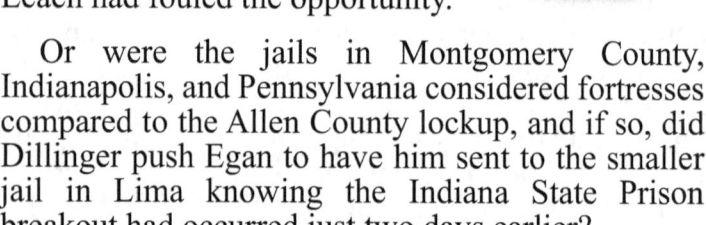

Indianapolis Police Chief Morrissey believed Captain Leach had fouled the opportunity.

Or were the jails in Montgomery County, Indianapolis, and Pennsylvania considered fortresses compared to the Allen County lockup, and if so, did Dillinger push Egan to have him sent to the smaller jail in Lima knowing the Indiana State Prison breakout had occurred just two days earlier?

Members of the press were stunned by the decision as much as police officials. *The Dayton Herald* press reporter Larry Andrews made a beeline to the Montgomery County Jail as soon as he heard that law enforcement from Lima was there to pick up the fugitive. John Dillinger had been incarcerated in Dayton for one week when Sheriff Sarber arrived at one o'clock in the afternoon.

Circa 1933: Downtown Dayton's Motor Car District 330 block of So. Main Street

The police had already released Dillinger's Hudson Terraplane and the cash to Jack Egan. The attorney ensured the automobile was placed in the care of his client's younger brother Hubert Dillinger.

Although some of the other confiscated items – guns and ammunition – were placed in the custody of Allen County, the money was not. The oddity of the fast-unfolded events that day motivated *The Herald* reporter to dig a little deeper into it.

Larry Andrews contacted Judge Patterson, and in gently questioning the court ruling, was advised that Dillinger stayed in Ohio because no charges had been filed in time by Indiana authorities while Allen County officials produced an arrest warrant.

Judge
Robert
Patterson

Montgomery County could not continue to hold the man without bringing charges, the judge reasoned.

When asked, the judge said he was unaware about the disposition of the cash seized from Dillinger.

The reporter had to admit to himself that there seemed to be solid grounds for the court's ruling.

Still feeling that something untoward was afoot – particularly after the press reporter learned that the $2,604 had been turned over by Montgomery County to Jack Egan – Andrews telephoned the attorney and they had the following exchange: [109]

Andrews: "You got [Dillinger's cash]? I don't understand. Wasn't that money supposed to be held for Indiana authorities as evidence in the Indianapolis bank robbery?

Egan: "I was paid that money for my fee."

Andrews: "Fee for what?"

Egan (irritated): "Legal services. I got him transferred to Allen County where I will represent him on a false charge of bank robbery. I will also oppose any extradition proceedings if they are brought by Indiana."

Attorney Jack Egan

Andrews: "But the money was evidence."

Egan (riled): "No one can prove that. We will insist it was his life's savings."

Andrews (persisting): "But some of those packages of currency were strapped with the Indianapolis bank wrappers!"

Montgomery County Jail alongside the Old Court House and new Court House.

Egan: "Never saw anything like that!" The phone went dead. End of story.

Having received a court ruling by a Montgomery County judge, Dillinger was prepared by turnkeys for conveyance north to stand trial for the Bluffton holdup. Allen County Sheriff Jess Sarber had arrived with two deputies.

Dayton Bureau of Identification photograph of John Dillinger.
Released to the press on the morning of the gangster's arrest.
Wright State University Special Collections and Archives

Dayton police officers were concerned that the Sheriff was not sufficiently appreciative of the danger John Dillinger and his gang posed, or as attentive to his custody as he should have been.

Years later, in an interview, Det. Russell Pfauhl recounted, "I tried to explain to the sheriff that this wasn't an ordinary criminal but Sarber just said, 'He's just another punk.'" [110]

The Allen County Sheriff got behind the wheel while one deputy sat next to him and the other deputy sat next to Dillinger in the back seat.

Sgt. Aldredge cautioned one of the deputies, "You won't get him there by yourself. He has gang members that will ambush you." [111]

Over the course of three days in Dayton, Ohio, John Dillinger was transported to and caged inside three jail

Dillinger's "limo" on two of three occasions.

Police Emegency No. 1 – Dayton PD's "Black Maria" paddy wagon.

cells at three separate locations – the Market House Police Headquarters, followed by the City Jail, and then the County Jail where he was isolated for six days.

In all three cases, Chief Wurstner and Sheriff Frick had the fugitive under tight security. They authorized extra police guards armed with shotguns and Tommy guns, as Inspector Yendes said, "to meet any possible attempt by confederates to free the prisoner."

After addressing the downside to traveling in a single car back to Lima, Chief Wurstner authorized a Dayton police escort using its armored Cadillac, the Bank Flyer, driven by Ptl. 'Big Frank' Johnson.

"Flying Squadron" motorman, Ptl. Frank Johnson, with the Bank Flyer.
Courtesy of Carolyn J. Burns, granddaughter.

Joining Ptl. Johnson's "land battleship" was a second wing car. In the caravan was a Montgomery County squad assigned by Sheriff Eugene Frick, under the supervision of Chief Deputy Sheriff Charles Hannabery. Both vehicles carried uniformed lawmen armed with shotguns and Tommy guns.

The motorcade traveled to Troy, Ohio. [112] There the escort met up with its northern counterpart: two Lima police cars carrying Chief John Cook, three of his police officers, the Sheriff's son, Deputy Don Sarber, and an Allen County investigator, Julius Callahan.

All heavily armed, these lawmen took over the protective detail for the remainder of the trip up north to ensure that this bank bandit would face justice.

The police transport of the outlaw, John H. Dillinger, to the County Jail in Lima, Ohio was without incident.

CHAPTER 9

OUTLAWS ON THE LAM – LAWMEN ON THEIR TRAIL

September 26, 1933: While Van Meter and Copeland roamed free, Makley, Pierpont, Clark, Hamilton and six other inmates broke out of prison. Transit Wanted Cards.
Allen County Museum and Historical Society

LAWMEN ON THEIR TRAIL

While the leaders of their respective law enforcement agencies – Dayton Police **Chief Rudy Wurstner** and FBI **Director J. Edgar Hoover** – exhibited their crime-fighting weaponry as an outlaw warning, public fascination with *"Famous Gangsters"* fueled their notoriety and pulp magazine publications.

"Crime Never Pays" was not heeded by **John Dillinger** and **Charley Makley**

MANHUNTS – John Dillinger was booked into the Allen County jail late in the afternoon of Thursday, September 28. He would face arraignment for the August 14 bank robbery in Bluffton, located 10 miles north of Lima.

Sheriff Jess Sarber had been made aware of Dillinger's buddies. He reported to the local press that they might try to spring him so the outlaw was placed under tight guard.

Many of those buddies were inmates that had escaped from the Indiana State Prison just after one o'clock in the afternoon two days earlier.

Indiana State Prison – Tuesday, September 26, 1933

Although frenetic in execution, Dillinger's scheme worked as planned. A bribed shirt delivery trucker arrived at the prison dock. Boxes were unloaded and taken into a prison shirt factory overseen by a single guard. Unbeknownst to him, some of the boxes were marked, indicating smuggled weapons inside.

On cue, several convicts with Dillinger ties collected the weapons and overtook the guard. He was then walked in the lead as a ruse that the filed trek was a work detail.

The other inmates in on the plan gathered together and armed themselves. The 10 inmates carried shirts to conceal the guns as they crossed the rainy prison yard and then through several gates. Making it to the administrative offices, they succeeded by locking the warden and employees in a vault and taking flight.

In the last rush to freedom, one clerk was shot and another beaten. Outside the front of the prison walls, some of the escapees overtook the car of Harrison

Indiana State Prison in Michigan City
Front Entrance

County Sheriff Charles Neel, abducting him with it, while the other cons jumped into another car.

Ten inmates sped away in the most daring and largest prison escape in Indiana history.

The alarm was sounded and a police manhunt began. Walter Dietrich, John Burns, Joseph Fox, and James Clark headed toward Chicago with the Sheriff as a hostage.

Harry 'Pete' Pierpont, Charles 'Charley' Makley, Russell Clark, John 'Red' Hamilton, Ed Shouse, and Jim Jenkins headed south to an Indianapolis hideout. Even though six of these 10 escapees comprised a core group, in fact the "Dillinger gang" was a fluid collection of like-minded criminals.

Gangsters already in Dillinger's fold were Harry Copeland, Homer Van Meter, and Hilton Crouch, among others. And joining Dillinger later were Tommy Carroll, Lester Gillis (aka Baby Face Nelson), Eddie Green, and John Paul Chase.

The connection Dillinger and his gang members had with St. Paul – Homer Van Meter and Eddie Green were from that city – fostered intermingling with the Karpis-Barker Gang. The breadth of unleashed hoodlums into society was certain to trigger mayhem and target lawmen who dared to recapture them.

But recapture or death would be their fate, although not before they became the scourge of the Great Depression era.

———————

On the lam, and having held Sheriff Neel kidnapped for three days, Dietrich, Burns, and Fox decided to shed themselves of burdensome cargo ... the Sheriff and fellow inmate James Clark were suffering stomach illnesses. Both were dumped on Friday, September 29 near Hobart, Indiana as the others sped off. Sheriff Neel was an incredibly lucky lawman. Clark was recaptured that evening and returned to the state prison where he served out his lifetime sentence.

The same Friday, in a hideaway on the west side of Indianapolis, Pierpont, Makley, Russell Clark, Hamilton, Shouse, and Jenkins were met after two days by Harry Copeland. They learned of Dillinger's incarceration in Dayton and transfer to Lima just a few days earlier (making Jenkins less needed). Copeland arranged a hideout for the gang in Hamilton, Ohio; they split into two groups and headed southeast.

Copeland, Hamilton, and Shouse took off in one car; Pierpont, Jenkins, Makley and Clark in the other.

Pierpont was a ruthless gang leader... and he did not like Jenkins – not one bit! He never wanted him to be part of the escape but had yielded to Dillinger's insistence.

Harry Pierpont

As Pierpont's band reached the community of Ben Davis, five miles west of Indianapolis, their stolen sedan was spotted by the Indiana State Police. A hot pursuit ensued. Suddenly, either by accident or maybe as bait, Jenkins was thrown from the chased car as it rounded a corner and then sped south at 80 miles per hour.

As Pierpont's sedan eluded police, Mary Longnaker's brother fled through a field, chased on foot by the law. He was able to dodge capture and then abduct at gunpoint the driver of another car.

Heading south to Bloomington and turning east to Nashville, Indiana, Jenkins' commandeered auto was low on gas. As the abductor inanely walked from the car to look for a gas station attendant the victim wisely sped away. It was about 2:30 in the morning.

Escapee Jim Jenkins

Soon, police throughout Brown County learned of Jenkins, and formed posses comprised of lawmen and farmers. Now, back on foot and tired, Jenkins laid low. But he was spotted Saturday evening, September 30, in Beansbottom, Indiana near a roadside cinder-block grocery store attached to a framed house.

Beanblossom Storekeeper Shot in Arm; Convict Dies En-route to Hospital

---

CAR THEFTS REPORTED

Sheriff Neel, Held Prisoner for Four Days, Enlarges Upon First Story

---

The stranger in the town was cautiously approached by the store owner and two farmers armed with double-barreled shotguns. Pulling a .38 revolver, Jenkins fired once, wounding the store owner by grazing his arm.

Sadly for Mary Longnaker, and few others, her brother Jim was mortally wounded from a return shotgun blast that blew away the side of his head as he ran. James Joseph Jenkins died an hour later. On either side of his prison term Jenkins had – in odd irony – bloody, deadly encounters with grocers.

Jenkin's body was returned to Bedford, Indiana for services the following Tuesday. Curiously, the town mayor, Henry Murray, and Police Chief Mahlon Rainboldt served as his pallbearers. He was buried in a family plot at Beech Grove Cemetery.

October 4 1933 newspaper articles
The Indianapolis Sunday Star

October 4, 1933 newspaper article
The Indianapolis Star

While in the Allen County jail, John Dillinger was given Mary's September 25 letter. It had been transferred from Dayton to Lima with his belongings. He read Mary's expression of love that said, in part:

> "Hello Honey: You remember you asked me to marry you. I am still willing to marry you.... I didn't know how much you meant to me. Just when I can't have you. [...] Loads of Love. Your sweetheart. Mary." *[sic]*

Sitting alone in his cell on October 1, Johnnie also read the tragic Sunday newspaper report about the killing of his former cellmate the day before. His thoughts were now on his Dayton gal, sweet Mary Longnaker.

Allen County Sheriff residence fronting the Jail and next to the Courts Building

So he tenderly wrote a long letter to her that said:

"Dearest Mary,

"I just read in the paper of Jimmys death and I know you must be heartbroken. I feel for you dear for I know how much you cared for each other, and I can understand your grief because Jimmy was the only real friend and Pal I had outside my family and I loved him like a brother. Honey this old world has delt you some heavy blows. I wish I were free so I could take you away and make you happy the least I can expect is ten years. *[sic]*

"Sweetheart if I had known two months ago that you would ever care enough about me to marry me I would have gotten a job somehow for I could enjoy working for a girl like you and having a home. Do you think I have enjoyed myself allways on the go, no place I could call home. I expect you were surprised to hear I was sent to Lima weren't you? I wish you would send me the pictures we had taken at the worlds fair. I will allways keep thems in remembrance of you. Darling I wont write you any more, I want you to forget me for ten years or more is a to long for any girl to wait, and as sweet as you are you will find the right man someday to make you happy. Dear I am heartbroken too about Jimmy for he was a wonderfull fellow. Goodbye and the best of luck to you allways. *[sic]*

"Love from Johnnie"

The two-page letter was postmarked October 2 and, even though it bore sincerity and affection, it started with "Dear Mary" when it might as well have begun, "Dear Jane."

Dillinger may have known what Dayton detectives never revealed when he was interrogated – that they knew, in his absence, Longnaker had grown restless and was keeping company with another man who had a room at the boarding house. She simply could not bear the boredom that comes with loneliness.

While Dillinger was writing his letter to Mary, Harry Copeland and five Indiana prison escapees were headed to a community an hour north of Dayton – the city of St. Marys, Ohio, atop the region known as the Greater Miami Valley. It was not unfamiliar in that one of the gang members was a native of the town.

Described as "Dillinger's lieutenant," **Charley Makley** was the toned-down counter balance to Dillinger's other "lieutenant," the volatile, Harry 'Pete' Pierpont. Charley was raised in St. Marys by a caring couple from a respectable local family who may have adopted him young in life from a circus performer. When his appetite for crime began is not certain, but a known arrest came at age 33. It was for receiving stolen property.

Charley Makley

Charley Makley specialized from that point forward in bank robberies.

He and his own gang were suspected of robbing Missouri banks in 1924, 1926, and in 1927, one in Kansas City of reportedly $79,000. Others included Indiana banks in Portland in 1926, the same Linn Grove bank in 1927 and again in 1928, as well as Ohio banks in St. Henry, Greenville, and Ansonia. He and his gang were captured in Hammond, Indiana in 1928.

St. Marys native and gangster, Charles Makley
Courtesy of Robert Makley, grandnephew

Circa 1933: First National Bank of St. Marys, Ohio *(right)*
Courtesy of Beth Keuneke, St. Marys Community Library

Charley was convicted and sentenced to the Indiana State prison where he met Dillinger and Pierpont, whose family lived in Leipsic, Ohio, an hour northeast of St. Marys. Now in a newly formed gang, Charley Makley was going to bank rob once again, this time in his small home town of 5,433 citizens.

On Tuesday, October 3, the First National Bank was the target of the heist, and it was directly across the street from the police headquarters.

The police chief, Gil Gerstner, had heard rumors that Charley was in town so he and a patrolman grabbed shotguns and drove to the Makley family homestead seeking him. While the lawmen were away, two cars pulled near the police station, one right in front, at around three o'clock. At least four of six gangsters entered the bank and spent 15 minutes inside. Meanwhile, Chief Gerstner returned to headquarters.

He later said he "strode in front of a car parked in front of headquarters and containing a couple of strange men." [113] *[sic]* Yet, the Chief continued on, walking into his police station.

A c r o s s the street, the bandits were polite as they waved their .45 caliber r e v o l v e r s. The three bank e m p l o y e e s and six patrons were placed in a vault. One bank employee recognized his fellow hometown native, Makley.

Circa 1933: Interior view of the First National Bank
Courtesy of Larry Kramer, St. Marys Hobby Center

The thieves calmly but hurriedly exited the bank with $12,050 in the unexpectedly huge heist ($241,414 today). The outlaws fled west on Highway 219 in a dark green Hudson and a black sedan long before the bank alarm sounded alerting the Chief.

After the St. Marys bank robbery, the gang traveled throughout Indiana and Ohio. They were as far south as Cincinnati a week later on October 10. In Dayton, the police department was back to its "routine" after the tension and bustle of the previous week.

On Thursday, October 5, Chief Wurstner forwarded Dillinger's wallet and contents, including a list of names, "evidently pals of John Dillinger in the Michigan City State Prison," to Indianapolis Chief of Detectives Fred Simon. Letters and "literature" seized from Dillinger were also mailed to Indiana State Prison Deputy Warden Harry Cloudy. The Chief's letter closed with this suggestion:

> "I wish to state that we have information that John Dillinger's brother flew here by airplane after John's arrest [to pick up the Terraplane]. I believe that if some kind of charge could be placed against Mary Longnacker [sic] and press her she could give you the inside information as to the escape of the prisoners, as she told a story in confidence which was related to me.

Deputy Warden Cloudy replied in writing on October 7 that he may be in Dayton in a few days. His arrival that date would not have brought him in contact with Longnaker. At the request of her attorney, Mary was allowed by Dayton investigators to leave the Gem

City for Bedford, Indiana to attend the October 3 burial of her older brother, Jim. Dayton police had looked for her since then but could not find her.

In Lima, John Dillinger lingered in the quiet solitude of the county lockup for nearly two weeks. He was well treated by turnkeys and staff. The Allen County jail, just as the Montgomery County jail, was fronted by the sheriff's residence. The jail

The Allen County Jail at rear of residence.

lobby had a north-side, first-floor entrance and jail cells were at the rear in an attached construction of massive stone blocks. The heavy guard from day one was no longer in force. Sheriff Sarber had allowed it to relax with the passing of time.

Allen County Jail – Thursday, October 12, 1933

At 6:30 in the evening, two cars pulled along the curb in the first block of West North Street. Harry Copeland, 'Red' Hamilton, and Ed Shouse remained with the automobiles while Harry Pierpont, Charley Makley, and Russell Clark strolled unhindered into the quiet, brick building that abutted the Allen County Jail in the middle of downtown.

Circa 1933: Stone jail at rear of residence.

What the escapees found was Sheriff Jess Sarber sitting at his writing table engaged in casual conversation with Deputy Wilbert Sharpe who was relaxing on a davenport.

The visitors claimed they were prison officials there to interview Dillinger – "We're from Michigan City," they proclaimed. When Sheriff Sarber asked to see their credentials, Pierpont pulled a pistol saying, "Here are our credentials." [114]

The Sheriff reached for his gun from behind his desk, but was instantly shot in the stomach ... it was a grave wound. The Sheriff's deputy could not take action or produce the jail keys upon demand. When the dying Sarber did not give the men the keys, he was viciously pistol whipped across his forehead as he lie helpless on the floor.

The sound of the gunfire and commotion brought the jail matron, Mrs. Lucy Sarber, running from the kitchen of their adjacent residence into the office. Seeing her bloodied husband, she begged, "Don't hurt him anymore. I'll get the keys and turn out Dillinger." [115]

Having heard the shot moments before, Dillinger nonchalantly stood telling the prisoners with whom he was playing cards in the bullpen that he was leaving. The captured fugitive, who had been in Dayton's jails only two weeks earlier, was freed from the cell block alone... a fugitive from the law once again.

The unarmed deputy and Mrs. Sarber were placed in another cell. The convicts left the jail unnoticed, fleeing the murder scene in their two get-away cars west to Indiana.

The jail break and mortally wounded lawman were discovered by Sheriff Sarber's son, Don, himself a deputy. Before he died, his father told him that he was shot by "Harry Copeland" but it was Harry Pierpont who was accurately identified by Deputy Sharpe.

Seated: Lucy Sarber and Sheriff Jess Sarber.
Standing: Son, Deputy Sheriff Don Sarber.
Allen County Museum and Historical Society

A striking reward of $5,000 was posted ($100,000 today) on the heels of the immediate formation of several sheriff posses from around Lima. Soon, other regional law enforcement agencies joined in. But Dayton police did not take part in the manhunt up north for a number of reasons:

1933: Allen County Jail Prisoner Register.
John Dillinger "discharged" entry on October 12, 1933.

On display by the *Allen County Museum and Historical Society* on loan from the *Allen County Sheriff's Department*

1) Inspector Yendes firmly believed Dillinger may come back into town looking for his girlfriend, Mary Jenkins Longnaker. He had his men keeping tabs on Mary until she traveled to Indiana for her brother's funeral. She was known to be back in town on Wednesday, October 11, but had since "mysteriously disappeared."

Police began a more intensive search for Mary on Friday. Dayton police believed she was aware of the jail break and might have left town to join Dillinger, *although* at the same time they wondered if she may be in hiding somewhere nearby waiting for him to show here. She was.

Longnaker had read the newspapers ... Johnnie was free to be with her. But she knew he could not show up at Mrs. Stricker's place. So how?

Mary paid for a hiding room at a three-story boarding house along the Great Miami River. It  was only a four-minute walk from her place on West First Street and even closer by car from the couple's night spot. Hoping for a rendezvous, Mary left a note at Pete's Greek restaurant to clue her beau as to where she could be found. [116]

"Dear Johnnie;

    "Thought I would leave this note at Pete's.... [I'm at] 228 N Robert ~~Bouvelard~~ Boulevard. Just come in the front door straight up the steps. It is the first door at the head of the stairs. Don't ask for me because they don't know me as my right name. See. If I am not at home leave a not or wait. I'll be seeing you. Mary." *[sic]*

Her sanguine wait turned to hard truth. She would not be seeing Johnnie. He never came for his "sweetheart" and probably never gave her a second thought. She should have known this from the "Dear Jane" letter ... if she believed it, or if she had even received it. The letter may well have been intercepted by Mrs. Stricker, the police, or even federal agents.

The police weighed conflicted thoughts about Mary's whereabouts. The truth was, the Dayton authorities simply did not know.

2) Police Chief Rudy Wurstner feared that the gang would be coming back to Dayton to commit a bank robbery as "reprisal" for Dillinger's local arrest three weeks earlier. The Chief had members of the police force and the public on high alert.

STILL WATCHING FOR DILLINGER TO SHOW HERE

Dayton Police Are Keeping in Touch With Bank Officials.

October 14, 1933 article
Dayton Daily News

Dayton Patrolman Clarence Colville received information that Friday. A citizen who was familiar with Russell Clark

Russell Clark

claimed he saw Walter Dietrich, a fellow Dillinger gang member, on a traction car headed downtown from Oakwood in the morning and then saw him meet up with Clark at two o'clock in the afternoon outside the Miami Loan Building at 25 S. Main Street.

The likelihood that those two gangsters were together and in town were remote but the Chief had Inspector Yendes personally contacting bank employees throughout the city advising they be on guard. He made sure that the bankers were given pictures of Dillinger and the escaped gang members.

Chief Wurstner

FEAR BANDIT'S PALS MAY STAGE HOLDUP

Dayton Police Are Placed on Guard Against Any Attempt at Reprisal For Arrest of John Dillinger Here.

October 13, 1933: *Dayton Daily News*

3) Lima police officials *came to Dayton instead.* Within one day of the killing there was a belief that the Dillinger gang was in southern Ohio in the city of Hamilton and wider Butler County.

Lawmen from Cincinnati, Hamilton and other cities took part in the southern Ohio manhunt and Dayton was a central meeting place for the northern police officials traveling south to participate. Chief Wurstner and Inspector Yendes met with the arriving party of Lima Police Chief John Cook, Inspector of Detectives Bernard Roney, and former Allen County Sheriff Benjamin Miller, Deputy Sheriff Hugh Moorman and Cal Crim of the Crim Detective Agency.

According to the news of the day, these police officials were "preparing for one of the most intensive manhunts in the state." [117]   As it turned out, the Dillinger gang was never found in southwest Ohio. Instead, it was on the move west across state lines.

The gangsters committed brazen crimes in three Indiana towns in only 11 days after Dillinger's escape by breaking into two police stations stealing entire arsenals of weapons (and bullet-proof vests!) and committing a bank holdup of nearly $75,000 ($1.5 million today).

October 16, 1933: *The Dayton Herald*
Lima and Allen County Authorities: Cook, Miller, Crim, Moorman and Roney.

Mary Ann Buchholz had seen Mary Longnaker only once since Dillinger was arrested in Dayton three weeks earlier. She expressed surprise at the sensational newspaper reports about a man as nice as Dillinger.

Longnaker bragged to her friend that she had been interviewed by the police, but told them she had never seen Johnnie with a gun. She instructed Buchholz, if she were ever questioned about Dillinger, not to say anything about the trip they had taken to Chicago, and "to keep [her] mouth shut regarding the guns, money or anything...." [118]

Longnaker also insisted Buchholz never say anything about the visit to the Indiana State Prison and the money secreted in the fruit. Longnaker's firm advice was ignored because late afternoon on October 17, Buchholz was brought into police headquarters by Sgt. Gross and Det. Pfauhl for questioning.

Buchholz spilled all that she knew of the trip to Chicago. She could offer very little else that was useful. Nevertheless, copies of the four-page interview transcript, for whatever value it might have, were mailed to Indiana State Prison Warden Walter Daly and Lima Police Chief John Cook.

The detective team of Gross and Pfauhl continued to pursue leads into Dillinger after his escape.

On October 25, they learned that Mary Longnaker was back at the West First Street boarding house, having returned from Richmond, Indiana.

Circa 1933: West First Street, a mere one block east of Longnaker's boarding house.

At the same time, Mary Ann Buchholz advised that she would not consent to any more interviews unless her parents were with her. The two Marys were not under any charges so cooperation was not forthcoming.

Still, Gross and Pfauhl remained on the lookout for the Lima jail escapee and his murderous associates.

Sidebar: Developing and Sharing Intelligence '30s Style

Ohio Association of Police Chiefs: Solid relationships were developed by police chiefs through the relatively new OAPC, but those bonds tightened in 1933 and 1934 under the weight of gang assaults. **Lima Police Chief Cook** had written to **Chief Rudy Wurstner** on October 25, 1933 with intelligence about a hangout "for all kinds of yeggs" in a village west of Montgomery County that might hold some of Dillinger's gang members.

In return, Chief Wurstner provided intelligence to Chief Cook about how the "wife or sweetheart" of Harry Copeland might be located through a former Dayton resident, now living in Louisville. Copeland was the one Dillinger gang member whose name locally surfaced most often, going back to The Pinkerton's National Detective Agency letter in August 1933. Intelligence sharing was by mail, telegraph, and, if urgent, telephone call.

Intelligence Gathering: Local information on gangsters was gleaned from the pounding of pavement by troops on the street and investigators. The detective team of **Sgt. Charles Gross** and **Det. Russell Pfauhl** persisted in running down whatever leads came their way. On October 25, they again found Mary Longnaker. On the same day, they dropped in on Mary Ann Buchholz. Despite applied pressure, neither woman was talking to the law.

 Intelligence on **Harry Copeland**, as well as his "wife or sweetheart" having a Dayton connection, persisted. On October 25, Sgt. Gross and Det. Pfauhl submitted a report to Chief Wurstner stating they had talked to a local relative of Harry Copeland's "wife," who ran into her at McCrabbs Grove on Germantown Pike. They learned she was "broke." She had taken up residence with a man on Crescent Street – which was one block directly south of Mrs. Stricker's boarding house, between the 300 blocks of West Second and West Third Streets – but, supposedly, had since moved to Muncie.

The movement of gangsters and accomplices in and out of towns and between states made the work difficult for law enforcement, its authority often restricted to their locales. Dayton detectives knew that the path and offshoots between two Ohio towns, Lima and Copeland's base of Hamilton, were well traveled by roaming bandits.

In November 1933, Harry Copeland was arrested in Chicago and sent to prison for 25 years. A month later, **Hilton Crouch** was nabbed there. Coincidentally, three of the Indiana prison escapees that had headed north together in one car were separately arrested in Chicago as well, including **Walter Dietrich** in January 1934. The other two escapees had disassociated from the Dillinger gang early on: **John Burns** was captured in December 1934 and **Joseph Fox** in June 1935. The manhunts for these three inmates, on the lam after their prison break, came to a close.

Circa 1933: One of the newspaper stands found on corners in downtown Dayton.

On October 26, Dillinger's captors observed two men at a newspaper stand at West Third and Ludlow Streets. Both men were absorbed reading a crime story. That in itself was not unusual but it struck the detectives as odd that newspapers were stuffed in their pockets.

When the detectives approached and started to question them, the men became jumpy. Suddenly, one started to pull a revolver but was instantly overpowered by Det. Pfauhl and Sgt. Gross. Both men were taken to police headquarters.

Further investigation revealed that Earl Holder and Frank Hawks Chews had committed nine holdups in Columbus, Indianapolis, Cincinnati, Zanesville and Springfield. The two bandits were picked up from the Dayton City Jail by Columbus detectives, armed with shotguns and machine guns, to answer for a $2,465 robbery in their city.

Chief Wurstner publicly lauded his men for another outstanding arrested. The citizens of Dayton needed to know they had the best in protection.

October, November, December 1933 – As the year closed out, John Dillinger and his gang were west of Ohio, as well as in and north of Chicago. They were hitting a bank per month in the states of Indiana, then Wisconsin, and then Illinois.

Bank robberies were not federal crimes, yet state and local agencies were asking the federal crime bureau, under J. Edgar Hoover, to take an active role. His bureau, the BOI, provided records to police agencies and investigative assistance but little else. Hoover and the U.S. Department of Justice would push for greater legal authority and federal law enforcement powers in the next year.

In 1934, the Dillinger gang intended to use the city of St. Paul, Minnesota for safe haven ... but the old standby was soon to undergo a change.

1933: A newspaper story in the *The Dayton Herald* about a **St. Paul, Minnesota** murder, robbery, and kidnapping - a harbinger of coming events and press coverage.

Circa 1935: An unidentified Dayton Patrolman downtown holding a little girl.
William Preston Mayfield Collection at Dayton History

PART FOUR

THE BADGES 1934 – 1941

Circa 1940 - Dayton Police Sergeant and Policewomen Badges *(above)*.
Identical to the badges worn by **Sgt. Lucius Rice** and **Plwn. Dora Rice**.
Courtesy of Dayton Fraternal Order of Police Lodge No. 44

CHAPTER 10

PUBLIC ENEMY NO. 1 AND PUBLIC ENEMIES

October 1937: "Dayton Gem Robber" – and Lima jewelry store bandit – Public Enemy No. 1, **Al Brady** meets his bloody end.

Circa 1930s: The Corridor Between Cincinnati and Toledo; the run from Hamilton to Lima through **Dayton, Ohio**.

1934 St. Marys' Newspapers
January 27 and February 23.

1934: Makley was the only one
of the three willing to look into the
camera lens of the Lima Police photographer.
The mug shots of Pierpont, Makley, and Clark.
Allen County Museum and Historical Society

1934: Mary Longnaker remained under the
watchful eye of Hoover's G-men into April.

Dayton B of I Russell Clark fingerprint card
and John Dillinger arrest records "jacket."
WSU Special Collections and Archives

THE CITIES – In **1934**, the Dillinger legend grew in the national press with each exploit.

During the East Chicago National Bank robbery in Indiana on January 15, Dillinger shot and killed a police officer. It was his first killing, thus joining many of his gang members as a wanted murder suspect. Captured on January 25 in Tucson, Arizona, Dillinger was extradited on January 31 to a county lockup in Crown Point, Indiana to face charges for the officer's murder during the bank robbery.

Pierpont, Makley, and Clark were arrested in Tucson as well but returned to Lima, Ohio to face Allen County trial for Sheriff Sarber's murder.

The Lake County, Indiana facility in Crown Point was hailed as an "escape-proof" jail by Sheriff Lillian Holley, the nation's only woman sheriff. But, on March 3, Dillinger escaped using a piece of wood carved in the shape of a gun, and dyed black with shoe polish. He fled in the Sheriff's car, further humiliating her in the national press.

Allen County
Sheriff Jess Sarber

J. Edgar Hoover had his government men (dubbed "G-men" by Machine Gun Kelly according to lore), organize a manhunt for the fugitive, Dillinger. A federal crime bill had been proposed in the U.S. Congress the month before, and would pass two months later. And, notably, Hoover had started arming his crime bureau agents to engage in war.

Now free, but without Copeland, Pierpont, Makley, and Clark, Dillinger united with Homer Van Meter, Red Hamilton, Eddie Green, Tommy Carroll and Baby Face Nelson. On March 6, they robbed a bank in South

Dakota, and a week later, a bank in Iowa. Then they sought refuge in the heretofore safe haven of St. Paul, where former Daytonian James Crumley, after three consecutive years, continued as the chief of detectives.

Eddie Green, a St. Paul native, arranged for John Dillinger to stay in a luxury apartment for nearly two weeks; however, a "tip" to Hoover's agents brought the lawmen and a city detective there. Coming across Van Meter at the front of the building, a gun battle erupted. Spraying the lobby with bullets from his Tommy gun, Dillinger fled out the back. Van Meter dodged the agents as well.

The outlaws met up with the others from the gang. But, three days later, on April 3, an unarmed Eddie Green was spotted alone in his hometown by G-men and mowed down with machine gun fire. The "heat" was blazing.

Homer Van Meter

While federal agents were in St. Paul, they were in Dayton, too, trying to track the elusive John Dillinger.

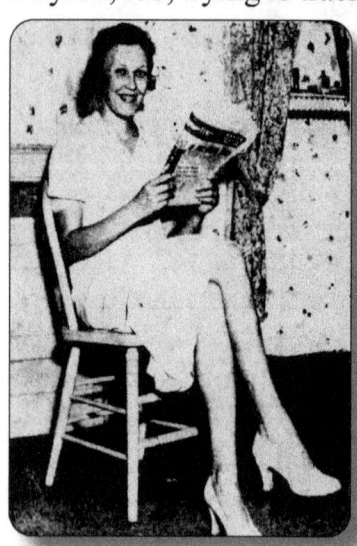

They knew that Claude Constable was intent on marrying Mary Jenkins Longnaker, but Special Agent Peter Nolan had heard that "she is of the opinion Dillinger will get in touch with her and ... would go with him in preference to marrying Constable as she loves Dillinger." [sic] [119]

1934: Mary Longnaker at her residence.

April 1934 St. Paul: A UPI story in *The Dayton Herald* on the fatal wounding of Eddie Green and greater peril to come in the Twin City.

The government agent contacted William Wallace of the Ohio Bell Telephone Company at 515 W. Second Street to determine whether Longnaker, Constable, or Mrs. Stricker had made or received any long-distance telephone calls. Wallace said he could provide the information by April 15.

The G-man also contacted Frank Harris, manager of the Postal Telegraph Company at 37 W. Third Street, regarding messages received or sent by these individuals. He advised he could have them by April 9.

Agent Nolan was especially interested in telegraphs sent or received by Jack Egan as well as the long-distance telephone records for both the attorney's office and home. He reported to superiors:

"Appropriate surveillance will be maintained in connection with John Eagan, Attorney, who is known representative of criminals who are picked up in Dayton or with so-called underworld connections and who formerly represented John Dillinger." [120] *[sic]*

The intrusive government effort was nonproductive.

A real concern that Dillinger may show in the Gem City during the month was apparent. Dayton Sgt. Clifford Croft and Ptl. Matthew Kirkpatrick reported on April 16 they had an informant who stated that Dillinger might come to a cottage on the east side of North Gettysburg Avenue near Wolf Creek. This came up empty as well ... with good reason.

On April 20, John Dillinger's gang, comprised of Van Meter, Hamilton, Carroll, and Baby Face Nelson, arrived at a Wisconsin resort known as the Little Bohemia Lodge. Alerted to the gathering of notorious gangsters at the remote location, federal agents surrounded the place on April 22. A gun battle ensued.

In the end, Dillinger, Nelson, and all of the gangsters escaped; however, the following day while driving to St. Paul, police spotted Dillinger, Van Meter, and

Little Bohemia getaway car

Hamilton in a stolen auto. Their astute observation initiated a wild car-chasing gun battle during which Hamilton was mortally wounded. Still

April 1934: The stolen car Hamilton was in when killed.
New Carlisle Historical Society

the bandits evaded capture. John 'Red' Hamilton died three days later; another gangster buried.

Two more banks were robbed, one each in May and June, although the gang was attempting to keep a low profile. Van Meter and Carroll purportedly robbed the First National Bank in Fostoria, Ohio, a small community 30 miles northeast of Bluffton. Allegedly, Dillinger, Van Meter, Baby Face Nelson, and possibly Charles 'Pretty Boy' Floyd committed the other heist at the Merchants National Bank in South Bend, Indiana.

In between these two robberies, on May 19, 1934, President Franklin Roosevelt signed into law the Federal crime bill that made bank robbery, transporting stolen property across state lines, killing a federal law enforcement officer, and other felonies federal offenses.

ROOSEVELT SIGNS MEASURES FOR FEDERAL CRIME CURBS

WASHINGTON, May 18. (P)— A group of bills requested by the Department of Justice to aid the Federal government in combating crime were signed today by President Roosevelt.

The measures—passage of which was hastened by the activities of John Dillinger, the outlaw—provide Federal penalties for offenses which messages in interstate commerce, fleeing across State lines to avoid prosecution or giving testimony in felony cases, fraud or robbery of national banks, assaulting or murdering a Federal officer or employee in line of duty and interstate transportation of stolen securities.

"There will be no relenting," said the President in signing the legislation.

May 1934: *The Los Angeles Times*

On June 22, 1934 – his birthday and exactly nine months after his arrest in Dayton – John Dillinger was declared America's first *"Public Enemy No. 1"* by J. Edgar Hoover, the director of the newly named Division of Investigation (the forerunner of the F.B.I.).

The Indiana prison escape, the Allen County escape, the Crown Point escape, the St. Paul escape, the Bohemia Lodge escape, the bank robberies, multiple thefts of police arsenals, the murders, the embarrassments… it was going to come to an end. Hoover's G-men were fully engaged in taking Dillinger down for good.

In Dayton, federal agents had kept Mary Longnaker under surveillance in the event the fugitive tried to rekindle his romance. Once again, Mrs. Lucille Stricker agreed to keep her eye out for the wanted desperado despite her fears.

The West First Street landlady "knew Dillinger was capable of killing her in retaliation. After the

Illustrated photo depicting Hoover's G-men taking down Public Enemy No. 1, John Dillinger, at the alley near the Chicago Biograph Theater. *Courtesy of William J. Helmer, author of "Dillinger: The Untold Story" and "Public Enemies: America's Criminal Past 1919-1940," et al.*

[Dayton] arrest, the woman lived in terror. Night and day, she feared the rampaging Dillinger gang would return to get even with her. At last, nerves shattered, she moved to California." [121]

Mrs. Stricker's anxiety and the local effort by federal agents were needless ...

... Dillinger had moved on to other women.

The bandit's notoriety extended to his gang members, and the gals that followed Mary Longnaker; women such as Evelyn 'Billie' Frechette, who succeeded Mary and was arrested with Dillinger in Arizona, and Edythe 'Polly' Hamilton, who lived with the operator of a lucrative brothel in East Chicago. The madam was Anna Sage; her real name: Ana Cumpănas.

On the Fourth of July, 1934, Dillinger took up residence with Polly and moved into Anna Sage's apartment. Forever known as the duplicitous "Woman in Red" because of the bright color of her dress – Sage later claimed it was actually orange – Anna and Polly accompanied Dillinger on July 22, 1934 to the Biograph Theater on Chicago's north side, the old gang territory of mob boss Bugs Moran.

Sage was fully aware that Dillinger was a marked man. Unknown to Hamilton, Sage agreed to set up the bandit for federal agents so as not to be deported to Romania. As the movie let out – Manhattan Melodrama starring Clark Gable, William Powell and Myrna Loy – the G-men spotted the gangster and he saw them.

Dillinger drew his gun as he tried to run toward an alley, but agents fired at least twice, instantly killing Public Enemy No. 1.

Dillinger's every escapade was reported in the three Dayton newspapers: the *Dayton Daily News*, *The Dayton Journal*, and *The Dayton Herald*. His death was no exception.

At the time, Mary was living with her new husband of three days, Claude Constable, in apartment number one at 214 Clay Street, the same row building she called home when she first moved to Dayton.

The Chicago authorities found a picture of a woman in Dillinger's pocket watch and identified the woman as Mary "Longacre."

When reporters learned of this, the speculative press wire service contacted her just days after his death. Longnaker denied the picture was of her.

The press later reported that the Chicago authorities "have abandoned the theory" regarding the pocket watch photograph. But photos of her at home made national news, allowing her to show off a liquor-serving set given to her by the outlaw.

When asked her thoughts about Dillinger, [122] Mary said Johnnie was...

..."one swell guy."

MARY LONGNAKER
Denying her picture was the one found in the watch of the slain desperado, John Dillinger, but admitting that she thought him "one swell guy". Mary Longnaker,

July 24, 1934: *The Dayton Herald and Central Press Wire Service*

Mary showing off her liquor-serving set.

Sidebar: The Life of a Dayton Girl after being a Dillinger Gal

Mary R. Jenkins Longnaker: She was never a gangster "moll," but was certainly a "girlfriend." Post John Dillinger, Mary found a new man in her life, ironically named Constable. She married Sherman Claude Constable, July 19, **1934**. Mary turned 24 a month later.

Briefer than her union with Howard Longnaker, her second marriage to Constable ended in divorce… this one _not_ paid by Dillinger. Mary did not stay single long. At age 26, she married Everett Titus on May 1, **1937** in Connorsville, Indiana. The two divorced in Richmond in 1945, but Mary may have been back in Ohio years before because Everett was drafted into the U.S. Army Air Corps in 1942. At age 39, on January 15, **1950**, Mary married Orval Johnson in Montgomery County but he died in 1960; and then, by May 9, **1972**, at age 61, she married a 38-year employee of Dayton's Inland Manufacturing Co., Willard Anderson, but he died in 1983. Her fifth marriage was her last.

Mary Ruth Jenkins Longnaker Anderson lived out her life in self-imposed obscurity. She worked under the name Mary Titus at "The Inland" factory at Abbey and Home Avenues. She became friends with a coworker named Frances Denton. The two women worked the assembly conveyer line during WWII producing M-1 carbines for the war effort. Mary and Frances worked side-by-side for over 20 years until 1967, when Frances took leave. Mary always dressed nicely, even to the point that she would wear a fur coat to the plant, although it never was as if she were flaunting. Mary would attend social gatherings and was particularly attentive to Frances' young daughter. [123]

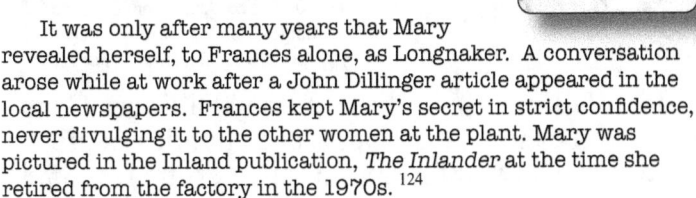

It was only after many years that Mary revealed herself, to Frances alone, as Longnaker. A conversation arose while at work after a John Dillinger article appeared in the local newspapers. Frances kept Mary's secret in strict confidence, never divulging it to the other women at the plant. Mary was pictured in the Inland publication, _The Inlander_ at the time she retired from the factory in the 1970s. [124]

Mary apparently never sought notoriety, or tried to profit on her infamous relationship with John Dillinger. In the end, she was a Huber Heights, Ohio resident when she died on May 10, **1991**, at 3:05 in the morning at Good Samaritan Hospital. Mary was 80 years old. There was no newspaper write-up. She was buried at the rural Pattonville graveyard in Indiana, separated by several miles from the cemetery where others in her immediate family are laid to rest.

The Gang's Reckoning – March to September 1934

THE DEMISE – John Dillinger had turned 31 exactly one month earlier when he met his deserved fate in Chicago, which was exactly 10 months from the day of his arrest in the Gem City. He was buried at Crown Hill Cemetery in Indianapolis. Dillinger had been paroled just 14 months before his death.

The 1933 Dayton police apprehension of bank bandit John Dillinger was his <u>first arrest</u> since his release from the Indiana State Prison.

It was one of only two captures *ever* of Dillinger while on the lam as a bank robber, and as a notorious gangster on the national scene, a deed matched by one other law enforcement agency, the local police department in Tucson, Arizona.

Dayton Police Department mug shot of Dilllinger from Kodak nitrate negative.
Miami Valley Regional Crime Lab

John Dillinger and those in the "Dillinger Gang" held up an estimated 26 banks and countless stores of more than $300,000 in conservative estimates ($5.81 million today).

The dead outlaw's cronies who had also been arrested in Tucson, Arizona – Harry Pierpont, Charley Makley, Russell Clark – faced their destinies four months earlier in Lima, Ohio. These three, who were responsible for the killing of Sheriff Jess Sarber, had trials held in an Allen County courtroom.

All three were found guilty in separate weeks of March. Clark was sentenced to life imprisonment. Pierpont and Makley received death sentences. All three had been locked away in the Ohio State

1934: Clark, Makley, Pierpont together in a courtroom.
Courtesy of Robert Makley, grandnephew

Penitentiary at the time Dillinger suffered his death penalty at the hands of Hoover's government men.

The other members of the "Dillinger Gang" who were captured and returned to prison – James Clark, Copeland, Shouse, Dietrich, and later Burns, John Paul Chase, and Fox – were newsworthy, but not similarly lofty fodder for the press.

Done in by a shotgun four days after his escape from Michigan City, Jim Jenkins' place in history is as a hanger-on, unlike the more dynamic standings given to the others cut down in manhunts: Eddie Green, Red Hamilton, and Tommy Carroll, who was the last of these three to die. Carroll's Catholic funeral and burial were held in June in St. Paul, Minnesota.

While St. Paul remained rife with criminals, there had been changes in the command of its police department since James Crumley's 1931 promotion to inspector of detectives by his police associate, Chief Tom Brown.

The Chief had been appointed, reputedly, with the backing of Leon Gleckman in 1930. But in May 1932, Brown resigned after he was suspected of tipping off the Karpis-Barker gang of coming arrests. This mix of murderous thugs and bank robbing thieves were also profiteering from kidnapping ransoms.

Despite his resignation, Brown was reinstated as a detective by June 1932. Eventually Tom Brown's connection to the underworld, particularly the Karpis-Barker gang, brought him under federal investigation. The suspected corruption did not keep Brown from running in a losing effort for county sheriff. Brown reportedly received funding support from Dillinger gang member Homer Van Meter.

Financial political loyalty only goes so far.

On August 23, Van Meter was tracked by four lawmen, including Brown, and slaughtered as he fled. Brown was accused of continuing his fire as Van Meter lie mortally wounded on the ground. The outlaw was betrayed by Baby Face Nelson with whom he had an earlier argument, according to lore.

Gang loyalty only goes so far.

This was a reckoning year for the core of the Dillinger gang. On September 22, 1934, exactly one year to the day that John Dillinger was captured in Dayton, Ohio, Makley and Pierpont decided they would not suffer his deadly fate at the hands of the state. They used his escape tactic from Crown Point.

After fashioning fake handguns using black shoe polish on carved soapstone, the two attempted to break out of the Ohio penitentiary. This time jail guards won out. Pierpont was wounded but Charley Makley was shot dead. He was buried in Pierpont's town of Leipsic, Ohio.

Less than a month later, Pierpont embraced his Catholic faith as he was executed on October 17. It was one year and five days after he shot and killed

Sheriff Sarber. Pierpont joined Makley in the city of Leipsic cemetery.

The Dillinger gang was responsible for at least 16 murders. It is believed the gang killed as many as 13 lawmen. In reflecting on the bandit and cohorts, Larry Andrews, *The Dayton Herald* reporter, wrote, "John Dillinger was a killer. Neither he nor his gang showed any mercy to a victim who pose[d] the slightest threat." In an understatement, the author noted that Dillinger "was no knight in shining armor."

After his Chicago death at the hands of G-men, John H. Dillinger was succeeded as J. Edgar Hoover's "Public Enemy No. 1" by Pretty Boy Floyd.

July 27, 1934: The FBI campaign on the **Top Six**: Dillinger, Nelson. Karpis, Barker, Van Meter, Floyd
Central Press Wire Service

In October, Floyd was taken down forever by Hoover's agents. Then Pretty Boy was succeeded by Baby Face Nelson.

When G-men eliminated Nelson's earthly existence in November, Al Karpis, the ruthless killer operating in St. Paul, Minnesota earned the title of "Public Enemy No. 1."

Law enforcement was fully engaged in the war against public enemies.

1933: Dayton Police
Bureau of Identification
"Wanted" file records
of roaming Ohio
gangsters
Clyde Barrow
and
**Charles Arthur
'Pretty Boy' Floyd**.

*Wright State University
Special Collections
and Archives*

WANTED FOR MURDER
$600.00 REWARD
JOPLIN, MISSOURI

On April 13, 1933, these men shot and killed Detective Harry McGinnis and Constable J. W. Harryman at Joplin, Missouri, suburban residence district.

Reward offered: $200.00 by the City of Joplin
$200.00 by the County of Jasper
$200.00 by the County of Newton
All rewards to be paid upon arrest and conviction

CLYDE CHAMPION BARROW
Age - 23 years.
Height - 5 ft. 7 in. BF.
Weight - 125 pounds.
Hair - Dark brown, wavy.
Eyes - Hazel.
Complexion - Light.
Occupation - None.
Home - West Dallas, Texas.
This man is very dangerous; his record shows that he has killed at least three or four men before this and participated in several highway robberies.

FINGER PRINT CLASSIFICATION:
29 - MO 9
26 U 00 9

Name—Charles Arthur FLOYD
Alias—"Pretty Boy" Smith—Frank Mitchell
Age—24 in 1931, height 5'7½", weight 155
Tattoo—Red Cross Nurse and Rose at Left Forearm Front.

REWARD

FLOYD is wanted for the murder of lawman Ralph Castner, who was shot on Apr. 1931 and died April 23rd, 1931.

The Commissioners of Wood County offer a reward of $1,000.00 for the arrest and conviction of Floyd, alias Mitchell.

Subject has record at St. Louis, Mo.; Kansas City, Mo. as No. 16930; Kansas City, Kans. No. 3099, Pueblo, Colo. as No. 1; Missouri State Prison as No. 29678; at Toledo, O. as No. 21458, Akron, O. as No. 19982.

Extreme caution should be used in approaching Floyd, alias Mitchell, as he will not hesitate to shoot.

Address all information to the undersigned.
Bruce C. Pratt.

Bowling Green, Ohio, May 15th, 1931.
(Circular 8A by Toledo Police.)

Clyde Barrow

March 31, 1930:
Middletown, Ohio
Police Bureau of
Identification
arrest record *(left)*
and mug shot of the
Southwest-Midwest
gangster
Clyde Barrow.

*Middletown
Police Department*

BUREAU OF IDENTIFICATION
MIDDLETOWN, OHIO

Name   Clyde Barrow
Residence   601 Liberty St., Dallas Texas
Occupation   None
Crime   Fugitive

Public Enemies – Dayton, Ohio 1930 to 1936

THE CORRIDOR – The first half of the 1930s is widely recognized as the age of the big-name Depression-era criminal. During this decade, the traditionally effective private Pinkerton's National Detective Agency was supplanted by Hoover's increasingly aggressive U.S. Division of Investigation.

Although Chicago and St. Paul, Minnesota, both Bugs Moran terrain, were the havens for Midwest gangsters, the 111-mile corridor between two Ohio towns, Hamilton and Lima – each dubbed "Little Chicago" – was well traveled by "public enemies" from 1930 to 1936. The major metropolis between the two was Dayton, Ohio, the nation's 41st largest city and growing.

The Dayton Police Department's Detective Bureau kept vigilant for the likes of Pretty Boy Floyd, who roamed Ohio towns to the north, but was feared to travel south, and Clyde Barrow. Dayton's Bureau of Identification (B of I) had mug shots and fingerprint cards at hand for both men the year John Dillinger landed in Dayton.

Clyde Barrow, the regional Texas-Oklahoma-Missouri outlaw of "Bonnie and Clyde" fame, surfaced along "the corridor." Awaiting trial in a Texas jail in 1930, Barrow escaped with a handgun slipped to him by Miss Bonnie Parker. He fled north, but was captured a week later committing a store robbery in Middletown, Ohio, a town of 30,000 people, 15 miles northeast of Hamilton (population 52,000). Returned to Texas to face time for his crimes, he later suffered an infamous death with his gun moll, Bonnie.

The Gem City exposure to public enemies stretched

past local hoodlum **Floyd Shawhan**, beyond George Remus' bootlegging network; beyond opportunistic bank-poaching by Fred 'Killer' Burke and Ray 'Crane Neck' Nugent; and beyond the oft convenient love tryst of John Dillinger. The *"Who's Who"* of underworld characters linked with Dayton in the '30s was reality:

Robert 'Bob' Zwick, known as "the Fox of Gangland," had his base in the Gem City for a time when he resided at 2826 Revere Avenue. In 1930, three members of Zwick's notorious gang were arrested in the Gem City; two of them were Daytonians living at 127 Knecht Drive.

Bob Zwick
The Dayton Herald
illustration in 1933

Zwick and the three attempted a bank robbery in Phillipsburg, Ohio for which Dayton police detectives were called in to investigate. He was bold and vicious in extorting other members of Dayton's underworld.

Zwick was a killer who terrified his own gang. Convicted in Hamilton County, Dayton Inspector Cy Yendes was commended by prosecutors for his investigation into the gang. The Inspector considered Zwick far more ruthless than Dillinger. Zwick was sentenced to life in the Ohio penitentiary in 1933, served 35 years, was paroled, and died in his sleep at nearly age 100 in 1997.

Al Fouts

Albert 'Al' Fouts, the native Daytonian, was well known to police for a crime career beginning in 1905. Convicted of murder in 1917, he was represented by Dayton attorney Jack Egan. Convictions between 1917 and 1930 landed Fouts in the Ohio Penitentiary, and San Quentin and Folsom prisons in California.

In 1931, Fouts was suspected of burglaries in both Hamilton and Lima, Ohio, and convicted for the latter. Al served time later this decade in the Atlanta federal penitentiary – another "big house" – that formerly held bootleggers **George Remus** and **John Friend**.

Fouts' story did not end with his parole in 1938. He would resurface the next decade, committing area robberies with **George 'Bugs' Moran** and St. Louis "gang lieutenant" **Virgil 'Doc' Summers**. Another comeuppance for Al would add Leavenworth federal penitentiary to his long list of fortified habitats.

Alvin 'Creepy Al' Karpis was the leader of the Barker-Karpis gang. He followed Dillinger, 'Pretty Boy' Floyd, and 'Baby Face' Nelson to the top on the FBI's most wanted list. Angered at being named "Public Enemy No.1," he wrote a letter to J. Edgar Hoover threatening to kill the director.

His 1935 letter, mailed from Dayton, Ohio, was widely reported in newspapers nationwide from Washington D.C. to Spokane, Washington. Karpis' local connection was certain. Whether the written threat was true or a publicity play by Hoover's recast agency, Karpis was captured by the FBI in 1936.

Al Karpis

Convicted in the federal court of St. Paul, Minnesota, Karpis was sentenced to life at Alcatraz penitentiary. He served 33 years, was paroled in 1969, and died in his sleep at age 72 in 1979.

Dolores Delaney, Al Karpis' gun-toting moll, was shot in the leg in a blazing battle in Atlantic City during which her fugitive boyfriend eluded police. She was captured, tried and sentenced to five years in the federal pen in Michigan.

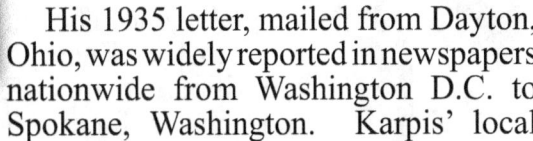
Dolores Delaney

Al Karpis retained the service of Dayton attorney Jack Egan – the same lawyer who represented Stimmel, Fouts, the Friends, and Dillinger – to appeal Delaney's conviction.

Never overturned on appeal by Egan, Delaney instead shared time in the same prison with other gangster molls, like Dillinger gal Billie Frechette, and Kathryn Kelly, wife of 'Machine Gun' Kelly. Released from prison in 1938, she faded from public view.

Jack Egan, while not a public enemy himself, was embedded in the world of underworld characters. His connection to Karpis during the Delaney appeal had placed him, once again, under FBI scrutiny.

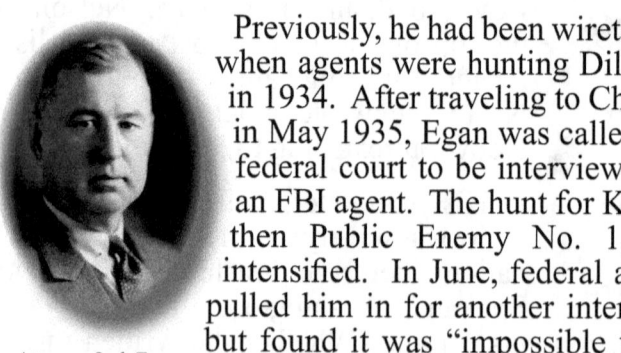

Attorney Jack Egan

Previously, he had been wiretapped when agents were hunting Dillinger in 1934. After traveling to Chicago in May 1935, Egan was called into federal court to be interviewed by an FBI agent. The hunt for Karpis, then Public Enemy No. 1, had intensified. In June, federal agents pulled him in for another interview, but found it was "impossible to get any information out of him which would incriminate himself." [125]

The shrewd underworld attorney was not one to be intimidated by Hoover's G-men.

Alfred 'Al' Brady, "Public Enemy No. 1," alias John Barton, was a killer whose arrogance was such he claimed his legacy would "make Dillinger look like a piker." [126] In April 1936, Al Brady and his gang robbed the Sol Partner jewelry store in downtown Dayton of $75,000 in

Al Brady

gems ($1.4 million today). This was in between the gang twice robbing the Kay Jewelry Store in Lima, Ohio of $34,000 total in jewels ($623,000 today).

The Brady gang was able to elude local authorities, but in "one of the greatest manhunts in the history of American crime," [127] federal agents tracked Brady to Bangor, Maine where he was killed in a gun battle.

It was not only gangsters in the G-men's crosshairs.

_____

A Police Reckoning – Shakeup in June 1935

THE POISON – In 1935, the United States' Division of Investigation (DOI) was officially renamed the "Federal Bureau of Investigation" under Director J. Edgar Hoover. The FBI war with gangsters continued, particularly against its newest Public Enemy No. 1, Al Karpis, who had been kidnapping for ransom in St. Paul. Karpis became the gang's lone leader at the end of January 1935 with the arrest of Arthur 'Doc' Barker in Chicago, and killings of Fred Barker and Ma Barker in a four-hour gun battle with the FBI.

Former Dayton detective, James Crumley, had a watershed year in 1935 in St. Paul. The former pro boxer found his calling to be police work in 1893. Including railroads, he had over 40 years of law enforcement service; 21 years in St. Paul; 10 years in Dayton.

Det. James Crumley
Dayton 1902

Whenever Detective Crumley returned to the Gem City, or advanced in his career, he was lauded by the local press. In 1931, the *Dayton Daily News* recalled his "enviable reputation" and his belief in "'fair play'." During a stay in Dayton in 1933, the St. Paul Chief of Detectives spoke about how the "wave of kidnapping" was the "underworld's substitute for liquor racketeering."

Inspector Crumley was a proud Irishman who found favor, or at the least kept in good graces with seven police chiefs of Irish descent. He was hired by Chief Farrell in Dayton and Chief O'Connor in St. Paul. Crumley continued in good stead under the 1930s St. Paul leadership of Chiefs Murnane, Brown, Dahill, Cullen and Culligan.

While Inspector Crumley was a constant "cog in the St. Paul police regime", the chief's position had incessant turnover – eight police chiefs were appointed in seven years from 1930 to 1936.

There was corruption within the police force, and Inspector of Detectives James Crumley was an underworld racketeering beneficiary. The last of the *Dayton Daily News* publicity for hometown favorite, James Crumley, were found in two summer newspaper articles leading with these headlines:

St. Paul Police Shakeup Hits Ex-Daytonian

Ex-Daytonian "Fired" When Lone Investigator Comes Along to Stop Gang Rule

These were not glowing stories in June and July 1935. *The Minneapolis Star* headline, as did the article, uncovered even more:

Police, Underworld Alliance Revealed
in St. Paul Inquiry

Inspector James Crumley had been caught in a wire-tapping sting operation that had gone on for months. A gambling syndicate was in cahoots with members of the police force.

Press reports in 1934 St. Paul - the police gun battle with Homer Van Meter and a suspicious police connection to the Barker-Karpis gang - followed in 1935 with accusations.

It should not have been a surprise. A year earlier, the U.S. Attorney General designated the St. Paul Police Department as "the poison spot of crime."

Crumley was ordered to resign, along with three officers of lower rank, and five others on the force were issued 30-day suspensions, including Chief Michael Culligan and former Chief Thomas Dahill. Sixteen charges were filed against Inspector Crumley, five of which were for bribery.

Dayton newspapers were quiet about the unfolding events, but *The Minneapolis Star* ran with the ongoing drama in exposé fashion. Criminal trials, appeals, grand jury hearings, and other proceedings lasted until 1938. Not only was it criminal, it became very personal with accusations and counter accusations. It was messy. Crumley went on the offensive and "shoveled the dirt."

The "massively built" former police inspector testified that his accuser, the public safety director, was himself involved in the racketeering. Crumley admitted to being involved in underworld collusion, but insisted it was under orders.

He was acquitted of 12 of 16 charges. He pushed for reinstatement to the police force, but that did not happen.

This trial was followed with one brought by federal authorities against former Chief Tom Brown, who had been suspended on charges of informing the Al Karpis gang of police activities.

Police Inspector
James Crumley
St. Paul circa 1937

Crumley became a prosecution witness, stating that Brown had him "tip off" a convicted kidnapper of the movements of police and federal agents. Brown's defense attorney tried to turn it around on Crumley. The animosity between two former fellow detectives with the link to Karpis made great press.

Then, on November 11, 1937, James Crumley was arrested for conspiring to bribe federal narcotics agents to "fix" a case of a "narcotics kingpin" for opium possession. Troubles for the "burley, grim-lipped" 75-year-old culminated two months later.

The disgraced former St. Paul police commander had exhausted the last of his "luck of the Irish." In January, he entered into a guilty plea agreement, and served a seven-month sentence in the Ramsey County jail.

In the twilight of his life, lawman James Crumley wrote a detailed letter to his family about a police career in which he took great pride.

He ended his letter by saying:

> "Have given my best efforts and have done everything in my power to keep [crime] at a minimum in the City of St. Paul."

The last article to appear in any local newspaper about James Crumley was one in *The Dayton Herald* six months after his release from jail. It announced that the "former member of the Dayton police force" died in St. Paul, Minnesota.

CHAPTER 11

THE GREAT DEPRESSION SEGUES TO WWII

December 8, 1941: The local press reports about a date which will live in infamy.

1943 Dayton, Ohio: During the middle of WWII, **Winters National Bank** on West Third Street at South Broadway. Factory workers cashing paychecks. A bank runner would be a target of **George 'Bugs' Moran** this decade.

The Downtown Gem City: The 1930s headed to WWII

West Fifth Street from Ludlow Street looking east *(left)*.

**1934 - 1941:
Automobiles
changing
the
landscape
of
Downtown
Dayton.**

1941: The railroad overpass
crossing South Main Street
looking north.

1934: The _new_ railroad
overpass crossing
South Ludlow Street
looking south *(above)*.

1939: Central downtown
South Main Street
looking north toward
the Great Miami River.

TRANSITIONS – The months-long investigations into the corruption of police officials in St. Paul, to include Inspector Crumley, was actually the beginning of reform measures over a five-year span.

While the end of Prohibition cut a mobster revenue stream, the St. Paul public safety commissioner cut out the "layover agreement" – the practice of safe harbor for gangsters. The 1935 introduction of a local police crime laboratory improved the quality of investigations, but the most significant reform would come in new procedures for making future appointments of St. Paul police chiefs.

Yet, as mid-1935 turmoil dogged the revolving police command far north, Chief Rudy Wurstner completed his 10th year at the helm of his police force in Dayton, Ohio. His longevity exceeded any other police chief in cities of 200,000 population or more.

Chief Rudy Wurstner

He was the embodiment of stability and propriety in a town that had experienced its share of disgrace in command since the inception of the police force in 1867.

The arrest of John Dillinger in Dayton, Ohio had earned Chief Wurstner professional stature on the national law enforcement stage.

Investigative techniques were being enhanced on many levels, and early on, Dayton's Chief took advantage of his connections with J. Edgar Hoover and Lt. Franklin Kreml, both of whom had newly established national training institutions. The two men would raise law enforcement standards, especially as pertains to investigative techniques.

Hoover's FBI National Academy opened in 1935 while Lt. Kreml's Northwestern University Traffic Institute (NUTI) opened in 1936.

1936: FBI Director Hoover left lower row. Sergeant Kirkpatrick right next row up.

These training schools have been described as the "West Point of law enforcement" and the "citadel of expertise in law enforcement." Dayton Sergeant **Matthew Kirkpatrick** was accepted into the FBI "Police School" in 1936.

Dayton Officer **Paul Price** was accepted to NUTI in 1938 (later the valedictorian of his class). Their attendance was a testament to the reputation of Dayton's police chief. Both policemen were in the earliest graduating classes of these two prestigious national training academies still in operation today.

Although underworld crime continued in this and decades ahead, Chief Wurstner's forward-looking approach regarding training for the purpose of improving police techniques – in the wake of the "gangster era" – was similarly applied to technologies and processes soon to come. The City administration provided additional funding in the police budget for these advances ... but not so for personnel costs.

The Chief's police force was feeling the weight of economic realities. Chief Wurstner's outstanding command staff, in place for over 15 years, was leaving. His three inspectors – Thomas Grundish, Otha Greger, and Cy Yendes – retired mid-decade. None were replaced until 1939 when just one inspector, Frank Krug, was promoted. After Captain Edward Poland retired in 1935, the number of captains dropped as well, from five to three, and remained that way until 1938.

Inspector Grundish's 1920-1935 Badge

Police Inspector Thomas Grundish

1935: Captain Edward Poland

Retires with bullet still lodged in his body from the 1920 shooting.

Courtesy of Dave Klippel, great-grandson, and Elizabeth Phillips, granddaughter

Even though a Great Depression citizenry was grappling at recovery in 1935, times remained hard on Dayton's economy as throughout the nation. Thousands lost their jobs. National Cash Register, Dayton's world-renowned avant-garde manufacturing company, alone laid off 5,000 people. The city's lost tax revenue resulted in lay-offs and reduced salaries.

By 1937, there were signs that Dayton was easing out of the Depression, due in large part to the city's diverse and specialized industries. Bread lines disappeared, people were no longer picking coal from the railroad tracks for heat, and employment increased. [128]

Under President Franklin Roosevelt's "New Deal," the Fair Labor Standards Act was first proposed in 1937. Eventually, local government employees were working a 40-hour work week. This was a benefit most Americans soon enjoyed ... but not Dayton police officers.

Circa 1936: Unidentified patrolmen with their 1936 Ford radio car in front of 338 Warren Street.

Patrolmen were still required to work an average 48-hour work week – cycling seven days on-duty, one day off-duty until the sixth calendar week when a Saturday and Sunday weekend finally rotated in.

Those men disposed to grinding out long days with ever-changing schedules for low wages were also men willing to face the real risks inherent in law enforcement.

Well over half of the citizens of Dayton at the start of the century were of German and Irish stock. The police department had many members from both backgrounds but men of Irish ancestry were prevalent on the force. Able-bodied men, emigrating from Ireland to urban centers on the U. S. East Coast, found policing to be their calling, most notably in Boston and New York.

That same dynamic was seen in the Gem City as well – such as with Andrew Walsh, born in Tipperary, Ireland, who became a Dayton police lieutenant. In the 19th century, Irish-born or Irish-American citizens often served in command positions, and as Dayton police rank-and-file members.

In June 1935, Matthew Maroney was appointed to the Dayton police force. After arriving in New York from County Clare, Ireland on May 23, 1927, Maroney made his way to Dayton by 1930. Anxious to join the police force at that time, he was rejected because his Irish brogue was so thick no one could understand a word he said.

Told to return when he could speak the English language, he did at a time when the police force was at a terrible manpower low. He was hired.

Irish Patrolman Matthew Maroney

When then Sgt. Maroney earned his police pension 25 years later in 1960, he still could hardly be understood by his own men.

While the City administration was willing to invest its resources into technology and equipment during the Great Depression, it was less inclined to do so with personnel. The decade saw the depletion in Dayton police ranks after 1935 even with the serious rise in crime.

The old timer and Dayton's "land battleship" motorman, Ptl. 'Big Frank' Johnson, retired in June 1935 after serving 33 years, replaced by Ptl. Maroney. Thereafter, the number of officers hired to replace those retiring or otherwise separating was not close to the same.

Ptl. Frank Johnson showcasing a new ballistic steel shield to the press a year before retirement.

The Dayton population was growing well above 200,000. By the close of 1935, the number of sworn personnel had dropped to 181 from 200 the year before "when a city the size of Dayton should have 300 officers." [129] The pay being poor, some patrolmen resigned. A few were activated away from the force, such as Sgt. William Aldredge, a captain in the 329th Infantry Reserves deployed to Montana as a company commander in the Civilian Conservation Corps (CCC), one of the New Deal alphabet programs.

Nine years into the Great Depression era, the FBI conducted a study on the rising criminal activity in Dayton. It attributed the high rate in 1938 to the low number of patrolling officers. Chief Rudy Wurstner released to the press the findings of Major Drane Lester, an administrative assistant to J. Edgar Hoover.

The report bluntly stated that Dayton's crime rate had "doubled." Yet, his warning did nothing to gain public or political support for adding troops at a time when the economy still struggled. Chief Wurstner made a more direct plea in the press for support by the end of the Great Depression. *The Journal Herald* exclaimed:

Dayton Needs More Policemen Badly!

By then Chief Wurstner's police force had dwindled to 152 sworn officers, its lowest number since the 1913 Great Flood. The Chief's plea was for the passage of a one-mill tax levy to add 30 officers, and to increase their pay. The levy failed.

War, and wartime rationing, was around the corner.

Dayton Police
Chief Wurstner

The dedication of many rank-and-file officers to protect their community never diminished in the face of low wages.

On February 21, 1935, Sgt. Charles Gross and Det. Russ Pfauhl received information on two wanted armed robbery/burglary suspects who were staying at a house at 13 Meigs Street in East Dayton. At ten o'clock in the evening, they began a stakeout.

Two and a half hours later, a car with two men pulled along the curb. The detectives approached and "threw a flashlight" on them, announcing they were the police. The suspects were told to step from the car with their hands up.

As Sgt. Gross removed a .32 caliber H&R pistol and held his man, the other character suddenly pulled a .32 Colt auto pistol and ran, firing a shot in the direction of Det. Pfauhl as he fled into the darkness.

The detective fired one shot in return and rushed in pursuit of the man. Having heard the shots, a neighbor telephoned the police desk.   When Det. Pfauhl spotted the suspect fleeing across the field, he fired twice more.   The robber dropped. Det. Matthew Kirkpatrick, Ptl. Horace Moore, and others arrived. The suspect had been shot dead.

Circa 1930
Detective Badge

The captured robber confessed to at least three burglaries committed a month earlier in 1935. He had come to Dayton from Corbin, Kentucky, having traveled northbound through the corridor.

Lost in the local retelling of the 1930s are the noncrime accounts of lifesaving actions taken by Dayton public safety officers. Chief Rudy Wurstner's police officers aided firemen at the scene of one of the more distressing incidents during this decade. Ironically, it occurred on Thanksgiving morning 1936, and the local community was gripped by this *Dayton Daily News* headline:

**14 TRAPPED IN ROBERT BLVD. FIRE;
ONE DEAD; THREE BELIEVED DYING**

It was exactly as the newspaper headline revealed. A horrific fire overtook an occupied large rooming house at 228 N. Robert Boulevard, the same dwelling where Mary Longnaker had hidden away three years earlier. It was a three-story 20-room double structure with seven apartments. The alarms came before eight o'clock in the morning. It was frigid outside;

the ground and rooftops were snow covered. The fire ignited on the second floor from a dropped cigarette, and then quickly spread to the third floor. The flames in the hall stairway cut off escape for many tenants.

Seven hose-and-wagon fire companies responded to the alarms. Police Captain Earl Yates "took charge for his division and ordered every available radio squad car and motorcycle officer to the scene." [130] There was a score of patrolmen, and eventually, three "ambulances" (paddy wagons).

Firemen climbed high on ladders in heroic efforts to save lives. Still, four of the 14 people trapped inside would die, but the others were mercifully rescued. A 16-year-old girl burned to death while her mother jumped from a third-floor window in what was a fatal fall. Two others were mortally injured. A number of those people that escaped suffered excruciating injuries.

Ptl. Thomas Dunlavey placing the first fire victim in the rear of the "ambulance."
Courtesy of Chuck Dunlavey, grandson

Sidebar: The Luck of the Irish – One Dayton Police Pensioner

Patrolman Thomas C. Dunlavey:
He had played semi-pro baseball for the
Davis Sewing Machine Co. as well as
the Dayton Veterans Class D pro team
(previously Dayton Old Soldiers). When
he was appointed to the Dayton Police
Department in **1916**, it was natural for
him to play centerfield for the Dayton
Police team managed by then **Sgt. Rudy
Wurstner**.

Their common thread was sports off-
duty and public service on-duty.

Ptl. Dunlavey manned Dayton's
"Emergency" wagon, the 1928 "Black
Maria" which served a dual role. Ptl.
Dunlavey had basic first-aid training
as a police "ambulanceman" but, in
responding to the most horrific injuries
imaginable, his was "load-and-haul" duty
that tends to take an emotional toll.

Circa 1920

As a prisoner wagonman, he engaged
in harsh business at a time when officers
had to be heavy-handed to survive. If
patrolmen
needed backup
(there were
no SWAT teams), they called for the
paddy wagon crew, often manned by the
toughest men on the police force.

On June 26, **1934**, Ptl. Dunlavey
responded to a machinists' strike at
the Brown-Brockmeyer Company, an
automotive plant at 1000 S. Smithville
Drive. A crowd of 150 had gathered and
were pelting autos with rocks. When
Ptl. Dunlavey attempted to arrest one,
the striking worker resisted and bit off
the top of the officer's right ear, causing

Circa 1940

Less a piece of his ear.

excruciating pain. Ptl. Dunlavey's assailant was subdued. [131]

Ptl. Dunlavey unquestionably earned his pension in **1942**.

Patrolman Dunlavey's working night stick.

All images and baton courtesy of Chuck Dunlavey, grandson

Ptl. Thomas Dunlavey, the operator of the same "Black Maria" that took Dillinger from Dayton jail cells to the county lockup, was the first on the scene of the fire with his wagon in the capacity of "ambulanceman."

In an era when the police department, not the fire department, was responsible for ambulance service, the few police paddy wagons often served as dual-purpose vehicles. They were used to convey prisoners, and equipped with stretchers, they removed the ill and injured for treatment by medical personnel.

Firemen immediately rushed critically injured victims to the paddy wagons where awaiting officers lifted them into the back. Ptl. Dunlavey cradled and covered one young burn victim as his emergency vehicle, holding two others, accelerated in transport to the hospital. Two of those removed would die.

Ptl. Dunlavey was later publicly criticized by a gawker for being insensitive in his actions. Chief Wurstner was quick to defend his officer's honor in writing. In addressing an onlooker's "denunciation" of Ptl. Dunlavey, the Chief replied to the man in a three-page letter, that said in part:

> "All these poor souls were suffering the very tortures of hell and with no time to lose, Officer Dunlavey ... sped to St. Elizabeth Hospital holding her in his arms the entire route ...

> "You can well imagine the suffering, moaning, writhing and screaming of the three victims, their very flesh and blood actually dripping to the floor of the ambulance, Officer Dunlavey, with one victim in his arms, and trying to take care of all three of them. [...]

> "The records shall show that [he] has been fully vindicated."

Having concluded his investigation, the Chief went on to say that the onlooker's circulated criticism was "an unwarranted rumor" that can only be rectified by his reporting to his "friends the true facts of the case…." His retort to this critic provided another reason for the troops to hold their Chief in high regard.

In 1937, the Dayton Bureau of Identification and the Detective Bureau were tightly joined. Both were under the command of Police Inspector Seymour Yendes as they had been for nearly two decades. The Dayton police force was a member of the National Bureau of Identification.

1937: Sgt. Walter Dempsey

Criminal forensic science advanced considerably within the Dayton police force under the Inspector's stewardship, and Chief Rudy Wurstner's direction. Two years earlier in 1935, the Chief authorized an investment of $800 ($14,000 today) in order to create a regional crime laboratory. It facilitated chemical testing, posmoulage processing, and helixometer measuring. [132]

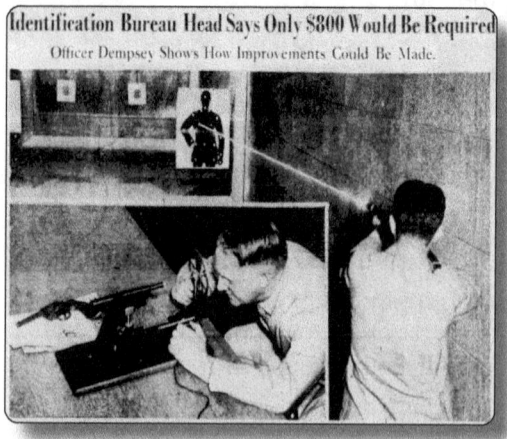

Identification Bureau Head Says Only $800 Would Be Required

Officer Dempsey Shows How Improvements Could Be Made.

August 30, 1935: *The Dayton Herald*

Later that same year, Dayton took local forensic science to another level, establishing the second ballistic laboratory in the state of Ohio following a practice set by the Cleveland Police Department.

In the 1930s, with only three police departments in the three incorporated cities in Montgomery County – Dayton, Oakwood, and Miamisburg – the county's 15 townships and eight villages had to rely on part-time constables and marshals. They had little infrastructural support for investigating and solving major crimes.

Attributable to the expertise of its crime lab and Bureau of Identification, in 1937 the Dayton Police Department formed its first "homicide squad" for county-wide "investigations and collection of evidence in murder cases." [133] [sic]

Under an agreement between Chief Wurstner, Sheriff Philip Kloos, [134] and County Prosecuting Attorney Nicholas Noland, the Montgomery County Sheriff investigator would "automatically" become a member of the squad when a murder case developed outside the city limits.

Montgomey County Sheriff Phillip Kloos

The county investigator was Detective Louis 'Lou' Janning at the time. He was a highly-experienced detective and well acquainted with Dayton's Bureau of Identification.

Det. Janning served on the Dayton Police Department for 26 years from 1904 to 1930, most of his time as a member of the Detective Bureau, before being appointed as the Sheriff's investigator, serving another 10 years.

Det. Louis Janning
Dayton Daily News
illustration in 1930

As one of the nation's major cities, Dayton was able to provide the entire Miami Valley region with a new crime laboratory under the management of its highly-sophisticated identification bureau (such as used by Troy, Ohio in prosecuting a robbery case).

The upshot was that the Dayton B of I also made Dayton's Detective Bureau second to none. Dayton detectives were "called in" by other jurisdictions to conduct major crime investigations, such as bank robberies, as it did with regional bank holdups by the Zwick gang and other bandits. The Dayton B of I was described at the time by Edwin J. Yantis, the Ohio Superintendent of the State Bureau of Identification, "as 100 per cent better than ... cities of the same size" and as advanced as many larger cities.

The 1937 City of Dayton *Civic Report* was published in early 1938. It announced that police officers were detailed to attend the American Red Cross School of First Aid to earn certificates as instructors. They, in turn, would train all members of the police force. The 1937 report also announced to the local community that "preparations [were] now underway for the installation of two-way radio reception" in police patrol cars. The report did not declare the hiring of more patrolmen or providing improved wage earnings.

A voice for fair pay and job conditions was needed, so Dayton police officers sought one in 1937. Sgt. Joseph Wells, Ptl. Harry Emmons, and Ptl. Melvin Fourman, traveled to Middletown to meet with other lawmen from Southwest Ohio.

Sgt. Joseph Wells
First Dayton FOP
Lodge President

A gradual grassroots campaign,

Police Fraternalism in the 1930s: Rank and file Dayton policemen *at Work*.

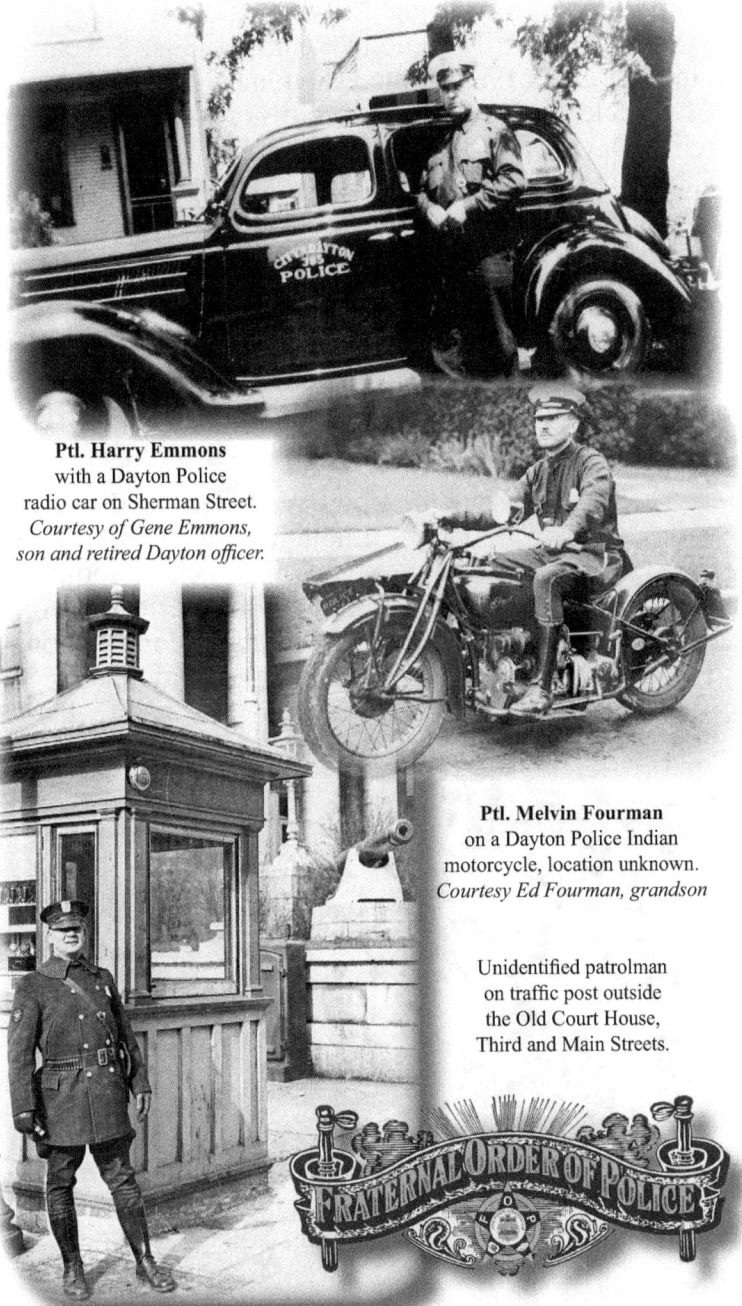

Ptl. Harry Emmons
with a Dayton Police
radio car on Sherman Street.
*Courtesy of Gene Emmons,
son and retired Dayton officer.*

Ptl. Melvin Fourman
on a Dayton Police Indian
motorcycle, location unknown.
Courtesy Ed Fourman, grandson

Unidentified patrolman
on traffic post outside
the Old Court House,
Third and Main Streets.

called the Fraternal Order of Police, had moved west from Pittsburgh crossing the Ohio River by 1920, but had broad growth in Ohio in the mid-1930s. Seventy-nine officers in 1938 formed Dayton FOP Captain John C. Post Lodge. While they did not find immediate relief, Dayton police officers' pay improved somewhat, and their work weeks were eventually reduced from an average of 48 to 44 hours (but not until 1952!).

The most ardent backers for the improvement of working conditions for cops on the beat were hundreds of local businessmen and professionals. Three years after the Dayton Lodge formed, and before WWII, these supporters would create the nation's first police "Associates" lodge, today FOPA Lodge No. 1.

The fourth decade of Chief Wurstner's career was winding down in 1938 (although he was not). The Chief and his officers had something to cheer about in December. The Dayton police tug-of-war team won the City Championship after four days of competition. The police team "disposed of the Dayton Steel Foundry" team among others in "record-breaking time," winning a cup and a cash prize for its victory.

Chief Rudy Wurstner proudly stood with his championship team for a photograph, just as he had 20 years earlier with his Jiu-Jitsu Squad.

Police Fraternalism in the 1930s: Rank and file Dayton policemen _at Play_.

Ptl. Lester Stockman
laughing at magician
Harry Blackstone tricking
an unidentified patrolman.
Courtesy of Ron Stockman, son

Magic Performance
at the Colonial
Theater in 1941.

Dayton Police
Band, May 1932.
*Courtesy of
Robert W. Six*

Dayton Police
Tug-of-War
Championship
Team, 1938.

The Chief proudly stands with his winning team.

Chief
Wurstner

D. P. D.
TUG OF WAR CHAMPIONS
DAYTON, O., DEC. 13-14-15-16, 1938.

Sadly, the competitive high would be followed by a terrible low a year later.

In January 1939, Dayton Policewoman Dora Rice was in poor health. She resigned from the Bureau of Policewomen after 10 praiseworthy years in service to her community. Her husband, Detective Sergeant Lucius Rice, was approaching his 30th year of police work at the time.

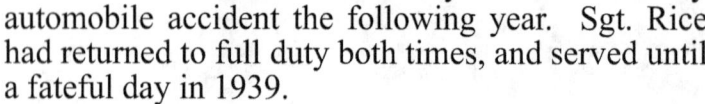

While he had accomplished much in his career, it had been a hard road. He had been badly injured and hospitalized six times, the worst when he suffered a near fatal gunshot wound to his stomach in 1926 followed by a critical on-duty automobile accident the following year. Sgt. Rice had returned to full duty both times, and served until a fateful day in 1939.

Dayton Policewoman
Dora Burton Rice

On September 30, Mrs. Rice experienced the greatest sacrifice that comes with a police career when she was telephoned at home by a police dispatcher. Her husband was needed for a manhunt in the killing of an individual at 629 S. Western Avenue.

She knew that Sgt. Rice was enjoying his day with their 28-year-old son, Robert. She called them, and together father and son drove to the crime scene.

Upon arriving, Sgt. Rice met up with his partner, Det. George Wheeler, and Detective Sergeant Fred Smith. Sgt. Rice developed a lead that indicated the murder suspect was at 515 College Street. He and Robert traveled there in search of the murderer, along with the other detectives.

Reassured by his father that he would not be long, Robert sat in the car as the detectives surrounded the home. Sgt. Rice took the lead in the search in the company of Sgt. Smith.

Entering the residence, the suspect suddenly emerged from a closet firing his revolver. In the gun battle, both sergeants were shot, Sgt. Rice most seriously having been struck several times. Wounded in the abdomen for the second time in his career, Sgt. Rice emerged from the house bleeding badly. Robert rushed his father to St. Elizabeth Hospital.

Sgt. Rice remained alert for a time and

DAYTON DAILY NEWS

2 DAYTON OFFICERS SHOT; 1 MAY DIE

October 1, 1939: *Dayton Daily News* headline

knowingly remarked, "I believe this will be the last time.... This is the end." [135] Robert stayed by his father's side. Notified, Chief Wurstner arrived at the hospital and spoke with his fearless detective one last time. An hour later, Sgt. Rice lapsed into a comma, and after five days, died from his wounds on October 5, 1939.

Sgt. Rice was the longest-serving area police officer to die in the line of duty (until 80 years later when Det. Jorge Del Rio was shot and killed in 2019).

Appointed in 1909. Killed in the line of duty in 1939.

Ailing and broken-hearted, the former Dayton Policewoman, Dora Rice, reunited with her husband less than six months after his death. She died on March 26, 1940.

Dayton Police Sergeant Lucius J. Rice

As for Sgt. Fred Smith, he recovered from his wound and returned to duty. Sgt. Rice's killer, Eugene Harris, was a "lifer fugitive," having escaped from an Alabama state prison. He, too, had been shot in the gun battle, but survived. Next to Dillinger, he was considered one of the most notorious prisoners ever held in the old Montgomery County jail (1875-1966). Tried and convicted, Harris was sentenced to death in the electric chair.

Eugene Harris and Old Sparky

A little more than a year after his capture, on October 23, 1940 the sentence was carried out as he sat under restraint on "Old Sparky." Harris is the only person in history to be legally executed for the murder of a Dayton police officer.

The very month Sgt. Rice was shot, war erupted in Europe after a decade of unease. The United States did not engage in 1939, 1940, and nearly through 1941.

In the new decade, Chief Rudy Wurstner was in command of the police force safeguarding the 40th largest city in the nation. The population of Dayton had managed to increase during the Great Depression to nearly 211,000 citizens, and would vault by the end of the 1940s … wartime industrialization having much to do with this. Under the oversight of Chief Wurstner, the Dayton police force continued to advance its radio technology.

Chief Wurstner

Although a Dayton patrol car had been outfitted with the first radio transmitter in 1938, a fleet-wide installation of radio transmitters had been in the planning stages for nearly two years but the technology was not quite there. Then, in August 1939, Motorola introduced the first practical and cost-efficient radio transmitter for police patrol cars.

Timing is everything and it happened at a moment when Chief Wurstner again crossed paths with Orville

Wright who served as host to President Franklin Roosevelt during a visit to Dayton on October 13, 1940.

October 13, 1940: Orville Wright sitting between the President and former Ohio Governor James Cox.

The local press reported that "for three days, technicians worked to install the first radio transmitter in a patrol car to help protect the president" during his election campaign stop in the Gem City. [136]

The radio transmitter was placed into practical police use for the first time as a "precautionary measure" for "the caravan of President Roosevelt."

Other police departments were much like Dayton in experimenting with two-way radio technology, [137] but with Motorola equipment and a presidential visit, Dayton became the nation's first municipal police department to equip an entire police fleet – 37 radio cars – with two-way radio communications. [138]

Sgt. Joseph Wells,
Dayton FOP president

Autumn 1940: Inspection of Dayton police fleet, now with two-way radios.

The advantage this innovation had for Dayton lawmen patrolling the streets was clearly demonstrated in action less than eight months later.

THREE SHOT IN ROBBERY CHASE

"Extra!" editions of the *Dayton Daily News* and *The Dayton Herald* hit the newsstands "after a spectacular 'honeymoon' holdup at the Gibbons hotel" led to a police chase and gun battle. Crime-scene photos spread across the front pages.

A Dayton patrolman and a 27-year old "gunmoll" were hospitalized. Another officer was grazed by a bullet. The moll's husband was behind bars in the city jail. Years later, the couple was spun by the press as "Dayton's Bonnie and Clyde."

On May 24, 1941, a honeymoon couple, Betty Austin and Raymond Rex 'Bus' Epperson, was rooming at the same hotel on South Ludlow at West Third Street that held the 1927 OACP Conference.

Earlier this same year, the groom had been freed from jail, while awaiting a new trial for a kidnapping, after having already served six years (since 1934) in the same Indiana State Prison in Michigan City that once held John Dillinger.

Hotel Entrance

The Gibbons Hotel on the southwest corner of South Ludlow and West Third Streets.

The couple were now suspected of a multi-state robbery spree in early May, and were wanted by authorities in Richmond, Virginia and Baltimore, Maryland. They had also been in Kentucky before traveling northbound through the corridor to Dayton.

During their stay at the Gibbons Hotel, the couple became very much aware of another lodger, a carnival manager. He had in his upper-floor room $1,700 in proceeds ($30,000 today). At four o'clock in the morning, the couple robbed him at gunpoint and placed him in a closet.

As the couple fled downstairs, the victim escaped his confinement and telephoned the lobby. The couple was slowed by a hotel watchman, and additionally by a cab driver. He tried without success to impede their escape with his taxi after the robbers piled into their car. All at once, Patrolmen Daniel Sammons and Walter Hammond rounded the corner in Radio Car 21.

Shouts of a robbery were heard by the officers as the getaway car sped away. Ptl Sammons accelerated while Ptl. Hammond instantly radioed the dispatcher:

"21 to dispatcher! 21 to dispatcher! 21
pursuing two armed bandits south on Ludlow
Street at a high rate of speed. Just pulled a
holdup at Gibbons Hotel. We are now crossing
Fifth Street at 70 miles an hour."

Had this occurred eight months earlier, the chasing
officers would not have been able to transmit their
pursuit to the dispatcher.

The chase reached speeds of 75 miles per hour
on South Patterson Boulevard, flying past the new
Carillon Historical Park until abruptly turning into
the Catholic Calvary Cemetery. [139]

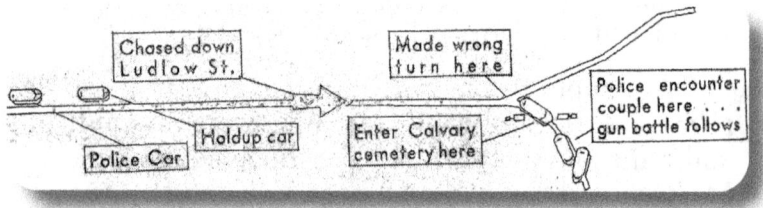

May 24, 1941: Police pursuit diagram (in part) from the *Dayton Daily News.*

Their car was trapped at the gateway – unnoticed
because it was recessed from the road – when the
officers pulled perpendicular to it. As the robbery
suspects exited the car, a "blazing gun battle [took
place] in the dark confines" of a graveyard. [140]

Bus Epperson was willing to give up, but his
moll, hell bent to get away, began blasting her Colt
Army Special .32-20 caliber revolver. Ptl. Sammons
was shot in the shoulder, and Ptl. Hammond's skull
was brushed by a bullet soaring through his hat. In
the return fire, a bullet seared the forehead of the
"gunmoll" who also sustained four wounds to her
back.

Other officers quickly arrived, but Patrolmen
Sammons and Hammond had already taken down the
two outlaws.

May 24, 1941: Front page of *The Dayton Herald.* Gun moll enjoys press celebrity.

Unlike Bonnie and Clyde, both suspects were taken into custody, later prosecuted in Montgomery County, and convicted of their crimes. Both patrolmen recovered from their wounds.

Betty Epperson made good press. She was photographed in her hospital bed, wound dressing on her temple, flashing a wry smile while holding a lit cigarette between her fingers.

A pulp crime magazine chronicled the "gunmoll's daring honeymoon" in a feature story.

The cover photo was of an attractive woman with her handgun held high. Less than eight months after the shooting, the *Complete Detective* article was on the newsstands.

Sidebar: *The Luck of the Irish – Another Dayton Police Pensioner*

Sergeant Daniel T. Sammons:
Appointed in **1937**, Patrolman Sammons was one of only 79 officers to risk their careers in **1938** by joining the newly chartered Dayton Fraternal Order of Police Lodge. As it turned out, unlike many police commanders in the nation, **Chief Rudy Wurstner** supported the F.O.P.

Promoted in **1947**, Sergeant Dan Sammons had an eventful 32-year career. When he earned his pension in **1969**, Sgt. Sammons was the last of those to retire from the police force who had been in the inaugural membership of Dayton's Capt. John C. Post F.O.P. Lodge No. 44.

Ptl. Sammons was of Irish descent; his paternal side rooted in County Mayo, Ireland while his maternal side was County Cavan.

Circa 1940

An Orignal Dayton
FOP Lodge member.

His legacy is his family. When he engaged in a gun battle in May **1941**, Ptl. Sammons' sons, Thomas and Michael, ages 5 and 2, were asleep in their beds only to afterwards discover that their father had been shot. Ptl. Sammons survived, and in spite of the distress it caused his family, he was later joined on the force by his two sons. **Lt. Michael Sammons** served 31 years, and his brother, **Ptl. Tom Sammons**, served 37½ years. The Sammons family served a combined 100+ years on the Dayton Police Department. [141]

As luck would have it, Dan Sammons grew up in Dayton with fellow Boy Scout and Stivers High School student, **Milton Caniff** who started professional cartooning in New York in **1932**. His boyhood friend surprised Dan later in life. The creator of the nationally syndicated comic *Steve Canyon*, debuted a new character, "Patrolman Dan Sammons," on January 14, **1986**. He appeared in three successive comic strips. [140 ibid]

All images courtesy of Michael Sammons, son and retired Dayton police lieutenant

The account of the Dayton police gun fight appeared in the magazine's December 1941 issue.

On December 8, 1941, the afternoon following the bombing of Pearl Harbor, President Franklin Roosevelt made his forever-remembered "Day of Infamy" address to the nation.

WORLD WAR II ... A closing to the ruinous effects of The Great Depression!

While there is no date certain for the end of a decade-long failed then frailed economy, the United States entry into war consigned it to being the great anxiety of the past.

It was a half score shy of "four score and seven years ago" since the first anniversary of President Abraham Lincoln's Gettysburg address to the nation.

Lincoln's speech marked the turning point of our Civil War. The nation, now unified in 1941, would prepare to combat outside threats to humankind.

At the close of the Civil War policing was a primitive practice at best, but had developed considerably by 1941.

Law enforcement adapted to emergent challenges during *three successive and distinct periods* in United States history. Dayton police had produced a legacy.

As 1941 closed, members of the police profession prepared for future engagements with threats, both at home and abroad.

In the oncoming war, the United States military will fight battles and be victorious in the end.

In the war on crime, American law enforcement fight battles that will never end!

EPILOGUE

THE WORLD'S WARS AND THE NATION'S DEAN

July 6, 1949: Dayton Police **Chief Rudy Wurstner** conducts his last police inspection in front of City Hall, 101 W. Third Street, across the street from the Gibbons Hotel..

In the last decade of a long and accomplished career, Dayton Police Chief Rudy Wurstner oversaw the safety of a city with an expanding population base. The municipality will thrive and grow post-WWII.

Circa 1945: West Fourth and South Main Streets in Downtown Dayton.

Detective Sgt. Charles McElhaney *(center)* flanked from the left by **Captain Matthew Kirkpatrick** and right **Sergeant Paul Price**.

Emil 'Russ' Guerra *(left)* being interviewed by WING radio's Jack Wymer. Guerra, a Battle of the Bulge POW, would become a Dayton police captain.

POSTSCRIPTS – As World War II beset the nation, Chief Rudy Wurstner was entering the fifth decade of his career.

Dayton's police chief saw to the safety of both the local and wider public throughout the anxiety of this second world war, from preparation in 1940 through cessation in September 1945. The city and public safety services were on high alert. The city of Dayton was classified by the federal government as a "highly strategic" city. [142]

The Dayton Signal Building, the communication center for both police and fire, was made the regional hub for the war siren system. City engineers installed equipment to warn of enemy invasion immediately following the Pearl Harbor attack: six five-horse-power, four two-horse-power, and fourteen one-half-horse-power sirens.

Given the state of the nation, the federal government was fully focused on threats to the American Home Front.

Chief Wurstner's professional relationship with the Federal Bureau of Investigation was such that he assigned two members of the Detective Bureau to handle all local anti-sabotage investigations in cooperation with the FBI.

A pipe bomb like those used by saboteurs is shown to Chief Rudy Wurstner by FBI Cincinnati Office Chief Raymond Suran.

The Chief also detailed his 1938 Northwestern University Traffic Institute graduate, Sgt. Paul Price, as a "special FBI instructor" to travel the nation.

In Columbus, Ohio, Sgt. Price taught a six-day "FBI war traffic school" for Ohio State Highway Patrol troopers, sheriffs and patrolmen from throughout the state. He did the same in Rochester, New York, Baltimore and other cities.

His week-long course was on military traffic and troop movements as part of vital domestic WWII defense planning. It was a three-part framework – military traffic; war-production traffic; and war-disaster traffic. [143]

Sergeant
Paul Price

The detailing of two detectives and Sgt. Price was done at a time when Chief Wurstner had to manage diminishing manpower and availability as young men enlisted for battle. There was patriotic fervor. Some active-duty officers volunteered to fight overseas, such as Ptl. Horace Moore who also fought in the Great War. Ptl. Moore requested a leave of absence in 1942 "for the duration of the emergency." Commissioned as a first lieutenant in the U.S. Army Air Force, he was quickly deployed.

The first half of the decade was all about rationing of material resources, but that also included police personnel. Dayton officers were required to advise the department of their draft classification and changes to their status. Ptl. Matthew Maroney was 3A (family hardship) but when he was reclassified 1A, Chief Wurstner immediately appealed to the draft board to retain his officer. Local protective staffing was at "a crisis" and he needed his troops.

On a temporary basis to increase its manpower, the Dayton police force hired "emergency patrolmen" until the honorable discharge of "regular patrolmen" from combat deployments.

Due to the war, automobile production virtually ceased for consumers in early 1942 because raw materials were limited. The police department did not buy any police vehicles from 1943 to 1946. Still, Dayton was a bustling place during the war. In 1942, local war industrialization was at full vitality earning Dayton, a major manufacturing town, the moniker of "Little Detroit."

The Gem City's automotive factories drew workers from around the country ranking Dayton third in the U.S. in cars per capita in 1942. [144] The Chief viewed this consumer product to be a more important tool for policing than the advances he experienced with forensic science and communication technology.

The arc of Chief Rudy Wurstner's long police career could be illustrated by the evolving forms of transportation. The main method was shoe leather in 1902 when he was appointed, although the police force could boast at having two horse-drawn patrol wagons.

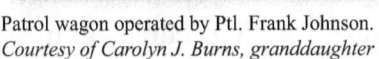

These wagons were in use during Ptl. Wurstner's first 10 years, but pounding the pavement on foot was the main means to get from Point A to Point B.

Patrol wagon operated by Ptl. Frank Johnson.
Courtesy of Carolyn J. Burns, granddaughter

In 1915, the police department obtained a single Model T Ford. The fleet expanded to six autos, but they were only deployed for special operations over the next 15 years. Then, in 1932, "radio cars" opened the way for actual auto patrol.

By the next decade's close, Chief Wurstner had 1949 Chevrolet cruisers and an estimated 50 patrol "squad cars" in his police fleet.

It was no wonder why Chief Rudy Wurstner believed that automobiles were the most significant modern development in the history of law enforcement.

Marked squad car operated by Ptl. Bob Swartz.
Courtesy of Sharen Neuhardt, daughter

———————

Troops came home after victory in the European and Pacific Theaters. It began with 23 war veterans rejoining the police force on March 13, 1946. They would be followed by other veterans returning from their military leave.

Chief Wurstner had the advantage of many of his newly hired police officers being disciplined military veterans. This, along with his tenure, allowed him to set the stage for future decades.

Chief Rudy Wurstner

The FBI established nationwide training standards a decade earlier. Now with the war over, Chief Wurstner charged his 1936 National FBI Academy graduate, Captain Matthew Kirkpatrick, with developing a new recruit training curriculum in January 1946 in a manner not seen since it had been done by Sergeants Wurstner and Thomas Grundish 30 years earlier. (There have been 111 Dayton Police Academy recruit classes in 75 years since then to present – 2021.)

Captain Kirkpatrick, who had a direct tie with FBI Director J. Edgar Hoover, would eventually become Chief Wurstner's immediate successor in command of the Dayton Police Department.

Sgt. Richard Grundish, the son of Inspector Grundish, was selected by Kirkpatrick in 1949 to be the second local officer to attend the National FBI Academy. He would make a mark for himself as chief of detectives, rising to the rank of captain.

FBI Academy graduate Sgt. Richard Grundish
Capt. Kirkpatrick and FBI Director Hoover.

When then Chief Kirkpatrick retired after his 30-year career, it was to move to Washington D.C. to become the worldwide police training envoy for the International Association of Chiefs of Police (reminscent of influence Chief Whitaker held exactly 50 years earlier).

Kirkpatrick's successor to head the Dayton Police Department was his longstanding counterpart and second in command, Police Inspector Paul Price.

The fortunes of Dayton police officers changed after the run-up to the wars' end. At the start of the wars, "among Ohio cities, no city paid a lower salary [to its police officers] than Dayton in 1941."

By 1946, "Dayton tied with Toledo for the first rank in both money and percentage increases made since 1941," [145] which was a misleading indicator in that wages remained meager even with the highest monetary raise.

1942: Dayton police Plymouth squad car inspection outside the Ford Street Staion.

Still, this improvement in police pay was a reflection of the post-war industrial boom, the advocacy of the Dayton FOP Lodge, and support of Chief Wurstner for his troops.

During the war years, there were a number of notable personnel changes as the old guard began new lives. Former Inspector Seymour Yendes, who had become the public safety director in 1937, retired from public service in 1941 after 33 years; but in 1946, he opened the private "Cy Yendes Detective Bureau" letting prospective business clients know that they were "protected" and that "thieves would be prosecuted."

In between 1941 and 1946, Ptl. Dunlavey retired in 1942, with 26-years of service; Sgt. George Wheeler in 1943 (33 years); and in 1944, Captain Earl Yates (37 years), Sgt. Charles Gross (25 years), and the supervisor of the Bureau of Policewomen, Lulu Sollers (30 years). Her career began when the bureau was first formed in 1914.

Plwn. Sollers was the first woman in Dayton to retire on a police service pension.

Plwn. Lulu Sollers
Ca. 1944 Retirement

Her bureau reported directly to the public safety director by design, not the police chief. The Policewomen's Bureau functioned more like a social service and probation agency. Neither she nor her five policewomen – with badges pinned to their dresses – ever carried firearms. Sollers admitted she would not know how to use one.

In April 1944, Plwn. Hazel Clark succeeded Sollers as supervisor. Clark had been a member of the Policewomen's Bureau since January 1924. She would see to its full transition into the police department by the end of the decade. [146] Unlike Soller's troops, Sgt. Clark's policewomen would be armed with snubnosed revolvers.

Plwn. Hazel Clark
Ca. 1924 Appointment

On January, 7 1945, the local newspaper, *The Journal Herald,* celebrated the 25-year-career milestone being reached by Det. Sgt. Russ Pfauhl. It gave the press an opportunity to once again recount the John Dillinger arrest from 12 years earlier.

Far more significant were press reports in 1945 announcing the end of six years of global wars. On May 8, the German high command signed a surrender agreement, and then on September 2, a similar signing was conducted with a Japanese delegation.

There was celebration throughout the country.

Two months later, on November 9, headlines unrelated to WWII appeared in the *Dayton Daily News* and *The Dayton Herald*:

Ansonia Bank Vault is Robbed of $20,000
Bank Robbers' Loot May Hit $100,000

The small village of Ansonia, Ohio was halfway the distance between Dayton and St. Marys, Ohio in the Miami Valley. Its population of 1,000 residents, protected by one night constable and one day constable, was shocked by the brazenness of the Citizens Bank robbery in their community.

This was a federal offense and FBI officials were called in to investigate. There was little known about suspects in the early stages but one thing was certain after examining the bank vault. These perpetrators had among their robbing gang ...

... a professional safecracker.

Al Fouts had laid low locally for quite a few years, not to be confused with being lawful. He was a bootlegger, swindler and active felon away from Dayton. He had over 27 arrests on his record dating back to 1905, but was 54 years of age in 1945. Small as he was, Al was a tough man of the underworld who had spent  much of his life in the slammer for his crimes. He was not one with whom to trifle. He once said, "I'll live a Christian life [but] I'm not a hypocrite, so I better not say more." [147]

 **George 'Bugs' Moran** had fallen from stature as a Chicago mob boss, and peer of Al Capone. When hitmen for "Scarface" took out Moran's gang on St. Valentine's Day 1929 intending to target him, Bugs knew

he was lucky to be alive. He still had a big name but his life was reduced to thuggery and swindling.

Moran left Chicago for his hometown of St. Paul, only to be rejected by that city's underworld. He returned to Chicago and formed a "professional" alliance with Capone's gang to be left unhurt. Still, he was on the police radar, and repeatedly served time in the Cook County jail. In 1944, he moved to Henderson, Kentucky to become an "oil man."

Virgil 'Doc' Summers was a St. Louis gangster. In 1933, he and six members of his gang committed  "a score" of holdups in Southern Illinois, during which Summers murdered one victim (later, Dayton police noted in its file that Summers may have been "one of John Dillinger's buddies"). Convicted in March 1934, Summers was in the Southern Illinois Penitentiary until December 1943.

Paroled, Doc quickly became the "chief lieutenant and 'strong-arm' man" of the Drewer gang in St. Louis. [148] After Lawrence Drewer was assassinated for purportedly cheating members of his own gang, Summers vanished for a short time.

Drewer's ready-made and now leaderless gang was taken over by Bugs Moran with Doc Summers tied to it as a henchman, and Al Fouts brought into the fold as a safecracker.

They, along with four other gangsters, were suspected by federals agents of being in a "syndicate that looted 22 small-town banks and bars," throughout the Midwest [149] including, it was later learned, the Citizens Bank in Ansonia (a town held up by Charley Makley and his gang 18 years earlier in 1927).

On June 25, 1946, Moran and Summers traveled to Dayton to again conspire with Fouts. The three toured Dayton the following day. Fouts knew of a runner for Silas Tavern [150] that would routinely withdraw money from Winters Bank at West Third and Broadway Streets. [151] The money was used by the bar to cash the paychecks of workers at the nearby Moraine Frigidaire plant.

The gangsters spent three days observing the activities of the runner and saloon keeper, John Kurpe, Jr., who lived at 515 Red Haw Avenue and journeyed between the two.

A little after ten o'clock on the morning of June 28, John Kurpe withdrew $10,000 in new $10 bills from Winters Bank ($133,000 today). He stuffed two bundles of $5,000 into each side of his coat and then walked to his Ford.

The Moran gang, spying nearby from a 1939 black Buick Century sedan with suicide doors, followed as Kurpe drove from Winters Bank south on Broadway. The ever-intense Bugs Moran was the wheelman.

Upon reaching the wide curve at Dona Avenue, John Kurpe slowed because of a large truck rounding the corner. At that point, the massive

The imposing black Buick driven by Bugs Moran.
WSU Special Collections and Archives

black sedan terrifyingly roared up from behind, swung around to his left and then cut in front, forcing Kurpe to stop.

Instantly, Summers and Fouts jumped from the sedan with guns drawn. Summers opened the driver's door and stuck the gun in the runner's ribs as Fouts entered the front passenger side, grabbed the back of Kurpe's neck, and forced his head between his knees. Summers sped away with Moran driving the black sedan directly behind.

After pulling next to a secluded dirt path off Vance Road, the car stopped and all exited. Fouts placed

a sweater across Kurpe's face so he could not see. Walking into the woods a short way, Kurpe was forced to lie down. His mouth, arms and legs were taped and shoes removed. He heard a third car drive up and speed away. A struggling Kurpe was able to

The woods off Vance Road where Kurpe was left.
WSU Special Collections and Archives

free himself. The gang stole the cash. Inexplicably, and fortunately for the victim – the one eye-witness – Kurpe was bound but left unharmed by three unabashed killers.

Left at the scene were the black Buick and his Ford, but Kurpe sensibly did not touch either because he thought there may be fingerprints in both. He was able to walk down Vance Road and flag a farmer who took him to a telephone where he contacted the sheriff and police. In the meantime, Summers drove Moran southward through the corridor. They stopped for breakfast, not surprisingly, in Hamilton. They then left to head to Henderson, Kentucky where Moran had a house. Fouts remained in the Gem City.

George 'Bugs' Moran Dayton Police Bureau of Identification fingerprint card.

WSU Special Collections and Archives

Sgt. Pfauhl *(above right)* looks on as Sgt. Teeter unhandcuffs gang.

Bugs Moran and Doc Summers enter a cell block of the Dayton City Jail handcuffed at 7:45 p.m. after transport from Kentucky.

Moran and Summers are escorted to the Montgomery County Jail by Sgt. Teeter and Deputy John Pratt.

Dayton police immediately began their criminal probe and were assisted by federal authorities.

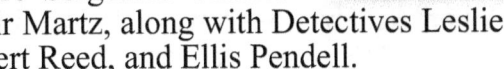

On July 6, Al Fouts was arrested at his home at 502 W. Fourth Street by the Dayton investigative team of three detective squads, led by Detective Sergeant Russell Pfauhl. The others were Sergeants Charles Teeter and Clair Martz, along with Detectives Leslie St. Pierre, Robert Reed, and Ellis Pendell.

A bundle of cash – $1,000 in $10 bills – was found inside Fouts' house.

The arrest was coordinated. The FBI had tracked Bugs and Doc to Henderson, Kentucky where they were apprehended that same day.

A Dayton police team in two vehicles, led by Sgt. Pfauhl, headed to Kentucky. The traveling team of six Dayton detectives was the same other than Sgt. Albert Gaylor replacing Sgt. Martz. After an extradition hearing, the two muggers were taken into custody by Sgt. Pfauhl's team, double-handcuffed, driven back to the Gem City, and booked at the Dayton City Jail on July 13, 1946.

The three men were arraigned in a preliminary hearing on July 15 and bound over to the Common Pleas Court for trial. They were then transferred to the custody of Montgomery County Sheriff Kloos, and into his jail. On August 16, Montgomery County Prosecutor Mathias Heck Sr. [152] turned the case over to his trial attorneys, Fred Kerr and William Wolff.

The defendants were the ideal clients for an attorney of Jack Egan's caliber. He could not represent them, however, because the underworld lawyer had died on August 19, 1936 ... exactly 10 years before FBI agents testified during the Moran gang trial about their surveillance techniques.

The decade before, two of Jack Egan's honorary pallbearers were Judge Robert Patterson, who authorized Dillinger's transfer to Lima, Ohio, and Albert Scharrer, who was representing Bugs Moran in this 1946 kidnap-robbery trial.

Scharrer did not have all three men as clients. It seems the gang had a falling out after their arrest. Fouts later called Moran a "double crossing, double-dealing bum." [153]

Moran's wife speaks with her husband inside the Montgomery Co. courtroom between Doc and Al.

Al Fouts chose Herbert Eikenbary and George Hurley to defend him while Summers dumped Scharrer in favor of St. Louis attorney Harold Brandy. In the end, it made no difference.

Before Judge Robert Martin, all three were convicted of the Kurpe kidnapping-armed robbery. They received prison sentences of no less than 10 years in the Ohio State Penitentiary. They were transferred there on August 29, 1946.

The Dayton holdup was the last crime committed by Bugs Moran, and arguably, the last conviction of a Midwest "celebrity gangster" of the Prohibition era.

After serving a decade at the Ohio State Penitentiary for the Dayton kidnapping-holdup, Fouts, Moran and Summers were tried and convicted of the 1945 Ansonia heist in 1956. Al Fouts tended to be more resourceful than the other two men (he was the only one to be released during the first trial on bail).

August 27, 1946: *The Dayton Herald* - Justice forthcoming to the town up north.

This time, he had a legal team that included Robert C. Knee, a Dayton lawyer who had testified in 1954 as the representative of the Teamsters Union before the 83rd U.S. Congress Special Anti-Racketeering Subcommittee regarding Cleveland, Ohio activities. Knee would later be the legal counsel for the Dayton FOP Lodge in successfully negotiating the officers' first police labor agreement in 1968.

Despite adroit counsel, all three convicts were, again, found guilty of robbery. All three convicts were sent to Kansas to serve sentences in Leavenworth Federal Prison.

None of the three would ever commit more crimes.

Bugs Moran died a month later, another Catholic gangster in need of the Lord's mercy at the end. Fouts and Summers were released five years later in 1961.

Former Gangster Had Only $12.95 in Pockets When Slain

Once Handled Large Sums of Loot;
No Leads or Arrests by Police

VIRGIL W. SUMMERS
—A. P. Wirephoto

December 4, 1962:
St. Louis Globe Democrat.

Doc Summers returned to East St. Louis and was "promptly killed" by a hit man.

The police suspected it was a gang assassination as "payback for hoarding the loot from the Ansonia robbery." [154]

Fouts, on the other hand, would live out a quiet life in Dayton. In December 1963, he was interviewed by a reporter from *The Journal Herald.*

He confessed, "My biggest regret is ... the wasted years ... and that I ever met Bugs Moran. I don't resent anything. The law has a duty to perform." [155]

Fouts may have been in a reflective mood that December. He sent a Christmas card to his attorney from 1946, Herbert Eikenbary, who replied with a two-page letter.

The lawyer ended with words of advice of a higher law: "Repent and be Saved! Come to the Shepard!" [156] The mobster had years for acts of contrition.

Al Fouts
Law Abiding

Al-Albert-Alfred Foutz-Fouts died in 1981 at age 90.

Fouts was a man of many names. It is curious that the original German spelling of his last name – his grandfather's name was "Pfautz" – was so oddly similar to the surname of "Pfauhl."

In June 1947, less than a year after the convictions of Moran, Fouts, and Summers, Det. Sgt. Russ Pfauhl accepted his earned pension after 27 years' service.

Having the arrests of Bugs Moran and John Dillinger as credits to his career, the retired sergeant opened a private investigation agency, the "R. K. Pfauhl Detective Bureau," which operated until 1976. He was also appointed in 1953 by newly elected Montgomery County Sheriff Bernard Keiter as his second in command – the "Chief Deputy" – a position he held until 1959.

Sgt. Russ Pfauhl
A New Career

The uniformed sergeant accompanying Pfauhl when Dillinger was arrested had been promoted to the rank of captain on the very day of the Ansonia bank heist. Captain William Aldredge also retired after a 25-year career which included time for his military service.

Captain
William Aldredge

Exactly a year to the day earlier, on January 1, 1947, Daytonian Milton Caniff's new *Steve Canyon* comic strip debuted. The cartoonist's character was an adventurer and WWII combat veteran who returned to the U.S. Air Force during the Korean War at the rank of lieutenant colonel.

Canyon's real-life counterpart, Ptl. Horace Moore – having taken leave from the police force five years earlier for military service overseas – was honorably discharged in 1947. His tour had been extended as a provost marshal to disarm German citizens. He returned to the police force on April 1, 1947.

A Great War and WWII combat veteran, Sgt. Moore would later reactivate in the U. S. Air Force during the Korean War, and be discharged at the rank of lieutenant colonel ... an authentic *Steve Canyon*.

On June 1, 1947, and exactly two months after returning from war-scarred Europe, Ptl. Moore was on patrol with his partner, Ptl. William Stevens. In the early evening, they spotted two men on Antietam Street, one carrying an object that he attempted to conceal.

Ptl. Horace Moore

When the officers told the men to put their hands up, one of the two drew a pistol, and aimed at Ptl. Moore. The combat veteran who disarmed Germans instantly fired two shots, killing the man.

Only a mile away and just two weeks earlier, on May 16, 1947, Dayton Ptl. Herman Drexler and his partner, James 'Jack' Tatom, responded to a burglary in progress. It was at Cooper's hardware store, 2512 W. Third Street. The officers separated to check the outside of the building.

Ptl. Herman Drexler

One of the two suspects was spotted running at the back of a shop by Ptl. Drexler, himself a WWII combat veteran. While being pursued, the suspect suddenly turned and fatally shot Ptl. Drexler.

Hearing the sound of gunfire, Ptl. Tatom rounded the building where he was taken to the ground with a gunshot blast to his hip. The killer then stood over the wounded officer and placed the gun to his head, declaring, "I'll shoot you, too, [expletive]."

Flat on his back, Ptl. Tatom snatched the gun cylinder, pulled out his black jack, and according to the press, "beat the man into submission." [157]

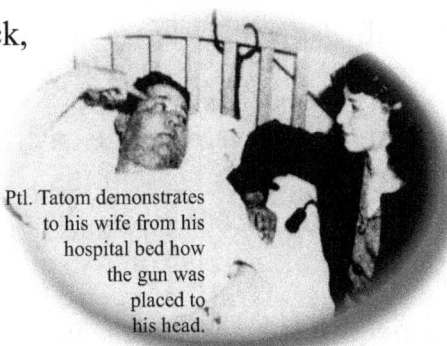

Ptl. Tatom demonstrates to his wife from his hospital bed how the gun was placed to his head.

His assailant, Emrick, was hospitalized with severe head injuries. His accomplice was captured and the two were later tried, convicted, and sentenced to life in prison for killing a Dayton police officer.

Julius A. Emrick, alias Joseph A., John A., and James A. Emrick

Emrick hospitalized with head injuries.

Two weeks before this murder, on May 3, 1947, another Dayton patrolman was killed in the line of duty.

Ptl. Sherman Nowlin had served in the U.S. Navy for three years during the war.

He had been on the police force for only 11 days. The patrol car in which the new officer was riding pursued a stolen vehicle which flew across the East First Street train tracks near Webster Street. The radio car, driven by Ptl. Edward Spiller, did not make it.

The vehicle was broadsided by a speeding locomotive, tragically killing the 22-year-old rookie police officer; his partner was only slightly hurt.

Ptl. Sherman Nowlin

Ptl. Nowlin was removed to Miami Valley Hospital. His 19-year-old wife was already there when her husband's lifeless body arrived. She had given birth to their son the day before.

The year 1947 proved to be another painful year in Dayton police history for all officers and the Chief once again. During the span of Chief Wurstner's long career, 17 of Dayton's 31 "fallen officers" were buried; he attended too many local funerals of fellow lawmen who suffered death while in uniform.

Police Chief
Rudy Wurstner

As the summer of 1948 approached, Chief Wurstner was closing in on 68 years of age and was in the twilight of his career.

Just as he had in making a murder arrest in 1925, the Chief would find within himself, once again, to be at the front lines with his troops. This time the Chief was on the scene of one of the nation's more violent labor strikes, certainly the most violent in local history.

There had been brutal labor strikes after the Great War, such as Browne-Brockmeyer in 1934. Disgruntled laborers on job walkouts, if unruly while on strike lines, always posed great risk for attacks on lawmen. This would be true in 1948 when the Univis Lens Company strike took place at 401 Leo Street at McCook Avenue. This was an industrial area with undeveloped land further west to the Great Miami River.

At the time, the labor movement was progressing with many war veterans entering the workplace at industrial plants. But a "Red Scare" was in its early years – prompted by disturbing news reports about Joseph Stalin, the Soviet Union, and the Cold War – and the labor movement was pegged by politicians and press as being under communist influence.

On May 5, a strike began when 600 production workers walked off the job. As time passed, the Univis workers drew the support of factory employees from DELCO, Frigidaire and GHR Foundry reportedly swelling the "mob" to somewhere between 7,500 and 10,000. By June it had become a dangerous setting and was worsening.

This strike caught the Dayton police, once again, undermanned. A *Time Magazine* article titled "Labor: Brass Knuckles" called it a "savage, three-month-old strike in which heads had been bloodied ... [and] ribs prodded by police billies."

Chief Wurstner was in the thick of the action. Archived film footage at the Ohio Historical Society shows the Chief standing nose-to-nose

Chief Wurstner at the scene of the Univis Lens Company strike.

with the labor leader, Louis Kaplan, in several heated exchanges.

It spilled over into boisterous City Commission meetings and had heightened community fears. In the end, the Ohio Governor came to the Gem City and called in 1,200 National Guard troops to secure the area. An imperfect settlement under pressure by state authorities was intensely negotiated between the two parties to end the impasse.

Ohio National Guardsmen join Dayton police officers in securing the strike scene.

Chief Rudy Wurstner conducted his last troop inspection on July 6, 1949. In front of City Hall, it was of the graduates of a Dayton police academy class. These rookie officers were sworn into service exactly 46 years and 7 months to the day since a much younger Wurstner had experienced the same.

The police force had increased to 253 sworn officers in 1949, and the city's population had nearly tripled in size to 244,000 citizens from when Wurstner was first appointed.

The first half of Rudolph Wurstner's police career crossed historic paths: first flight in 1903 – in having the Wright Cycle Shop and the inventive proprietor brothers on his beat – the Temperance Movement, the 1913 Great Flood, World War I, war production, the Spanish influenza pandemic, and the fast-rising automotive industry. The second half was his time as chief of police beginning in 1925. He traveled through the Roaring '20s, Prohibition, the Great Depression, the New Deal, the "gangster era," World War II, wartime industrialization, the labor movement, and the start of the Cold War.

To place his time in command in perspective, he became chief seven years before Franklin Roosevelt had become the U.S. President ... and he would still be the Chief four years after our four-term-elected, longest-serving president had died.

Upon retirement on July 11, 1949, Chief Wurstner was recognized in newspapers and the FBI Law Enforcement Bulletin for being what he had been since 1935 – the Nation's Dean of Police Chiefs for 14 consecutive years. His tenure as the most senior metropolitan police chief in the nation was previously equaled by only three others in U.S. history. [158]

"Chief Wurstner, then and now."

In the Gem City, his was the longest police career, and also remains the longest tenure as chief in the history of Dayton police with 24 years in command.

At a farewell banquet at Suttmiller's Supper Club on North Main Street, the Dayton Fraternal Order of Police Capt. John C. Post Lodge presented the Chief a retirement badge with six diamonds inlaid along a banner draping the eagle. It was time for the old warrior to enjoy his family, his garden, and his time relaxing at his cottage in Michigan while fishing on Bear Lake.

Standing alongside his successor, Matthew Kirkpatrick, Chief Wurstner appreciatively accepts his retirement badge.

Chief Wurstner was a humble man. He was often quizzed by news reporters about his past exploits. He preferred not to talk about, what he termed, "water over the dam." He said, "I don't enjoy reading about what other men have said they have done in capturing notorious robbers, so I [don't] indulge in any kind of boasting myself." [159]

The Chief was genuinely respected by his troops as demonstrated by his farewell banquet and by the way he was remembered long after he retired. Why?

One reason was he was known for his keen sense of fairness. A veteran patrolman once said, "If you were right, you had a champion… in your corner.

If you were wrong, you could expect to be handled in the same firm way." Chief Wurstner always held that a police officer should "be a square shooter and observe the golden rule." [160]

DAYTON DAILY NEWS

"Well-Informed People Read The Dayton Daily News"

DAYTON, OHIO, WEDNESDAY, JUNE 8, 1949

Dean Of Nation's Police Chiefs Plans Fishing Vacation, Then Stay In Dayton

Even when the community was caught in tumultuous affairs – and there were many in the first half of the 20th century – the Chief always focused on his relationship with his community from his time as a patrolman through his retirement as chief. He once said: "On my beat I always made it a habit to drop in and learn to know those who ran business establishments or persons in the neighborhood, whether they were cobblers or bankers." [161] Or, it could be added, even world-renowned aviation pioneers.

At the close of an incredible 47-year career, he remarked, "I value nothing more highly than the confidence I feel I have gained from the public I have tried to serve." [162]

———

The modest police chief was remembered this 21st century by the good citizens of **Dayton, Ohio** who bestowed their highest honor to **"The Dean"** in recognition of his long, eventful, and meaningful career. **Chief Rudolph F. Wurstner** was inducted into the Dayton Region Walk of Fame posthumously. He had passed away on July 12, 1969, nearly 35 years to the day after the meaningless life of **John Dillinger** was extinguished by lawmen.

The man who deserves national legendary acclaim is properly Chief Rudy Wurstner ... but, regrettably, history affords that distinction to a killer, John Dillinger.

Sidebar: *Dayton Region Walk of Fame - Law Enforcement Inductees*

The Dayton Walk of Fame, formed in 1996, "has recognized 156 outstanding individuals and groups for their enduring personal or professional contributions to the community, nation, and the world." Only three law enforcement officers have been inducted; all three were nominated by *Dayton Police History Foundation, Inc.*

Dayton Police Chief Rudolph F. Wurstner (2012): His career speaks volumes about his character. Long after his police career had concluded, Chief Wurstner crossed paths with the Wright brothers one last time. When 'Rudy' was inducted into the Dayton Walk of Fame, he joined **Wilbur** and **Orville Wright** and many other celebrated Daytonians. He is rightly the first law enforcement officer to be so honored.

Dayton Police Chief Richard Biehl spoke at the ceremony and Chief Wurstner's grandson, **John A. 'Jack' Barstow**, accepted the induction plaque on behalf of the Wurstner family.

Dayton Police Sergeant Lucius J. Rice and Dayton Policewoman Dora Burton Rice (2018): These two law enforcement officers were inducted, fittingly, as a couple. They shared a 30-year marriage, two children – Robert and Lillian, who themselves led accomplished lives – their police careers, and religious faith. Lucius' career and deeds are well documented.

Dora's deeds are a quiet reflection of the person. She was exceedingly active and chose to live in a way that validated her spiritual beliefs. She was described in a Wesleyan Methodist Church publication: "Always an outstanding figure in the community; in Y.M.C.A., club work and civic affairs, Mrs. Rice played an important part in the development of Negro life in Dayton." Her devotion to the welfare of children is what led to her becoming a policewoman, breaking a barrier for women of color. As an inductee, she joined in the Dayton Walk of Fame the accomplished poet who lived with her at the time of his death, her first cousin, **Paul Laurence Dunbar**. His last poems were of her.

Chief Richard Biehl gave a video address, laden with history, at the ceremony. Dora and Lucius' grandson, **Robert B. Rice, Jr.**, accepted their induction plaque on behalf of his family.

The National Law Enforcement Officers Memorial (1991)

A half century after his tragic death, the name *"Sgt. Lucius J. Rice"* was engraved on the marble wall at the National Law Enforcement Officers Memorial in Washington D.C. on October 15, 1991. In addition to personal achievements, Lucius and Dora Rice personify the sacrifices of all 87 regional law enforcement officers who have forfeited their lives in service to their community – the ultimate sacrifice – as well as all "fallen officers' survivors" who surrendered their loved ones' lives for the sake of public safety.

Above - **September 2012:** Jack Barstow proudly stands with Dayton Police Chief Richard Biehl at the Ceremony for his grandfather, Chief Rudolph F. Wurstner.

Below- **September 2018:** Robert Rice proudly stands with Mr. Harry Seifert, Wright Dunbar, Inc. CEO, at the Ceremony for his grandparents, Sgt Lucius and Plwn. Dora Rice.

AFTERWORD

BOOTLEGGERS, BANDITS, AND BADGES:

FROM DRY TIMES TO HARD TIMES IN DAYTON, OHIO

1920 Model T Ford Hack on display at the **Carillon Historical Park** exhibit.
It looks like a lumber hauler, but is designed for smuggling bootlegged liquor
It is one of three vehicles, along with a 1930 Diamond T paddy wagon and a
1932 Packard Eight Club Sedan with gangster whitewall tires, on display.

Artist renderings of the two custom cases by Exhibit Concepts, Inc. holding
Chief Wurstner's service revolver and Dillinger's auto pistol *(above)*,
and the Montgomery County Sheriff's Tommy gun *(below)*.

AFTERWORD

THE VISION – Whereas the *Introduction* explained my reason for writing this book, the *Afterword* takes this one step further by describing the exhibit and, hopefully, advancing Dayton Police History Foundation, Inc.'s principal goal.

Bootleggers, Bandits, and Badges is hosted by Carillon Historical Park (CHP) through the close of 2023 thanks to **Brady Kress**, President and CEO. This exhibit is in CHP's main building – the Kettering Family Education Center – and located in the north wing, the Kenneth Quinter Family Exhibition Gallery. It presents the *three slices* of time in Dayton area law enforcement history as recounted in this book: the **Temperance Movement** (1860-1919); **Prohibition** (1920-1933); and **Great Depression** (1929-1941).

The 2,500 square-foot gallery holds a number of period exhibit items, both small and large, but two major displays are the centerpieces of two distinct time periods.

The first is the Prohibition Era with a custom case holding a model 1921 AC Colt Thompson submachine gun. This Tommy gun with drum magazine has been in the **Montgomery County Sheriff**'s arsenal since being received in a 1927 shipment from Pennsylvania. It is exhibited thanks to the authorized donation in 2018 by then **Sheriff Phil Plummer**. The acquisition was facilitated in 2019 by **Sheriff Rob Streck**.

The second centerpiece display is in the Great Depression Era. It is a custom case that holds John Dillinger's 1933 Colt Super .38 auto pistol taken from him when arrested in Dayton. It is shown in stark contrast to and alongside Dayton Police Chief Rudy Wurstner's 1920 Colt service revolver. Both firearms are exhibited thanks to the **Wurstner family**.

In between, linking the two guns, are the handcuffs placed on Dillinger by Dayton detectives. It is exhibited thanks to **Wright State University Special Collections and Archives**.

What else is there to take in?

Large scenic murals and audio tracks that transport onlookers to Dayton of yesteryears; a replicated 19th century saloon bar; display cases with many police artifacts; a 1920 Ford Model T Hack with a disguised haul of "moonshine" barrels; accounts of police liquor squads combating bootleggers; a bootlegging still; episodes from the "Roaring '20s" and cultural garments – from period police uniforms, to a flapper dress, to a 1920s Klan hood – a full-size patrol call box mounted on an iron stanchion; filmed accounts and imagery; the John Dillinger saga, of course, and even more to take in....

The **City of Dayton** and the **Dayton Police Department**, through the backing of **Chief Richard Biehl** and authorization from the City Manager's Office, furnished two outstanding elements for the tour in addition to some vintage police artifacts. One is in a display case. It holds over a dozen criminal weapons seized by Dayton police officers in the '20s and '30s, similar to those depicted on page 110.

The other is an actual old city jail cell that was also used in a 2014 movie production. Thanks to **Matt Miller**, owner of **Carl's Body Shop**, the cell was disassembled, stripped, returned to original condition, and then assembled at the exhibit site by his restoration team.

A few of the exhibited criminal weapons seized by Dayton patrolmen while arresting bandits and felons during The Roaring '20s and The Great Depression.

DAYTON POLICE DEPARTMENT CONTRIBUTIONS

This particular city prisoner cell was used in the 2014 filming of a "New York City" jail scene for the movie *Miles Ahead*. That movie premiered in 2016 and was an important early project for Academy Award-winning film production designer, Daytonian Hannah Beachler (*Black Panther*, 2019). *Miles Ahead* starred Don Cheadle and it was his directorial debut in feature film. The cell is a popular photo-taking exhibit feature.

Top Left:
St. Marys First National Bank
teller window.

Top Right:
1930 Diamond T paddy wagon.

Center:
1932 Packard Eight Club Sedan.

Bottom Left:
New Carlisle National Bank
teller window.

Two other period vehicles, in addition to the "bootlegger" Model T, are on display. One is a 1930 Diamond T "Black Maria" from the classic car collection of **Jim Day**, owner of **Esther Price Candies**, and the other is a 1932 Packard Eight Club Sedan with gangster whitewall tires from **America's Packard Museum** through its director, **Dan Badger**.

Large gangster cars, such as Packard hardtop sedans, had rear windows that served as gun ports to discourage police chases. As for the exhibited, fully restored 1930 police paddy wagon, it was originally from the police department of Forest Park, Illinois, a community five miles from Al Capone's Cicero home.

Two teller windows from banks robbed by the Dillinger gang are featured as well. **Larry Kramer**, the proprietor of **St. Marys Hobby Center**, provided through **Robert Makley** a teller window from his city's First National Bank, held up by Charley Makley and other members of Dillinger's gang.

And, retired Clark County **Chief Deputy Carl Loney** facilitated the acquisition of a teller window from the old National Bank of New Carlisle, the first bank John Dillinger himself robbed.

James Dailey II was incredibly generous with rare photographs by opening *The Dailey Archives* to the exhibit. Words express a story but pictures visually transport the reader. There is considerably more on display thanks to CHP, the **Dayton Fraternal Order of Police Lodge**, DPH Foundation, and many individual contributors of police 'tools of the trade' and other notable items, such as both Dayton Walk of Fame plaques, iconic badges, et al.

Yet, the item of greatest interest to many visitors is the Colt .38 Super auto pistol, confiscated from Dillinger when he was arrested in Dayton.

"Taken from
John Dillinger on...."

In 1933, it was inscribed and warmly presented to Dayton Police Chief Rudy Wurstner by his detectives. The Colt auto pistol remained in the Chief's family until 2004 when they selflessly gifted it to the Dayton community, believing this rare artifact belonged in the public domain and not in private hands. In the January 2011 edition of *Ohio Magazine* – in its annual feature titled "Best of Ohio" – the Dillinger Colt .38 Super semi-automatic handgun was named "Ohio's best historical artifact."

More than the Artifacts and Exhibits

The evolution of law enforcement, as it adapted to the changing nature of the country, is the central storyline of this exhibit, but social and cultural accounts are presented throughout the journey.

Certainly, the story of the temperance cause is chronicled in depth. Other historical, interrelated narratives of the three eras include the suffrage movement, race relations, politics, business, manufacturing, the economy, arts, entertainment, sports, transportation and city infrastructural improvements.

While this exhibit is a story about the Greater Dayton Area's presence on local, statewide, and national stages, it also captures the tale of our nation's decade-by-decade development from the 1860s to 1950.

OTHER VIEWS
FROM
THE EXHIBIT

Chief John
Allaback's
1910 Badge,
Nightstick,
and Colt
Service
Revolver.

Policing is an often unnoticed component of society's growth... but not with this exhibit.

A Larger Vision and Fuller Story to be Told!

Bootleggers, Bandits, and Badges is sponsored at a cost of $60,000 by Dayton Police History Foundation, Inc. thanks to generous financial donations made by its supporters, many of them retired police officers.

Bootleggers, Bandits and Badges was designed to bring attention to our greater goal of producing a permanent Dayton Metropolitan Police museum facility on the Carillon Park grounds. There are nearly 225 years of Dayton law enforcement history to be shared. This cannot be accomplished without major philanthropic sponsorship by businesses and individual benefactors willing to adopt this project, estimated to be $1.5 million. **Concept renderings of <u>Our Vision</u> are depicted** on the next few pages. They are a glance into the past as well as to the future.

Interested parties that recognize the genuine value a police history museum offers the community are asked to please contact DaytonPoliceHistory.org.

Finally, our sincerest gratitude is extended to everyone involved too numerous to name herein. They are listed on the exhibit's *Wall of Recognition.* The loans of artifacts, individual donations, business sponsorships, and the work of Dayton History staff and volunteers have made this a special gift to our local community and visitors to the Greater Dayton Area.

— Stephen Grismer

Proposed Exhibit Building modeled after the 1902 Dayton Police Patrol House, 15 South St. Clair Street.

OUR

VISION

OF THE

FUTURE

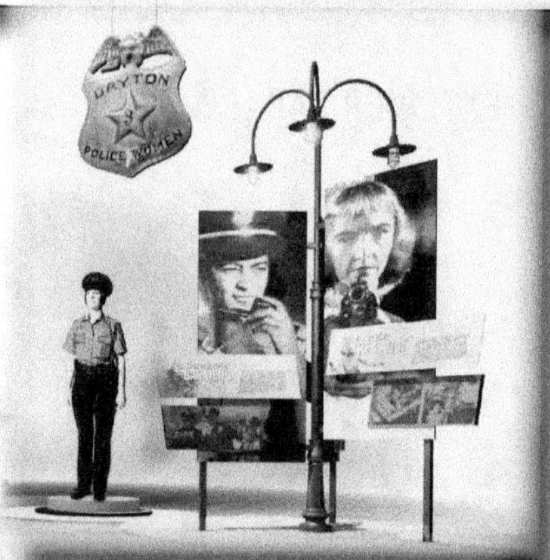

DAYTON POLICE HISTORY FOUNDATION, INC.

DAYTON METROPOLITAN POLICE MUSEUM

OUR VISION OF THE FUTURE

WALL OF RECOGNITION

SPONSORED BY DAYTON POLICE HISTORY FOUNDATION, INC. (DPHF)
IN MEMORY OF DPHF CHAIRMAN JOHN A. 'JACK' BARSTOW

ENDNOTES

PROLOGUE

[1] William Martin was preceeded by Patrick O'Connell, Amos Clark, and Thomas Steward. A year after the police force was formed in 1867 under O'Connell, political wrangling at the state level resulted in the 1868 repeal of the law that allowed the formation of police departments in cities of the second class (only Dayton and Columbus). An organized force continued under the authority of the mayor and a marshal (technically sanctioned by the state) until the Ohio law was reenacted in 1873.

[2] Mace Crable's Saloon was located where Don's Pawn Shop stands today.

[3] In-house written and illustrated by the Brown Bierce Co., *Illustrated History • Dayton Fire Department* (Dayton, Ohio: J.E Brelsford "Job, Book, and Catalogue Printer," Callahan Bank Building, 1900). Chapter: The Paid Firemen, p. 14.

[4] Born **Alfred** George Fouts on October 19, 1890. He was more often identified as **Albert** Fouts than his given name on Dayton police records as well as in newspaper articles. It is for that reason, he is referred to as Albert (and Al) throughout this book. On far fewer Dayton police records, his first name is identified as Alfred. His police rap sheet carries both names.

Also, worth noting is that early in his life, Al Fouts' last name was also spelled "Foutz" and appears that way on a few police records. As a point of interest, his oldest brother Clifton was identified as Clifford in various documents and his other older brother Earl, a convicted thief, went by the nickname Pete. Earl's last big crime in 1936, a large securities scam, netted him three years in prison. He was indicted under 13 aliases. Clearly, name identity was a family issue.

[5] Howard Burba. "The Downfall of Chief Farrell," *Dayton Daily News*, 25 April 1937.

CHAPTER 1

[6] "Detective Crumley on Visit to City," *Dayton Daily News*, 3 August 1918.

[7] Four sources for quotes on fighting acumen: 1) "BIFFED, A Copper in the Eye, and Then–," *The Dayton Herald*, 18 February 1899; 2) "STRUCK with Crumley's Good Strong Right Fist," *The Dayton Herald*, 16 May 1899; 3) "He's 'Some Pumpkins' Himself," *Dayton Daily News*, 10 June 1901; and, 4) "Exciting Capture and Escape of a Daring Negro Sneak," *Dayton Daily News*, 7 July 1902.

[8] James Crumley letter about his personal life and law enforcement career, 1872 to ca. 1938, courtesy of Bridget Sperl.

[9] "Exciting Capture and Escape of a Daring Negro Sneak," *Dayton Daily News*, 7 July 1902.

[10] "CRUMLEY, Crumley Landed.... a Celebrated Crook," *Dayton Daily News*, 6 September 1904.

[11] The source of the inquiry is not known for a note marked: "Filed Dec-15-16" and leading with "Dayton Ohio Dec., 12 --". It concludes with "Journal 730pm 140 words bt" and is from the archives at the St. Paul Library courtesy of Bridget Sperl. The replying person from *The Dayton Journal* is not identified on the note.

[12] Source for all related quotes to this account: Howard Burba, "When Carrie Nation Came to Dayton," *Dayton Daily News*, 17 December 1933.

[13] Recommended reading on the 19th century murders in Dayton: Curt Dalton, *Spilt Blood: When murder walked the streets of Dayton* (Dayton, Ohio: C. Dalton, 2004).

[14] Recommended reading on Dayton lawyer Jack Egan and his clients: David C. Greer, *God is Merciful – The Colorful Career of John E. Egan* (Wilmington, Ohio: Orange Fazier Press, 2017).

[15] Or were the murders solved? Recommended reading on Dayton's serial killings: Brian Forschner, *Cold Serial • The Jack the Strangler Murders* (New York, NY: Morgan James Publishing LLC, 2016).

[16] Op. cit., Alfred George Fouts, Endnote [4].

[17] Ohio Senate Bill No. 4; AN ACT to amend Section 5: "An act providing against the evils resulting from the traffic in intoxicating liquors." Passed 13, May 1886; Filed 25 March 1909.

[18] "Initial Ball Given by the Dayton Police Benevolent Association Proves Big Success," *The Dayton Journal*, 8 January 1910.

CHAPTER 2

[19] The City Railway tracks that ran along the 3rd Precinct Police Station on the south side of the street at 1828 W. Third Street is where Haerlin Lane is situated today.

[20] "Why Saint Paul?: A Quick History," online at *VisitSaintPaul.com*. Post undated. Visit Saint Paul. Official Convention and Visitors Bureau: Internet, 27 April 2020.

[21] Two sources for all related quotes in three paragraphs of this account: 1) John C. Hover, et al., editors *Memoirs of the Miami Valley - Volume Two*; (Chicago: Robert O. Law Company, 1919), Section: "Practical Results in the Division of Health, Public Welfare, Chamber of Commerce," pp. 210-211; and 2) Larry Herron, "May We Present, Lulu Sollers, Policewoman," *Dayton Journal Herald*, Sunday Spotlight, 17 December 1939.

[22] "Have Narrow Escapes in Warning Others," *The Dayton Journal*, 2 April 1913.

[23] Marshall Everett, *The Tragic Story of America's Greatest Disaster* (Chicago: J.S. Ziegler Company, 1913). "Orders Looters Killed." P. 177.

[24] Recommended reading on police rescue and relief efforts during 1913 Great Dayton Flood: Stephen C. Grismer, *Drenched Uniforms and Battered Badges: How Dayton Emerged from the 1913 Flood* (Dayton, Ohio: DPH Foundation, Inc., 2013).

[25] The area of horse carcass disposal was described as six miles south of West Third Street on grounds of the Great Miami River, placing it near modern-day Moraine Air Park.

[26] Earlier printings of this book listed **Patrolmen Edward Branch** and **Thomas Cavanaugh** as duty-related Spanish influenza deaths. In 2022, Rocky Geppert, *Officer Down Memorial Page* researcher, notified this author about on-duty influenza deaths of Patrolmen Harsh and Hennessey (now listed), leading to a fuller death records review. Ptl. Cavanaugh died from "stomach trouble" in October 1918 but not influenza, while Branch had resigned from the force in 1917, months before he died from the Spanish Flu.

[27] Recommended reading on the local involvement in World War I: Paul D. Lockhart and Gwen Haney, *Over There: Dayton in the Great War* (Dayton, Ohio: P. Lockhart; G. Haney, 2017). Quote: "The High Price of War," p. 72.

[28] "Jiu-Jitsu to be Taught Soldiers," *Dayton Daily News*, 4 May 1918.

[29a] The *Bootleggers, Bandits, and Badges* exhibit at Carillon Historical Park, Dayton, Ohio. One of the text panels authored by Steve Lucht, Dayton History, as exhibit coordinator, 2019.

[29b] Ibid.

CHAPTER 3

[30] The *Bootleggers, Bandits, and Badges* exhibit at Carillon Historical Park, Dayton, Ohio. One of the text panels authored by Gwenyth Haney, Dayton History, exhibit collections manager, 2019.

[31] Op. cit., James Crumley Letter, Endnote [8].

[32] "John Dillinger," online at *History.com*. Posted 9 November 2009; updated 21 August 2018. The History Channel: Internet 24, April, 2020.

[33] Recommended reading on Dayton in the 1930s: Philip McKee, *Big Town* (New York: The John Day Company, 1931). Chapter 9: "The Noble Experiment." P. 169

[34] Curt Dalton, *Breweries of Dayton – A Toast to Brewers from the Gem City: 1810-1961* (Dayton, Ohio: C. Dalton 2013). Chapter Two, Part Two: "Prohibition Takes Effect." p. 83.

[35] F.O. Eichelberger, City Manager, *Annual Report of the City of Dayton for the Year 1922* (Dayton, Ohio: The City Commission, 1923).

[36] The name Pfauhl is pronounced "Fall". In a word play, this story could have been titled "Pfauhl takes a Fall."

[37] There are four sources for all related quotes to this account:

1) R.K. Pfauhl (detective, liquor squad), Special Report to J.N. Allaback, Chief of Police, dated June 28, 1922 (Dayton, Ohio); 2) Chief of Police, Report to H.E. Myers, Director of Safety, dated July 5, 1922 along with "Charges and Specifications for violations of Rule One and Rule Thirteen; 3) R.K. Pfauhl, Patrolman 98, handwritten letter to J.N. Allaback, dated July 11, 1922; and 4) H.E. Myers, Director of Safety, Change of Plea form with disposition.

[38a] "New Chief of Police to get More Salary," *Dayton Daily News*, 8 November 1922.

[38b] The C. H.& D. is the Cincinnati, Hamilton and Dayton Railway.

[39] "Booze Trade "Honor' is Nil," *Dayton Daily News*, 7 August 1922.

[40] "Liquor Disappears Soon After Tossed from Car; Constables Puzzled," *Dayton Daily News*, 25 June 1925.

[41] Dr. Margaret Peters interview, 111 Building, Suite 1100, Dayton, Ohio, 25 September 2010.

CHAPTER 4

[42] "U.S. May Hear of Bomb Blast at University," *Dayton Daily News*, 21 December 1923.

[43] William Vance Trollinger, Jr, "Forgotten Flames," University of Dayton Magazine. Winter 2013-14. p. 35.

[44] "Bootleg Gang may be Guests in Local Jail," *The Dayton Herald*, 3 April 1925.

[45] "Two Others in Case Not Yet Arrested," *Dayton Daily News*, 21 January 1927.

[46] "Federal Grand Jury to Begin Probe of Charge Against 100 on Monday," *Dayton Daily News*, 1 May 1927.

[47] The headline actually named the constable but since his name is not referenced in the account herein, his police position was more relevant. The headline is: "Woman Says Severs Told Her to Give Him $100," *The Dayton Herald*, 20 May 1927.

[48] The exact location of Jefferson Road was not determined but is believed to be in the area of today's Free Pike.

[49] "Uniform Comes Into Its Own for Dayton's Police Chiefs," *Dayton Daily News*, 20 June 1925.

[50] "Lindbergh Fiasco Back Alley Trick Says Police Chief," *The Dayton Herald*, 23 June 1927

CHAPTER 5

[51] "Second Racketeer Dies," *The Dayton Herald*, 17 June 1933.

[52] Ross Rice, Special Agent, Chicago FBI (ret.), commentator. *Melvin Purvis: The Gangbuster*. American Lawmen. Cinefix Productions, 2016.

[53] Nate Hendley, author/commentator. *Melvin Purvis: The Gangbuster*. American Lawmen. Cinefix Productions, 2016.

[54] "Dayton Bankers Battle Bandits," *The Dayton Journal*, 16 April 1930.

[55] The banker, Phillip Kloos, whose first name is also spelled "Philip" in newspaper articles, was later elected to the office of Montgomery County Sheriff.

[56] All quotes in this account: "Bandit Dead, Another Dying After Xenia Av. Bank Raid," *Dayton Daily News*, 6 May 1930.

[57] H. Jamison Redder, *Paper, Mister? Downtown Dayton-- 1935.* (Dayton, Ohio: 1 January 1995). pp. 182-183.

Pages from this book were provide by Dayton police retired Lieutenant Thomas Tunney. The Cincinnati company that "refitted" the Bank Flyer was not identified in the story. In conducting further research, the staff at the Dayton-based *America's Packard Museum* advised that cars of this nature during this time frame would have been customized in Cincinnati by Hess and Eisenhardt. In addition to customizing Capone's Cadillacs (similarly bullet-proofed), it also customized U.S. Presidential limousines, including the one John F. Kennedy was in when he was assassinated in Dallas, Texas in 1963. The "Bank Flyer" was in regular service for a little more than 10 years, then "retired from duty" in 1941.

[58] "Ohio Man is Sentenced on Pistol Charge," *The Richmond Palladium*, 24 November 1931.

[59] "Dry Officer Will Attempt to Link Foutz with Raid," *The Dayton Journal*, 5 February 1931.

[60] "Years Change Styles in Garb of John Law," *Dayton Daily News*, 13 August 1933.

[61] "Wurstner and Yendes Back from World Police Meet," *Dayton Daily News*, 24 October 1931.

CHAPTER 6

[62] Source for both paragraph quotes: *Civic Report of the City of Dayton for the Year 1933*, published by the City Commission.

[63] Miami County Children's Home Index. Longnaker, Clara Ann. Longnaker, Betty Jean. Troy, Ohio: The Troy Historical Society, 1930-1970.

Recommended reading: Ellen Poulsen, *Don't Call Us Molls – Women of the John Dillinger Gang* (Oakland Gardens, NY: Clinton Cook Publishing Corp., 2002). On pp. 37-38, Poulsen cites that Mary Longnaker filed for divorce due to "cruelty and neglect," that Howard vindictively refused to let Mary see her two daughters, and that the courts refused her custody. Poulsen makes a compelling case that Mary was emotionally wrought and this was the basis for the fight that Dillinger later had with Howard Longnaker. It was as much over the matter of custody as it was hastening the divorce.

[64] There is a question as to whether the eldest of the two daughters, Clara Ann, was Howard Longnaker's child. Also, his life ended on May 20, 1956 when he committed suicide at "Lover's Lane" in Pleasant Hill. He was sitting in his car that he had purposely rigged with a hose from the exhaust pipe so that he would succumb from carbon monoxide poisoning.

As for both girls, they were adopted by families with the means to properly raise them. Their first names were changed as were their last names by virtue of the adoptions. Raised by different families, and in different states, they had long and seemingly prosperous lives, reacquainting years later. Clara Ann died at age 77 in Rockford, Illinois in 2006. Betty Jean, now 90 years old, lives in Flagstaff, Arizona.

[65] Mrs. Stricker died in 1968 at age 83. The boarding house at 324 W. First Street was torn down with little fanfare the year before in 1967; *The Journal Herald*, 25 October 1967. Today, the location is a parking lot west of the AT&T building at the corner of North Perry Street.

[66] The building still exists. Since its banking days, it has housed a number of businesses, the most current at this writing is a collectibles shop called "Abe's Hidden Treasures".

[67] Today, this is Ohio State Route 571.

[68] The general story rings true but accounts vary: One has it that Marshal Orth Stocker was trapped when Dillinger rolled up the window on his arm while another has the marshal intending to ride on the running board but had to hold on for dear life because the auto unexpectedly accelerated. The marshal either fell from the car or was knocked or pushed off. As for his Dillinger's encounter with Howard Longnaker, it was one in which Howard later said, "I didn't think he'd be as strong as he was." Ellen Poulsen contends in *Don't Call Us Molls*, the fight was over Dillinger's attempt to get Mary child custody of her two girls.

[69] The Pony House saloon was located between East Fourth and Fifth Streets but no longer exists; however, its mahogany bar is located inside Jay's Seafood at 225 E. Sixth Street.

Lore: Other notable patrons who drank at the bar include Buffalo Bill Cody (reportedly while on his horse) and heavyweight boxing champions, John L. Sullivan (the Boston Strongboy), 'Gentleman Jim' Corbett, and Jack Dempsey (the Manassas Mauler).

[70] Vargo's Restaurant no longer exists but was located at 2374 W. Riverview Avenue at Vernon Drive alongside the old Dayton Tire and Rubber factory.

[71] This house at 1106 Oakridge Drive is the only Dayton building still standing where Dillinger was known to be. Whether Dillinger was inside, outside on the porch, or waited in the car is unknown.

[72] Mary Ann Buchholz police transcript dated October 17, 1933. Source: WSU Archive Collection..

[73] Ibid.

74 John Toland, *The Dillinger Days*. New York: Random House 1963 (1st edition); reprinted De Capo Press, 1995. The quote is from Toland, *The Dillinger Days*, p. 77. The timeline and letter excerpts from this section are from pp. 76, 77.

CHAPTER 7

75 Lib Hedges is a story unto herself. Born in 1840 in Germany, her true name was Elizabeth Richter. She immigrated to the U.S.A. and found home in Dayton. She became the Gem City's infamous madam, owning 38 mostly Victorian houses, many operating as houses of ill fame. She and her sister "Louisa La Fontaine" were in business until the late 1910s. Hedges died in 1923 leaving an estate valued at $202,546 ($3 million today). She was very generous with financial donations during the 1913 Flood relief.

76 The length of time of the stakeout, as being seven (7) weeks, has been oft repeated in newspaper articles, as far back as 1945, and in books. This claim, made by Det. Pfauhl himself, is misconstrued. It would mean August 4, 1933 as the start of the stakeout relative to the date of the arrest. The detectives would have had to have known Dillinger's girlfriend was Longnaker at that point. Documents show the earliest her identity was learned was likely August 30 making September 1 or 2 as the most logical start of the surveillance – thus, an operation lasting three (3) weeks. The "seven weeks" is likely how long Dayton police were aware of Dillinger's presence in the Greater Dayton Area based on a Cy Yendes statement.

77 Jessie Nicodemus, "On a September Night in 1933 a Man Called on his Girl...," *The Journal Herald*, 6 April 1963.

78 Steve Clark, "2 Daytonians Recall Day They Caught Dillinger." *Dayton Daily News*, 25 September 1970.

79 Sgt. William Joseph Aldredge as told to grandsons Tom and Joey Huddleston. "Additional notes about the capture of John Dillinger in Dayton, Ohio," 17 July 2019.

80 Dale Huffman, "The Word Went Out: John Dillinger's In Town," *Dayton Daily News*, 19 September 1973.

81 "Dillinger's Arrest in Dayton was Planned So Well He Didn't Have a Chance." *Dayton Daily News*, 23 July 1934.

82 Op. cit., Dale Huffman, "The Word Went Out....", Endnote [80].

83 Ibid.

84 Ibid.

85 Ibid.

86 Ibid.

87 Jessie Nicodemus, "On a September Night in 1933 a Man Called on his Girl...," *The Journal Herald*, 6 April 1963.

[88] Op. cit., "Dillinger's Arrest in Dayton was Planned So Well He Didn't Have a Chance," Endnote [81].

[89] Op. cit., Dale Huffman, "The Word Went Out....", Endnote [80].

[90] Op. cit., "On a September Night in 1933....", Endnote [77].

[91] Lewis F. Carr, "May We Present Horace Moore – Among the Youngest in the AEF." *The Journal Herald Spotlight*, 9 November 1941.

[92] The old Market House was razed in 1956. Today, it is the location of the Greater Regional Transit Authority Central Hub.

[93] "Dillinger Was Impressed By the Lawmen's Vests." *Dayton Daily News*, 29 September 1970.

[94] Op. cit., Jessie Nicodemus, "On a September Night in 1933...," Endnote [77]; and Steve Clark, "2 Daytonians Recall Day They Caught Dillinger," Endnote [78].

[95] Larry Andrews, "I Was There When They Captured John Dillinger in Dayton, Ohio." *Dayton Daily News*, The Magazine. 29 July 1984: p. 4.

CHAPTER 8

[96] Op. cit., Sgt. William Joseph Aldredge; additional notes about the capture of John Dillinger, Endnote [79].

[97] "QUESTION SUSPECT IN SIX BANK ROBBERIES." *Dayton Daily News*, 22 September 1933.

[98] As had the Police HQ (see Endnote [92]), the Ford Street Central Police Station was also razed in 1956 when all Dayton police operations were centralized into the Dayton Safety Building at 335 W. Third Street. Today, the location of the Ford Street Station is a parking lot between Sears and Webster Streets behind The Steam Plant at 617 E. Third Street.

[99] Op. cit., Steve Clark, "2 Daytonians Recall Day They Caught Dillinger," Endnote [78].

[100] Ellen Poulsen, *Chasing Dillinger – Police Captain Matt Leach, J. Edgar Hoover and the Rivalry to Capture Public Enemy No. 1* (Jefferson, North Carolina: Exposit, 2018), p. 88.

[101] Source for quotes in first two paragraphs: Op. cit., "QUESTION SUSPECT IN SIX BANK ROBBERIES," Endnote [97].

[102] Joanne Huist Smith, "Dayton's connection to Dillinger: Bank robber came here for love," *Dayton Daily News*, 28 June 2009.

[103] Op. cit., Dale Huffman, "The Word Went Out: ... In Town," Endnote [80].

[104] The "Black Maria" (pronounced "Mariah") was a large 1928 patrol wagon that was also utilized as a police ambulance. Regarding the old Montgomery County Jail at 29 W. Third Street, it was razed in 1974 to make way for Dayton's Court House Square.

[105] "Dillinger Held at County Jail," *The Dayton Journal*, 24 September 1933.

[106] Fred D. Parsons is believed to be the first African-American Montgomery County deputy sheriff. Newspapers during this period did not classify a white citizen in its news articles but were certain to identify a black citizen as "Negro" or "colored".

[107] "Deputies Guard Jail Prisoner," *The Dayton Herald*, 27 September 1933.

[108] Op. cit., Ellen Poulsen, *Chasing Dillinger*, Endnote [100].

[109] Op. cit., Larry Andrews, "I Was There When....," Endnote [95].

[110] Op. cit., Dale Huffman, "The Word Went Out: John Dillinger's In Town," Endnote [80].

[111] Op. cit., Sgt. William Joseph Aldredge; additional notes about the capture of John Dillinger, Endnote [79].

[112] "Dillinger is Under Guard in Lima Jail," *Dayton Daily News*, 28 September 1933, is the only report found that identifies the stopover as being in Piqua, while other references have surfaced, including first-hand accounts, indicating Troy, Ohio to be the meeting place.

Piqua in Miami County is closer to the midpoint; however, Troy is the city where the Miami County jail is located. Besides, there is no mention of the stop in the *Piqua Daily Call* which is a curious omission, had a stop been made, given the notoriety of Dillinger.

CHAPTER 9

[113] Marion Esterline, "Chief Recalls Bank Theft by Dillinger", *The Journal Herald*, 11 October 1948.

[114] "Reward Spurs Killer Hunt," *The Lima News*, 13 October 1933.

[115] Ibid.

[116] The timing of the <u>undated</u> letter written by Mary Longnaker to "Johnnie" and left at Pete's Greek restaurant has been probed. Immediately after his escape is the most logical timing. There was no reason for Mary to hide to meet Dillinger before his Dayton arrest and, in the months after his escape, there was no other triggering event that would lead her to believe he might return to her. As time passed, the chances of a reunion diminished.

The letter was probably left undated by Mary purposely. If found by the police, it would be more difficult to use against her in prosecuting for aiding a fugitive. An analysis by and debate with Susan D. Jansen, Esq. helped draw the author's conclusion to this puzzle.

[117] "Plans Laid at Dayton Conference for Man-Hunt," *The Dayton Herald*, 14 October 1933

[118] Op. cit., Mary Ann Buchholz police transcript, Endnote [72].

CHAPTER 10

[119]   Federal Bureau of Investigation File No. 62-19777-1, "John Dillinger. Serials 1-28," 3 April 1934 to 23 July 1934.

[120]   Ibid.

[121]   Jessie Nicodemus, "Dillinger Recalled in Pleasant Hill," *The Journal Herald*, 9 April 1963.

[122] Two sources: "HIS GIFT – SWEETHEART – WOMAN IN RED," *The South Bend Tribune*, 26 July 1934; and "Dillinger's Former Dayton Girl Friend 'Sorry'," The Dayton Herald, 24 July 1934 *(see Sidebar below)*.

[123]   Stewart, Virginia 'Ginny,' Trotwood Madison Historical Society (Ohio), Re: Mary Longnaker, 24, February 2015.

Thanks to a connection facilitated by local historian Curt Dalton, the author of this book had a telephone conversation with Ginny Stewart at 9 a.m. on Tuesday, February 24, 2015. Ginny's mother, Frances Denton, was a co-worker of Mary Longnaker who she knew as Mary Titus. (*Note:* Ginny's mother passed away in 2005 at the age of 85.)

Frances and Mary met at "The Inland" plant located on Abbey Street. The two worked a conveyer line assembling guns and, post-war, metal ice cube trays. Closely together on the assembly line, the two women develop a friendship and talked about their lives.

[124]   Ibid.

Mary kept her romance with Dillinger a life secret to all except Frances. It was through her mom's friendship that Ginny Stewart herself came to know Mary from about 1947 to 1961. Ginny remembers first meeting Mary at one of Inland's social gatherings when she was small, around 1947. She said that, as her mother and Mary's friendship grew, Ginny would see Mary at other times. She last spoke with Mary when Ginny was in her early 20s (after 1961). It was years long after this when her mother confided that her coworker, Mary Titus, was Mary Longnaker.

The Ending Note: The Former Dillinger Gal – in Her Own Words

Mary Jenkins Longnaker: "I haven't cried yet. I felt like it ever since Johnny was killed." The first press quote in July 1934 under *The Dayton Herald*'s bold, front page headline **Dillinger's Former Dayton Girl Friend "Sorry"**. "I was sleeping when I heard a boy shouting of Johnny's death. I got up and read everything about it. I guess his end had to be that way - but I hated to see it. To tell the truth, I thought he was just too smart to be caught by the police."

The photo in Dillinger's pocketwatch was not of her, she told the press, because her nose was different than the woman in the photo. The picture turned out to be Polly Hamilton. "I'm sorry the law caught up with John - killed him just like they killed my brother.... John and he were such good pals. They both died the same way."

125   Op. cit., David C. Greer, *God is Merciful.* Endnote [10].

126 "Blame Brady Gang in Ohio, Indiana Raids," *Dayton Daily News*, 18 December 1936.

127 "FBI HISTORY – Famous Cases and Criminals – The Brady Gang," *FBI.org*. Post updated; 31 May 2020 (website).

CHAPTER 11

128   The *Bootleggers, Bandits, and Badges* exhibit at Carillon Historical Park, Dayton, Ohio. One of the text panels authored by Steve Lucht, Dayton History, as exhibit coordinator, 2019.

129 "Traffic Big Police Problem," *The Dayton Herald*, 22 October 1935.

130 "Two Dead, Three Injured in Fire," The Dayton Herald, 26 November 1936.

131   The striking worker was indicted for "Maiming." The prosecutor called the man who assaulted Ptl. Dunlavey a "professional agitator." Officers on the scene were "unable to find the half of the ear which he chewed off." When the prosecutor asked the defendant what he did with it, he replied he "spit it out because if I swallowed it, it would have poisoned me." The whole upper half of the patrolman's ear was gone. It made what Mike Tyson did to Evander Holyfield in 1997 look lame in comparison.

132   *Examples* of these various laboratory procedures: 1) Chemical testing could be conducted on blood stains, et al.; 2) Posmoulage processing, plaster casting, could preserve shoe or hand impressions; and 3) Helixometer measuring could ascertain the rate of twist of a rifled bore of a firearm.

133 "Homicide Squad Needs Studied," *The Dayton Herald*, 19 August 1937.

134 Sheriff Philip Kloos was the same man who managed the Xenia Avenue Trust Company when it was bank robbed on several occasions in 1930. He survived the blazing gun battle that took place inside and outside his bank. He was the Montgomery County sheriff from 1936 to 1944 and again in 1946.

135 "Rice Dies 4 Days After Gun Fight with Murder Suspect," *The Dayton Herald*, 5 October 1939.

136   Bob Nangle, "'Ford Squads' Replaced Pedal Cops in 1910," *Dayton Daily News*, 14 February 1961.

137   Rudimentary two-way radio systems were experimentally installed in patrol cars during the 1930s, such as in Bayonne, New Jersey (1933) and Piedmont, California (1934) according to various online sources. The challenge was in developing an affordable and practical radio system. This occurred when the Galvin Manufacturing Company introduced a Motorola transmitter in 1937.

[138] A framed picture of the 1940 two-way-radio Dayton police fleet (depicted on page 282) was on display at the Chicago Motorola World Headquarters as late as 1987. It is by renowned Dayton photographer, William Preston Mayfield, the first man to take an aerial photograph (while in a flight piloted by Orville Wright). Lt. Barry Bales (ret.), the Dayton police point man with NCR and Motorola for the 1987 installation of innovative computer-aided dispatch technology, provided much in the way of history.

[139] Calvary Cemetery is directly next door to Carillon Historical Park which opened in 1940 and is the location of the exhibit upon which this book is based, *Bootleggers, Bandits, and Badges: From Dry Times to Hard Times in Dayton, Ohio.*

The gate entrance to Calvary Cemetery sits back from the main street. It was constructed to secure the grounds a year earlier, 1939.

[140] Mary Sikora, "No comic strip cop; Dan is real-life guy in Caniff's cartoon," *Dayton Daily News*, 23 January 1986.

[141] Among other assignments at his rank, Lieutenant Michael Sammons was the Investigations Division Violent Crimes Bureau commander and the Dayton Police Academy commander. He was No. 1 on the Civil Service list for promotion to Captain but denied when that rank was abolished after 1979. Officer Tom Sammons served for 37 years and 7 months, making him the 18th longest-serving law officer in Dayton history (1797 to present), just ahead of Captain Earl Yates.

EPILOGUE

[142] Benton, Perry, Superintendent, Division of Telegraphs and Signals, "Sirens Installed for Safety," *City of Dayton 30th Annual Report – Municipal Activities*. Dayton, Ohio: 1943, p. 3.

[143] Sergeant Paul Price would use a magnet traffic "blackboard" during his presentations, invented in 1940 by Dayton engineer A. R. Will of 1250 Demphle Avenue.

[144] Switzer, W. F, Chairman, "What the Transportation Committee Has Accomplished," *City of Dayton 30th Annual Report – Municipal Activities*. Dayton, Ohio: 1943, pp. 50-52.

[145] Dayton Chamber of Commerce, Department of Governmental Affairs, "Comparative Data – Dayton, Ohio, and Comparable Cities," Dayton, Ohio: May 1946, p. 6.

[146] Sgt. Hazel Clark had the second-longest woman's sworn career at 27 years to Plwn. Lulu Soller's career. Both were surpassed in 1988 by Police Officer Nancy Breen. In 1949, the Bureau of Policewomen was transferred under the Division of Police. In 1950, Plwn. Clark was conferred the rank of sergeant, the first woman to hold a police supervisory rank. When Sgt. Clark unexpectedly died from natural causes in 1953 she became the first Dayton woman afforded a police funeral.

[147] Keilman, John "Bugs Moran meets Dayton bootlegger Al Fouts," *Dayton Daily News*, 27 December 1999.

[148] "Last of Drewer Gang Captured; Named in Killing," *St. Louis Globe Democrat*, 7 July 1946.

[149] Keilman, John "Moran takes the stand in Dayton robbery trial," *Dayton Daily News*, 30 December 1999.

[150] Silas Tavern is today named Upper Deck Tavern. It is located at the corner of Pike and Blanchard Avenues in the city of Moraine, Ohio. It was previously The Lighthouse and John Bull's Restaurant. John Kurpe's father-in-law, Gabor Silas owned the tavern. Research courtesy David Miller, Moraine Community Service Coordinator.

[151] The Winters Bank branch located on West Third Street was one of a number of branches of Winters National Bank, which was established in 1882. The Dayton Exchange Bank (est. 1851) was its forerunner, which was controlled by Valentine Winters, and then his son, Jonathan Winters. As an aside, they are the great-grandfather and grandfather of Jonathan Winters III, the comedian and actor who was born in Dayton and raised in the Greater Dayton Area; specifically, Bellbrook and Springfield.

[152] Mathias Heck, Sr. is the father of the current and long-serving Montgomery County prosecutor, Mathias H. 'Mat' Heck, Jr.

[153] Jessie Nicodemus, "A Lifetime Wasted, But Fouts Happier," *The Journal Herald*, 2 December 1963..

[154] Keilman, John, "'Old Man' Moran dies in obscurity," *Dayton Daily News*, 31 December 1999.

[155] Op. cit., Jessie Nicodemus, "A Lifetime Wasted, But Fouts Happier," Endnote [153].

[156] Herbert M. Eikenbary, defense attorney for Al Fouts. Typed letter to Al Fouts on 17 December 1963. Letter courtesy of David Greer, Esq.

[157] "Patrolman Dies in West Side Battle," *The Daily Herald*, 16 May 1947.

[158] "Dean of Nation's Police Chiefs Plans Fishing Vacation, Then Stay in Dayton," *Dayton Daily News*, 8 June 1949. Quote: "Chief Wurstner's 24 years as chief is a record equaled by only three men in the nation in cites of 200,000 population or over. The cities were Milwaukee, Akron and Syracuse. The last of those men... retired in 1935, so for the past 14 years Wurstner has been the dean of police chiefs...."

[159] Bruce, Malcolm. "---- Chief of Police," *The Journal Herald*, the article undated 1949.

[160] Op. cit., "Dean of Nation's Police Chiefs...." Endnote [158].

[161] Ibid.

[162] Ibid.

Circa 1918: Sgt. Rudy Wurstner oversees police recruit Jiu-Jitsu training inside the gymnasium at Dayton's other Market House on Wayne Avenue. *NCR Lantern Slide Collection at Dayton History*

BIBLIOGRAPHY

Every author selects the manner by which to present the sources that are the basis for his or her book. Some writers divide the resources by chapter; others in alphabetical order in full or by grouping. As relates to *THE DEAN, DILLINGER, AND DAYTON, OHIO*, this bibliography is divided by category. This author then found it preferable (i.e. easiest) to list within each category the sources of information in the order in which they first appear in this book (general reference sources being the one exception).

General Reference Sources

• Lucht, Steven; Haney, Gwenyth; Grismer, Stephen. *Bootleggers, Bandits, and Badges: From Dry Times to Hard Times in Dayton, Ohio*. Carillon Historical Park, Dayton, Ohio, 2019.

• Williams' Dayton City Directories. Numerous volumes/editions from the 19th century. Cincinnati: The Williams Directory Company, 1858-1900.

• U.S. Bureau of Census. Data: Table 1, "Rank by Population of the 100 Largest Urban Places." Table 9 (1860), Table 13 (1900), Table 17 (1940) 18, Table 20 (1960). Internet release date: 15 June 1998.

• Wilson, Joe. "Sheriffs of Montgomery County, Ohio - 1803 to present." Compiled List. Dayton: Montgomery County Sheriff Office History Committee, 2016.

• Ohio Census. Data: "Decennial Census of Population, 1900 to 2000, by Place." All Ohio cities. Prepared by the Office of Strategic Research, Ohio Department of Development, 3/2001.

• Inflation Calculations: Data from U.S. statistical indexes. See "Websites" sources for Friedman, S. Morgan, 2019.

• Ancestry.com. Researched postings, papers and legal documents related to Mary Jenkins Longnaker and relatives, Alfred (Albert) Fouts (Foutz) and relatives; James Crumley, and William 'Tom' Wilson. 2017-2020.

Books

• Edgar, John F. *Pioneer Life in Dayton and Vicinity: 1796-1840*. Dayton, Ohio: L. Stebbins, 1896.

• Sharts, Joseph W. *The Biography of Dayton*. "Evolution of Police
  Protection." Dayton, Ohio: The Miami Valley Socialist, 1922.

• Stebbins, Jane. *Fifty Years History of the Temperance Cause*.
  Cincinnati: L. Stebbins, 1874.

• Dalton, Curt. *Spilt Blood: When murder walked the streets of
  Dayton*. Dayton, Ohio, C. Dalton, 2004.

• Greer, David C. *God is Merciful – The Colorful Career of John E.
  Egan*. Wilmington, Ohio: Orange Fazier Press, 2017.

• Forschner, Brian. *Cold Serial • The Jack the Strangler Murders*.
  New York, NY: Morgan James Publishing LLC, 2016.

• Hover, John C.; Barnes, Joseph D.; et al., ed(s). *Memoirs of the
  Miami Valley - Volume Two*. Chicago: Robert O. Law Company,
  1919.

• Everett, Marshall. *The Tragic Story of America's Greatest
  Disaster*. Chicago: J.S. Ziegler Company, 1913.

• Grismer, Stephen C. *Drenched Uniforms and Battered Badges:
  How Dayton Emerged from the 1913 Flood*. Dayton, Ohio: DPH
  Foundation, Inc., 2013.

• Lockhart, Paul D. and Haney, Gwenyth. *Over There: Dayton in
  the Great War*. Dayton, Ohio: P. Lockhart; G. Haney, 2017.

• Bauer, C. A. *The Detective*. Dayton, Ohio: Burkam-Herrick
  Publications, 1920.

• McKee, Philip. *Big Town*. New York: The John Day Company,
  1931.

• Dalton, Curt. *Breweries of Dayton – A Toast to Brewers from the
  Gem City: 1810-1961*. Dayton, Ohio: C. Dalton 2013.

• Herigstad, Gordon. *Colt Thompson Serial Numbers & Histories*
  (pp. 296, 418, 443, 459). Santa Ana, California: Graphic
  Publishers, 2015.

• Redder, H. Jamison. *Paper, Mister? Downtown Dayton-- 1935*.
  Dayton, Ohio: 1 January 1995.

• Dalton, Curt. *On This Date in Dayton's History: Remembering the
  Gem City One Day at a Time* (p. 80). Dayton, Ohio: C. Dalton,
  2017.

• Poulsen, Ellen. *Don't Call Us Molls – Women of the John Dillinger Gang*. Oakland Gardens, NY: Clinton Cook Publishing Corp., 2002.

• Toland, John. *The Dillinger Days* New York: Random House 1963 (1st edition); reprinted De Capo Press, 1995.

• Poulsen, Ellen; Hyde, Lori. *Chasing Dillinger – Police Captain Matt Leach, J. Edgar Hoover and the Rivalry to Capture Public Enemy No. 1*. Jefferson, North Carolina: Exposit, 2018.

• Testa, D. M. *Defending the Dillinger Gang: Jessie Levy and Bessie Robbins in the Courtroom*. Jefferson, North Carolina: McFarland and Company, Inc., 2020.

• Greer, David C.. *The Little Man Who Wasn't There: In Search of Al Fouts*. Wilmington, Ohio: Orange Fazier Press, 2021.

Government Publications

• The Brown Bierce Company. City of Dayton. Dayton Fire Department. *Illustrated History • Dayton Fire Department* . Dayton, Ohio, Callahan Bank Building: J.E. Brelsford - Job, Book, and Catalogue Printer, 1900.

• Whitaker, John C., ed. City of Dayton. Dayton Police Department. *Dayton Police Department 1902 • Police Souvenir Book*. Dayton, Ohio: Published for the benefit of the Dayton Police Benevolent Association, 1902.

• Whitaker, John C., ed. City of Dayton. Dayton Police Department. *History of the Police Department Dayton, Ohio: From Earliest Times to October First 1907 • A Souvenir*. Published for Convention of the Ohio Police Association. Dayton, Ohio: U.B. Publishing House – Printing, Binding & Engraving, 1907.

• Ballard, John Milton, ed. City of Dayton. Dayton Police Department. *Dayton Police Department with Complete Biographical Sketches of Each Member, Illustrated*. Dayton, Ohio: Published by and for the Benefit of the Police Pension Fund, Dayton, Ohio, 1910.

• Eichelberger, F.O., ed. City of Dayton. *Annual Report of the City of Dayton for the Year 1919 [... to 1930]*. Dayton, Ohio: Published by the City Commission, Dayton, Ohio, 1920 to 1931.

• University of Dayton, ed. City of Dayton. *Annual Report of the City of Dayton for the Year 1931.* Dayton, Ohio: Published by the City Commission, Dayton, Ohio, 1932.

• University of Dayton, ed. City of Dayton. *Civic Report of the City of Dayton for the Year 1932* [... to] *1935.* Dayton, Ohio: Published by the City Commission, Dayton, Ohio, 1920 to 1932.

• City of Dayton. *Headquarters, Division of Police, Dayton, Ohio, Dec. 31, 1932.* Police Detail effective January 1, 1933 (p. 1). Dayton, Ohio: Published by Division of Police, 31 December 1932.

• Cooper, Charles, ed. City of St. Marys. *History of the St. Marys Police Department.* "The Dillinger Gang in St. Marys." pp. 15, 16, 37. St. Marys, Ohio: Published by SMPD, 2010. Courtesy of St. Marys Police Chief Jacob K. Sutton, 2019.

• University of Dayton, ed. City of Dayton. *Civic Report of the City of Dayton for the Year 1938.* Dayton, Ohio: Published by the City Commission, Dayton, Ohio, p. 47.

• Eichelberger, F.O., ed. City of Dayton. *30th Annual Report – Municipal Activities.* Dayton, Ohio: Published by the City Commission, Dayton, Ohio, pp. 3, 50-52.

• Department of Governmental Affairs. *Comparative Data – Dayton, Ohio, and Comparable Cities.* Dayton, Ohio: Published by the Dayton Chamber of Commerce, May 1946, pp. 6-12.

• Federal Bureau of Investigation. *FBI Law Enforcement Bulletin,* Vol. 18, No. 11. "Police Personalities – Dean of Police Chiefs Retires." Washington D.C.: Published by the Federal Bureau of Investigation, United States Department of Justice, November 1949, p. 19.

Ledgers/Registers/Records

• Township/City Council Meeting Minutes. Dayton Township/City of Dayton. Numerous original volumes from the 19th century. Dayton, Ohio: Official Recorders, 1800-1875.

• Dayton Metropolitan Police Commission Meeting Minutes. City of Dayton. Original ledger from the 19th century. Dayton, Ohio: Official Recorders, 1867-1882.

• City Council Meeting Minutes (regular session). City of Dayton. Courtesy of David Klippel. Dayton, Ohio: C. N. Greer, Secretary, Reference---Finance, 27 February 1911.

• Dayton Police Department, Dayton Police Relief & Pension Fund Ledger, 31 January 1913 to 26 June 1924; and Dayton Police Relief & Pension Fund Ledger, 22 August 1924 to 27 April 1935.

• County Probate Court, Montgomery County, Ohio, Record of Birth Ledger, p. 87, Line 38, Fouts, Alfred George, 19 October 1890.

• Department of Police. City of Dayton. Bertillon Record No. 4525, Albert Foutz. Wright State University (WSU) Archive Collection. Dayton, Ohio: Official Arrest Record, 15 April 1908.

• Department of Police. City of Dayton. Criminal Record Photo No. 631, Albert Fouts. WSU Archive Collection. Dayton, Ohio: Official Arrest Rap Sheet, 26 November 1905 to 3 December 1916.

• Division of Police. City of Dayton. Bureau of Identification Form F 355. Albert Fouts No 1507. WSU Archive Collection. Dayton, Ohio: Official Arrest Rap Sheet, 16 December 1943.

• County Registrar. William C. Olt, Sheriff. Montgomery County, Ohio. Registration Card No. 68, Fouts, Alfred George, 2 June 1917.

• State Prisons of California. Register and Descriptive List of Convicts Under Sentence of Imprisonment. Entry Number 12214. A.G. Fouts. When Received, 30 July 1922; 9 August 1922. Paroled 15 September 1925.

• Ohio Association of Chiefs of Police, Inc. Listing of "Past Presidents, OACP Year, and Police Department. Terms 1928-1929 through 2010-2011. Revised 25 September 2012.

• Department of Police. City of Dayton. Bureau of Identification, Albert G. Fouts (also Alfred G. Fouts). WSU Archive Collection. Dayton, Ohio: Official Mug Shot Card File Card, 8893 undated circa 1930.

• State of Ohio. London, Ohio. Bureau of Criminal Identification. Ref. No. 448-374. A. Owen Fouts No. 19075-6369. WSU Archive Collection. Dayton, Ohio: Official Arrest Rap Sheet, 23 February 1933.

• Miami County Children's Home Index. Longnaker, Clara Ann. Book #2, Page #50, Inmate #1727. Longnaker, Betty Jean. Book #2, Page #50, Inmate #1728. Troy, Ohio: The Troy Historical Society, 1930-1970.

• Repair Order No. 3790A from Supreme Motor Sales, Chicago for "Mr. Donovan" (Dillinger) dated September 15, 1933. Source: WSU Collection.

• Department of Police. City of Dayton. Criminal Record Photo No. 10587, John Dillinger. WSU Archive Collection. Dayton, Ohio: Official Arrest Card and Mug Shot, 22 September 1933.

• Department of Police. City of Dayton. Bureau of Identification, John Dillinger. WSU Archive Collection. Dayton, Ohio: Official Fingerprint Card, 22 September 1933.

• Record of Prisoners in Jail. Allen County, Ohio Ledger. Page 142. Entry Number 276. John Dillinger. Bank Robbery 30. When Received: 28 September 1933; Discharged: 12 October 1933; 2:00 P.M.

• Federal Bureau of Investigation File No. 62-19777-1. Subject: John Dillinger. Serials 1-28. FBI reports and documents including Biograph shooting scene ledgered diagram (52 pages). 3 April 1934 to 23 July 1934.

• Department of Police. City of Dayton. Criminal Record Photo No. 21458, Charles Arthur Floyd. WSU Archive Collection. Toledo, Ohio: Official Fingerprint Card and Mug Shot, 15 May 1931.

• Department of Police. City of Dayton. Criminal Record Photo, Clyde Champion Barrow. WSU Archive Collection. Joplin, Missouri: Official Wanted Card and Mug Shot, 13 April 1933.

• Department of Police. City of Dayton. Bureau of Identification, John Barton (alias of Alfred 'Al' Brady). WSU Archive Collection. Dayton, Ohio: Official Mug Shot Card File Card, C73661 undated circa 1935.

• Federal Bureau of Investigation File No. 7-576. Subject: Barker/Karpis Gang Bremer Kidnapping. Section Sub A - 21. FBI-gathered newspaper clippings from the nation (146 pages). 21 August 1935 to 5 September 1934.

• Family of Andrew F. Walsh and Mary J. Clegg. Andrew F. Walsh. Born 30 Nov 1862. Emigrated 12 May 1883, Co. Tipperary, Ireland. Police Officer 7 Feb 1896. Lieutenant 1 Aug 1906. Died 16 Jul 1909.

• Secretary of Commerce and Labor of the United States. List or Manifest of Alien Passengers for the United States Immigration Officer at the Port of Arrival. Maroney, Matthew D., age 18. Scarriff, Ireland. 23 May 1927.

• Department of Police. City of Dayton. Radio Equipment Service Record. "Installation Data on Radio Eqpt". Sept. '32, Police Dept. Western Electric 98; Aug. '40, Police Dept. Two Way 3178OKC Motorola Eqpt.

• Department of Police. City of Dayton. Criminal Booking Record, Albert G. Fouts. Officer Sgt. Teeter-Det. Pendell. WSU Archive Collection. Dayton, Ohio: Suspicion Blank card, 6 July 1946.

• Department of Police. City of Dayton. Criminal Booking Record, Alfred Geo. Fouts. Reg. by Sgt. C. Wilkin. WSU Archive Collection. Dayton, Ohio: Form F 452 Record of Arrest–Criminal card, 6 July 1946.

• Department of Police. City of Dayton. Criminal Record Photo No. 19075 (Al Fouts). WSU Archive Collection. Dayton, Ohio: Official Full-length Mug Shot, 6 July 1946.

• Department of Police. City of Dayton. Criminal Booking Record, George C Moran. Officer Reed-St. Pierre. WSU Archive Collection. Dayton, Ohio: Suspicion Blank card, 6 July 1946.

• Department of Police. City of Dayton. Criminal Record No. 20774-8216, George Clarence Moran, "Bugs". WSU Archive Collection. Dayton, Ohio: Official Fingerprint Card, 13 July 1946.

• Department of Police. City of Dayton. Criminal Record Photo No. 20774 (George Moran). WSU Archive Collection. Dayton, Ohio: Official Mug Shot, 13 July 1946.

• Division of Police. City of Dayton. Bureau of Identification Form F 355. George Clarence Moran No 20774. DPHF Archive Collection. Dayton, Ohio: Official Arrest Rap Sheet, 13 July 1946.

• Federal Bureau of Investigation. United States Department of Justice. FBI No. 320989. George Moran. DPHF Archive Collection. Dayton, Ohio: Official Federal Arrest Rap Sheet, 13 July 1946.

• Department of Police. City of Dayton. Criminal Record Photo No. 20774 (George Moran). WSU Archive Collection. Dayton, Ohio: Official Full-length Mug Shot, 13 July 1946.

• Department of Police. City of Dayton. Criminal Booking Record, Vernon Summers. Officer Dets. Pendell, Reed-St. Pierre. WSU Archive Collection. Dayton, Ohio: Suspicion Blank card, 13 July 1946.

• Department of Police. City of Dayton. Criminal Record Photo No. 20775 (Virgil Summers). WSU Archive Collection. Dayton, Ohio: Official Mug Shot, 13 July 1946.

• Federal Bureau of Investigation. United States Department of Justice. FBI No. 768236. Virgil Summers. WSU Archive Collection. Dayton, Ohio: Official Federal Arrest Rap Sheet, 25 July 1946.

Papers/Documents/Reports

• Typed reply from an unidentified person with *The Dayton Journal*. Source of the inquiry also unknown. Note marked: "Filed Dec-15-16", leading with "Dayton Ohio Dec., 12 --" and concluding with "Journal 730pm". Source: Saint Paul Public Library (archive collection). St. Paul, Minnesota, 1916. Provided by Bridget Sperl, 2018.

• Treadway, Francis W., President of the Senate. "An act providing against the evils resulting from the traffic in intoxicating liquors" [Senate Bill No. 4]. Columbus, Ohio: Filed with the Office of the Ohio Secretary of State, 25 March 1909.

• Dayton Police Department records, documents, photo images (underline: multiple and varied), and other sourced documents; e.g. Board of Police Directors, *25th Annual Report of the Department of Police of the City of Dayton for the Fiscal Year Ending February 28, 1898*, J. W. Johnson, Dayton, Ohio 1898; authorized strength reports; "Department of Safety, Dayton, Ohio Division of Police" photo collage, 1917; et al.) as well as other corroborating general Dayton Police records including departmental unsourced documents.

• Pfauhl, R.K. (detective, liquor squad). Special Report to J.N. Allaback, Chief of Police, 28 June 1922. Source: Dayton Police History Foundation (DPHF) Archive Collection.

• Chief of Police (John Allaback). Report to Myers, H.E., Director of Safety, along with "Charges and Specifications. 5 July 1922. Source: DPHF Archive Collection.

• Myers, H.E., Director of Safety. Change of Plea form with disposition issued to Pfauhl, R.K. 11 July 1922. Source: DPHF Archive Collection.

• Wesleyan Methodist Church, 201 Bruen Street. Biographical Account on Mrs. Dora Burton Rice. Circa 1943. Excerpt from a church publication, courtesy of Curt Dalton. Source: DPHF Archive Collection.

• Two Sources of photographs with identifying information regarding Dayton and Montgomery County Ku Klux Klan gatherings: **1)** Ohio Historical Society (Ohio History Connection). Columbus, Ohio: 20 April 1923 (KonKlave); 11 September 1923 (women class); 21 September 1923 (cross burning); 21 September 1923 (parade). **2)** Dayton Daily News, 25 October 2015. Dayton, Ohio: 24 July 1923 (KonKlave women); 21 September 1923 (demonstration).

• Dayton Police Department, Bureau of Identification, Form F 97, Dayton, Ohio. Dayton police arrest of Albert G. Fouts on a Federal Warrant for two Kentucky post office burglaries. 31, August 1933. Source: Wright State University (WSU) Archive Collection.

• Dayton Police Department, Bureau of Identification, Envelope No. 8893, Dayton, Ohio. Dayton police arrest of Albert G. Fouts on an Allen County warrant for three burglaries. 3, February 1931. Source: WSU Archive Collection.

• Ridgeway, Pete & Mary. "Pa's Stories – A Short Historical Setting for Pa's Dillinger Story," 13 September 2010. Extremely well sourced document with bibliography and endnotes citing book passages by authors: Burrough, Bryan; Cromie, Robert and Pinkston, Joseph; Girardin, Russell with Helmer, William; Gorn, Elliot J.; and Matera, Darcy. Document provided by local author Dalton, Curt. 15 November 2015.

• Gross, Sgt. C.E.; Pfauhl, Det. (R.K.). Handwritten "Report of Arrest," Form F 97, to Dayton B of I file No. 10587, listing date of arrest, September 22, 1933. Source: WSU Archive Collection.

• Gross, Sgt. (Charles E.); Pfauhl, Det. (Russell K.). "Report," Form F64, three handwritten reports from Sgt. Gross and Det. Pfauhl, Complaint No. "General," on September 22, 1933. Re: Dillinger witness escorts. Source: WSU Archive Collection.

• Eyer, Ptl. L. M. (Lee M.) Handwritten report, Form F-196, to Chief R. F. Wurstner through Capt. Edward Poland and Inspector Otha Greger marked "Information" on September 22, 1933. Source: WSU Archive Collection.

• Wurstner, R.F., Chief of Police. Western Union Telegraph to Michael F. Morrissey, Indianapolis Police Chief dated September 23, 1933. Source: WSU Archive Collection.

• Makley, Robert A. "Charlie Omer Makley 1889 – 1934 • Member of the Dillinger Gang in the 30's." undated.

• Colville, Ptl. C (Clarence). Typed report, Form F-196, to R.F. Wurstner on October 13, 1933. Re: Russell Clark and Walter "Detrich." Source: WSU Archive Collection.

• Buchholz, Mary Ann. Typed 4-page transcript of "Statement" to Sgt. Charles Gross at Dayton Police HQ in the presence of Det. Russell Pfauhl dated October 17, 1933. Source: WSU Archive Collection.

• Gross, Sgt. (Charles E.); Pfauhl, Det. (Russell K.). Handwritten "Report," Form F64, Complaint No. "General," on October 25, 1933. Follow-up with Buchholz and Stricker. Source: WSU Archive Collection.

• Gross, Sgt. (Charles E.); Pfauhl, Det. (Russell K.). Handwritten two-page "Report," Form F64, Complaint No. "General," on October 25, 1933. Re: Harry Copeland. Source: WSU Archive Collection.

• Croft, Sgt. C. (Clifford C.); Kirkpatrick, Ptl. (Matthew C.). Typed two-page Typed "Report," Form F64 Complaint No. "Information," on April 16, 1934. Re: Dillinger acquaintances. Source: WSU Archive Collection.

• Wack, Larry E., Special Agent (ret.). Federal Bureau of Investigation July 20, 1936 National Academy, Third Session class photograph. Dayton Police Sgt. Matthew Kirkpatrick, second row, third from right; Director J. Edgar Hoover, front row, sixth from right. Source: FBI Archive Collection.

• Wurstner, R.F., Chief of Police. Typed Special Report to F. O. Eichelberger, City Manager and Director of Public Safety on June 7, 1935. Re: Matthew Maroney appointment to Dayton Police Department. Source: DPHF Archive Collection.

• Aldredge, W. J., Capt. Inf-Res, 329th Inf. Typed Special Report to Typed Special Report to Hon. Civil Service Commission, City of Dayton, Ohio through R. F. Wurstner, Chief of Police on December 31, 1935. Re: Extension of Leave of Absence (CCC Service). Source: DPHF Archive Collection.

• Three Sources of typed Special Reports regarding the February 22, 1935 Det. Russell Pfauhl shooting incident: **1)** Sgt. P. J. Roche to R. F. Wurstner, Chief of Police dated February 22; **2)** Captain D. C. Wetzel to R. F. Wurstner, Chief of Police dated February 22; and **3)** Inspector S. E. Yendes to R. F. Wurstner, Chief of Police dated March 22, 1935. Source: DPHF Archive Collection.

• Two Sources of typed transcript of "Statement" to Inspector of Detectives S. E. Yendes at Dayton Police HQ dated February 22, 1935 of: **1)** Sgt. Charles Gross at 10:15 AM; and **2)** of Det. R. K. Pfauhl at 11:00 AM. Source: DPHF Archive Collection.

• Newman, Sgt. W. E. (Walter E.). Typed report, Form F-196, to R.F. Wurstner on June 26, 1934. Re: Disabling Injury to Ptl. T.C. Dunlavey." Source: DPHF Archive Collection.

• Keen, Det. Robert (ret.), editor. "History and Program of the Department of Police – 1938-1968." Capt. John C. Post Lodge newsletter. Publication undated but most likely in 1968.

• Wurstner, R.F., Chief of Police. Typed report on Dayton police letterhead to All Members of the Division of Police on December 20, 1938. Re: Congratulations to the Dayton Police Tug of War Team winning the City of Dayton Championship. Source: DPHF Archive Collection.

- Wurstner, R.F., Chief of Police. Typed Special Report to F. O. Eichelberger, City Manager and Director of Public Safety on July 2, 1942. Re: Patrolman H. C. Moore commission in the United States Army Air Service. Source: DPHF Archive Collection.

- Cy Yendes Detective Bureau. Metal sign with blue print posted at business locations that contracted the services of the private detective agency. Circa 1946. Source: DPHF Archive Collection.

- Wurstner, R.F,, Chief of Police. Typed Special Report to F. O. Eichelberger, City Manager and Director of Public Safety on July 1, 1947. Re: Investigation into the shooting by Patrolman H. C. Moore. This report along with five typed Special Reports and seven pages of transcribed interviews. Source: DPHF Archive Collection.

- Division of Police, Dayton, Ohio. Complete Personnel Record of Public Safety on July 1, 1947. Re: Sherman Edward Nowlin, Bureau of Identification No. 2335; TA 9734. Reports dated: 16 April 1947 to 15 August 1947. Source: DPHF Archive Collection.

- Wurstner, R.F., Chief of Police. Typed letter to Russell E. McClure, City Manager and Director of Public Safety on Jun 8, 1949. Re: Retirement from the Dayton Police Department. Source: DPHF Archive Collection.

- Greer, Esq. David C. PDF file of 115 newspaper clippings regarding Al Fouts, Bugs Moran, and Virgil Summers and the attorneys who defended and prosecuted these criminals. The news articles date from July 6, 1946 to November 25, 1963. The file also includes the following letter:

- Eikenbary, Herbert M., defense attorney for Al Fouts. Typed letter to Al Fouts on December 17, 1963 in response to a Christmas card received from the paroled convict.

- Dayton Police History Foundation, Inc. Completed 2012 Dayton Walk of Fame Nomination Form. Dayton Police Rudolph F. Wurstner. 28 February 2012.

- Dayton Police History Foundation, Inc. Completed 2018 Dayton Walk of Fame Nomination Form. Dayton Police Sergeant Lucius J. Rice and Policewoman Dora Burton Rice. 28 February 2018; confirmed 1 March 2018.

Other Publications/Periodicals

• Burns, Carolyn J., granddaughter. "My Life in Montgomery County • Biography of Frank William Johnson." Paper 9. Dayton, Ohio: C.J. Burns, 23 August 2008.

• Trollinger, William Vance. "Forgotten Flames." University of Dayton Magazine. Winter 2013-14: pp. 34-39

• Trollinger, William Vance. "Hearing the Silence: e University of Dayton, the Ku Klux Klan, and Catholic Universities and Colleges in the 1920s." History Faculty Publications. Paper 11. Spring 2013: pp. 1-22.

• Wurstner, Rudolph F., ed. City of Dayton. Ohio Police Chiefs Association. *Official Manual of Ohio Chiefs of Police Association* (237 pages). Dayton, Ohio: The Central Printing Company, 1927.

• John C. Post Lodge No. 44. Constitution and By-Laws (34 pages). Dayton, Ohio: Adopted by the State of Ohio, Fraternal Order of Police, 17 January 1939.

• American Journal of Police Science, Vol. 1, No. 5. "The Detroit Police Department Radio System." Indiana University, Bloomington: Northwestern University Press, Sep/Oct, 1930; digitized 16 July 2010. pp. 456-465.

• Pleasant Hill History Center Newsletter, Vol. 4, Issue 2. "Howard Longnaker, Mary Jenkins and John Dillinger." Pleasant Hill, Ohio: December 2, 2016.

• Oliver, Mary. The Montgomery County Historical Society Newsletter. *Columns.* "John Dillinger's Dayton Connection." Dayton, Ohio: Published Quarterly, November 2004. pp. 3-4.

• Oliver, Mary. Dayton History at Carillon Historical Park. *The Heritage*, Vol. 9, Issue 4. "John Dillinger's Dayton Connection." Dayton, Ohio: Winter 2013.

• Dayton History at Carillon Historical Park. *The Heritage*, Vol. 16, Issue 1. "John Dillinger's Ties to Dayton Highlighted in Gangster Era Exhibit." Dayton, Ohio: Spring 2020.

• Berry, Bill. New Carlisle Historical Society. "The Heist That Put New Carlisle on the Map." Undated.

• Young, Roz. Montgomery County Historical Bulletin. "Mrs. Hedges' House." Dayton, Ohio: Published Quarterly, Summer 1967.

• Andrews, Larry. "I Was There When They Captured John Dillinger in Dayton, Ohio." *Dayton Daily News*, The Magazine. 29 July 1984: pp. 8-11, 15.

• McEnnis, L. J. Jr. Journal of Criminal Law and Criminology, Vol. 42, Issue 5. "Background and Development of the Traffic Institute of Northwestern University." Indiana University, Bloomington: Northwestern University Press, Winter 1952, pp. 663-673.

• Roberts, C. V. "Gunmoll's Daring Honeymoon – Love and Kisses Mingle with Guns and Bullets as a Lady of the Streets Shoots It Out with Unromantic Cops." *Complete Detective*. December 1941: pp. 20-23, 57-58.

• Miller, David. "'Bugs' Moran's Moraine Connection" *Moraine Messenger*. Moraine, Ohio: October 2017. p. 7.

• Time Magazine. "Labor: Brass Knuckles." *TIME • The Weekly Newsmagazine*. Vol. LII No. 6, National Affairs – The Nation. 9 August 1948.

• WONE Radio. "Chief Rudolph Wurstner." Transcript of *Police Beat Program*. Broadcast Date: 8 June 1949.

• WHIO Radio & Television. "Chief Rudolph Wurstner." Transcript of *An Official Opinion WHIO Radio & Television*. Broadcast Date: 16 July 1969.

Letters/Journals/Diaries

• Crumley; James. Letter about youth and law enforcement career, 1872 to ca. 1938. Provided by great-granddaughter, Bridget Sperl, 2018. St. Paul, Minnesota, ca. 1938.

• Pfauhl, R.K., Patrolman 98. Handwritten letter to J.N. Allaback (chief of police), dated July 11, 1922. Source: Dayton Police History Foundation (DPHF) Archive Collection.

• Grundish, Thomas, Inspector. Record. "Circumstances surrounding major crimes – accidents." Bound booklet with pertinent notes on pp. 10-11 (re: Ptl. George Clark) and 20-21 (re: Ptl. Perry Heywood). Entries from 24 March 1922 to 22 December 1926.

• Yoes, Patrick, National Secretary (today, National President). Letter to Steve Grismer regarding Dayton F.O.P. Lodge charter date and number. Nashville, Tennessee: National Headquarters, 1 April 2009.

• Longnaker, Mary. Handwritten letter from to "Johnnie" John Dillinger, dated August 25, 1933. Source: Wright State University (WSU) Archive Collection.

• Clark, E. S., Division Manager, Pinkerton's National Detective Agency. Typed letter to Dayton Police Inspector of Detectives "C. E. Yendes," dated August 25, 1933. Source: WSU Archive Collection.

• Chief of Police (Wurstner, R.F.). Typed letter to Mr. Walter H. Daly, Warden, Indiana State Prison, Michigan City, Indiana dated August 28, 1933. Source: WSU Archive Collection.

• Clark, E. S., Division Manager, Pinkerton's National Detective Agency. Typed letter to Dayton Police Inspector of Detectives Cy Yendes, dated September 2, 1933 and forwarded to Sgt. Gross and Pfauhl. Source: WSU Archive Collection.

• Constable, Claude. Handwritten letter to "Honey" Mary Longnaker, undated, early in the romance, likely between September 2 and September 17, 1933. Source: WSU Archive Collection

• Jenkins, James "Jim." Handwritten letter to Claude Constable, undated, likely near September 17, 1933 (see next entry for date reference). Source: WSU Archive Collection.

• Jenkins, James "Jim." Handwritten letter to Mrs. Mary Longnaker, dated September 17, 1933 and postmarked from Michigan City on September 19. Source: WSU Archive Collection.

• Jon Bergstrom, step-grandson of Captain William Aldredge. An account as told by Captain to his grandsons Tom and Joey Huddleston. 31 July 2019.

• Six typed letters from police officials. Re: Requests for Dillinger's picture and description: 1) Lawrence County in New Castle, Pennsylvania, dated October 2, 1933; 2) Delaware County in Muncie, Indiana dated October 14, 1933; 3) Detroit, Michigan dated October 20, 1933; 4) Indianapolis, Indiana dated October

21, 1933; **5**) Los Angeles, California dated January 10, 1934; and **6**) Orlando, Florida dated January 17, 1934. Source: WSU Archive Collection.

• Morrissey, Michael F., Indianapolis Chief of Police. Typed letter to Dayton Inspector of Detectives S. E. "Yendes," dated September 23, 1933. Source: WSU Archive Collection.

• Longnaker, Mrs. Mary. Handwritten letter to John Dillinger, dated September 25, 1933, with envelope marked ℅ Sheriff Frick and addressed to the Montgomery County Jail. Source: Allen County Historical Society Archive Collection.

• Chief of Police (Wurstner, R.F.). Typed letter to Mr. Walter H. Daily, Warden, Indiana State Prison, Michigan City Indiana dated September 27, 1933. Re: Jenkins' father. Source: WSU Archive Collection.

• Oftedahl, Jasper, Captain, Pennsylvania State Police. Typed letter to "The Chief of Police" (R. F. Wurstner) dated September 28, 1933. Re: Dillinger return. Source: WSU Archive Collection.

• Dillinger, John "Johnnie". Handwritten letter to "Dearest Mary" (Longnaker), dated October 1, 1933 with envelope postmarked October 2, 1933. Source: REA online marketing post.

• Chief of Police (Wurstner, R.F.). Typed letter to Mr. H. D. Cloudy, Deputy Warden, Indiana State Prison, Michigan City, Indiana dated October 5, 1933. Re: Charging Longnaker. Source: WSU Archive Collection.

• Chief of Police (Wurstner, R.F.). Typed letter to Mr. Fred A. Simon, Chief of Detectives, Indianapolis, Indiana, dated October 5, 1933. Re: Forwarding pocketbook. Source: WSU Archive Collection.

• Cloudy, H. D., Deputy Warden, Indiana State Prison. Typed reply letter to Chief of Police (R.F. Wurstner) dated October 7, 1933. Re: Receipt of papers. Source: WSU Archive Collection.

• Longnaker, Mary. Handwritten letter to "Johnnie" John Dillinger (undated, most likely to have taken place right after Dillinger escaped from the Allen County jail on October 12, 1933. See endnote [77] for explanation). Source: WSU Archive Collection.

• Chief of Police (Wurstner, R.F.). Typed letters dated October 23, 1933 to two officials: **1**) Mr. Walter H. Daly, Warden, Indiana

State Prison, Michigan City, Indiana; and **2**) Mr. J. W. Cook, Chief of Police, Lima, Ohio. Source: WSU Archive Collection.

• Cook, J. W., Chief of Police, Lima, Ohio. Typed letter to R. F. Wurstner, Chief of Police dated October 20, 1933. Re: Yeggs hangout in Lewisburg. Source: WSU Archive Collection.

• Press Release. Typed report from the Office of the Director on April 13, 1936. Re: Police Training Schools of the Federal Bureau of Investigation." Source: FBI Archive Collection. Courtesy Larry E. Wack – FBI (ret.), Historical Research/ Consulting, 25 October 2016.

• Press Release. Typed report from the Office of the Director on July 20, 1936. Re: Third Session FBI National Police Academy." Source: FBI Archive Collection. Courtesy Larry E. Wack – FBI (ret.), Historical Research/Consulting. 25 October 2016.

• Wurstner, R.F., Chief of Police. Typed letter to Mr. Melvin K. Kuntz, Ohio Metal Products Company on December 9, 1936. Re: Citizen complaint filed against Ptl. Thomas Dunlavey at fire scene, 228 Robert Blvd. Source: DPHF Archive Collection.

• Wurstner, R.F., Chief of Police. Typed letter to Mr. E. W. Davies, Chairman, Local [Draft] Board No. 6 on April 6, 1944. Re: Ptl. Matthew Maroney I-A classification. Source: DPHF Archive Collection.

• Dayton Police Department. Handwritten file note 20775 (Virgil Summers DPD number) unsigned, undated in the Dillinger archive file. "One of John Dillingers Buddies Virgil Summers". Source: WSU Archive Collection.

• Hallford, Fred, Special Agent in Charge, Louisville, Kentucky. Typed letter to Mr. R. F. Wurstner, Chief of Police dated June 2, 1949. Re: Advising that three firearms seized in Kentucky with Moran arrest and turned over to Dayton for prosecution were not needed by federal authorities. Source: DPHF Archive Collection.

• Eikenbary, Herbert M., defense attorney for Al Fouts. Typed letter to Al Fouts on December 17, 1963 in response to a Christmas card received from the paroled convict. Source: David C. Greer, Esq. (see Papers/Documents/Reports)

E-mails

- Barstow, John 'Jack'. Various titles on topics related to Dayton Police Chief Rudolph Wurstner. Series of email exchanges with Stephen Grismer. 12 May 2008; 19 May 2008; 11 August 2008; and 9 March 2013.

- Barstow, John 'Jack'. Unknown title on topics related to Dayton Police Chief Rudolph Wurstner. Correspondence to Carol Sampson, Wright Dunbar Association. 13 July 2011.

- Murphy, Dennis. Unknown title on topics related to 'Jack' Barstow and Chief Rudolph Wurstner. Correspondence to Stephen Grismer. 30 January 2008.

- Sperl, Bridget. Dayton police career of Dayton Det. James Crumley. Series of e-mail exchanges with Stephen Grismer. 29 November 2018 to 20 January 2019.

- Siler, Gary. Al Fouts' Murder of Sweetheart. Series of e-mail exchanges with Stephen Grismer. 30 April 2020 to 5 May 2020.

- Siler, Gary. 372nd Infantry Regiment (WWI) related to Dayton Ptl. William 'Tom' Wilson in correspondence to Joe Keeble (great-grandson). 12 May 2016.

- Dalton, Curt. Mary Longnaker and her divorce. Exchange initiated by Stephen Grismer. 15 November 2015.

- Murphy, Dennis. Mary Longnaker and her family. Series of e-mail exchanges with Stephen Grismer. 13 February 2016.

- Huddleston, Tom; Bergstrom, Jon. Dayton Sgt. William Joseph Aldredge. Several e-mail exchanges with Stephen Grismer during which a family document was provided. 8 August 2019 and 9 August 2019.

- Siler, Gary. Mary Longnaker and her family. Series of e-mail exchanges with Stephen Grismer. Beginning 14 March 2019 through 26 March 2019.

- Sperl, Bridget. Later police career of St. Paul Chief of Detective James Crumley. Exchange initiated by Stephen Grismer. 22 April 2020.

- Wack, Larry E., FBI Special Agent (ret.). National FBI Academy Class records 1935 and 1936. Exchange initiated by Stephen Grismer. 25 October 2016

• Moore, Steven. The police and military career of Horace C. Moore. Series of email exchanges with Stephen Grismer. 25 March 2013 to 27 March 2013; 15 June 2015.

Films/Documentaries

• PROHIBITION. Episode 1: A Nation of Drunkards. Dir. Ken Burns and Lynn Novick. Narr. Peter Coyote. National Endowment for the Humanities. PBS, 2011.

• American Experience The Vote. Directed and produced by Michelle Ferrari; executive producers, Mark Samels and Susan Bellows. Narrated by Kate Burton. National Endowment for the Humanities. PBS, July 6-7, 2020.

• American Lawmen. Episode 3: Melvin Purvis: The Gangbuster. Dir. Jeff Vanderwal. Commentator: Ross Rice, Special Agent, Chicago FBI (ret). Commentating Authors: Nate Hendley, *American Gangsters, Then and Now*; and Paul Maccabee, *John Dillinger Slept Here*. Cinefix Productions, 2016.

• "UE-CIO – Univis Lens Co. Strike Action from July 26 to Aug. 3, 1948... Filmed by Radio Station WHIO..." (no audio), 1948. Source: Dayton Police History Foundation (DPHF) Archive Collection.

DPHF-conducted Interviews

• Barstow, John A. 'Jack'. Topic: Chief Rudolph Wurstner career, 1902-1949. Interviewer, Dr. Judith Monseur. Interviewed at 111 Building, 111 W. First Street, Suite 1100, Dayton, Ohio at the law firm of Doll, Jansen & Ford. Archived. 3 April 2010 (filmed).

• Peters, Dr. Margaret. Topic: Black Dayton police officers, 1910-1930. Interviewer, Dr. Judith Monseur. Interviewed at 111 Building, 111 W. First Street, Suite 1100, Dayton, Ohio at the law firm of Doll, Jansen & Ford. Archived. September 25, 2010 (filmed).

• Stewart, Virginia 'Ginny.' Trotwood Madison Historical Society (Ohio). Topic: Mary Longnaker (Titus). Interviewer, Stephen Grismer. Telephone conversation, Dayton, Ohio. Tuesday, 24, February 2015.

Newspapers

- No bylines. Four related news articles: "The Temperance Crusade," *The New York Times*, 22 February 1874; "Excited State of Feeling in Dayton," *The New York Times*, 25 February 1874; "A Movement Gaining Strength in Dayton," *The New York Times*, 24 March 1874; and "End of the Crusade in Dayton, Ohio," *The New York Times*, 8 April 1874.
- Burba, Howard. "Dayton's First 'Wet and Dry' Campaign." *Dayton Daily News*, 3 May 1931.
- No bylines. Two related news articles: "Murder – Office Lee Lynam Shot Down," *The Dayton Democrat*, 17 January 1880; and "The Murdered Patrolman *The Dayton Democrat*, 18 January 1880.
- Burba, Howard. "The Downfall of Chief Farrell." *Dayton Daily News*, 25 April 1937.
- No byline. "Detective Crumley on Visit to City," *Dayton Daily News*, 3 August 1918.
- No bylines. Five related news articles: "BIFFED, A Copper in the Eye, and Then–," *The Dayton Herald*, 18 February 1899; "STRUCK with Crumley's Good Strong Right Fist," *The Dayton Herald*, 16 May 1899; "He's 'Some Pumpkins' Himself," *Dayton Daily News*, 10 June 1901. "Exciting Capture and Escape of a Daring Negro Sneak," *Dayton Daily News*, 7 July 1902; and "CRUMLEY, Crumley Landed.... a Celebrated Crook," *Dayton Daily News*, 6 September 1904.
- No bylines. Two related news articles: "FIVE KNIFE WOUNDS," *The Dayton Herald*, 24 December 1894; and "Christmas at Dayton," *The Saint Paul Globe*, 24 December 1894.
- No bylines. Two related news articles: "Investigation as to Detective Crumley's Conduct in Progress," *Dayton Daily News*, 24 September 1902; and "Chiefs Issues an Order," *Dayton Daily News*, 25 September 1902.
- No byline. "Found a Trunk of Stolen Goods," *Dayton Daily News*, 16 March 1903.
- Burba, Howard. "When Carrie Nation Came to Dayton," *Dayton Daily News*, 17 December 1933.
- No byline. "Seek Slayer of Dayton Girl," *The New York Times*, 7 February 1909.
- No byline. "Initial Ball Given by the Dayton Police Benevolent

Association Proves Big Success," *The Dayton Journal*, 8 January 1910.

- No byline. "Have Narrow Escapes in Warning Others," *The Dayton Journal*, 2 April 1913.

- Herron, Larry. "May We Present, Lulu Sollers, Policewoman," *Dayton Journal Herald Sunday Spotlight*, 17 December 1939.

- No byline. "Police Women's Chief Resigns," *The Dayton Herald*, 5 November 1918.

- No byline. "City Suffrage Pioneer, 1st Policewoman Dies" *Dayton Journal Herald*, 20 April 1960.

- No byline. "Public Places May Be Closed Indefinitely," *Dayton Daily News*, 3 October 1918.

- No bylines. Two related news articles: "Has a Criminal Record in Xenia," *Dayton Daily News*, 5 December 1916; and "Murder Charge Placed Against Alfred Fouts," *Dayton Daily News*, 16 December 1916.

- No bylines. Two related news articles: "Cuts Own Throat and Falls Across Dead Woman's Bed – Albert Pfoutz," *The Dayton Herald*, 2 December 1916; and "Foutz Endeavors to Tear Stitches from His Throat," *The Dayton Herald*, 7 December 1916.

- No byline. "Fouts Convicted of Manslaughter in Mullen Case," *The Dayton Journal*, 10 June 1917

- No byline. "Jiu-Jitsu to be Taught Soldiers," *Dayton Daily News*, 4 May 1918.

- No byline. "Dwyer Will Take Appeal From Verdict," *The Brooklyn (NY)*, 27 July May 1926.

- No byline. "Clay Says Inspector Knocked Out One of His Teeth," *The Dayton Herald*, 30 September 1921.

- No byline. "Passing of the Bungaloo Gang," *Dayton Daily News*, 20 February 1916.

- No byline. "New Chief of Police to get More Salary," *Dayton Daily News*, 8 November 1922.

- No byline. "WANT BLOODHOUNDS," *Dayton Daily News*, 17 September 1904.

- No byline. "Woodward Rapped in Report of Police Probers; Manager Cautious in Announcing Official's Fate," *Dayton Daily News*, 12 June 1925.

- No byline. "Booze Trade 'Honor' is Nil," *Dayton Daily News*, 7 August 1922.

• No byline. "Eighteenth Amendment to be Read in All Dayton Schools by Instructors," *The Dayton Herald*, 15 January 1923.

• No byline. "Liquor Disappears Soon After Tossed from Car; Constables Puzzled," *Dayton Daily News*, 25 June 1925.

• No bylines. Three related news articles: "Crowd Throngs Streets Where Klan Parades ," *Dayton Daily News*, 22 September 1923; "Same Methods in Dayton as Used in South," *Dayton Daily News*, 9 September 1921; and "Ku Klux Klan to Conduct Meeting in Memorial Hall," *Dayton Daily News*, 25 May 1921.

• No bylines. Three related news articles: "Dayton Events for Twelve Months Pass in Quick Review," *Dayton Daily News*, 30 December 1923; and "Sold Upon Streets; May Be Suppressed," *The Dayton Herald*, 7 February 1923.

• No bylines. Two related news articles: "Dayton Mecca for Meeting of Klansmen," *The Dayton Evening Herald*, 21 September 1923; and "Crowd Throng Streets Where Klan Parades," *Dayton Daily News*, 22 September 1923.

• Archdeacon, Tom. "Tackling Hatred," *Dayton Daily News*, 25 October 2015.

• No bylines. Two related news articles: "U.S. May Hear of Bomb Blast at University," *Dayton Daily News*, 21 December 1923; and "Crosses Burned," *Dayton Daily News*, 7 December 1924.

• No byline. "Crosses Burned in Celebration," *The Dayton Herald*, 7 May 1924.

• No bylines. Two related news articles: "An Attempted Hold-Up," *Mooresville Times* (via History Treasure Trove), 11 September 1924; "Sentenced by Court," *Mooresville Times* (via History Treasure Trove), 19 September 1924; and "Circuit Court," *Mooresville Times* (via History Treasure Trove), 17 October 1924.

• No bylines. Three related news articles: "Robertson Case Goes to Grand Jury," *The Dayton Herald*, 20 January 1923; "Federal Drive on Liquor Ring Corrals Eight," *The Dayton Herald*, 8 February 1924; and "Indict Wagman as Liquor Gang Chief," *Dayton Daily News*, 16 May 1925.

• No bylines. Three related news articles: "Dayton Jail Term Bars Remus Parole," *The Dayton Herald*, 11 March 1924; "Bootleg Gang may be Guests in Local Jail," *The Dayton Herald*, 8 April 1925; and "George Remus First to Face Dayton Charge,"

• No bylines. Seven related news articles: "Tell of Buying $3,760

Liquor," *Dayton Daily News*, 11 May 1922; "Constables to
Learn Fate Next Tuesday," *The Dayton Herald*, 30 May 1927;
"Two Others in Case Not Yet Arrested," *Dayton Daily News*,
21 January 1927; "Woman Says Severs Told Her to Give Him
$100 Sum," *The Dayton Herald*, 20 May 1927; "Federal Grand
Jury to Begin Probe of Charge Against 100 on Monday," *Dayton
Daily News*, 1 May 1927; "Gambling and Liquor Paraphernalia
Seized in Rad on Xenia Pike Home," *The Dayton Herald*, 12
June 1931; and "Tavern or Not? '400 Club' Sign Brings Stir,"
The Dayton Herald, 21 August 1947.

- No byline. "Former Noted Jockey Faces Liquor Charge," *Dayton
Daily News*, 20 November 1927.

- No byline. "Wurstner in as Chief; Plans to Study Situation,"
Dayton Daily News, 18 June 1925.

- No byline. "Uniform Comes Into Its Own for Dayton's Police
Chiefs," *Dayton Daily News*, 20 June 1925.

- No byline. "Wurstner is Given Diamond Studded Badge," *Dayton
Daily News*, 1 July 1927.

- No byline. "Dayton Police Receive Shipment of Machine Guns
and Gas Bombs," *The Dayton Herald*, 14 September 1927.

- No byline. "Thugs Shoot Detective in Pistol Fight," *The Dayton
Herald*, 30 April 1920.

- No bylines. Two related news articles: "Officer Rice is Near
Death of Bullet Wound," *Dayton Daily News*, 25 July 1926;
"Condition of Rice, Wheeler Held Critical," *Dayton Daily News*,
19 April 1927.

- Roberts, C.V. "The Dead Man Who Talked," *Dayton Daily News*,
30 November 1941.

- No bylines. Two related news articles: "Two Police Officers
Wounded; Negro Killed ," *The Dayton Evening Herald*, 24
September 1927; "Officer Invades Hospital, Fires 'Blanks'
at Negro Who Shot Capt. Post; Latter's Condition Critical,"
Dayton Daily News, 25 September 1927.

- No byline. "Lindbergh Fiasco Back Alley Trick Says Police
Chief," *The Dayton Herald*, 23 June 1927.

- No byline. "Liquor Squad of Police is Made Smaller," *The Dayton
Herald*, 30 December 1927.

- No byline. "Zwick's Story is that of Gang which Infested Southern
Ohio," *The Cincinnati Enquirer*, 9 April 1933.

- No byline. "Dayton Bankers Battle Bandits," *The Dayton Journal*,
16 April 1930.

- No byline. "Five Bandits Get $35,000 at Dayton Bank," *The Dayton Herald*, 4 April 1930.
- No bylines. Three related news articles: "Bandit Dead, Another Dying After Xenia Av. Bank Raid," *Dayton Daily News*, 6 May 1930; "Dayton Policeman Kills Bank Bandit, Wounds Another in Running Gun Fight," *The Dayton Herald*, 6 May 1930; and "Identify Pair Shot in Holdup of Branch Bank," *Dayton Daily News*, 13 May 1930.
- No bylines. Two related news articles: "Count Seconds in Fight on Bank Holdups," *Dayton Daily News*, 24 December 1933; and "Moves Only on Signal of Bank Alarm," *Dayton Daily News*, 26 December 1937.
- No bylines. Two related news articles: "Local Authorities Seeking Gangsters," *The Dayton Herald*, 22 September 1930; and "3 of 5 Dayton Bank Bandits Held or Dead," *Dayton Daily News*, 2 August 1932.
- No byline. "Robbery in Dayton Said to be Work of Notorious Gangster," *Dayton Daily News*, 1 February 1930.
- No bylines. Five related news articles: "Robbery in Dayton Said to be the Work of Notorious Gangster," *The Dayton Herald*, 1 February 1930; "Floyd Shawhan Near Death in Hospital Here," *Dayton Daily News*, 15 April 1935; "Floyd Leg Amputated," *The Dayton Herald*, 15 August 1936; "Floyd Shawhan is Sentenced," *Dayton Daily News*, 17 September 1935; and "New Sidelights," *Dayton Daily News*, 31 July 1938.
- No bylines. Three related news articles: "Leon Gleckman is Kidnapped; Ransom Asked," *The Minneapolis Star*, 29 September 1931; "Kidnappers of St. Paul Man Ask $250,000," *The Minneapolis Star*, 30 September 1931; and "One Admits Killing Hotel Man on Ride, Police Report," *The Minneapolis Star-Tribune*, 5 October 1931.
- No bylines. Two related news articles: "Prisoner Has Police Record," *The Dayton Herald*, 16 July 1931; and "Ohio Man is Sentenced on Pistol Charge," *The Richmond Palladium*, 24 November 1931.
- No byline. "Fugitive Will Be Returned," *Dayton Daily News*, 23 December 1933.
- No byline. "Dayton Man is Arraigned for P.O. Robbery," *Dayton Daily News*, 1 September 1933.
- No bylines. Two related news articles: "Foutz is Held as Suspect in Lima Robbery," *The Dayton Herald*, 5 February 1931; and "Dayton Man Given Sentence at Lima," *Dayton Daily News*, 25 April 1931.

• No byline. "Action Filed to Recover $9,000," *Dayton Daily News*, 11 December 1935.

• No bylines. Two related news articles: "Tunnel Found by Officers in Hamilton Raid," *The Dayton Herald*, 15 December 1930; and "Dry Officer Will Attempt to Link Foutz with Raid," *The Dayton Journal*, 5 February 1931.

• No byline. "Years Change Styles in Garb of John Law," *Dayton Daily News*, 13 August 1933.

• No byline. "Wurstner and Yendes Back from World Police Meet," *Dayton Daily News*, 24 October 1931.

• No byline. "Police Radio Cars and Dedication Principals," *Dayton Daily News*, 25 September 1932.

• No byline. "Marriage Announced," *Martinsville Reporter Times*, 15 July 1932.

• No byline. "Repeal in Effect Year Ago Today," *The Circleville Herald*, 5 December 1934.

• No bylines. Five related news articles: "Dayton Pistol Team is Victor," *Dayton Daily News*, 23 April 1932; "Local Police Pistol Team Retains Joint Leadership in Loop," *The Dayton Herald*, 7 April 1932; "Police Pistol Team Leading in Interstate," *Dayton Daily News*, 28 February 1932; "Dayton Police Officers Win Medals... at Camp Perry," *Dayton Daily News*, 5 September 1929; and "Dayton Police Miss Only 44 Out of 1000," *Dayton Daily News*, 9 April 1931.

• No bylines. Five related news articles: "Small Son Died of Diphtheria," *The Bedford Daily Mail (Indiana)*, 8 November 1913; "PNEUMONIA," *The Bedford Daily Mail (Indiana)*, 23 February 1917; "Three Men Held in Bedford Jail; Holdups Charged," *The Palladium Item (Indiana)*, 25 June 1928; "Massman Gets Conviction," *Jackson County Banner (Indiana)*, 19 June 1929; and "By United Press," *The Muncie Evening Press (Indiana)*, 19 June 1929.

• Huist Smith, Joanne. "Dayton's connection to Dillinger: Bank robber came here for love," *Dayton Daily News*, 28 June 2009.

• No byline. "Dillinger's Former Dayton Girlfriend 'Sorry'," *The Dayton Herald*, 24 July 1934.

• No bylines. Three related news articles: "New Carlisle Bank is Robbed of $10,000," *Dayton Daily News*, 21 June 1933; "Bandits Grab $10,000 in Holdup of New Carlisle Bank, Escape in Auto," *The Herald*, 21 June 1933; and "New Carlisle Bank Robbed of $10,000 by Bandit Gang," *Springfield Daily News*, 21 June 1933.

• Nicodemus, Jessie. "Dillinger Recalled in Pleasant Hill," *The Journal Herald*, 9 April 1963.

• No byline. "Delivery Attempts Feared," *The Indianapolis News*, 13, October 1933. Reference: "Correspondence" (not dated) from John Dillinger to Mary Longnaker.

• Huffman, Dale. "The Word Went Out: John Dillinger's In Town," *Dayton Daily News*, 19 September 1973.

• No byline. "Bandit Gained Notoriety After His Arrest Here," *Dayton Daily News*, 26 January 1934.

• Nicodemus, Jessie. "On a September Night in 1933 a Man Called on his Girl...," *The Journal Herald*, 6 April 1963.

• Carr, Lewis F. "May We Present Horace Moore – Among the Youngest in the AEF," *The Journal Herald Spotlight*, 9 November 1941.

• Clark, Steve. "2 Daytonians Recall Day They Caught Dillinger," *Dayton Daily News*, 25 September 1970.

• No byline. "Fear Bandit's Pals May Stage Holdup," *Dayton Daily News*, 13 October 1933; p.2, column 4.

• No byline. "Dillinger Was Impressed By the Lawmen's Vests," *Dayton Daily News*, 29 September 1970.

• Batz, Bob. "Dillinger Endorsed Bulletproof vest use," *Dayton Daily News*, 18 March 1979.

• No byline. "Pfauhl Rounds Out 25 Years on Dayton Police Division," *The Journal Herald*, 7 January 1945.

• No bylines. All local news articles for every day beginning 22 September through 28 September 1933 from three Dayton newspapers: *Dayton Daily News*, dates: September 22, 26, 27, and 28, 1933; *The Dayton Herald*, dates: September 22, 23, 25, 27, and 28, 1933; *The Dayton Journal*, dates: September 22, 23, 24, 27, 28, 1933.

• No byline. "Fear Bandit's Pals May Stage Holdup," *Dayton Daily News*, 13 October 1933. p.2, column 5.

• Bottsford, W.P. "Police Track Bank Bandits Into Ohio, Then Lose Trail," *The Pittsburgh Press*, 13 September 1933.

• No byline. "Dillinger is Under Guard in Lima Jail," *Dayton Daily News*, 28 September 1933.

• No byline. "Dillinger Held at County Jail," *The Dayton Journal*, 24 September 1933.

• No byline. "Deputies Guard Jail Prisoner," *The Dayton Herald*, 27 September 1933.

• No byline. "Prison Official Tells How Convicts Escaped," *The Indianapolis News*, 27 September 1933.

• No bylines. Three related news articles: "Motorist Escapes at Nashville," *Muncie Evening Press*, 30 September 1933; "Jenkins, Escaped Prisoner is Slain ," *The Indianapolis Star*, 1 October 1933; and "Mayor and Police Head Jenkins Pall Bearers," *The Star Press* (Richmond, Indiana), 3 October 1933.

• No bylines. Four related news articles: "Seized Alleged Bank Robbers," *The Lake County Times*, 5 June 1928; "Ohioans Are Held as Bank Suspects," *The Pittsburgh Press*, 5 June 1928; "Makley Named as One of Gang in Bank Robbery," *The Indianapolis Star*, 4 October 1933 and "Seek Bandit Chief as St. Marys Bank Robber," *Dayton Daily News*, 4 October 1933.

• Esterline, Marion. "Chief Recalls Bank Theft by Dillinger" (this is the 14th in The Journal series about Miami Valley police chiefs), *The Journal Herald*, 11 October 1948.

• No bylines. Eight related news articles: "Slayer of Sheriff at Lima is Identified as Fugitive," *Dayton Daily News*, 13 October 1933; "Fear Bandit's Pals May Stage Holdup," *Dayton Daily News*, 13 October 1933; "Reward Spurs Killer Hunt," *The Lima News*, 13 October 1933; "Dillinger Gang Reported in Indiana; Officer Freed," *The Dayton Herald*, 13 October 1933; "Still Watching for Dillinger to Show Here," *Dayton Daily News*, 14 October 1933; "Sister of One Desperado Has Left Her Room," *The Dayton Herald*, 14 October 1933; "Plans Laid at Dayton Conference for Man-Hunt," *The Dayton Herald*, 14 October 1933; and "Dillinger Hunt Centers at Hamilton," *The Dayton Herald*, 16 October 1933.

• No byline. "Chief Praises Officers, Who Seized Gunmen," *Dayton Daily News*, 31 October 1933.

• No byline. "Machine Guns Blaze as Jury Whitewashes Police," *The St. Paul Daily News*, 31 March, 1934.

• No byline. "The Night John Dillinger Died," *Dayton Daily News*, 1 August 1954.

• Scarupa, Henry. "House Where Dillinger Slept Will Fall Soon," *The Journal Herald*, 25 October 1967.

• No bylines. Two related news articles: "Outlaws of Dillinger Type are Aimed at in Proposed Federal Crime Code," *The Indianapolis Star*, 8 February 1934; and "Roosevelt Signs Measures for Federal Crime Curbs," *The Los Angeles Times*, 19 May 1934.

- No byline. "Bandit Gained Notoriety After His Arrest Here," *Dayton Daily News*, 26 January 1934.
- No bylines. Three related Central Press Service articles: "HIS GIFT – SWEETHEART – WOMAN IN RED," *The South Bend Tribune*, 26 July 1934; "Dillinger 'Swell Guy'," *Montana Standard, Butte*, 26 July 1934; and "One Swell Guy," *Longport Pharos-Tribune (Indiana)*, 26 July 1934.
- No bylines. Six related news articles: "Death Penalty for Pierpont," *The Dayton Herald*, 11 March1934; "Dillinger Aide Found Guilty in Sheriff Murder," *The Dayton Herald*, 17 March1934; "Clark Given Life Sentence for Murder," *The Dayton Herald*, 16 March1934; "Makley Dead; Pierpont Shot," *The Evening Leader (St. Marys, Ohio)*, 22 September 1934; "Last Rites for Charles Makley Held at Leipsic This Afternoon," *The Evening Leader (St. Marys, Ohio)*, 26 September 1934; and "Pierpont Takes Secret of Crime to His Grave," *The Dayton Herald*, 17 October 1934.
- No bylines. Four related news articles: "Officials Quiz Alleged Zwick Gang Members," *The Dayton Herald*, 26 May 1930; "Zwick Faces Cincinnati Charges," *The Dayton Herald*, 9 January 1933; "Thank Police for Their Aid in Zwick Case," *Dayton Daily News*, 19 March 1933; and "Dillinger's Arrest in Dayton Was Planned So Well He Didn't Have a Chance," *Dayton Daily News*, 23 July 1934.
- No bylines. Four related news articles: "Wire Threat Signed 'Karpis' is Sent to J. Edgar Hoover," *Washington D.C. Star*, 22 August 1934; "Karpis Threatens to Kill J. E. Hoover," *New York Times*, 21 August 1934; "Karpis Threat for J. E. Hoover Citing 2 Barkers," *Chicago Tribune*, 21 August 1934; and "Threatens Chief of 'G' Men; J. Edgar Hoover Receives Death Threat Letter," *Spokane Daily Chronicle*, 20 August 1934.
- No bylines. Two related news articles: "G-Men Kill Al Brady and Pal," *The Dayton Herald*, 12 October 1937; and "Blame Brady Gang in Ohio, Indiana Raids," *Dayton Daily News*, 18 December 1936.
- Powell, Lisa. "Brady Gang made a $75K Dayton jewelry store heist in 1936," *Dayton Daily News*, 6 April 2017.
- No bylines. Two related news articles: "Ex-Policeman Here Promoted," *Dayton Daily News*, 11 January 1931; and "St. Paul Detective, Once Dayton Officer, Is Visitor," *Dayton Daily News*, 16 September 1933.

- No bylines. Two related news articles: "Shakeup Hits Ex-Daytonian," *Dayton Daily News*, 24 June 1935; and "Ex-Daytonian 'Fired' When Lone Investigator Comes Along to Stop Gang Rule," *Dayton Daily News*, 28 July 1935.
- No byline. "Police, Underworld Alliance Revealed in St. Paul Inquiry," *The Minneapolis Star*, 24 June 1935.
- No bylines. Five related news articles: "Link Gamblers in Police Sift," *The Minneapolis Star*, 25 June 1935; "Bribery Charges Against St. Paul Detectives Filed," *The Minneapolis Star*, 10 August 1935; "Officials Hear Alleged Record of Police Graft," *The Minneapolis Star*, 27 August 1935; "Warren Denies Charge He Allowed Gambling," *The Minneapolis Star*, 25 June 1935; and "St. Paul Jury Frees Crumley," *The Minneapolis Star*, 25 April 1936.
- No bylines. Three related news articles: "Crumley Links Brown to Gang," *The Minneapolis Star*, 5 September 1936; "Brown Denies Kidnapper Tip," *The Minneapolis Star-Tribune*, 5 September 1936; and "Linking of Crumley in Tip-Offs Foiled," *The Minneapolis Star-Tribune*, 24 September 1936.
- No bylines. Four related news articles: "Ex-St. Paul Detective Jailed in Dope Fix," *The Minneapolis Star*, 27 November 1937; "J.P. Crumley, Ousted Chief, Held for U.S.," *The Minneapolis Star*, 11 November 1937; "Crumley is Guilty in Dope Bribery Case," *The Minneapolis Star*, 6 December 1937; and "Crumley, Hildebrandt Get 'Fix' Case Terms," *The Minneapolis Star*, 16 January 1938.
- No byline. "Former Officer Dies in St. Paul," *The Dayton Herald*, 9 February 1939.
- No byline. "Dean of Nation's Police Chiefs Plans Fishing Vacation, Then Stay in Dayton," *Dayton Daily News*, 8 June 1949.
- No bylines. Two related news articles: "Officer Price to Return Following Graduation," *The Dayton Herald*, 23 May 1938; and "Policemen Honored," *The Newark Advocate*, 24 May 1938.
- No byline. "Police Order Plans Dinner," *The Journal Herald*, 22 September 1940.
- No bylines. Three related news articles: "Traffic Big Police Problem," *The Dayton Herald*, 22 October 1935; "Dayton Police Department Seriously Undermanned is Opinion of F.B.I. Official," *The Dayton Herald*, 21 February 1938; and "Policemen on Stand in Suit for Back Pay," *The Dayton Journal*, 17 February 1940.

• Zurlinden, Pete. "Police Undermanned by a Ratio of 4-1, Study Shows," *The Journal Herald*, 4 August 1940.

• Wurstner, Rudolph F, Police Chief. "Dayton Needs More Policemen Badly!" *The Journal Herald*, 19 October 1941.

• No byline. "Man Gets Prison Term on Robbery Conviction," *The Dayton Herald*, 3 December 1926.

• No bylines. Two related news articles: "Two Dead, Three Injured in Fire," *The Dayton Herald*, 26 November 1936; and "14 Trapped in Robert Blvd. Fire; One Dead; Three Believed Dying," *Dayton Daily News*, 26 November 1936.

• Curnutt, Bob. "War Puts Pressure on Police Identification Bureau," *The Dayton Herald*, 8 March 1942.

• No bylines. Two related news articles: "Homicide Squad Needs is Studied," *The Dayton Herald*, 19 August 1937; and "Homicide Squad Will Be Organized by City," *Dayton Daily News*, 18 August 1937.

• No bylines. Two related news articles: "Bites Off Ear of Patrolman," *Dayton Daily News*, 27 June 1934; and "65 True Bills," *Dayton Daily News*, 1 October 1934.

• No byline. "Observatory: History," *The Dayton Herald*, 17 October 1938.

• Sikora, Mary. "No comic strip cop; Dan is real-life guy in Caniff's cartoon," *Dayton Daily News*, 23 January 1986.

• No bylines. Two related news articles: "Pair Wounded While Probing Murder Report," *Dayton Daily News*, 1 October 1939; and "Rice Dies 4 Days After Gun Fight with Murder Suspect," *The Dayton Herald*, 5 October 1939.

• No byline. "Some Mighty Mean Ghosts Going Out with Old Jail," *The Journal Herald*, 31 May 1966.

• No bylines. Three related news articles: "2-Way Radios for Police Seen as a Possibility," *Dayton Daily News*, 17 February 1940; "Police to Have 2-Way Radios by Oct. 1," *Dayton Daily News*, 28 August 1940; and "Two-Way Radio for Police Cars Get Its Initial Test," *Dayton Daily News*, 13 October 1940.

• Nangle, Bob. "'Ford Squads' Replaced Pedal Cops in 1910," *Dayton Daily News*, 14 February 1961.

• No byline. "Defense Mobilization Test Here Tomorrow," *The Dayton Herald*, 21 November 1942

• No byline. "Price Instructor in Columbus," *The Columbus Dispatch,* 9 March 1942.

• No byline. "53 to Complete Regional 6-Day FBI War Traffic

School Today," *The Baltimore Sun*, 7 March 1942.

• No byline. "Traffic Class Aids Defense," *The Rochester Times Union*, 30 March 1942.

• No byline. "23 War Veterans Join City Police Force on Monday," *Dayton Daily News*, 9 March 1946.

• Cull, Dick Jr. "Dayton Police Officer is Latest FBI Academy Graduate," *Dayton Daily News*, 6 November 1949.

• No byline. "Kirkpatrick to Take Job with Unit in Washington," *Dayton Daily News*, 9 March 1955.

• No byline. "Cy Yendes Opens Detective Agency Here," *The Dayton Herald*, 3 September 1946.

• Herron, Larry. "May We Present .. Lulu Sollers Policewoman," *The Sunday Journal Herald Spotlight*, 17 December 1939.

• No byline. "Mrs. Hazel Clark Dies at 61; Veteran Policewoman Here," *The Journal Herald*, 13 October 1953.

• No byline. "Liberal Law Enforcement Education Given Rookie Policemen," *Dayton Daily News*, 20 November 1949.

• No byline. "Ansonia Bank Vault is Robbed of $20,000," *Dayton Daily News*, 9 November 1946.

• No byline. "Bank Robbers Loot May Hit $100,000," *The Dayton Herald*, 9 November 1946.

• No byline. "Former Gang Chief and Aide Under Bond," *Dayton Daily News*, 7 July 1946.

• No bylines. Two related news articles: "Mt. Vernon Bandit Roundup Solves Holdups, Slaying," *Alton Evening Telegraph, Illinois*, 8 January 1934; and "Four Mt. Vernon Men Get 17 Years Each," *St. Louis Globe Democrat*, 3 March 1934.

• No bylines. Two related news articles: "Lieutenant of Slain Gang Boss Missing," *St. Louis Star-Times*, 11 January 1946; and "Last of Drewer Gang Captured; Named in Killer," *St. Louis Globe Democrat*, 7 July 1946.

• Keilman, John (print); Powell, Lisa (online post). Six-day series of feature articles: "Special Report: Bugs Moran in Dayton" (all editions with different titles), *Dayton Daily News*, 26 December 1999 to 31 December 1999; posted 11 August 2016.

• John Keilman. "'Old Man' Moran dies in obscurity," *Dayton Daily News*, 31 Dayton 1999.

• No bylines. Two related news articles: "Killer Lurks with Shotgun in Ambush," *St. Louis Globe Democrat*, 3 December 1962; and "Former Gangster had Only $12.95 in Pockets When Slain," *St. Louis Globe Democrat*, 4 December 1962.

• Jessie Nicodemus. "A Lifetime Wasted, But Fouts Happier," *The Journal Herald*, 2 December 1963.

• No byline. "Patrolman Dies in West Side Battle," *The Daily Herald*, 16 May 1947.

• No byline. "Dayton Policeman Killed Chasing Stolen Auto," *Dayton Daily News*, 3 May 1947.

• No bylines. Seven related news articles: "600 Production Workers Strike at Univis Lens," *The Dayton Herald*, 5 May 1948; "Pickets Intercept Univis President," *The Dayton Herald*, 10 June 1948; "Picket Violence at Univis First Since Middle 30's," *The Dayton Herald*, 15 June 1948; "Police Officials Say Pickets Broke Ruling," *Dayton Daily News*, 16 June 1948; "Herbert to Meet with Univis, UE Officials today," *The Dayton Herald*, 7 August 1948; "National Guards in 'Full Charge'," *The Dayton Herald*, 4 August 1948;and "Univis Workers Return to Posts as Peace Reigns," *Dayton Daily News*, 10 August 1948.

• Carr, Lewis F. "Chief R. F. Wurstner in His 39th Year of Service," *The Journal Herald Spotlight*, 1 December 1940.

• Bruce, Malcolm. "---- Chief of Police," *The Journal Herald*, undated 1949.

• No byline. "Police Chief Wurstner Resigns," *The Journal Herald Spotlight*, 8 June 1949.

• Osler, Jack. "New Car Given Chief Wurstner in Surprise Move," *Dayton Daily News*, 6 July 1949.

• No byline. "Ex-Police Chief Wurstner Dies," *The Journal Herald Spotlight*, 13 July 1969.

Websites

• Friedman, S. Morgan. "The Inflation Calculator." *westegg. com.* Data from U.S. statistical indexes (see site explanation). Updated annually through 2019. Web. 24 April 2020.

• No author cited. "John Dillinger." *History.com.* The History Channel. Publication date 9 November 2009; updated 21 August, 2018. Web. 24 April 2020.

• Two related sources: 1) No author cited. "Bugs Moran – The Life and Crimes of George 'Bugs' Moran." *BugsMoran.net.* No publication date. Web. 2 May 2020. 2) No author cited. "Bugs Moran." *en.wikipedia.org/wiki/Bugs_Moran.* Last edited 15 April 2020. Web. 2 May 2020.

• Dalton, Curt, ed. "When Influenza Came to Dayton in 1918." *DaytonHistoryBooks.com.* Dayton History Books Online, undated. Anthology of 49 *Dayton Daily News* articles dated beginning 4 October 1918 to 6 January 1919. Web. 2 May 2020.

• No author cited. "The American Influenza Epidemic of 1918-1919." *InfluenzaArchive.org.* Influenza Encyclopedia. University of Michigan Center for the History of Medicine, undated. Web. 2 May 2020.

• No author cited. "Why Saint Paul?: A Quick History." *VisitSaintPaul.com.* Official Convention and Visitors Bureau, undated. Web. 27 April 2020.

• Reicher, Matt. "O'Connor Layover Agreement." *mnopedia.org.* MNOPEDIA, 14 July 2014; modified 25 November 2019. Web. 27 April 2020.

• No author cited. "Dayton Marcos." *Wikipedia.org.* Wikipedia Free Encyclopedia. Last updated 20 December 2019. Web. 27 April 2020.

• No author cited. "Dayton Triangles." *Wikipedia.org.* Wikipedia Free Encyclopedia. Last updated 24 March 2020. Web. 27 April 2020.

• No author cited. "How Prohibition Fueled the Rise of the Ku Klux Klan." *History.com.* The History Channel. Publication date 15 January 2019; updated 19 February , 2019. Web. 28 April 2020.

• Buckley, William R. "Dillinger's Hometown Holdup." *mplindianaroom.blogspot.com.* History Treasure Trove Mooresville, Morgan County, Indiana. Publication date 22 March 2018. Web. 28 April 2020.

• Hanson, Ph.D., David J. "George Remus: 'King of Bootleggers' During Prohibition." *Alcoholproblemsandsolutions.org.* Alcohol Problems and Solutions. Publication © 1999-2019. Web. 28 April 2020.

• Cosgriff, Chris, founder. "Search for a Fallen Officer." *odmp.com.* Officer Down Memorial Page, Inc. Publication © 1996-2020. Web. 28 April 2020.

• No author cited. "FBI History Timeline." *FBI.org.* FBI • Federal Bureau of Investigation. Publication updated. Web. 15 May 2020.

• Jones, Richard O. "The Little Chicago Chronicles: End of the Line for Foxy Bob Zwick." *justhamilton.com.* The Hamiltonian. Publication 2019. Web. 15 May 2020.

• Jones, Richard O. "Hamilton's checkered 'Little Chicago' past: Gangsters, booze and John Dillinger." *journal-news.com*. The Hamilton Journal-News. Publication date 22 August 2009; republished 4 March 2020. Web. 15 May 2020.

• Park, Sharon. "Crooks' haven: The gangster era in St. Paul." *mnopedia.org*. MNOPEDIA, 10 November 2015. Web. 17 May 2020.

• No author cited. "Jay's History • The Pony House Restaurant and Bar." *jays.com/history*. Jay's Seafood Restaurant, Dayton, Ohio: undated. Web. 17 May 2020.

• No author cited. "History of Beer Part 3: Beer and Prohibition." *nocoastbeer.co/blogs*. Plains Simple, Oskaloosa, Iowa: 25 May 2018. Web. 1 May 2020.

• Federal Bureau of Investigation File No. 62-29777 Section 10. Subject: John Dillinger Gang. *Archive.org*. Freedom of Information and Privacy Acts. FBI reports and documents. Internet Archive, 5 April 2016. Web. 7 June 2020.

• Robinson, Amelia. "How a Dayton landlady helped nab infamous bank robber John Dillinger." *Dayton.com*. Dayton Daily News: undated. Web. 1 June 2020.

• Robert Edwards Auctions. "Extraordinary 1933 John Dillinger Two-Page Handwritten Love Letter from Prison." *robertedwardsauctions.com*. Chester, New Jersey. Posted Date Spring 2012. Web. 31 May 2020.

• Swift, Tammy, reporter. "Fargo woman was with gangster John Dillinger when he was killed in 1934." *grandforksherald.com*. Grand Forks Herald. Published Date 28 June 2009. Web. 13 May 2012.

• Legg, Lisa. "St. Paul's seedy past at center of Eagan author's true cop caper." *Twincities.com*. Pioneer Press. Publication date 2 December 2013; updated 7 November 2015. Web. 23 June 2020.

• Bianco, Juan Ignacio. "John Herbert Dillinger." *Murderpedia.org*. Updated 11 April 2017. Web. 23 June 2020.

• No author cited. "Homer Van Meter." *en.wikipedia.org/wiki/Homer_Van_Meter*. Last edited 14 May 2020. Web. 2 May 2020.

• Pack, Lauren, Staff Writer. "Clyde Barrow, of Bonnie and Clyde fame, was arrested in Middletown 90 years ago. Here is what he did." *Journal News.com.* Journal-News, Butler County's Local News Now, 19 January 2020. Web. 27 April 2020.

• No author cited. "Clyde Barrow Crime Spree Through Middletown." *Midpointlibraryblog.org.* The Pointe, Midpointe Library's Official Blog, 23 May 2019. Web. 2 May 2020.

• No author cited. "FBI HISTORY – Famous Cases and Criminals – The Brady Gang." *FBI.org.* FBI • Federal Bureau of Investigation. Publication updated. Web. 31 May 2020.

• No author cited. "Chiefs of Police." *spphs.com/history/chiefs.* Saint Paul Police Historical Society. Publication © 2020. Web. 24 June 2020.

• Steenberg, Edward J. "St. Paul Police Department Reform, 1933–1940." *mnopedia.org.* MNOPEDIA, 7 March 2018; modified 10 February 2020. Web. 26 May 2020.

• Robinson, Amelia. "Honeymoon mayhem: How Dayton's Bonnie and Clyde let police on a chase that ended in a shootout among the tombstones." *projects.dayton.com.* Dayton.com. Web. 14 February 2016.

• No author cited. "The War – At Home – War Production." *pbs.org.* PBS.org. Based on the Ken Burns and Lynn Novick documentary, *The War.* Publication © September 2007. Web. 6 May 2020.

Circa 1922: Ptl. Russell Pfauhl, Sgt. Newton Haywood, and Ptl. Lawrence Morrell with seized bootlegging stills in storage at the old Central Police Station on East Sixth Street. *William Preston Mayfield Collection at Dayton History*

INDEX

DAYTON POLICE HISTORY THROUGH THE DECADES AND THROUGH PHOTO IMAGES

Bernard 'Ben' Meyer: Appointed to the Dayton police force in 1904. He is seen here in **1910** as a Patrolman; circa **1925** as a Sergeant; and in **1942** as a Captain when he retired.

Ptl. Clement Francis *(left)*, appointed in 1916, he died from the 1918 Spanish Influenza Pandemic.

Ptl. Francis on a traffic post with a semaphore.

Circa 1942

Sgt. Paul Geralds *(above)* at a traffic accident scene (see page 7).

Photographs

The Dean, Dillinger, and Dayton, Ohio, in addition to the written account, offers a **visual history** of the lawmen, law breakers, and the times. The contributors to the book cover are identified on Page ix. Again, they are: Amy Simpson, Julie Utley, Miami Valley Regional Crime Lab (MVRCL) and Wright State University (WSU) Special Collections and Archives. Former Dayton police officer Amy Simpson, a talented artist and photographer, has an eye for lighting and uncommon angles. The image she captured of the Dillinger archive is her vision and a wonderful gift to DPHF.

Where possible, **attribution is beneath the image depicted**. Along with the credits are the noted relationships of many of the photo contributors to the pictured police officers.

The photographs in this book that could not be credited due to space restrictions on the page in which they appeared are the following:

- Major John Thomas, **Page iii** – Valerie Lemmie Thomas, wife.
- Sgt. Amer Keller, **Page 20** – Linda Yonkers, twice great-granddaughter.
- Ptl. William Dalton, **Page 20** – Patricia Silver, great-granddaughter.
- Chief Thomas Farrell, **Page 31** – Illustration by "Faris."
- John E. 'Jack' Egan, **Page 36** – David C. Greer, Esq., author.
- Ptl. John Boes, **Page 36** – Jeanette Patton, granddaughter.
- Alfred/Albert Fouts, **Page 57** – Gary Siler, retired USAF.
- Ptl. Horace Moore, **Page 60** – Steven Moore, grandson.
- Chief John O'Connor, **Page 73** – Minnesota Historical Society.
- Flying Squadron, **Page 76**– Carolyn J. Burns, Ptl. Johnson granddaughter.
- Ptl. Russell Pfauhl, **Page 77** – Darlene Snyder, granddaughter.
- Chief James Woodward, **Page 78** – WSU Special Collections and Archives.
- Al Fouts mug shot (CA), **Page 91** – Gary Siler, retired USAF.
- Sheriff Howard Webster, **Page 93** – WSU Special Collections and Archives.

- FBI Academy Class, **Page 262** – FBI Collections via Larry Wack, retired special agent.
- Inspector Thomas Grundish's badge, **Page 263** – Tom Grundish, grandson.
- Ptl. Frank Johnson, **Page 266** – Carolyn J. Burns, granddaughter.
- Sgt. Walter Dempsey, **Page 272** – WSU Special Collections and Archives.
- Sheriff Phillip Kloos, **Page 273** – WSU Special Collections and Archives.
- Det. Lou Janning, **Page 273** – *Dayton Daily News* illustration by O'Dell Dean.
- Plwn. Dora Rice, **Page 279** – Robert Rice, Jr., grandson.
- Eugene Harris, **Page 280** – Curt Dalton, author.
- WWII Emil 'Russ' Guerra, **Page 290** – Tom Guerra, son.
- Capt. Richard Grundish (with Chief Kirkpatrick & FBI Director J. Edgar Hoover), **Page 295** – Tom Grundish, son.
- Plwn. Hazel Clark, **Page 297** – Sue Ann Patrick & Clarissa Wittmann, granddaughters.
- Moran, Fouts, Summers, Pages **298**, **299**, **303** – WSU Special Collections and Archives.
- Chief Rudy Wurstner's badge, **Page 314** – Eric Wurstner, great-grandson.
- 2012 Walk of Fame, **Page 317** – Bill Barstow, Chief Rudy Wurstner's grandson.
- 2018 Walk of Fame, **Page 317** – Robert Rice, Jr., Sgt Lucius & Plwn. Dora Rice's grandson.
- Capt. Ben Meyer, **Page 404** – Jeanette Grantham, granddaughter.
- Ptl. Clement Francis, **Page 404** – Cathy Harlow and Sally Francis, granddaughters.
- Sgt. Paul Geralds, **Page 404** – Tina Young, granddaughter.

All other photographs, illustrations, and images shown without attribution are from these sources: The Dayton Metro Library, City of Dayton, Dayton Police Department, Dayton Fraternal Order of Police, Dayton History, Montgomery County Historical Society (now Dayton History), Newspapers.com, online public domain, as well as the private collection of Dayton Police History Foundation, Inc.

DAYTON POLICE HISTORY FOUNDATION, INC.

Dayton Police History Foundation, Inc. is an outgrowth of a 2008 six-month police exhibit at Carillon Historical Park, *Patrolling the Streets of Dayton*. It was the largest temporary exhibit held at the park's newest museum facility at that time, the Dicke Family Transportation Center. It was visited by 20,000 students, and by that measure alone, it was considered a success. In 2019, it sponsored its most ambitious project to date, *Bootleggers, Bandits, and Badges: From Dry Times to Hard Times in Dayton, Ohio*.

Dayton Police History Foundation, Inc. was officially chartered by the State of Ohio on January 1, 2010. It is a private, non-profit, 501(c)(3) charitable organization strictly dedicated to the preservation of local police history. DPH Foundation, Inc. is independent but operates in cooperation with the City of Dayton Police Department, the Dayton Fraternal Order of Police, the Dayton History-NCR Archive Center, Carillon Historical Park and many other organizations. More can be learned about DPH Foundation at the following website:

DaytonPoliceHistory.org

Contact or Comment:

info@DaytonPoliceHistory.org

***DONATIONS** to support the efforts of DPH Foundation, Inc. are gratefully accepted and receipted. Please mail to:*

DPH Foundation, Inc.
P.O. Box 293157
Dayton, Ohio 45429-9157

1939: Dayton Police Sergeant Paul Price interviewing school safety patrol boys for a police radio program. This photo taken four years after WHIO first began radio broadcasting and 10 years before WHIO-TV came into existence (1949).

ABOUT THE AUTHOR

SGT. STEPHEN GRISMER (RET.) is a 25-year veteran of the Dayton Police Department. He entered the police academy in 1976 and was later assigned to uniform patrol duties in the Fifth District. Promoted in March 1986, he experienced a broad career in investigations, staff, internal affairs, drug enforcement, intelligence and training. He was a long-serving member of the hostage negotiation team and the vice president of the Dayton Fraternal Order of Police.

The author participated in a WHIO-TV internship before graduating from the University of Dayton in 1984 with a degree concentration in journalism and a minor in criminal justice. He is currently a legal assistant in the employ of the law firm Doll, Jansen and Ford.

In 2008 the author helped produce the successful police history exhibit at Carillon Historical Park, *Patrolling the Streets of Dayton*. In 2019, the author was one of the architects for the current police exhibit upon which this book is based, *Bootleggers, Bandits, and Badges*, also located at Carillon Historical Park. He is one of the founders of Dayton Police History Foundation, Inc. and is currently a member of the DPHF Board of Trustees.

In addition to THE DEAN, DILLINGER, AND DAYTON, OHIO, Steve has authored and co-authored two other books which were commemorative to Dayton episodes in 1913 and 1992:

DRENCHED UNIFORMS AND BATTERED BADGES:
HOW DAYTON POLICE EMERGED FROM THE 1913 FLOOD
(100th anniversary © July 2013)

THE CHRISTMAS KILLINGS: 40 HOURS TO JUSTICE
(25th anniversary © December 2017)
The Christmas Killings co-authors:
DR. JUDITH MONSEUR & DET. DENNIS MURPHY

www.ingramcontent.com/pod-product-compliance
Lightning Source LLC
Chambersburg PA
CBHW050739030726
47505CB00002B/331